SINS OF THE GODS

By K. Llewellin

Acknowledgements

A big f-you to Covid-19, who sapped my will to do anything, so delaying the release of this third novel! Let's hear it for perseverance!

"If you know the enemy and know yourself, you need not fear the result of a hundred battles."
Sun Tzu

CONTENTS

Title Page

Copyright

Dedication

Epigraph

Prologue   1

Chapter 1 - Ressen   5

Chapter 2 - Leo   11

Chapter 3 - Shar   17

Chapter 4 - Sin'ma   25

Chapter 5 - Grelt   34

Chapter 6 - Arron   41

Chapter 7 - Ressen   48

Chapter 8 - Leo   53

Chapter 9 - Sin'ma   57

Chapter 10 - Ressen   65

Chapter 11 - Tia   75

Chapter 12 - Sin'ma   79

Chapter 13 - Leo   85

Chapter 14 - Walks   98

Chapter 15 - Tia   125

Chapter 16 - Ressen   147

Chapter 17 - Tia   155

Chapter 18 - Sin'ma   166

Chapter 19 - Shar   171

Chapter 20 - Tia   179

Chapter 21 - Ressen   188

Chapter 22 - Grelt   200

Chapter 23 - Leo   205

Chapter 24 - Walks   220

Chapter 25 - Chione   238

Chapter 26 - Walks   255

Chapter 27 - Sin'ma   263

Chapter 28 - Walks   268

Chapter 29 - Tia   298

Chapter 30 - Leo   306

Chapter 31 - Tia   366

Chapter 32 - Kan   429

Chapter 33 - Tia   446

Epilogue   458

About The Author   461

Prologue

"**W**ould someone like to explain to me how we lost at Ciberia?"

Fleet Admiral Imahu was pacing up and down the room, the ceaseless clacking of his cane filling the oppressive, drawn-out silence. It had been three months since the Orion Alliance's trouncing in hyperspace, and those at the top were still licking their wounds. The men sat around the table may have all been in their prime, with decades of battle experience to their names, but none dared speak, or give the fleet admiral eye contact. In turn, Imahu stared at the assembled leaders. His one, big, triangular eyeball, set in the centre of his head, never blinked, as he cast its gaze on each of them in turn. They had become cowed prey before the hunter; one who could take their lives as easily as their jobs.

Imahu continued his tirade. "Ten battleships. Ten! Nine were destroyed, and from what my sources tell me, the tenth helped!" Colour was beginning to flush the admiral's cheeks, but as his blood was green, it gave his pale skeletal face a sickening hue.

Admiral Ujiri decided to speak up, and the translator terminal before him buzzed into life as he clicked his response. All available eyes fixed on him, and the more he spoke, the more he felt like he was offering himself up as a sacrifice. "They had help," came his tremolos answer. "You said yourself that two Karee vessels were aiding the combatants."

"The Karee do not fight," Imahu exclaimed. "By keeping our

conquests outside of Zerren space, we should not have been interfered with. My sources had assured me this would be the case."

"With all due respect sir, your sources do not seem to know what they are talking about."

The two commanders sat either side of Ujiri tried to shift as far away from him as possible, as the eye of Imahu rounded on him. "Watch your tongue!" he warned, with an unmistakeable tone.

Ujiri's two stomachs tightened, and he shrank back into his seat. Like the other officials around the table, he wasn't entirely sure as to who Imahu's sources were. There were whisperings and conspiracy theories bandied about; mentions of ancient races, warmongering civilisations, and the like, but the truth was well above his pay grade. All he knew was if they had supplied the intel the fleet had relied on, they had been misinformed…or had lied. But those were words he was never going to utter, lest he lose his life on the spot.

Imahu was still ranting. "…and what of the battleship that was captured? Our own people must have helped in some way." He banged his cane hard on the floor, making several in the room jump. "Strands of treachery are starting to weave themselves into the fabric of the Orion Alliance and must be purged. Any hint of insubordination must be dealt with swiftly and terminally. We cannot allow a plague of turncoats to spread and destroy what took our leaders so long to build. All within the Orion Alliance must be committed to our cause, to ensure it becomes the greatest civilisation this galaxy has ever and will ever know."

Ujiri understood what Imahu's words meant. The Humans called it a witch hunt. Anyone believed to be questioning or veering away from the Alliance was to be killed. No trial and no second chances. The Alliance would use them as an example. Put a toe, talon, hoof, or tentacle over the line, even just a millimetre, and death was assured. And, in a lot of cases, no line would have been crossed. It would be a pre-emptive killing to rattle the souls of those entertaining doubts.

Despite his position among the warriors, Imahu's hints made Ujiri uncomfortable. He may have been a battle-monger of some sixty years, but the combatants he had killed had always been opposing warriors. They had been the males and females charging at him with weapons drawn, and despite his service in the Orion Alliance, he had regarded them with respect. They had fought with honour and strength, just as he always hoped he had. What they had not been were simple family members; those who had just been trying to live their lives quietly out of harm's way. In the grand scheme of things that didn't mean much, as non-combatants were usually enslaved once the warriors were erased, but Ujiri's selective view on whom he'd had a direct hand in slaughtering helped him sleep a little better.

"Everything we throw at these primitive races is missing the mark, what with the Karee race protecting Zerra, this interfering A'daree stirring up an army, and these seemingly rogue Karee lending their firepower" Imahu was saying. "We need better intelligence gathering. We need to know what they know, as soon as they know it, and as the Humans say, throw a spanner into their works at every available opportunity. All of you, select your best infiltrators. Spies or assassins, I don't care, I just want that damn space station filled to the brim with our own eyes, ears, and mind-set. We need feet on the ground, and weapons hidden in the shadows."

"But how do we get them on undiscovered when there's an A'daree aboard?" asked Colonel Y'tellos from across the table. "She can telepathically track them down and deal with them, like she did with the station's original Alliance crew."

"Have no fear of that," Imahu answered. Already, one of my men has managed to infiltrate the Scientia and has assassinated Tia's trusted servant Aben. It drove her mad, and now the rebels are in chaos, and the station is on lockdown. Trust me, I have the means, you provide me the men."

A look of scepticism passed across several faces, and Ujiri

didn't blame them. He was sure his own expression was mirroring their dubiousness, as a further glare from Imahu in his direction attested to. He tried to keep his face neutral, but doubt niggled at him. *Are the sources telling Imahu that the Karee emissary has gone crazy the same sources that had assured us the Karee wouldn't interfere in our attack of Ciberia? If so, then their reliability is looking unreliable, and with disastrous results.* However, none dared question Imahu's words, least of all Ujiri. He was their superior, and they could not deny him his request. They had to trust that the Fleet Admiral's source's success rate increased substantially.

"Do we have agreement?" Imahu asked the room. Slowly, each official present turned on a white light in front of him; a universal way to show agreement when head nods did not come naturally to all races. "Excellent, send me your men, and let us finally turn this war back in our favour, before the masses start questioning our competency."

I think it's too late for that, Ujiri thought to himself.

Chapter 1 - Ressen

All he was aware of was pain, pain and darkness. Every part of him was on fire, although he couldn't discern what part of him was what. All he knew, was that he was a ball of agony, though the pain ebbed and flowed like the tide. Drugs? Every so often, he would be aware of something more, a muffled voice in an alien language here, an urgent machine beeping there; short-lived moments that told him he was alive, at least in some form.

Ressen found the tide metaphor an interesting analogy, as he'd never visited the sea. A moment of sadness welled up within him, as he contemplated the thought that it was something he was never going to do. Then the circadian pain washed over him once more, and he lost the tenuous ability he had to hold a rational thought. Yet, while the fire lapped back and forth, he had the odd idea that he wasn't alone in his darkness. It was as if somewhere, just beyond the corner of his eye, something was watching him intently.

He had no idea how long he'd been a slave to the pain, as time didn't exist in the limbo universe he inhabited. Occasionally, titbits of what had happened to him floated back into memory. A pursuit by big ships, a world burning, cries of people he didn't know, the smell of death, a wall of fire wrapping itself around a body that couldn't defend itself. The nightmarish tableau would sometimes give way to a comforting sight; the blue and white striped face of his brother, Grelt. His cheeky dark-blue eyes and cocksure smile would appear, making Ressen feel warm and safe, if for just a moment.

Occasionally, he could hear snippets of his brother's words, "It's fine.... I got you.... Don't move.... Stay with me...." But he had no idea if they were memory or real-time. Other times, it would be voices and words he didn't recognise. Hushed worried whispers, matter-of-fact conversations, all in languages he couldn't translate, and it left him feeling alone and frightened in his out-of-body state.

Then there was the other feeling...the feeling of being watched. It never seemed to waiver in its existence. It was forever there when he was. Every day he tried to push his mind further into the darkness, to try to catch a fleeting glimpse of who or what it might be, but it had always stayed just out of reach. But he was determined to discover its source, and so every time he felt himself becoming lucid in his mind, he did his best to push the images and pain away and go hunting.

At first, it was an indefinable shape; a thing of mist and mirrors, as if whatever it was, wasn't ready for him to catch it. It skirted in the periphery of his vision, that is, if he could actually open his eyes. He would see it for the briefest of seconds, turn his mind, and in a flash, it would be gone. It was like tracking a wisp. Soon, all his lucid moments were concentrated on this one flighty thing, the searing pain a vague nagging in the back of his mind, the images of memory, ephemeral afterthoughts.

After a while, the sprite seemed to stay longer. When he turned to see it, it didn't vanish immediately. Rather, it remained awhile, before the indecipherable form slowly melted away. However, throughout his hunting, Ressen never felt afraid. It never occurred to him to feel afraid. There was some weird, alien entity inside his mind, and by rights he should've been scared, but he never was. There was overwhelming curiosity, and a desire for the thing to stay, just so he could speak to it, and say a word of greeting, and to know that, even in his current state, he wasn't alone. He never felt any animosity from his visitor either. He even sensed his own intrigue mirrored off the smoke, as if the thing were trying to fathom what he was too. *Is it inside my mind, or am I inside its?* Ressen wondered.

Then, one time, when chasing the phantom, and feeling its presence once again wane, readying to vanish, Ressen took charge. *"Don't go!"* he called out to the blackness in his head. *"Please stay. I want to see you."*

He felt an odd sensation go through him, as if he could feel its indecisiveness. Then, when he thought the entity had gone, he became strongly aware someone, or something, was stood right behind him. In the disconnected realm of his mind, he didn't really have eyes to see, nor hands to feel, just facsimiles made by his imagination to give him centre. Yet he knew, if he turned his disembodied head around, he would finally see it. He took a breath with his imagined lungs and turned.

He wasn't sure what he'd been expecting. Perhaps some demon of his childhood, born of primitive fear brought on by the dark. What faced him, with its head slightly cocked to one side, was an alien of a species he had never met before, but one he knew the name of. *A Human?*

The Human, he guessed female from what he'd picked up from news articles, was looking at him intently; just as intently as he figured he was looking at her. She seemed to be in no hurry to change back into smoke and vanish, and so he took his time to take her in. She was shorter than he had expected a Human to be. She was certainly shorter than him. *That is if I've imagined myself to be my correct height.* Ressen was around two-and-a-half meters tall, so he estimated the female to be a little over one-and-a-half meters. Her skin was text-book Human, being light flesh-coloured, and her head was topped with long blonde hair. She was clothed in a long, turquoise dress, which covered her from throat to toe, and her bright blue eyes regarded Ressen as a small smiled played across her lips.

"Hello?" he said, a little unsure of what else to say to the interloping apparition.

"Hello," she said back.

"My name's Ressen." Ressen said, trying to keep the conversation light, in a bid to prevent her from taking flight again.

He was also trying not to over-think the fact that she had understood his alien words and had spoken to him in his own language.

The Human paused for a while, and Ressen wondered if she was going to be in a sharing mood. Eventually, she answered. *"My name's Emma."* Then a look of confusion passed across her face, and her eyes crinkled slightly at the corners as she looked to be trying to remember something. *"Or is it Tia? I'm not entirely sure."*

"Well, what would you like me to call you?" Ressen asked, trying to be helpful.

Emma/Tia gave him direct eye contact. *"I don't know why, but I think Emma...for now. Tia...she's someone...somewhere else."* Again, the look of confusion.

"Well, Emma, what can I do for you?"

Emma looked startled. *"Do for me?"*

"Well, you're inside the head of a dying man, talking to him, so I assume you're here for a reason."

"Oh." Emma looked like she was desperately trying to remember what had brought her into the mind of an unconscious alien. Her eyes darted this way and that, as she seemingly tried to grab hold of whatever fleeting thoughts were going on in her head. *"I'm lost,"* she finally declared.

"Metaphorically or physically?"

Emma gave him another sideways look. *"You're very rational about all this."*

"To be honest, I'm just trying not to freak out and scare you off. First contact impressions are always important."

"You sound like you've done this before."

"Not this. Nothing like this! But I have encountered other little-known races. I got them to trust me and helped them in return." Without warning, an image of huddled humanoids flooded his mind. Muffled screams, and the memory smell of effluent, made him reel back. Emma looked shocked, and for a moment, her form became slightly transparent, as if she were about to make a dash for the door.

At the last moment, she pulled herself together, and became solid. *"Are you okay?"*

"I was just remembering...something...."

"There were people," Emma said, with an encouraging tone.

"Yes," Ressen answered, trying to put memory to the images. *"We were running...."* A phrase popped into his mind. *"The Orion Alliance."* It was as if saying those words was a magic key, unlocking the story behind his current predicament. The once broken images swam towards him and fitted into place, revealing the timeline for both he and Emma to see. He had saved a handful of primitive aliens, as the Alliance had swooped down on their planet. Their screams of panic, as the black alien ship had flown over them, taking pot shots at people who had no defence other than spears and axes, filled the air between Emma and him. They watched his apparition usher the survivors into his small ship, and then as his brother Grelt had manoeuvred them away from the Alliance battleships. They watched a verdant planet became a burning ember, torched by the giant vessels, and they shared in the loss felt as those refugees, too injured to survive the long journey, succumbed. Then, as he remembered the moment of elation he had felt on arriving at the Scientia, a wall of flame encased him. Without thinking, he screamed, before realising the flames of memory had no heat. Then darkness returned; nothing else left to remember.

Ressen looked at Emma, feeling more emotional than he had in a long time. *"Did they survive? Please tell me they survived."* After everything they'd been through, he hoped and prayed that the refugees had avoided the explosion on his ship. He lamented over his own predicament, but that paled in comparison to his wish for the others to have made it to safety.

Emma closed her eyes, and her face scrunched again, as if she was trying to push out, past the dark, to what lay beyond. Her apparition pulsed between solid and transparent. Then, during a solid phase, she opened her eyes. *"Yes,"* she confirmed, without elaborating, but that was enough for Ressen. His relief must have been palpable because Emma smiled in response.

"I wonder if I'll survive," Ressen mused aloud. There was no doubt in his mind, from the sea of flames that had engulfed his body, that he was in an extremely bad way. The nagging pain was testament to that.

Emma, however, surprised him. *"Your mind is strong. You will survive."*

"You're sure of that?" he questioned, dubious.

"Yes, I am. I'm not entirely sure how I know, but I know." Then, Emma gave a start, and her form waned. *"Tia,"* she muttered. She looked at Ressen. *"She's waking, I have to go."* Before Ressen could protest, Emma had blinked out of existence, leaving him alone once more.

"Now what?" he pondered.

Chapter 2 - Leo

Passing hours and endless waiting were taking their toll on Leo. Not to mention the fact that he was camped out in proximity to what was, in all intense and purpose, a wild and unpredictable dragon. In reality, it wasn't a dragon, though its countenance would've fooled a layman. Wrapped in the black beast of talons, wing, horns and teeth, Leo prayed that Tia still existed.

As he watched over the slumbering beast, he held on to who Tia was, and why he was staying within striking distance of her. Tia was a reluctant leader. She had infiltrated the Scientia during its days under Orion Alliance rule, and had helped, in no small part thanks to a team of covert hackers and mercenaries, to rip the station out of the Alliance's clutches. She was an emissary of an enigmatic race, the Karee, who had bestowed their protection on the planet Zerra and her people, thereby preventing yet another massacre of an ill-prepared race, the Zerrens. She was seen by many Zerrens as a goddess; her abilities, her link with the Karee, and her subsequent evolution into one providing all the confirmation they needed. She was at once good and terrifying. She would put herself on the line to protect those weaker than herself, yet at the same time, she could shred minds, and the strongest of steel, with thought alone. Above all, she was loyal. Loyal to those who served her, and loyal to those who stood by her. And that loyalty remained, even in death.

Leo figured that was why she was where she was, doing what she was doing, even though it was inappropriate. He was still a bit hazy over the facts, but he had a good idea what had happened. Some unknown assailant had murdered Aben, her good friend and attaché, shooting the fragile-looking alien point blank in the stomach. Tia, meanwhile, had been fighting a dangerous foe, deep in the bowels of the station, thanks to an unknown enemy having smuggled on board a scorpiad; a mindless drone built to kill, and who was akin to Tia in form and viciousness. They had battled, she had been victorious, but the price she had paid for her victory was that she couldn't save Aben. Leo had stumbled across the two in a corridor, Tia already in her demonic form, and had watched as she had scooped up her fallen comrade, and headed for the Scientia's only natural area, the arboretum. He had followed as part of the funeral procession, and there he had remained, watching over Tia, unsure of what else to do.

Nobody had dared enter the arboretum once Tia had set up home there. Nobody except for Chione. In another life, he had been the scientist responsible for Tia's conception as a scorpiad queen. A secret known to very few; even fewer on Aben's passing. After developing a conscience, and being near killed because of it by the Alliance, Tia had transferred his psyche into a cat. The acceptance of this reality still made Leo's brain hurt, especially when Chione talked to him, but he was glad of the companionship, especially as Tia wasn't conversational in her monstrous form. He was also glad to see Chione because of what he brought him, namely gifts from his extremely missed Zerren wife, Pra'cha.

Leo hadn't seen Pra'cha in over five months. She had gone off with the Scientia's captain, and fellow Zerren, Sin'ma, to hack an Alliance battleship. What they had ended up doing was lending a hand to a mutiny on the vessel, wiping out the remaining enemy crew, and piloting the ship into war. There they had helped save the Ciberian planet from sharing the same fate as so many other worlds caught in the Alliance's crosshairs. Pra'cha had finally come home, but Tia going nuts over Aben's death had delayed their reunion. Still, Leo was glad to know he was still in the forefront of his mate's mind. He lived for the moments when he spotted Chione trotting towards him, carrying in his mouth a small basket filled with freshly baked biscuits, or bread and preserves, as well as little notes of support. Every so often he'd appear with a flask strapped to his back, filled with either Zerren fruit tea, or cocoa in the form of Liverden hot-bean. Even Leo's friend Arron had got in on the act, and the odd bottle of ale would surreptitiously find its way to him, along with updates on station business.

Despite his use of the phrase, Leo wasn't sure if Tia had actually 'gone nuts'. However, he figured if Tia was still in charge of her mental faculties, then she would have reverted to her normal form, which was a combination of lanky Human and scary scorpiad-dragon. Yet she stayed a hulking monstrosity, guarding the lifeless form of Aben. Aben too was becoming an issue. It had been a little over two months since his murder, and his body was horrendously ripe. Even Chione's nose wrinkled in the corpse's presence, and the pair's meetups were more down-wind with each passing day.

Leo gave a sigh and looked forlornly off into the distance. Movement caught his eye, and he turned to see Chione making his way down the path. Leo heaved himself up to go and greet the feline. The animal looked as immaculate as ever, and his white fur was well-groomed, and his green eyes were bright. This was in stark contrast to Leo. His hair was a greasy dishevelled mess, his eyes were red and dull through lack of sleep, and for the first time since hitting puberty, he had a beard. Chione raised his tail in greeting as he got closer but dropped the day's basket of goodies to the ground well away from Tia.

Leo, after giving a cursory, "Morning," in return, went ahead and delved into the basket to see what treats awaited. The basket wasn't big, as neither was Chione, or the strength of Chione's jaws, but there was always something good to be found, which Leo often supplemented with herbs and vegetables from the arboretum. *When this is all over, I'm going to be shelling out for a lot of replacement seeds.* Leo was pleased with the morning's fair. There were marmalade sandwiches, a round yellow fruit, which he recognised as coming from the Pann's homeworld, and that would be crisp and juicy, and a small bag of jelly-like sweets. There was also a small scrap of paper with 'Thinking of you' written on it.

"Pra'cha is making you some vegetable soup, so you have that to look forward to this evening," Chione informed Leo, as Leo wolfed down the sandwich.

"I hope she's keeping you well-fed," Leo answered, after swallowing his mouthful. With Aben dead, and Tia incapacitated, Leo had asked Pra'cha to look after Chione. She didn't know the cat's secrets, but she did know him to be the pet of Tia, and that was more than enough to get her to agree to babysit. Leo had initially considered asking Walks, as the Chief of Security did know about Chione's past, but the man had his hands full with Shar, and Leo hadn't wanted to add to his burden.

"Oh yes," Chione confirmed. "She still leaves a bowl of food out for me most nights. Last night was fresh meat night. Not sure what it was, but it tasted a lot like chicken, and was a welcome change from rat. And she bought a stack of tins of gourmet pet food, so it looks like I'm going to be good for a while."

"And she still hasn't questioned the fact that you can bring a basket of food to me unaided?"

"Not out loud. To be honest, I think she just thinks that's just something an Earth cat can do, seeing as she's never dealt with one before." The cat looked past Leo's shoulder to the slumbering black mound. "Any change?" he asked, getting down to business.

"She's getting snarlier," Leo confided. He'd noticed that if he got too close to her, she'd growl, and the previous night she had snapped her jaws at him in warning.

"I wager the scorpiad in her is getting stronger, and whatever sentient side to her there is left is losing its grip," Chione postulated. "I'm not sure how safe it is for you to still be here. It certainly won't get any safer. Frankly, I'm surprised she's hung on to her sanity this long."

"I made a promise that I'd stay with her until the end, whatever that end may be."

"I know, and I respect that, but that end could very well be your death. You may not care, but I'm sure Pra'cha will."

Leo sagged a bit. "I know you're right, but I can't leave her alone here. I talk to her when she's alert, and it seems to calm her. If I go now, I'm sure she'll go downhill faster, then what of this station and the people in it? Everyone will be in danger."

"We can easily evacuate to Zerra and live to fight another day, but not if we leave it till the last minute. In full scorpiad mode she'll be fast and lethal."

"When that day comes, if that day comes, then that's what we'll do. Until then, I'll wait with Tia. Frankly, I must believe her vessel has something in the works. It's still around, and it helped rescue that incapacitated vessel, and saved the life of its captain."

Chione pulled a face. "Saved is a bit of a grandiose word for his condition. From what I've heard, he's still a char-broiled mess. The doctors are doing their best, but it looks like it's a waiting game until he dies of his injuries."

"Still, her vessel has got to be doing something more than running around doing errands. Jarell too for that matter. I refuse to believe that they're just going to leave her like this."

"You're probably right, but we have to prepare for the worst."

Leo gave a protracted sigh. "I know, I know. Look," he said, fishing for a pen, and scribbling on the back of Pra'cha's note, "take this to Sin'ma. It says what you've just said: that we need to prepare for the worst, and asks what, if any, contingency plans he has in place, or can put in place. Once he gets back to me, I'll think about moving. Until then, keep the coffee coming."

Chione nodded in confirmation.

"I don't suppose Shar or Kan can come?" Leo asked, as an

afterthought. "Their presence could help unlock Tia. Maybe they know some magic word we don't."

"Doubtful," was Chione's unhelpful response. "Shar's still locked-up, resisting the urge to break out, and Kan is doing his best to run interference to prevent any kind of trial from starting, because once it does, Shar is screwed without Tia's help. Besides, if I don't know the magic word, neither do they."

"Figured as much. I suppose Tia going berserk wouldn't be a completely terrible thing. It'd give Shar a chance to escape. What about Ambassador Kiskin?"

"Not so quietly seething, badgering Sin'ma every day, and trying to tie down the surprisingly hard-to-find Walks and Kan."

"Well, the longer they keep it up, the longer Shar survives. Keep me posted on everything."

"Will do, and you, try to get some sleep. No offence, but you look more haggard than any lad your age should." Chione split before Leo could give him a snide retort.

Chapter 3 - Shar

Shar sat slumped on his prison cot, seething, with every fibre of his being telling him to run. His cell had all manner of devices to keep prisoners incarcerated: guards, force-fields, stun emitters, alarms, and a distinct lack of gravity. To Shar, they were mild inconveniences, especially if Kan surreptitiously got in on the act, and helped him break out by disarming the systems, but so far, Shar had held his tongue. His ever-growing conscience was getting the better of him, and he didn't want to have to kill the guards. They were all young lads of varying races, and more importantly, were innocent of any wrongdoing towards him. He also didn't want to cause Walks more problems. The Chief of Security had looked at Shar with abject guilt when he'd handcuffed him, and Shar knew he couldn't get mad at the man. He had simply been doing his job, albeit under quiet protest. At the end of the day, it was all the Karee's fault. Them and that damn alien Kiskin!

Shar didn't know the race of Ambassador Kiskin. He just knew that he, or she, or it, was an overly self-satisfied arsehole, and an attack dog of the Karee, who were running their own private vendetta against their newest member, Tia. What little he did know seemed to confirm this theory. The ambassador had turned up while the rebel leaders had been at war, busying themselves with saving the lives of billions of Ciberians. It had then threatened, on the Karee's behalf, to leave the Scientia unprotected if Shar wasn't arrested for his crimes. If anybody was Tia's right-hand man, it was Shar. He was an unyielding warrior, a canny captain, and an excellent strategist, and it wasn't just his ego that told him that. Tia, despite all her godly abilities, lacked when it came to leadership and strategy, something she had occasionally admitted to in private, so removing him, by way of death, was a clever way to drive Tia away from the Karee hive, and possibly the war. *They **really** don't like her,* he reflected, with just a hint of satisfaction. With the Karee not liking Tia, Tia was less likely to become like the Karee, namely a self-serving git uninterested in the goings-on of those races that were a little lower down the evolutionary tree.

Unfortunately for Shar, Kiskin's charges weren't baseless. It had accused him of the murder of four billion, six hundred and seventy-five million, nine hundred and thirty-five thousand, one hundred and seventy-two Verek. Although he had never known the actual total, he figured the number Kiskin had given to be correct. The Verek were the downfall of his species, and ultimately him. His own race, the Skarren, had inhabited a neighbouring system to the Verek, and as the two species had evolved, they had discovered each other. But while the Verek had been out for discovery, the Skarren race had been out for conquest, and much like the Orion Alliance, Shar's people had seen the Verek system as a prize commodity. However, the Verek weren't a primitive people, and were more than capable of protecting themselves, and their planet, against marauding Skarren forces. So, instead of the usual quick annihilation, such as the Alliance enjoyed against lesser races, a war had raged for a couple of hundred years.

As the end loomed, Shar had been conscripted, and had quickly grown in rank and brutality. When the time came for the final push for conquest, he had been in charge, and as he had watched the Verek's extermination, he had born witness to his own race's demise. At the end, there had been no more Verek, but at the same time, hardly any Skarren had been left to enjoy the fruits of victory. Shar had fled, as everything had crumbled around him. It may have seemed like weakness, but it had been more about self-preservation. Those Skarren that had been left would have wanted answers and a sacrificial scapegoat, and as the one who had given the commands, it would have been him atop the flaming pyre. Shar figured he was probably the only Skarren now left in the universe, especially as the war had officially ended some three hundred years ago. *No, two hundred,* he recalculated, remembering some not entirely linear travelling in Tia's presence.

The Verek massacre had been the reason for his servitude to Tia. Every life lost at his hand contributed to his sentence, though whether that contribution was arbitrary, or was part of some directly correlated calculation, only Tia knew. Shar had no idea if he'd spend the next four billion plus years under Tia's command; his time spent only ending when thousands of stars and races had winked out of existence.

He gave out a long sigh, which made the guard outside his cell look up nervously.

"Don't worry, I'm still here," he said to the Zerren, though it didn't seem to relax him any. A noise made the guard's head whip round, and Shar followed his gaze to see a man that was both his friend and enemy enter the room. Shar was supremely glad to see a familiar face, though as it was Kan's, and they had a tolerate-hate relationship, he'd never admit to his joy. Kan looked as though he needed a good night's sleep, and his blood-shot green eyes had noticeable dark circles under them. He also hadn't had shaved his blond hair back into its regimental cut, having let it grow out during his and Shar's deep space escapade to find Tia, this despite having been back 'on shore' for some time, and he was neglecting his facial hair again. *Less five-o-clock shadow, more a quarter past midnight the next day,* Shar mused, as he took in Kan's ragged stubble.

Kan also looked to be having trouble with the micro-gravity. Shar, who had four arms, had no problem, and he could brace two of his arms against the wall, and still have a free pair to do the required necessities of life, like eat, or take a leak. Conversely, Kan had to take on the universal stance of bipedal, bibrachial hominids when in a low-grav environment, which made him look like a well-muscled starfish. Shar gave a slight grin as he watched his sparring partner wedge himself in the door frame to Shar's cell. Kan's face was so close to the re-inforced Plexiglass door, his breath fogged it, and every couple of seconds, a wall of white obscured his face.

"Quit enjoying this," Kan grumbled, catching Shar's smirk.

"I'm stuck in a five-by-five room with no bar or gym, and **very** public amenities. I'll take my enjoyment where I can." Shar responded, with a sneer.

Kan rolled his eyes. "That's hardly the way to speak to the person that's trying to keep you alive. Though gods only know why I'm bothering."

"It's because you love me," Shar explained, with a be-fanged smile, and an exaggerated flutter of his eyes.

"The hell I do," was Kan's gruff retort. "Aben should be doing this, but some arsehole murdered him. I'm doing this more in memoriam for him than for your thanks."

"As good a reason as any." Shar agreed. He too had liked the little alien, though more as a colleague than a friend. He had been intelligent and inoffensive. He hadn't been the kind of person Shar had normally hung out with, and he was certain Aben had been terrified of him, but to him, Aben's murder was inexcusable. He was a defenceless creature taken out for some unknown reason, and Shar hoped he'd find those responsible, so he could flay them alive. However, that was reliant on him living long enough to do so. If Kiskin got its way, then that would put the kibosh on things. "So, you're to be my defence council?" he asked Kan.

"If the need arises, then yes…and before you say it, no, you won't be screwed!"

"Really? Kiskin turns up here, with the Karee's blessing, to reveal me to be the perpetrator of a world-wide genocide, and you think everything's going to be okay?"

"Look, I get being a mass-murderer isn't going to get you a 'not guilty' if Kiskin gets her way," Kan said, tersely, "but here's the thing, the Karee know you're serving the sentence under Tia. I mean, why else would you be with her? Not only that, but we all signed on knowing death was the easier choice. So, why the hell would they let another race come and arrest you for time already being served, with the end game being execution? It just doesn't make sense."

"It's probably for just the reason you've said," Shar said. "They've already sentenced me via Tia, and to go back on that would make them look bad. Better to get another party to lay charges and kill me off that way. Though to be fair, threatening to abandon Zerren space probably already makes the Karee look pretty petty in a lot of eyes."

"The Karee seem to be playing a chaotic game," Kan mused.

"Yeah. It's clear they're desperate to shake off Tia, and are willing to try anything, no matter how bloody-minded."

Kan nodded in agreement. "Which takes me back to my original point. From what the Ambassador is now saying, the Karee only said what they did to lay gravitas to the issue of apprehending you, and that they had no intention of leaving Zerra defenceless. It was a miscommunication, and misconstrued wording."

Kan enunciated the syllables of several of the larger words hard, as if it were the first time he was trying them out loud. Something that Shar didn't fail to notice. "Whoa, those are some big words. Your head not hurting?" he ribbed.

"Don't be an arse, I'm trying to help. And for your information," he added, sharply. "I'm just as intelligent as you. It's just that my skills lie in electronics, not in being a dick." He threw Shar a stink-eye look.

Shar gave a grin in response. "Apologies counsellor, do continue."

"What I'm getting at, is the ambassador has been rather careful to downplay any direct connection with the Karee. She's making it out to be them kinda lending a helping hand in apprehending you, but it not being of Karee interest, so their reputation as a benevolent race remains intact. However, it's clear to us that's bullshit, and that they're rescinding on their word by proxy."

"Did you swallow a law book or something?" Despite Kan's

earlier protestation, Shar had visions of Kan lip-reading documents with the help of a thesaurus.

"Shut up! The point I'm trying to make is that we have evidence that can prove that a deeper connection between the Karee and Kiskin's race exists. One that'll show them to be the shitty, co-conspiring liars they really are. And with any luck, that'll cause enough problems to invalidate any trial."

Shar sat bolt upright. "How the hell did you manage that?"

"Talon."

Shar gaped at him. "You mean to tell me that greasy little barman could get me freed?" He'd never been so surprised in his life. He knew Talon to be a petty thief, a two-faced gun-runner, and a smug git. He had never come across as a miracle worker, except when piloting ships through small gaps.

"Possibly. We'd need Tia to put her weight behind the facts, but yeah, it's a good possibility."

"How?" Shar was flabbergasted.

"The plaque that led us to the dead world, did you ever see it?"

Shar thought back to their mission. "No, Tia and Tartarus plotted the course."

"I figured as much. For whatever reason, Tia was secretive about the plaque. She didn't let it far out of her sight, and kept it locked away when not needed. There is only one person who studied the plaque in detail, has a surprisingly good memory, and has put two and two together...Talon."

"What about the Ciberians who got the plaque for him?"

Kan shrugged. "The plaque had been in their collection for donkey's years gathering dust. Besides, they're more about the finding than the figuring out."

"So, what did our sneaky little bastard figure out?"

"Well, on the plaque were runes and pictograms, some were words, some imagery. The glyph that triggered our journey was a depiction of the orb, but with it were a couple of small images that Talon took to be depictions of the race that had once lived on the dead world. They had small squat bodies, with four legs and two arms, but their most interesting feature were their heads. They looked like crescent moons on their sides, as if they had horns coming out from each side of their skulls. Sound familiar?"

"Son of a bitch!" Shar's loud exclamation drew another worried stare from his warden.

"Exactly."

"So those bastards were surviving off a Karee egg." Shar stated, joining the dots.

"Yep, and whether they knew it at the time doesn't matter. Their continuing existence is a direct result of a Karee. Not only that, but their discovery of the orb also led to the transformation of Tia into a Karee. The races are as good as linked."

"Why couldn't Talon tell me this himself?" Shar asked, curious.

"He's got his hands full watching Walks' back, keeping him from Kiskin's clutches so keeping you from hers. Ditto me."

"Where is Walks anyway?"

"I think he's hiding in the walls."

Shar gave a guffaw, which was more of a release of relief than he cared to admit. Then his mood darkened again. "So, all we need now is Tia to snap out of her funk and give Kiskin what for."

"That's basically it."

"And how are we doing with that?"

Kan grimaced. "Leo's still watching over her, but there's been no change."

"That kid's got some balls, I'll give him that."

"Agreed. I just hope he hasn't taken on more than he can handle."

"Any word from Jarell or Morrígan?"

"No, and that's worrying. Everyone I've spoken to has said the same thing, that the Karee, or at least Tia's vessel, must have the situation under control, but the longer things drag on, the more I wonder. Are we putting blind faith into these creatures? What if they're not inclined towards helping her, hoping she'll somehow sort herself out? Or it's a test of her metal, one she could be about to fail, with disastrous consequences to us."

Shar mulled over Kan's theories. "I disagree. Neither Jarell nor Morrígan will leave Tia the way she is now. Why? Precedence. The Karee came to save this station and the Zerrens on it, and then Jarell stayed to watch over the station and its inhabitants, including Tia. There's no way they, especially Jarell, who's joined us in this war, would let a scorpiad run rampant on the Scientia, killing off the populous. I'm sure there are those saying we can evacuate the station if the danger gets to a certain point," Kan nodded in confirmation, "but let me tell you, it won't stop Tia in her present form. During our time together, she drip-fed me information from her past lives, and from what I've heard, I'm positive she can just as easily get down onto Zerra's surface and run amok there. Mark my words, she will be unstoppable, especially if she somehow taps into the abilities of her Karee self. There is absolutely no way Jarell and Morrígan are letting her be. Besides, Morrígan is part of Tia, whatever Tia feels, so does her vessel. It'll know when the time's right to step in."

"So, you think they'll intervene." Kan said, not sounding convinced.

"You know what? I bet they've already put things in motion." Kan pulled a face. "I have centuries of experience with Tia, so trust me the way I'm trusting you to keep my head out of Kiskin's noose."

"I'll do my best," Kan promised. "Anything I can get you in the meantime?"

"I suppose a female visitor is out the question."

The guard, who had been doing his best to look as though he wasn't listening, choked on his tongue. Kan turned back to Shar. "I'll get you a magazine."

Chapter 4 - Sin'ma

It had taken Pra'cha months of digging through hidden files and sub-folders, and no small amount of hacking and data decryption, but she had finally found the answer to the rebel's confusion at the Ciberian battle. The cause of their confusion was, on attacking the Alliance's battleship's jump engines, they had found their weapons useless. The answer was the ships had new, classified shielding. The files about the hows and whys were buried so deep, only those at the top had known of their existence. But their discovery revealed one important fact, their captured battleship, the Victory, formally the Vengeance, had the shields as well.

This news delighted Captain Sin'ma. Reading the documents, he learnt that only the captains and admirals of the individual vessels knew of their existence. The secret wasn't made common knowledge in case it ended up being leaked to the rebels, but the resulting defences could be brought online once at Ciberia, if the Ciberian forces had caused problems. It was a nasty surprise that could've cost the rebels the entire battle. However, the Alliance hadn't been prepared for a Karee vessel, Morrígan, and a Karee-built vessel, the Tartarus, to be in the fray. The Alliance's advanced modulating shielding, while supremely effective against the static-frequency weapons of the more primitive rebel vessels, had failed to stand against the quick-thinking brains of Tia's vessel and the Tartarus. *Had it not been for them, we would have been decimated,* Sin'ma reflected. *The sooner we get our own battleships up and running the better.*

As it was, the GR battleships wouldn't be ready for another

year or so, even with all the engineers the rebel systems had to offer working flat out. It was a worrying time for all concerned. *How many more battles will we have to narrowly win before we can truly hold our own? That is, of course, if Tia is with us once again.*

Tia's continuing absence was a daily headache for Sin'ma, not least because she was no longer a fully functioning member of the GR. He had learnt that she had reverted to some beast-like form, and was hunkered down in the arboretum, standing guard over her murdered attaché's body. Sin'ma's second in command, Leo Jackson, on witnessing her retrieval of the body, had opted to stay with her. It was a worrying development, as there was no knowing if she'd suddenly decide to go on a rampage through the station. If so, Sin'ma knew Leo could do nothing to prevent it. She had taken out a fellow beast in the depths of the station; a plant by the Alliance to cause murder and mayhem within the GR's ranks, and the resulting pile of disintegrating goo made it clear a weak and squishy Human, such as Leo, would stand no chance if Tia went fully feral. Sin'ma had done as much as he could in preparation, namely putting Security on high alert, and ensuring evacuation plans were mapped out in infinite detail.

Yet there was a thread of hope. Tia's new vessel remained close by, and Ken'va's knowledge of the history of the Karee made him believe all was not lost. Despite the obnoxious behaviour of the Karee over Shar, and the subsequent dumping of Kiskin in his lap, the ex-priest still talked about the extraordinary abilities of the ancient race with conviction. He had almost convinced Sin'ma that Tia had the wherewithal to save herself. However, it was one thing to regurgitate the lauding of an ancient text, it was another thing entirely to be on the verge of staring down the throat of a rabid monster that had once been a friend.

A long buzz of his intercom made Sin'ma look up from the shielding schematics Pra'cha had given him. They looked unnecessarily complicated, and Sin'ma had no idea if the technicians within the rebel races could duplicate them. Indeed, the equations and diagrams he was looking at were far beyond his area of expertise, and even Pra'cha had pulled an unconvinced expression when he'd asked her if they were doable. Yet the distraction proffered by the intercom's buzzer didn't fill him with much cheer. He recognised the overly long press as belonging to Ambassador Kiskin, who he guessed was on the other side of the door, getting ready to lean on the button again. He rolled his eyes to the sky before pressing a button to open the door, while bracing himself for the daily onslaught. He'd resorted to locking the door, even when in his office, as the ambassador was apt to just walk in without so much as an invitation. *I have never known a creature so rude,* he reflected, *and I had to deal with the Alliance for five years.*

On cue, Kiskin scuttled in, the tips of her carapaced legs clicking on the faux wood floor as she came. Sin'ma didn't even manage to open his mouth in sarcastic greeting.

"Have you spoken to Lieutenant Commander Walker yet today?" she asked, forgoing pleasantries as usual.

Sin'ma knew full well the chief of security was doing his best to hide, and buy some time for Shar, but it was getting increasingly difficult for all those concerned to cover for him. "I am afraid not," he answered, in his best, professionally polite tone. "There have been some serious thefts in the biochemistry department, and Lieutenant Commander Walker is having to follow up with enquiries." The thefts had been of little concern to those in the know. They had involved Petri-dishes of mould spores, which were likely simply misplaced, but it had given Walks a chance to be gone to do other things. It was also likely the staff had misplaced them on purpose, and had then cried foul, because Shar had helped save the station from the Alliance, and those who knew it were determined to see him safe.

"Why can't his sergeants see to it," was Kiskin's indignant reply. "I hardly see how missing mould spores would warrant the Lieutenant Commander's time."

Sin'ma took a deep breath and thanked the universe that

Kiskin's questionable aid wasn't present. Sin'ma was pretty sure the creature was a telepath, and that it could read his mind, despite not being the same species. "The spores in question could, if in the right hands, be used as a biological weapon against us," he lied, hugely, as the spores in question would only cause a mild cough if inhaled by, and only by, a Toch.

Kiskin grunted but seemed disinclined to leave. Sin'ma gave her a questioning look. "Can you not sanction his release into our custody?" she finally asked. "You are, after all, the one in charge of the station...are you not?" She made it clear she was trying to goad Sin'ma by suggesting he was under Tia's thumb. Sin'ma wasn't biting.

"We have protocols on this station. Without protocols, we are, at best, lawless. At worst, we are no better than the Alliance. Lieutenant Commander Walker needs to review the paperwork and confer with the station's legal department about setting up a trial date. Then, and only then, when all agree, and the paperwork is complete, can I sign, confirming the trial. However, there is no knowing when that is to be as we have several trials in the queue, and some of them could last days, if not weeks." That was also an extreme stretch of the truth. There were three trials in the pipeline, all for petty offences, and all would be over in a couple of hours. Though if push came to shove, Sin'ma could make sure they dragged on. "It would also not be fair on the accused to reschedule their trials as they have been waiting patiently for their day in court, just as you have been." *As patient as a fly trapped in a jar,* he thought, wryly. "Further, as Tia is incapacitated, and as Shar is on a Zerren station, in Zerren space, if he were to be released into anyone's custody, it would be an appointed Zerren, not an outside race. However, considering his 'alleged' past, and his abilities as a soldier, it would be better for all concerned that he stays under lock and key. Shar is going nowhere, so I am afraid you will have to be content with that for the time being."

The anger radiating off Kiskin was enough to give him sunburn through his green fur, but it appeared their daily verbal battle was over. "Very well." She spun round and scurried out of Sin'ma's office without so much as a, 'Thank you and good day.' Sin'ma knew full well he hadn't seen the last of her, and that he'd have to go through the same rigmarole the following day.

It almost made him wish the Alliance would attack again, so he had a valid excuse for not being in his office. As it was, they were taking their frustrations out on innocent races that couldn't defend themselves, something that made Sin'ma's blood boil even more than normal, and had it not been for the strange alien pair, Grelt and Ressen, that event may have never been uncovered.

The two males, males as far as Sin'ma knew, had prevented the near extinction of the Filteth; a primitive farming culture located way beyond what should have been the borders of the Orion Alliance. The Alliance had flamed their planet, presumably as it was only suitable for mining. *Probably to make more battleships to refill the gap we made when we destroyed their fleet,* Sin'ma theorised. *It seems they are having to travel further afield for their resources.*

All but a handful of the Filteth race remained, having survived the journey to the Scientia in the brothers' hold. There was a question mark over whether the species was still viable with such a small number, or whether the Alliance had inadvertently succeeded in their bid to eradicate them from the galaxy. Sin'ma's government was determined that they would at least have a fighting chance, and plans were under way to relocate them to an out-of-the-way area of Zerra, until a new world could be found for them. While they waited for the paperwork to be finalised, Sin'ma had found the refugees shelter in one of the station's privately-run hostels. He had also given them a small allowance to buy their own food, thereby giving them some semblance of independence. Word was, they still spent most of their time hiding out in their rooms, perhaps scared of the modern-day hubbub the station's residents called normal.

Sin'ma returned his attention to the shielding schematics, desperately trying to bring his old school knowledge out of long-term memory storage. There were equations with more letters than numbers, and too many figures written in subscript. Eventually, his brain clouded over, and he had to admit defeat. His mind drifted back to the Filteth homeworld. *Why exactly did they choose that planet?* he wondered. *Most of a battleship's components are made of metal; steel plating, copper wiring, and the like, and there should be more than enough buried in their planets, or extractable from moons and asteroids. Why traipse all the way out to the Filteth's world? What did they have that the Alliance has in short supply?* He could think of only two people who could provide him with the answer, but as the head of engineering, Kan, was also being scarce for Shar's sake, he chose, reluctantly, to contact Pra'cha.

Her communicator rang for a minute before her face appeared on Sin'ma's computer screen. He saw instantly that she looked exhausted, and he suspected it was a culmination of covering for Kan, translating the engine diagrams, and worrying about the fact that her mate was spending his days in the presence of a monster. "I think I know better than to ask how your day is going," he said to the weary face.

Pra'cha rolled her yellow eyes. "Work has been frantic," she replied, tersely, "but we are cracking the equations."

"Anything unusual standing out?" Sin'ma asked.

"You say that like you are expecting the unusual. Care to enlighten me?" Her voice was clipped, and it had been that way towards him ever since he'd ordered her to execute the Alliance soldiers hunkered down on the Vengeance, so they could capture the vessel.

"I never could get anything past you," Sin'ma responded lightly, trying, and failing, to break the tension between them. He carried on regardless. "I was wondering why the Alliance flamed the Filteth's home planet. They cannot be that short of metals for their battleships, which makes me wonder if the planet was harbouring something rare, but no less important;

something that could in some way be linked to the engines and the new shielding."

Pra'cha considered his point for some time before answering. "The jump engines contain enormous crystals that vibrate in such a way that when combined with a huge amount of energy, can rip through the fabric of space, allowing entry into hyperspace. The Alliance call them Kipechtean Crystals after their discoverer, a scientist named Kipecht from the planet Lesk. Their natural state is not as big as we see them in jump engines, but rather, they tend to be small, ranging in size from pencil-size, to as big as two Zerrens. They are then grown and augmented to create the jump engine crystals. However, as far as I know, there are several large deposits of the smaller natural crystals dotted throughout the galaxy, including inside the boundaries of Orion Alliance space. There should be no practical reason for them to take out the Filteth's world. Especially as Kipecht also formulated the method that makes them grow big, and quickly."

"The Kipechtean Method," Sin'ma interjected, recalling his university teachings.

"Correct. I can think of only two reasons which would change this. One, the Alliance was furious over their defeat, and decided to eradicate a race while at the same time getting some crystals. What the humans would call, a two birds one stone deal. Or two, the crystals usually used for jump engines interfere with this new shield's energy somehow, and that the Filteth's planet harboured different crystals that have a modified or rarer composition that works in combination with the shielding."

"Which option do you think it is?" Sin'ma asked.

"If it is a different kind of crystal, it would go some way to explain why the models I have been using to test the equations have been off slightly. We have been working under the assumption that they are Kipechtean Crystals. The outputs of my models are not far off, but enough off for a couple of my computer simulations to destroy the universe. It is amazing the chaos a different fraction can cause when dealing with the fabric of space and time."

"I do not doubt it. The equations needed to create a route through hyperspace are hugely complicated. One wrong calculation, and you can end up coming out inside a sun." Pra'cha nodded in agreement. "Is there any way you can check what crystals the engines are using? If they are different, we are going to need to completely rethink our battleship building."

"If you are right, then this is a problematic development. I will send a scanner into an engine on the Victory and run some tests to be sure. It is strange it was not mentioned in the schematics."

"It could have been another way for the Alliance to cover themselves in case of a leak, or as a preventative against industrial espionage. Just think of the money someone could make selling this shielding to outside worlds, or the deals they could make."

"Agreed. The planet Lesk was a non-Alliance world, and still is, which is why even non-Alliance worlds have jump engines. Kipecht shared the information with all in the spirit of collaborative science and space exploration. However, if the Alliance have created these crystals and shielding, they will not share easily, primarily to keep the upper hand in this war."

Sin'ma didn't like the sound of that. "If we find it is different crystals, how will we build our shielding?"

"We will not," Pra'cha stated simply. "Not unless we find our own deposits."

"In that case we will have to send scanner probes out as soon as possible. Gods, it could take years to find a viable source." Sin'ma's head spun at the implication.

"Then we will have to do without and put our skills into improving other parts of our battleships, like the weaponry."

"Pra'cha the pragmatist."

"Not simply pragmatism. We have a great collection of races and knowledge at our disposal, and I am sure we will create things the Alliance has not even thought of."

"I wish I could share in your confidence," Sin'ma said, sadly. "As it is, this news has me feeling even more depressed than when I started this day."

"Ambassador Kiskin still making her presence known?" Pra'cha asked, finally showing him a bit of sympathy.

"Regular as clockwork," he grumbled. "I keep having to make lame excuses for Lieutenant Commander Walker's prolonged absence. What about you, have you laid eyes on Kan at all?"

"He turned up in his office this morning and purposefully locked the door. It seems he has achieved all he can to help Shar, and much like us, he is waiting on Tia to revive herself. It looks like he is catching up on his backlog."

"A backlog with you in charge? I never thought such a thing possible."

Pra'cha gave an embarrassed smile. "Actually, he is mostly just counter-signing my work." Then a thought seemed to hit her. "Actually, I can ask him to help in the matter of the crystals. Or rather, get help from the Tartarus. Their ship is of Karee technology, with a brain to match, and it managed to outwit the Alliance's shielding. There is a good chance that if we give it the equations, and the idea that it is a new crystal form, it can finish translating the diagrams much faster than us. It may even be able to figure out the crystal's composition and start scanning for it."

"Do it! The sooner we know what we are dealing with, the sooner we can play catch up to the Alliance."

Pra'cha nodded, and with a brusque goodbye, hung up on Sin'ma.

Sin'ma gave a long groan. "What is it the Humans say? One step forward, two steps back," he said to the room.

Chapter 5 - Grelt

Grelt sat outside one of the little cafés that dotted the thoroughfare. A bowl of he knew not what, but seemed to contain mostly red grains, shredded white meat, and green sauce, sat before him. It had been made for him by a lizard-like creature with light-green skin covered in dark-green stripes, large pointy ears, opalescent eyes, and who had two green spiralling horns on its head. It was a Maisak, and one of the few species Grelt recognised, but as the creature had been busy serving its other customers, Grelt had been unable to draw it into conversation.

To escape the hubbub inside the café, Grelt had opted to sit outside, despite the inevitable problem that came with that choice, which was people tended to give him sideways glances as they passed. However, he figured it was more out of curiosity at the uncommon alien now present amongst them, rather than from rudeness and mistrust. He too was aware of how unique he was, as he'd spent several days wandering the Scientia's street, marvelling at all the strange races, but never coming across anyone that looked remotely like him. He was a good deal taller than most, and his striking blue-and-white striped skin made him stand out amongst the crowds. Still, nobody had taken issue with his presence, and he'd never had to explain to the general populous who he was, what he was, or what he was doing on the station. That conversation had been reserved for the station's command staff, though as he hadn't spoken a word of their language, it had been a one-sided, monosyllabic discussion.

He wasn't sure how much the green furry alien had taken from their conversation. Grelt had gathered the individual's name was Sin'ma and took him to overseer of the station. Sin'ma, in turn, had seemingly understood that Grelt was Grelt. There'd also been a bout of pointing at star maps, so Grelt knew where he was, and Sin'ma knew where Grelt had originally come from. Then there had been the explaining of the refugees. Grelt had resorted to pointing at the refugee's equally confused spokesperson, to the map, then finishing by flinging his arms wide, making his best explosion noise, and capping it by saying, "Alliance." This triggered a response of comprehension, and the Sin'ma individual started conversing intently with another of his race, whom Grelt had learnt was called Ken'va. There was a lot more map pointing, and grumbled words, but Grelt and the refugee were no longer needed for that part of the discussion and had been dismissed.

The meeting hadn't just been befuddled pointing though. Both Grelt and the refugee had been given a suitable sum of the station's currency. The refugee's spokesperson, a female of advancing years who'd become their leader in the intervening days, had been given enough for the rest of her tribe to be able to afford food and drink. Grelt had been given enough just for himself and was making effective use of it in the local cafés. He'd made it his mission to try as many types of cuisine as he could before his inevitable departure, though when that departure was to be, he didn't like to guess. His brother, Ressen, was a permanent resident of the intensive care ward in the Medicentre, his blue skin still unrecognisable under the burns that covered him from head to toe. Grelt had visited him a few times, but seeing him as he was, with no way of helping him, made him morose. The doctors and nurses in the Medicentre seemed to be looking after him well, so Grelt felt inclined to leave him be, knowing if there was any change, for better or worse, he would be contacted. Instead, he was using his time to repair their little vessel, which had taken a beating trying to make it through hyperspace, and whose dying throes had done their best to kill Ressen.

In fact, Grelt still marvelled at the miracle that was his brother's survival. He'd heard the explosion and had sprinted to the control room to find the place engulfed by flames, and his brother's lifeless body lying a distance away, his clothes still smouldering. Grelt had pulled his brother to safety, doused his flames, and made to tackle the control room inferno. It was then that two things had happened almost simultaneously. First, their ship's generators had died with a shuddering bang. This had drawn a cry of anguish from Grelt, as he realised he couldn't accelerate their ship to the sanctuary that was the Scientia to save Ressen's life. Then the second thing happened, which was a huge, strange, organic-looking turquoise vessel had uncloaked above them, latched onto the brother's stricken vessel with some unseen energy beam, and had whisked it, and its cargo of injured, to the station.

Grelt, extinguisher still in hand, had been met at the hatch by a group of medics, who had swarmed on to Ressen. In barely a couple of minutes, they'd salved him, bound him, and had hoisted him onto a gurney, before whisking him out of sight. Grelt had managed to make the nurse attending his minor burns follow him to the hold of his vessel, where the survivors of the Alliance's attack were still huddled. There then followed another wave of medic and security personnel, as the refugees were escorted away from their ripe hovel. Despite security personnel trying to remove him too, Grelt had managed to dig his heels in. After he'd helped the morgue staff remove the dead bodies, people seemed content to leave him be, and other than his meeting with Sin'ma, he'd gone undisturbed. It seemed that, despite nobody understanding him, or knowing him, he was trusted.

This trust mirrored itself in Grelt, and instead of feeling paranoid, and constantly watching over his shoulder in case he was about to be nabbed by security, he felt more open to the station's inhabitants and crew. As the days had passed, he'd been having conversations with those he'd met, and although much was nonsense to the other, he was starting to pick up words. He knew his word glart translated to bread, horgger was water, and torl was salad. He could ask for a simple meal, point at extras, and he'd figured out the different currency he was handing over, which had the bonus of him not getting short-changed by the occasional, shifty-looking seller.

However, despite the geniality of those he met, Grelt couldn't help but feel there was an undercurrent of nervousness displayed by those he spoke to. Once or twice, a sudden noise had made the people in his vicinity flinch noticeably, and the loud sneeze of an alien, with a shock of green hair, had caused a fellow patron to drop their plate in fright. Grelt wasn't sure if this reaction were down to his strange presence, the fact that the Alliance could appear at any time, or something else, and his lack of words meant he was in the dark.

Nevertheless, he tried not to let the unknown worry get to him, and he spent his free time observing the station's inhabitants instead. He was in awe over just how many species called the place home, or temporary home. There were creatures with horns, creatures with fur, creatures with multiple limbs, creatures with multiple eyes, and more creatures still with a mixture of the previous. Yellow skin, green skin, grey skin, pink skin, orange fur, white fur, green fur…the combinations seemed endless. It was an eye-opener for Grelt. Sure, he'd seen some aliens in his time, the refugees for one, but never of the magnitude and variety the Scientia possessed.

As time had worn on, and people had got accustomed to his presence, he had got to learn more about the individuals he met. Through broken English and sign language, he'd learnt the heart-breaking stories of the races that filled the station; of those swallowed up by the Alliance; of family, friends, and worlds lost. He'd seen the defiance in the eyes of some, and the hope in others, as they'd spoken excitedly about the organisation called the GR, and what it could achieve. He'd also noticed one important thing, though there was a myriad of species on the Scientia, many had only a few individuals representing them on the station. He soon came to learn that was down to one factor, which was the Alliance having exterminated them nearly to extinction. He learnt of their escapes, and how others had stayed behind to give them that chance. The wars that had consumed their worlds had been brief and effective, leaving only a handful to rebuild their species: scientists, farmers, mothers, and children.

As he sat, eating his meal, it struck Grelt that the most needed individuals were missing, or reduced in numbers, namely the fighters. It was a simple reason, those that had faced the Alliance had lost, and been lost. Those fighters that did exist in substantial numbers were from colonies that had never tackled the Alliance, so were inexperienced. The authorities on the station seemed to be aware of this, and posters plastered the walls of the station, incomprehensible videos ran on public screens, and aliens in military attire handed out fliers. Grelt may have not known what the words meant, but he knew a military recruitment drive when he saw one. His world hadn't seen a full-on war for over a century, but skirmishes between countries occasionally happened, so compulsory military service was still a thing. He had spent four years of his life dividing his time between studying for a future in polite society and learning how to blow people up. It was there that he'd learnt of his aptitude for piloting, and on being discharged, had teamed up with his brother to smuggle alcohol. Although smuggling was a criminal act, it was hard to police, and the customs officials of his world were rather lax, and easily bought off, so as criminal occupations went, it was a pretty safe one. Or at least it had been, until the day the Alliance had turned up to ruin a species' existence.

Grelt finished up his meal, left a handful of currency on the small rickety table, and wandered back onto the thoroughfare. His route took him past one of the recruiters; a red-skinned, reptilian-looking individual, with opalescent red eyes, who was wearing imposing purple body armour. The alien thrust a leaflet in Grelt's direction, and for once, he didn't decline the proffered material. A thought had hit him, and he accepted the document politely, with a quiet nod.

*****

Grelt waited until he'd trekked back to his ship before opening the leaflet. Once there, he went searching for a long-lost bit of tech in the bottom of a trunk in Ressen's bunk room. It was something Ressen had picked up from another race they'd 'traded' with, having got it in exchange for a wiring job he'd done on some random local's ship. Grelt smiled for a moment, remembering his brother's love for gadgets. After some rummaging, his hand hit a familiar-shaped target, and he extracted the object from underneath a mass of clothes and cabling. It was a primitive translator, programmed to scan words and loosely translate them into a chosen language, so long as both languages were in its database. Ressen had accepted it as payment because his ability to learn languages was lacking, especially compared to Grelt's.

Grelt plugged its charger into a wall socket, turned it on, and checked its index. The good news for him was that it contained rudimentary Human, the bad news was that it didn't have Grelt's language. However, it did have the next best thing, simplified, albeit bastardised, Maisak, which was a language Grelt knew the basics of to read thanks to him and his brother having traded with the race's outermost colony. He slowly moved the device over the leaflet, allowing it to capture the words to its memory, and once he'd covered every side of the paper, he let the device go to work. The resulting text wasn't that much easier to read, but if Grelt let his eyes glaze over the sentences, rather than focusing too hard on grammatical structure, he could get the gist of what was being said.

It was as he'd figured. The GR, otherwise known as the Galactic Revolutionists, were seeking paid volunteers to fill positions in their developing armies. There was a roll call for cooks, electricians, mechanics, ground troops, and of course, pilots. There was mention of their captured battleship and talk of more ships being built. Having seen the size of the Alliance battleships, Grelt knew they needed an inordinate amount of people to fill them to make them functional. *This station may be big, but I doubt all the people on it could fill even one battleship. They're going to need an awful lot more bodies if they're to go to war.* He wondered how many people had already signed on, and what their motivations were. After he had carried out his military service, Grelt hadn't considered for a minute joining the army full time. Yes, there were occasional spats between neighbouring countries that needed to be sorted out, but his own country was at peace, and he saw no reason to get involved in other people's bickering. Plus, he liked being alive.

However, as he sat, sipping a nightcap, he couldn't get out of his mind the stories he'd heard from the unfortunates. Many had seen their worlds come to an end but were in no position to do anything about it or help prevent it happening to other people. The GR could hardly expect barely weaned children and aged mothers to take up arms. He reflected on how far his own world was to the ever-encroaching border of Orion Alliance space. His home lay on the opposite side of the galaxy's heart to Alliance space, and chances were, his planet had several hundreds of years' grace. But what then? Also, it may have been far away, but it was by no means safe, as the decimation of the refugee's world testified to. If his people weren't prepared, then they'd go the same way as every other race, military-enabled or otherwise. It was a sobering thought, and Grelt gave up on his drink.

Will future generations look harshly on me if I'm able to do something, but don't? he pondered, as his eyes fell upon the one word in the leaflet that spoke the loudest to him; pilots.

Chapter 6 - Arron

Ensign Arron Collins went through his daily bridge routine. He arrived on deck the same time as Commander Emell Nyon, Leo's temporary command replacement, and stood to attention as she, and Commander Veth Herrin, exchanged pleasantries and issues of note. That done, Arron accepted a datapad from his night shift counterpart, which listed the night's coming and goings, and as he familiarised himself with the updates, he made a hot beverage for Commander Nyon. By the time the brew was ready, he could present both to the Commander, and get her up to speed on any critical issues, as well as any meetings that could crop up. As it was, because she was only a temporary fixture, and not fully trained in what was expected from her in meetings, she didn't have many on her schedule. Mediation and the like were reserved for Captain Sin'ma and Ken'va, leaving the Commander to concentrate on overseeing the bridge, as well as attending meetings with staff to go over menial issues like systems checks and rota changes.

Commander Emell Nyon was a Ciberian, like Commander Herrin, but that was where the similarities ended. Whereas Herrin was a male, Nyon was female, and had the large curving black horns and blue eyes indicative of her dominant gender. Her fur was of her species' normal colour of tan with deep brown stripes, unlike Commander Herrin, who had a rare mutation that gave him orange, brown-striped fur. She also lacked the mass of gold earrings and gold capped fangs of her nocturnal counterpart, instead, she wore a black adornment attached to one of her horns. It looked like a diamond brooch with long tassels, but every bit of it was carved out of obsidian. It was something some other Ciberian females seemed to wear, and Arron occasionally pondered what, if anything, it signified.

Beyond the physical difference, Arron also found Commander Nyon to be much more gentile, and a pleasant antithesis to Commander Herrin's roguish brashness. Although she had no experience of commanding a station like the Scientia, she had been chosen to fill in for Leo after much consideration by Sin'ma and Ken'va; their decision driven partly by sudden necessity, and partly because she had plenty of experience from within the ranks of her own kind as, like many Ciberians, she had been a deep space explorer. With the Ciberian's penchant for disappearing into the depths of space, Arron often wondered how many Ciberians remained on their home planet at any one time.

His morning routine complete, Arron positioned himself at his assigned station. He was scheduled to man long-range communications, which meant his day was to be spent listening for incoming messages from outside the Zerren system. This usually boiled down to warnings from vessels heading towards the system that they were going to appear at some point, either through the massive jumpgates, or under their own steam via jump engines. Arron would need to make the relevant notes in the station's log of the vessel's name, and ETA, then respond that the message had been received. After which, he moved onto the next. When the ship finally arrived, it became the responsibility of whoever was covering short-range communications.

Arron methodically switched between bandwidths, listening for any direct messages, while trying to stop his thoughts from wandering off during the long stretches of silence. He had to admit, it was one of the least stressful posts, at least during the current lull in battle. The guys dealing with internal communications barely got a moment to themselves, thanks to having to relay massages from departments and docked ships, as well as responding to random requests. The only other quieter post was weapons, and the Zerren posted there looked to be already nodding off.

Arron felt for the guy, as he'd found it equally soporific the last time he'd been sat behind the controls. He'd been running the gamut of stressful and boring posts because he had his eye on a promotion and needed to be up to speed on all the various positions, otherwise Sin'ma wouldn't consider raising his rank. Arron wanted to prove his worth as a senior member of staff, and though he didn't begrudge Leo his quick assent up the ranks, he wanted to achieve his without the helping hand of an alien demigoddess. So he sat, glassy eyed, while trying desperately not to think about what he was going to eat for lunch.

After an hour or so, during which time he'd decided he was going to have Zerren-caught fish and chips, a faint call-sign directed towards the Scientia caught his ear. He fiddled with the settings to enhance the signal, and caught the name of the ship, the Eiden Selz. A quick side check told him it was a Rolst explorer, out charting some barely visited region of space. The message was a self-contained report on a repeat loop, and Arron knew it would remain so until any response he sent was received by the sending vessel. Which, because of the distances involved, could take anywhere between several hours, or several days, depending on the reliability of the jumpgates when it came to relaying the answer.

Arron listened intently to the message, making sure to jot down the important points. It was in the Rolst dialect, which Arron understood fairly well, meaning he could translate most of the message directly, and it listed two sets of coordinates. The first linked to the ships name, which Arron took to mean the vessel's position on sending the message. The second set of coordinates was paired with the phrase 'hokellza', which was something Arron didn't completely understand. He knew 'hokell' meant planet and 'za' meant dark, which he assumed grammatically meant dark planet, but what a dark planet was, was an enigma to him. As the message played over in his ear, he called up a new screen, and ran a search for the phrase in Rolst scientific literature.

The answer took barely a millisecond to come back to him. "So dark planet means rogue planet," Arron muttered under his breath. He knew what rogue planets were; they were worlds without suns, sent aimlessly wandering through space because of some catastrophe that had befallen them in their home system. A cross-check with the station's star charts revealed it to be an unidentified body, its co-ordinates putting it in the vast expanse of nothingness that was deep space. Arron was unsure of what to do next. He turned to check on Commander Nyon and saw that she was sat quietly in the captain's chair, reading her datapad. He decided not to yell across the bridge, choosing instead to go to the commander to give her the news up close.

"Commander, sorry to interrupt," he said, politely, as he reached her, "but I've received some information, and I'm not sure what to do with it."

"What sort of information?" Emell asked, looking up from her list of figures.

"Well, apparently the Rolst explorer Eiden Selz has located an uncharted rogue planet way out in interstellar space. In fact, it's so far out it's in a region not even named under Zerra's Sector System, it's just referred to as deep space. What should I do?"

Emell's eyes had lit up at the mention of an unexplored world, indicating the Ciberian adventuring spirit was still alive and well within her. "Protocol says we should get an independent verification of the discovery," she stated, trying not to sound too excited. "Contact the Observatory Institute on Zerra, give them the co-ordinates, and get them to check. Those co-ordinates put it a long way out, but if they array their telescopes, they may be able to spot it."

Arron went back to his station. He threw together a quick communique to the head scientist at the Observatory Institute, then formulated a message to the Rolst vessel, thanking them for their input, and telling them further investigations were in hand. That done, he went back to listening for his next random message, as he watched Commander Nyon get up to patrol the workstations.

As efficient as Commander Nyon was, Arron missed Leo. He hadn't seen his friend for ages, and spent the quiet moments worrying about him. He missed their daily chats about their lives past and present and missed having a friendly face to catch the eye of, and nod at, during rare lulls. Not that his fellow crewmates were horrible. The Zerren, Ciberian, and Maisak personnel, to name a few races, were all good people, but he didn't share the bond with them that he had with Leo. Leo and he were akin to brothers. They were two Humans of similar pasts, and of similar ages, who could talk of relatable things, and he hoped that whatever was happening with Tia didn't result in his best friend being taken from him.

Arron didn't know Tia well, having only met her once after the battle to claim the Scientia, as she went about deciding who amongst the Human crew might be a future danger to the station. She had barely given him a sideways glance as she'd declared him fit to continue duty; Arron's heroics in the Medicentre already common knowledge by then. In those few seconds, Arron had decided she was tall and intimidating, but that was about all he could surmise. Leo had enlightened him on his escape from the arboretum, when she had shredded the double steel doors, and a lot of Alliance soldiers. Then her storming of the bridge, where she had mentally taken out a group of high-level Alliance telekinetics, and even more soldiers. All of which made her sound even more scary to Arron, and now his best friend was in the arboretum with some horrendously metamorphosed version of her, as she guarded the body of her fallen aide.

Because of Leo's current predicament, being sat within earshot of the internal communications posts was nerve-wracking for Arron. Every time he heard an individual stationed there raise their voice, his stomach would leap as, for a split-second, he entertained the idea that the shit had hit the fan, and Tia was about to run amok. The only thing worse than sitting beside internal communications was manning internal communications, as there was every possibility that Arron would be the one to get that message. He did not want to be the one to receive the news of his friend's abrupt death. He'd known training for a promotion was going to be stressful, but the added worry of Tia and Leo was leaving him feeling emotionally drained at the end of every day. He just hoped that he'd hear some good news, and soon.

*****

It was three days later when Arron heard back about the rogue planet. In truth, he'd forgotten all about it, as he'd been too engrossed with learning the ropes of the other bridge positions to spare it a second thought. However, as he made his way onto the bridge for his morning shift, contemplating the mind-numbing day he had ahead at the weapons console, he was stopped short by Ensign Bell'ka. She bounded up to him, an excited look in her bright yellow eyes.

"I heard back from the Observatory Institute last night," she stated, "and they confirmed the discovery of a new rogue world."

"And a good morning to you too Ensign Bell'ka," said Arron, cheekily.

Bell'ka looked a little abashed. "Apologies, I guess I was a little excited to tell you. I have been thinking about it all night, waiting to let you know…. Good morning Ensign Collins."

"I never thought you'd be the kind of person to be excited about space." Arron said, heading to his assigned seat.

"Oh yes, I enjoyed astronomy as a child," she revealed, as she tagged along after him, her shift already at an end. "Unfortunately, I struggled with physics. All those equations," she added, glumly. "The role of communications officer is not the one I dreamed of when I was young, but at least it gives me the chance to see above Zerra's atmosphere."

"So, what did the scientists have to say?"

"Not much, which is not surprising, given its distance. Microlensing confirmed its existence, and its location, which is where the Rolsts said it would be. They are now doing further observations to try to work out its size, and to track its movement, so they can figure out where it came from. They also plan to do some spectroscopy work to detect what it is made of."

Arron had to smile. "You sound as excited as Commander Nyon tried not to when I told her there was a world out there that hadn't been explored."

Bell'ka smiled back. "I guess I am what you Humans would call a nerd about this kind of thing. Oh, and the scientists have been discussing what to call it. As you sent the message, they thought about putting Arron in the name."

Arron shook his head profusely. "No no. It was discovered by the Rolsts aboard the Eiden Selz. If it's to be named after anything, it should at least be that, or after their science officer. I'll chase up their personnel logs when I have a free moment and pass the information on to the Observatory Institute. I wonder if they'll discover anything interesting about it."

Bell'ka shook her head. "I do not think so. From what I know, they are usually the size of a gas giant and devoid of life. Although, this one appears to be a lot smaller because of its minimal thermal signature, so it may be a rare rocky body. Even so, as exciting as it is to have found it, it would look boring close-up. I doubt even a Ciberian would spend long exploring it."

Arron chuckled at her joke. "Well, I guess any future excitement over it will only be had by astronomy nerds." He gave Bell'ka a wink.

She rolled her eyes at him. "I'm not that much of a nerd," she said, before heading off the bridge, leaving Arron to face the encroaching boredom of the day.

Chapter 7 - Ressen

Time had passed some more for Ressen, though he had no idea how much. One thing he was sure of was his pain was easing, though that didn't mean a lot, as he'd come to realise that his whole body had been nigh on incinerated when the control panel of his ship had overheated and exploded into him. Less pain was a relative feeling. However, the ebbs seemed to be increasing, and the pain itself was more tolerable. Or it could be *I'm just becoming used to it,* he reasoned, in the inky blackness of his mind.

Another thing he'd noticed was that he was picking up more from the outside world. At the beginning, there had been only fragments breaking through his coma, in the form of worried whispers, and electronic beeps, but his senses seemed to have expanded their range. It still came in dribs and drabs, but he could often hear a general hubbub, say from a bustling emergency ward. Occasionally, there'd be a shout, or a moment of laughter as two, he figured nurses, shared an unheard joke.

Smell also wafted into his mind. There was a clear smell of chard meat, which could only be coming from one source, *Me,* but there were others. Mostly they were what Ressen classed as hospital smells: strong bleach and disinfectant, and the occasional welcome waft of freshly laundered linen. However, he hadn't tasted anything, but as he'd had no discernible hunger pangs, he could only assume he was being intravenously fed.

The only other thing he was missing was his one-time corporeal visitor, Emma. Since their odd conversation, she hadn't resurfaced, and Ressen was concerned. She had left mentioning someone, or something, named Tia. He didn't know who or what they were, but Emma had looked decidedly unnerved before she'd vanished, and Ressen hoped that Tia hadn't done harm to Emma. He'd even got into the habit of calling out her name in his mind, whenever he was feeling lucid, yet no answer had been forthcoming. But he didn't let a lack of success stop him. He had nothing else to do, what with being comatose, and stuck in his head all day and night, so he kept up the ritual. And as time imperceptibly passed, he got into the habit of counting how many times he had called Emma's name, for no other reason than for something else to occupy his brain.

By his reckoning, he was on call number six hundred and fifteen when he finally got an answer, and Emma appeared, looking drawn, frail, and exhausted.

"Gods, what's happened to you," Ressen asked, taking in her tired face.

Emma gave a long sigh. "I'm losing the battle." She shook her head sadly.

"What battle?"

"The one for Tia's sanity."

*"Who **is** Tia?"*

"I am Tia. At least I would be, if I could break through her wall and remind her of the fact."

"You've lost me."

Emma gave another protracted sigh. *"Once I was Emma, then the fates dealt me some pretty major hands. As the years passed, I became Tia. Who you see before you is a fragment, a part of a personality long buried, but very much alive. A small, Human part, which gave a monster a soul. The problem is that monster has walled itself off from me, driven by a moment of rage and grief. Not completely mind, I can still sense it, and I'm sure it can sense me. However, the wall is getting harder to penetrate, and if we can't unite, I fear for what may come."*

"So, the monster is Tia...as are you?"

"Yes."

"Seems to me, despite the way you look, you have a better han-

dle on things. The first time we met, you didn't seem to know who you were."

Emma nodded. *"I've been busy, granted, but because of that, my energy is waning fast. I know who I am, I know what I am, more or less, but I don't think I can do anything about it."*

"I see...." The words hung in the air between them, and then Emma gave Ressen a look that he knew he couldn't interpret any other way. *"Me?"*

"Yes."

"But why?"

"I have my reasons," was Emma's unenlightening response.

"What kind of reasons would make you ask a stranger, burnt to a crisp, and in a coma, to do...who knows what?"

"You don't know the real me, what I am, what I can do...if I was whole. Though, to be honest, even I don't know what I truly am. I just know I need to be made whole with Tia again. I know this sounds all vague, and I'm sorry. There's been a notion that's niggled me day in and day out, and that is; I need to trust my instincts, and right now, so do you. Something buried deep within me guided me to you, and every rational voice in my head is screaming it should be you. I agree, considering the condition you're in, it seems laughable that you could help, yet here I am, and here you are."

"So...what is it I'm supposed to do?"

"There's a necklace, in a room...mine I believe. It's a delicate thing of silver strands and sapphire crystal. You need to take it to Tia."

"Give the monster 'you' a necklace?" Ressen asked, incredulous.

"I believe so. I can't recall what the necklace means, I just know it's the key to ending my limbo."

"And when am I supposed to do the impossible?"

"Now!" With that word, Emma's eyes turned into pools of blue light. The word, unlike every other one she had uttered, was harsh and demanding, and it rang in Ressen's head, echoing over and over in a maddening cacophony. Through it came an urgent, single note; a mechanical thing was wailing like an

alarm. Emma's form vanished, replaced by a blinding light that made Ressen's eyes hurt, and his head scream in pain. Then came a moment of unprepared for lucidity, as he realised the white light was real light, not some dream. His eyes were open, and he was staring at the ceiling. The alarm was the machines by the bed, alerting anyone who would listen that he was awake. But he had barely time to process anything, as some inexplicable force was willing him to sit up, to get up, and to walk.

Every nerve in his body shrieked in protest as he righted himself. His eyes became marginally less sensitive, and he could take in more of the scene about him; the white linen covering the bottom half of his torso, the intravenous wires snaking into his body, and the two unrecognisable limbs that he saw, to his horror, were his arms. He wanted to throw up. What had once been strong limbs covered in blue and white striped flesh were instead bloody, red, and weeping, despite the gauze that covered them.

As shadows swam in his periphery, he eased his legs gently from under the sheets. Two limbs, just as horrific to behold as his arms, appeared, and touched the ground. The shadows took on the appearance of medics, as they hurried towards him, desperately trying to make him understand their words. Ressen understood what they wanted him to do. They wanted him to do the sensible thing, and get back into bed, but he knew, deep down, that was not an option. He was a corpse with a purpose, perhaps about to fulfil his last good deed for the universe, and he had to go on. As the medical staff came to usher him back into the safety of his bed, he had the urge to utter a protest, but he doubted anyone would understand his language, so he chose one of only two words he thought they'd understand. "Tia," he croaked.

It was as if the oncoming nurses had been stunned into immobility. Ressen's eyes couldn't see much detail, but he didn't miss the exchange of shocked looks that were shared among the crowding personnel. Then, in unison, they stepped back.

Only one stayed within reach of him, and gently removed the wires that were still adhered to his oozing flesh. As the last wire fell, the pain that had been kept at bay with strong meds came crashing down on him. His body swayed, and several hands reached forward, readying to catch him, but somehow, he held his balance, and took the tiniest of shuffling steps forward, then another, and then another. His speed was less than that of a glacier, but he was under way, guided by the invisible, urgent force.

Chapter 8 - Leo

Leo was sat a good distance away from Tia, and what was left of Aben. As she hadn't moved for hours, he felt it safe to not be standing sentry. She was like the slumbering dragon protagonist in so many of the fantasy tales he'd read as a child. Growing up on a farm, he hadn't had much time for reading, just an hour or so before lights out, but it had been his escapism from the humdrum existence of hoeing and sowing.

Fantasy and science fiction novels had been, in part, his drive to join the Alliance's Space Academy. They had ignited his sense of wonder, bolstered his desire to explore the strange and unusual, and had overridden any desire to remain on his home planet and plant vegetables. The other push he'd had to join the academy had been through the peer-pressure he'd felt from his other family members who'd joined at one time or another. The words had never been said, and in truth, he could've easily become a farmer and faced no judgement, but his family had set the bar high, and his ego wasn't going to let him limbo under it, so he had followed in the footsteps of his long-since retired father, two eldest brothers, and younger sister.

However, wonder and exploration hadn't been initially forthcoming, and Leo had instead found himself sat in front of an engineering terminal checking readouts. At the time, he'd taken a certain amount of satisfaction from knowing his siblings hadn't fared much better. His sister was a computer tech, stationed back on his homeworld, where she helped oversee the planet's defence satellites. And his brothers were as Leo had been, engineers, and they spent their days maintaining the Alliance's jumpgates out on the edge of their home system. None of them, not even his father, had been officer material, or had seen action, and Leo was grateful for that, as it had made his defection to the rebels a lot easier to stomach.

Things had changed a good deal since his engineering days, and not just because he'd been made a lieutenant, and promoted to second in command of the Scientia. It was still pretty much soul-destroying, monotonous work, but the lead up to it, namely the battle for the station, had brought with it an excitement he could relish, especially as he'd survived. But now he found himself in a situation akin to one of his beloved fantasy books, and he was starting to miss the good old days of mind-numbing numbers. He also missed his shower, his bed, and his wife.

He picked up a pebble and tossed it into the pond he was sat beside; watching as the ripples and fish expand away from its entry point. He noticed a small, purple, dragonfly-like creature, not much bigger than his finger, resting on a twig. Its iridescent scales shone, and its four wings trembled slightly in the breeze generated by the arboretum's fans. Though pretty, they had been a source of irritation for Leo during his self-imposed secondment, and one would routinely buzz his head at a low level when he was trying to get a bit of solitude. They seemed to bug Tia too, and were one of the few things she snapped at if they got too close, though they always managed to stay just out of reach of her fearsome maw. Not even the flies collecting around Aben's corpse elicited the same response from her.

An uncharacteristic pang of anger filled Leo, fuelled by his frustration at his current situation, and with barely a thought, he picked up a stone, and with the practised marksmanship that came from shooting vermin on his farm, he whipped the stone at the dragonfly with barely a side glance in its direction. He had half expected the creature to fly off at the last moment, as insects and their ilk so often did, but the direct and unsuspecting hit brought the creature down. However, Leo's guilt at having made the bullseye was overridden by the distinctly audible ping that had occurred on stone meeting bug. His head snapped round at the sound, and he stared at the creature, which was lying on the ground immobile. He went over to it, and carefully picked it up. A soft, barely perceptible buzzing reached his ear. As an engineer, it was a familiar sound, and spoke to him of an electrical short. *What the hell is this thing?* he wondered, turning the creature over in his hand, and inspecting its big, multifaceted eyes. Then the thought hit him. *This damn bug is an actual bug! Someone, somewhere, has been spying on the goings-on of the arboretum.* Leo figured the bug had only one real target; Tia. *She's the person of most importance on the station, is a thorn in the Alliance's side, and spends an inordinate amount of time in the arboretum. Where better place to spy on her? And now they know she's turned into a monster.* Anger boiled inside Leo, and with a flick of his wrist, he broke the device in two. The buzzing stopped, and he dropped the thing on the ground in disgust. He strained to hear any more buzzing over the rustling plant life. He had only ever seen one of them at a time, *which could mean there's only ever been one of them,* but he wasn't taking any chances. He grabbed some more pebbles from the path and was about to begin a circuit of the arboretum when a flash of white, coming towards him fast, made him stop in his tracks. Chione was sprinting up the path, minus any hamper.

The cat braked hard in front of Leo, and between pants, managed to get out, "Something's happening."

"You're not wrong, I just took out a spy drone," Leo responded, giving the defunct device a kick with his foot.

"That's not even close to what I meant," Chione answered, giving it a cursory sniff.

"What's your something then?" Leo asked.

"You remember the alien captain that was brought in after being burnt?"

Leo nodded. "You mean the crispy guy who everyone was waiting on to die."

"That's the one. Well, he's still crispy...he's also up and walking."

"Well, that's good...if extremely creepy. But why the fuss."

"Because of the only word he's uttered...."

"Yes?"

"Tia."

"Oh...."

Chapter 9 - Sin'ma

Sin'ma was going through his daily log. It listed his things to do for the day, warned him of upcoming events, and mentioned other issues of notes. He stopped to study a long-awaited report, that of the hulls in the Scientia V and Scientia II being fixed after Tia's escapades. The holes she had created when exiting and re-entering the station had been big enough for her, but though her form had been large at the time, the resulting damage had been relatively small and contained, as opposed to what it would have been like after a weapons strike or accidental explosion. The mechanics and engineers had done a thorough job, although Sin'ma expected nothing less, and the station's structural integrity and wiring were once more at one hundred percent.

It also meant the engineers could shift their attention to the next pressing matter, such as installing backup artificial gravity in key areas in case the station ever stopped spinning. The notion had come to Sin'ma after Tia had damaged the station. Whilst her actions would have nowhere near interrupted the Scientia's spin, an attack by a more determined foe could, and during a time of war, it paid to be prepared. As it was, the old station had been created before the invention of reliable artificial gravity generators. Afterwards, as the Scientia had been stationed closer to home, the Alliance had considered it unnecessary, and when it had been sent in pieces to the Zerren system, they had decided it was unnecessary weight. But now, pitched in Zerren space, with enemies breathing down its neck, Sin'ma figured there was no time like the present to prepare. With a couple of engineering groups being on down

time, due to the battleship engine build being stalled, he figured their time could be put to better use.

After a final glance through, Sin'ma signed off the repair
report, and flagged the artificial gravity request as a priority.
Overall, it meant he had a couple of things less to worry about,
though that didn't entirely help his stress levels. Ambassador
Kiskin was being an ever-present thorn in his side, and him
having to constantly fob her off was fraying the nerves of
both parties. Conversations between them were barely cordial,
and the simmering resentment each had for the other was decidedly audible.

The final blow had been when Kiskin had turned up with
her attaché, Wrymiesk. Sin'ma hadn't trusted the creature
from the moment he had laid eyes on it. In many ways, it
looked like Kiskin. It was a squat creature that looked somewhat like a crab (an Old Earth creature Talon had told him
about during a much needed unwind in his bar) and had
the four carapaced legs and crescent moon-shaped head of
its species. However, while Kiskin was cream coloured, Wrymiesk was brown. Further, it had insect-like wings on its back,
the function of which confounded Sin'ma, as despite being
smaller, and more low-set than Kiskin, it was still too big to
get off the ground. Additionally, it creeped Sin'ma out that the
creature had no arms or hands, and nobody he'd spoken to had
ever seen it eat. It just wandered the corridors of the station,
occasionally staring over-intently at an individual.

Sin'ma's earlier belief that the creature was a telepath, capable of reading multiple species, seemed to be gaining more
evidence, and even the voice of reason, Ken'va, had agreed with
his concerns.

"We cannot have an individual like that freely roaming the
station and invading people's private thoughts," the ex-priest
had stated. "That goes against everything we stand for. Most
people on this station are innocent individuals, without malice
of forethought, but what of those who work deep within the
GR? Secrets could be learnt that could end up in the enemy's

hands."

"Ambassador Kiskin is in league with the Karee, so I doubt that would be the case," Sin'ma had reminded him.

"Even so, it is setting a dangerous precedent, and it will not be long before murmurings, comparing these individuals to the Alliance and their telepath vanguard, start surfacing. That is talk the GR could do without."

Sin'ma had concurred. The bonds holding the GR together were a lot stronger than they had been, thanks to their victory at Ciberia, but the races within the rebellion were a skittish bunch. It was bad enough Tia was otherwise transformed, and Sin'ma knew that one wrong rumour, or another disconcerting occurrence, could send them all running for deep space. Then Wrymiesk had appeared in his office, and Sin'ma's last good nerve had been well and truly trodden on.

He knew full well why Kiskin had brought it. There was no doubt she was suspicious of his misdirection over Walks' continuing absence and was ready to argue against any line he gave her. Conversely, Sin'ma wasn't going to let her get her way, especially as the Scientia was his domain, and all those in it were his responsibility. Before she had even opened her mouth to begin her daily tirade, Sin'ma had rediscovered his captain's voice.

"No! That thing stays outside," he had said, standing up, and pointing at Wrymiesk.

"That **thing** is my attaché," Kiskin had replied, defensively.

"Whatever he or she is to you does not matter. It is, without doubt, a telepath, and it has been wandering about the station, illegally reading the minds of the crew and populous. This is against our rules. From now on, it is confined to your quarters until the time you leave."

With no official proof on his side, he had expected Kiskin to deny the accusations, but unlike withholding the truth, lying didn't seem to come naturally to the alien. Instead, she had decided to throw petty arguments his way. "You let Tia wander this station," was Kiskin's belligerent response.

"That is different. Tia has earned our trust and has fought tooth and nail for the people inside this station, not to mention for a good section of this galaxy. What have you done? Thrown accusations around, threatened a man who fought valiantly for this station with execution, and have been underhandedly spying on people. You are as far from trustworthy as anybody can be right now without belonging to the Alliance."

"I have the support of the Karee," was her best argument in the face of Sin'ma's rage.

"So does all of Zerra, and right now, there are way more of us than there are of you." Kiskin had given him a look of utter contempt. "More than that, Shar is one of Tia's men. I do not care if Lieutenant Commander Walker's calendar suddenly becomes empty. I refuse to order a trial until she can defend her soldier. You will just have to wait, for however long it takes." Sin'ma had been aware his words could've caused the Karee to be stroppy again, and threaten to leave, but he was getting sick of being pushed around while having to deal with thinly veiled threats. He was prepared for the consequences.

The consequences where that Kiskin and Wrymiesk had vanished to their allotted quarters and had barely been seen since. Single-serving food orders had been requested and delivered, but other than that, they'd remained scarce. Sin'ma was cautiously happy, and for the last couple of days, their continued absence had meant he'd been able to concentrate on more important things, like paperwork. Alongside the structural reports were weapons and component requests he could finally read and approve; a request for advancement from Ensign Arron Collins he could mull over, before signing off; and several mediation requests he could schedule. Sin'ma prayed the two aliens stayed gone and weren't plotting some stress-inducing comeback.

A polite rap on his door made him start, and for a moment, his mind went to Kiskin. *No, if that was Kiskin, she would be trying to break the buzzer,* "Come," he said, opening the door. He was still not entirely confident in Kiskin's absence to keep it unlocked.

Pra'cha entered. This was a pleasant surprise for Sin'ma as, since their return from Ciberian space, she had avoided his presence, apparently not yet comfortable being in his vicinity after having fulfilled his genocidal orders. Sin'ma gave her a weak smile. He felt awful for what he'd done, but it had been the only workable answer to a life-threatening problem, namely several hundred enemy soldiers hunkered down in a weapons store. The pair's actions, whilst unsavoury, had resulted in the capture of the Victory, and the freeing of her rebelling crew. The vessel had then been able to come to the aid of the rebels at the battle for Ciberia. Tia had seen the issue with the same mind, and though she had been sombre in her response on hearing the news, she hadn't admonished them, or threatened them with servitude. She had simply nodded in understanding and had responded that it had been a difficult answer to an incredibly difficult problem.

However, Sin'ma knew Pra'cha was a sensitive soul. Her having gassed several hundred men, even evil men, was going to weigh hard on her shoulders for a long time. The animosity towards the individual who had commanded her to do such a thing would, likewise, take a long time to ease. He didn't want her to be angry at him, as he knew rifts within the core of the GR could have a knock-on effect on the behaviour of others. If those in the lead couldn't agree on action, or remain resolute in the face of adversity, what chance was there that all the other easily spooked races could? Moreover, he didn't want to lose her as a friend. Pra'cha was a good and just person, and he understood he needed someone like her beside him to help him remain on the right course. Thanks to his actions on the Victory, and Kiskin's omnipresence, his thoughts had become a lot darker, and his warrior alter-ego Le'eth was in danger of making a return. But it was clear he couldn't rush her, and he hoped that the olive branches he put her way would eventually bear fruit.

"What can I do for you?" he asked, as lightly as possible.

"I thought you would like to know what we found out about the Victory's engines," she answered, in a tired voice.

Sin'ma took her presence to be a good sign, not about the engine, but the fact that she had chosen to come and see him personally. She could have much easily video called him, as opposed to traipsing all the way up to his office, and he hoped her presence meant her coldness towards him was receding. "Good or bad news?" he probed.

Pra'cha sat in the chair opposite his desk and gave an exhausted sigh. "It is as we feared. The crystals used within the jump engines are hybrid crystals, not standard Kipechtean Crystals. They are morphs of some kind, which are needed for the engines to work with both the modulating weaponised shielding and the hypershields. Tests show that there are other rare elements mixed in with the crystals, and our readings are comparable to what the Tartarus came up with, so there can be no question over our results. I fed as much of what we know into my computer simulations, and they finally work, and the Tartarus agrees with me. Which means, if we are to make more ships with the same shielding, we need these crystals."

Sin'ma was crestfallen, and there was little he could do about the discovery. "I do not suppose you know what kind of conditions are needed for these crystals to form?" he asked. "There is a good chance that knowing such a thing will give us a clue as to where to look for them. Who knows, maybe they are present on our world."

"There is a possible answer," Pra'cha responded, and Sin'ma lent forward, eager for some good news. "As I said, chemical analysis shows that the crystals contain rare impurities, but we have identified them, or rather the Tartarus did. The elements were created by certain supernovas. I can only assume these explosions seed protoplanetary disks with the elements, then, when the planets form, they become infused with the Kipechtean Crystals to form this new type. Seeing as the Alliance took out the Filteth's world, as opposed to making their own, I can only conclude that the natural aberration is the only way to get them. If, and this is a big if, we could historically track some of these supernovas, we may be able to find the crystals too. We may also prevent other species from being made extinct if we get to them first." Then Pra'cha gave a downcast look. "The trouble is, these elements tend to be formed by an ancient supernova, a kind that lived and died well before beings could record them. Finding traces of these elements is not easy, even with modern-day probes and scanners."

Sin'ma took time to think. "So, what you are saying is, we need the help of a race, or races, that have been around for an extremely long time." He looked pointedly at Pra'cha.

"I may have hinted at that," she confirmed, "but I doubt the Karee would help us, especially as we have been giving Ambassador Kiskin problems."

"But do we need the Karee race as a whole?" Sin'ma queried out loud. "We have two Karee vessels, and at least one Karee within our midst. Does that other vessel have a symbiont?"

"I honestly do not know," Pra'cha answered. "I do not think anybody knows."

"Well, either way, we have Tia. I know she is indisposed at present, but I believe she will not remain so. Chances are, she will know, or can find out, where we need to search."

"I hope you are right on all counts, and if so, this will be huge." Pra'cha confirmed. "We will be, as the Humans say, level pegging with the Alliance. Whatever they have done to their battleships, we can do likewise."

Sin'ma smiled in answer, and was about to say something to the affirmative, when the communicator to his office door buzzed urgently. "That better not be Kiskin," he grumbled. Pra'cha pulled a face as Sin'ma buzzed the door open.

Ensign Arron practically flew into the room, his eyes open wide. "Sir! You remember the burnt guy that got rescued?" he gabbled, dispensing completely with protocol, and without even waiting for a go ahead from Sin'ma.

"Yes, the alien in the coma. What of him?" Sin'ma answered,

realising, by the look on Arron's face, that it wasn't the right moment for admonishments.

"Well, he's still burnt to a crisp, pardon my crudeness, but he's awake, and heading off on a mission through the station, apparently for Tia."

Sin'ma and Pra'cha exchanged equally wide-eyed looks. "Finally!" Sin'ma cried, clapping his paws together.

Chapter 10 - Ressen

I f Ressen had known how arduous the journey was going to be, he may have relented to the medics' advances and gone back to bed, instead of heeding the unknown call in his soul to press on. Pain pulsed though him with each shuffle, breath, and blink. He tried not to dwell on what he must have looked like; a horrific burned corpse slowly making its way along the corridors, guided by an unseen hand. He had no idea of his destination, yet he seemed to know where he was going, and after a walk that lasted an aeon, he found himself before the doors to an elevator.

Another Human was holding the elevator doors open, but this one was not as delicate in appearance as Emma, and Ressen took it to be a male of the species. He had messy grey and black hair, stubble across his face, and brown eyes with dark circles under them. He was also wearing a uniform. The man looked Ressen up and down with wide eyes but made no attempt to send him back to the ward.

"I have no idea if you can understand me," Ressen didn't have a clue to what the man's words meant, "but my name is Lieutenant Commander John Walker, and I'm in charge of security. I'm also here to make sure you get to wherever the hell it is you're supposed to be going."

Ressen stepped forward, and for a moment, the Human before him looked unsure. Ressen pointed to a button on the elevator's wall that showed a downward arrow, accompanied by some lettering. He didn't know what they meant, but he was sure it was the correct choice.

"You want to go down to this wheel's hub?" The man's words washed over Ressen. "You don't want to go round to the arboretum?"

Ressen wasn't sure what the delay was about. Mutely, he again pointed to the button. The man shrugged and stepped back, allowing Ressen to step into the elevator. Ressen watched as the man strapped himself into one of the seats that filled the small structure. He took stock of the straps, and a moment of reluctance came. He didn't like the idea of the material digging into his raw flesh, but the man was gesturing that he needed to do it. Ressen gingerly lowered himself onto a seat and swallowed a scream as more pain hit him around his rear. One of the medics, the one who had removed his medical paraphernalia, and was a curious creature with horns sticking out of its head, maroon eyes, and grey-striped blue skin, took charge. Carefully, it arranged the straps around Ressen's body in a way that would cause him the least discomfort. Then it too got seated, and strapped itself in, evidently with the intention of being Ressen's guardian for the rest of his journey.

With a jolt, the elevator started. The two other occupants of the lift stared at Ressen, he in turn, not knowing their language, stared back. Eventually, the Human decided to break the silence. He pointed at Ressen and stated, "Ressen." Then he pointed at himself and said, "Walks." Ressen could only assume the man was saying his title. It also told him that his brother had managed to make himself understood and had supplied his name to the medic staff. He wondered where Grelt was. *Could he be readying the ship for our return journey home?* Then a sad thought popped into his head. *Perhaps he has already gone, thinking I'd never wake.*

Ressen turned to the medic. It pointed to itself, and in a voice that was considerably less gravely than the Humans' it announced itself as Tah-Gel. Ressen took their names to memory, but that was all he could do. He let his mind drift to the refugees he had managed to bring to the station. Emma had told him that they had survived, and he assumed that meant the ones that had managed to survive the trip through hyperspace. *Have they been found a home and a new life?* he wondered. Before the console had exploded, he had seen the planet the station circled. It had been no more than a tiny smudge on the screen, its details barely discernible, but it had been enough to fill him with hope for the refugees; people who had been no more than farmers. *I hope they've been found a place and purpose on the planet on their own little island. That would be nice.* The straps digging into his shoulders snapped him out of his thoughts, and he winced. Tah-Gel lent forward, and gently moved the straps to a position better protected by gauze. Ressen said a quiet thank you in his head.

The reason for the straps digging in was that the gravity was easing off, and Ressen figured, from what he knew of the layout of the station from his brief glimpse, was that meant they had travelled to the centre of one of the huge wheels. After a few more minutes, and with his tender backside a few centimetres above his seat, the sense of movement provided by the elevator stopped.

Ressen looked towards the opening doors, to be greeted by a crowd of curious onlookers. "Back off! Out the way!" the Human male boomed, in an authoritative voice, as he flung his arm in the direction of the crowd. The crowd parted to stand and stare at a more respectful distance.

I don't know who this Walks is, but he wields some dominance, Ressen reflected, as he waited for Tah-Gel to unbuckle him. The medic then gently pushed Ressen out of the door, towards a guide rope that wound off out of sight down the corridor. Ressen took a moment to let the instinctive force get its bearings, then made his way off down the corridor, with Walks and Tah-Gel in slow pursuit. His going was even slower than when he'd been walking, because in the micro-gravity he had to pull himself along the rope, hand over hand, and he felt every fibre dig into his palms, and his joints and muscles ached from too long spent prone in bed.

Too often he had to stop and catch his breath, and push

back against the nausea and dizziness, but neither Tah-Gel nor Walks protested his regular breaks. In fact, the Human seemed as relieved to stop as Ressen did, as each time they paused, he would release a long sigh, and massage his left shoulder. After a long time wandering, Ressen found himself in front of another elevator door. Walks overtook him and opened the door. Ressen pointed to the button with a downward facing arrow, and the indecipherable letters that formed the word 'Scientia III - Hub'.

"Down again?" Walks said, then a look of round eyes and mouth appeared on his face. "Tia's quarters?" He turned to Tah-Gel. "That's got to be his destination. It's the only thing that makes sense." The medic remained mute but made an exaggerated shrug with its shoulders. Ressen wasn't sure what was being discussed, but he recognised Tia's name, so he dared hoped they had partially worked out the purpose of his journey. He took a seat once again and waited for his new companions to join him.

His instinctive journey took him on another lift journey through micro-gravity, then a hand over hand trip to a third shuttle lift. There Ressen pointed to the phrase 'Scientia III - Quarters' and found his journey went in reverse of the first, with the gravity getting stronger as they travelled. As the lift doors opened after the third journey, he was faced with an even bigger crowd of people. Word had spread, and all manner of peculiar races and faces had come to stare at him, with what Ressen could only assume was horrified curiosity, judging by the looks on their faces. Walks and Tah-Gel formed a protective barrier around him, making sure no one accidentally bumped his fragile body. Not that Ressen cared. He was in so much pain that an accidental knock wasn't likely to register above the fiery din.

After and arduous shuffle, followed by an ever-growing entourage, Ressen found himself at an unknown door. He looked hopefully at Walks, who nodded in comprehension and keyed the door open. Ressen stepped into a comfy looking room, and a moment of relief washed over him as the door swiftly closed, leaving him and his two compatriots safe from prying eyes. He took a moment to look around the room, the dim lighting making it easier for his sensitive, tear-filled eyes to focus on his surroundings.

There was a small table, surrounded by large chairs in one corner, and a small kitchen annex. A door led off into an unseen room, and that was the direction he tottered, where he found himself in what could only be Emma's bedroom. *Necklace,* was his only thought. Whatever it was, it frustratingly wasn't on show. *Figures. Emma described a delicate adornment, so it's probably in a safe box.* Ressen let his eyes wander the room, and on the opposite side of the room, on a low table, was a medium-sized box. *Please let it be this,* he prayed, as he shuffled around the bed towards it. Getting there, he gingerly picked up the box, and fumbled with the clasp, his damaged fingers unable to get a purchase on the tiny mechanism.

"Here," Walks said, as he lifted the box from Ressen's unprotesting hands. The man flicked the clasp open with ease, and present the now open box to Ressen, who looked at its contents.

It was as Emma had described. It was a necklace, made of silver chains as thin as a strand of his hair, and woven into the mesh were tiny blue gems as delicate as dewdrops. Unthinking, Ressen made to touch it, but drew his hand back at the last minute, not wanting to defile it with his broken flesh.

Walks, seemingly satisfied, closed the box. "Now what?" he said.

But Ressen wasn't listening to his words, instead, he was listening to the invisible voice within him. He looked back at Walks. "Tia," he croaked.

"Are you sure this time? You want to go to Tia?" the man said.

Ressen stared at him blankly. "Tia," he said again.

"Okay, Tia it is, but this time we'll take my route, away from those gawkers out there." Walks led the way out, and Ressen felt it was the done thing to follow him, and he trailed slowly, and painfully, in his wake.

Ressen hadn't understood Walks' words, but he figured he must have said something about a private way, as after they'd got past the throng, Ressen found himself in a different elevator. He took it for a service lift, as it was roomier, and several piles of boxes were anchored down in a corner. Even their route through the micro-gravity sections was quieter, and the corridors they pulled themselves through were sparsely populated with people in uniforms who gave him curious glances but seemed more concerned with going about their day than taking in a freak show.

Walks kept his lead, keying doors open when needed, and Tah-Gel brought up the rear, the box containing the necklace held against his (or hers, Ressen couldn't discern any gender defining qualities) chest. Then it was another service elevator trip, during which Ressen found himself surrounded by trays of purple-leaved plants, and several clear tubs with small creatures floating about in them, before gravity brought him, and they, down to earth.

Once back in an inhabited area with full gravity, Walks led Ressen to a pair of double doors. He stopped in front of them, simply pointed at them, and said "Tia." Tah-Gel, in almost ceremonial fashion, handed the box to Ressen, bowing as they did so, then backing off a couple of steps.

Up till that point, Ressen had been nothing more than an extremely tender leaf buffeted in the wind, going where he was pushed. The few times he'd had a moment to think, it had been to try to consciously push his agony to the back of his mind. But now, the unknown force was gone, he was at his goal, and he was acutely aware of his nerves. He had no idea what Tia looked like, what he'd find, if he'd survive finding her, and what the hell the necklace had to do with things. However, he had little time to dwell on his worries, as the doors had been opened, and Tah-Gel was gesturing him through with their hand.

Neither Walks nor Tah-Gel seemed inclined to follow him through, and so Ressen found himself alone in an airlock, and as the main doors behind him closed, the ones in front of him parted, to reveal the last place he'd expected to come out in on a space station. *A garden!* It was huge, at least it seemed that way because of his lack of vision. A giant domed glass ceiling let the light of the galaxy in, a gentle warm breeze buffeted his fragile body, and the smell of flowers, grasses, and decaying plant matter overtook the smell of his charred skin in a mix that was sweet, green, and peppery. A barely discernible swishing sound met his ears, as all manner of plants, in a range of purples and turquoises, bowed to the unseen wind. A small creature with transparent wings came to hover barely a centimetre from his nose, and Ressen, for the first time since waking, smiled; his joyous reaction causing his face to sting.

Ressen allowed himself a few minutes reprieve, and let the sights, sounds, and smells cocoon him. Then he let his feet take over, and he began an arduous, meandering journey down one of the paths. He had no idea where Tia was, as there were no monstrous roars to give him a direction of travel, so he hoped they'd eventually bump into each other, although he prayed that wasn't because of her hunting him.

After a couple of minutes, a small, curious creature appeared on the path before him. It was covered in white fur, had two bright green eyes, and an erect tail. It also appeared to be making an intercept course for him. It stopped in front of Ressen, did a one-eighty, took a couple of steps, then peered over his shoulder back at Ressen. Ressen wasn't sure what to make of it. It looked to be a primitive creature of sorts, yet there it was, undeniably giving the indication that it meant for Ressen to follow. He gave a mental shrug and fell in line as the creature slowly padded down the path ahead, its tail held at half-mast.

After a slow and circuitous trip, Ressen encountered the third Human he'd ever met. He too looked to be a male of the species but seemed to be a good deal younger than Walks.

Ressen judged him to be about Emma's height, so a good bit shorter than himself, and he had blue-grey eyes and dishevelled, ear-length dark-blond hair. Like Walks, he supported a fair amount of facial fuzz. Unlike him, his white uniform was crumpled beyond decency, and Ressen, despite his damaged senses, could pick up a ripe odour from the young male, which Walks had not displayed. It brought to his mind the refugees. *He has not bathed in a long time.*

The male touched his chest "Leo," he said, in a voice that even Ressen could translate as being exhausted. Then he pointed behind him. "Tia."

Ressen hadn't even noticed it, or rather, hadn't registered what he was seeing as an entity. There was a huge black mass that he had mistaken for the side of a building, and it wasn't until he focused on it that he could see it moving slightly, as if it were breathing.

"I don't know what you intend to do," Leo was saying, "but you better make it quick. Her mood-swings are getting worse."

Ressen made his way slowly to the mound, still completely in the dark as to what he was needed to do. *Am I supposed to put the necklace on her?* He didn't like that idea one bit. The Tia creature, whatever it was, looked huge, even when curled in a ball. The beast was a mass of black scales, but as his vantage point changed, Ressen could pick out details. There were wings on its back, each bigger than him, made of claws and dark flesh. A tail, thicker than his torso, curved itself around the hunched form, and on top of it rested a huge head, with an elongated muzzle. The head itself was crowned in huge horns, and an eye, like a pool of obsidian, stared unblinking at him. A low rumble started from deep within the terrifying mound. It was a warning growl that ended in a snarl, and as the creature opened its mouth, it revealed dagger-like teeth, just as black as every other inch of it.

As it shifted its body to release the snarl, another smell caught Ressen's nose. It was unmistakable. It had filled the hold of his ship as they'd made their journey to the space

station. It was the smell of death. Something was decompos-
ing, and by the stench, it had been rotting for some time. *Has
it already killed?* Ressen panicked. *Emma made no mention of
that, although she did say things were getting strained. No,* he
reasoned, *what I smell has been dead for some time. Emma would
have told me...I hope.*

Ressen tried to open the box still in his grasp. Thankfully,
Tah-Gel had had the foresight to loosen the latch, and he got
it open easily. Though he wasn't happy about it, he picked up
the fragile necklace, and let it drape over his hand. He wasn't
sure, but it almost felt like the necklace was vibrating, sending a hum through his already delicate nerve endings. Then he
took a hesitant step towards the beast. He could hear another
growl forming, but he refused to back down. He held out his
hand, so the beast could see the necklace. "Tia," he croaked.
The creature jerked its head towards him and bared its fangs.
Ressen didn't know what else to do but use his species' own
words, and hope that Tia, like Emma, could, through some cosmic magic he had yet to fathom, understand him.

"Tia, you don't know me, but I'm Ressen." His throat blazed
in pain, and his voice threatened to give up. "Emma sent me.
You remember her? She says she's your soul. I don't know if
soul means the same thing to you, but to me it means the
good part of you, that part that makes you do good things. I
like to think I have a good soul, and Emma, she seemed good
too. She's been trying so hard to make you remember who you
are, but now she's too tired, and fading, and if you don't accept
her back, you'll be lost, and so will she. I don't know anything
about you, but your name resonates with those around you.
You seemed to be revered, and I think, if you were lost, much
more than you will be lost, if you get my meaning. Forces
beyond my understanding seem to think likewise. Why else
would they reanimate a corpse like me to make you understand, and to bring you this...?" Ressen took another step forward, brandishing the necklace.

Tia turned her head towards the proffered jewellery. The

little gems caught the light of the garden and reflected it back on to her smooth scales in tiny sparkling dots.

"Do you know what this is?" Ressen asked hopefully. "Do you know what you need to do?" The creature remained fixated on the necklace, but it didn't move. Then Ressen had an idea. "Emma, if you can hear me, I'm here, but I need you to focus all your energy for one last time and help me. I don't know where to go from here."

He had no idea if it had been the Emma part of Tia that had heard him, or whether it was Tia herself, but something within the beast was triggered. Tia unfurled slightly, and stretched out a long arm, tipped with talons, towards Ressen. Ressen's eyes nearly popped out of his head with fear, but he held his ground, as a hand, bigger than his head, touched the necklace with surprising delicacy.

Chapter 11 - Tia

Over the years, and through her different forms, Tia had experienced dreams. Images from the day would play out in weird scenes, as her mind made sense of, and filed away, the day's comings and goings. From darkness would come fractured imagery, brought on by REM sleep, then, just before waking, there would be a sliver of realisation that she was dreaming. In that brief, glorious while, she could have dominion over her surreal realm, changing story direction and outcome to suit her whim. Then awareness would claim her. Only when she had become Karee had the need for dreams left her but locked as she was in the mind of an animal, the cycle had returned, and was beginning to play out once again.

First, the dream. She was flying through space, blinding explosions cutting through the vacuum, as giant vessels lumbered past her, and smaller vessels zipped past her, yet she didn't appear to be cocooned by metal. The strange blue void around her seemed crisp to her eyes, yet she never questioned whether there was, or should have been, glass between her and it. Suddenly, there was a burst of cyan lighting that at once had sound and no sound.

The flash brought her directly to a new scene: a personal battle with an unknown monster. Its face was a grinning man she was sure she knew, but it seemed vaguely out of place on the creature's body, which was black, and huge, and seemed to meld into the shadows.

Then a cut scene came that jarred against the other violent imagery. A female she didn't recognise, yet somehow knew, was stood on the shore of a tumultuous turquoise sea, telling her to wake up. But Tia didn't understand the meaning behind the words. She didn't even know she was sleeping.

Then she returned to the violence, and a face she knew only too well lay prone in a pool of his own blood. Tears stung her eyes. He looked so small and helpless; a fragile alien, with pastel green skin, his eyes closed, and a hole where his stomach had been; his life already extinguished. She leant down to hug him, but her arms had been replaced by a demon's; long, black, and taloned.

Realisation dawned, and as she concentrated, the monster's arms became her own, and she held the little alien close to her chest and howled in anguish. She knew if she concentrated hard enough, she could bring him back to life, but another part of her knew that he would be alive only in her dream world, which was fading fast.

"Tia?" A voice, distant, barely discernible, and rasping.

She quashed her rational side, and the little alien opened his huge eyes. Dark blue and almond-shaped, they stared up at her, and a weak smile broke on his face.

"*I'm sorry it took me so long,*" she said to Aben.

"*It wouldn't have made a difference,*" he answered. "*You remember your promise to me, the one you promised to never break.*"

Guilt stung her insides. "*That, if you were ever mortally wounded, I would not revive you, no matter what. You are not one of my men, you are not serving time, so you are not shackled to me. Your soul is free to leave when the time comes.*"

"*Indeed.*"

"*But you were taken from me. I envisioned those words happening when you'd lived to an old age.*"

Aben smiled sadly. "*I may, in the grand scheme of things, be still young, but thanks to you I have lived a long and full life. Thank you.*"

Tia felt her whole body shake as she sobbed. "*I'm not ready for you to go.*"

"Tia?" There was that voice again. It was at once rasping and gentle, but it hadn't come from Aben. Tia's unconscious mind tried its best to hold on to the dream, to make it her reality, but it was becoming warped and surreal.

"I'm sorry," she whispered, as the world she so desperately wanted to last dissolved around her, and Aben's face melted into light.

She blinked, and reality, in all its gory glory, flooded her senses. Decomposition, sweat, burnt flesh. Tia's mind reeled as she staggered upright. Feelings of overwhelming fear and pain hammered at her brain from sources unknown. She tried to focus, but the disassociated sleep she had endured had left her befuddled. She groaned, and the air filled with the sound of a snarl that took her by surprise. It took her just a second to realise it had been her. She was not the Tia she had expected to be. She looked down at herself and saw the huge body of a beast.

Dreams became memory. Her taking on Mister Ward and the scorpiad, then finding Aben and losing her mind. She had succumbed to her scorpiad psyche, and had taken on its form, in all its monstrosity. Looking beyond herself, she saw where all the physical and mental intrusion was coming from. Prone on the floor, were the remains of her beloved Aben. Trying to stand downwind of them, were a dishevelled Leo, her feline companion, Chione, both of whom she recognised instantly, and a third, unknown and ghastly form.

She couldn't discern its race, or gender, just that it was a walking mass of burns and bloody gauze, but she did recognise what was held in its wavering, outstretched hand. *My necklace!* Understanding came to her, at least about what had snapped her out of her scorpiad state, but how the humanoid before her had figured it out eluded her. An image of the female by the sea broke into her thoughts, and this time she knew her. *Emma.* By some miracle within her, her human psyche had found a way to reach out.

The humanoid seemed to finally give up, and sat heavily on the ground, releasing a wail of pain as he did so. Tia flinched in sympathy, as his raw emotion flowed unwittingly into her mind. *What I couldn't do for you my friend, I can do for someone else*. She dug one of her talons deep into her palm, then reached out and gently touched the broken skin of the fallen hero. She could feel his fear, and see it in his eyes, but he held his nerve, and didn't flinch away as Tia's blood mingled with his own. A couple more seconds, and she removed her hand, to let nature and time take its course.

Chapter 12 - Sin'ma

Sin'ma was giddy with a feeling he hadn't experienced in seemingly forever: happiness. "Tia is awake!" He'd been saying the same phrase over and over in his mind in a bid to convince himself it wasn't a dream. Saying it out aloud, when in private, also had the benefit of making him smile. Tia was alive, and well, and normal, and that could only mean good things.

After Arron's proclamation regarding Ressen's journey, Sin'ma had sent Walks to intervene, to give the alien an escort and a fighting chance. From the details he'd been getting from the medical staff, the creature shouldn't have been alive, let alone mobile, yet a miracle had happened. Sin'ma had then readied himself for the inevitable news, his heart practically jumping out of his body. He'd stayed glued to his communicator, waiting for every new detail to be relayed to him. Pra'cha hadn't left his office, seemingly just as transfixed and desperate for news as he'd been.

While they marked time, he and Pra'cha had talked in hushed whispers, not wanting to jinx the outcome, and had mulled over every little detail, their animosity at least forgotten for the time being. They had remotely followed the alien's journey from the Medicentre, to Tia's quarters, for a piece of her jewellery, and onward to her resting place in the arboretum. Then word had come from Leo that Tia had regained her mind, and it was as if the universe had suddenly expanded outwards, releasing its squeeze on Sin'ma.

That hadn't been entirely the end of it though. Tia had

eventually skulked off back to her quarters to recoup and change back into her more usual shape. There had also been the recovery of Aben's corpse, which Sin'ma had ordered to be placed in cold storage, knowing the final decision over his interment would come from Tia. However, the worst was over, and he could breathe a little easier. Pra'cha had left him in a much better mood too.

Since the turn of events, several hours had passed, and Sin'ma checked the time to find it was long past the official time for his shift to be over. For once, he didn't feel like going straight back to his quarters to rest. His nerves were vibrating, and his hormonal flight-or-fight response was still affecting his system. He could barely sit still, let alone commit to an evening of trying to unwind. Then an idea hit him, and he checked the employee manifest. One name was missing from the evening's roster: Ensign Bell'ka. The female Zerren had become the object of his affection since turning up as a communication's officer on the bridge. In turn, Sin'ma had become hers, her actions towards him at Leo's wedding a clear sign that she had designs on him. But with everything that had been going on, their courtship had stalled, to be replaced by polite nods of recognition as they passed in the control room and corridors, so Sin'ma decided to move things forward before the next upheaval came along. The lack of her name on the list meant she had the night off, and Sin'ma, basking in his good mood, decided to throw caution, and Zerren dating protocol, to the wind, and ask her out for a meal.

He dialled her quarter's number, and on her answer, got right to the point. "Would you like to go to dinner with me tonight?" Bell'ka, being the typical forthright Zerren female, had answered affirmatively, and so, a short while later, he found himself sat opposite her in a Zerren restaurant.

The air about them was lively, and patrons were talking and joking. Their waiter told them it was the first time in days that his establishment had been fully booked, despite the station being on lockdown, and people still needing to eat. Sin'ma knew it was down to the news of Tia's reanimation filtering its way through the station. The undercurrent of depression that had permeated the station was starting to lift, and people once more had a reason to eat, drink, and be merry.

Over a four-course meal, Sin'ma and Bell'ka talked shop, life, and the future, but buoyed by the atmosphere about them, they didn't dwell on dark moments. An outsider, listening in on their conversation, wouldn't have imagined they were in a system surrounded by war, or that they had lived for days in fear of a monster in the shadows.

Through their salad, they chatted about what their colleagues had been up to, and Sin'ma discovered Bell'ka was quite the gossiper. She talked about the hook-ups, the split-ups, and shared her not too unkind opinions of the two. Listening to Bell'ka's recap of Scientia life not only allowed Sin'ma to learn more about what had happened in his absence, but also let him get to know those working under him a little better. For too long they had been just faces and ranks, but not by choice. Sin'ma knew it was important to understand those that worked for him, and their quirks, strengths, and weaknesses. However, since becoming captain, and with the GR and the forging of allegiances taking up so much of his time, he had fallen behind. Thankfully, Bell'ka was a font of knowledge, and as their meal progressed, his staff became less hard-working carbon copies, and more well-rounded individuals with families, hobbies, hopes, and dreams.

As they had their soup, they discussed menial moments at work, and speculated over the origins of the rogue planet that had been discovered. Its trajectory wasn't linear, indicating it had been slingshotted from somewhere, and its course showed it could have come from a red dwarf system many light years away. Initial long-distant scans showed it to be a nondescript body of rock and iron, but that was as much as the scientists could tell. How long it had been wandering the depths of space was anybody's guess.

During their main course, they reminisced about their lives

growing up, their parents, siblings, and friends. Sin'ma talked fondly of his time growing up on his parents' farm, and Bell'ka shared the enforced over-achieving joys of having a lawyer for a mother and a judge for a father.

When dessert came, they talked about where their relationship was going, which was when the conversational ball landed squarely in Bell'ka's court. She was the female, and as such, she got to choose the direction of their partnership. Sin'ma waited anxiously as she considered their future. "I understand why Leo and Pra'cha got 'married' before she left," Bell'ka began. "Humans are like most races, and in times of hardship, the bonds between allies are strengthened. That is also true for romantic allies. For me though, there is too much chaos and uncertainty right now. I am more of a realist, and I am not prepared to make this pairing official; not yet. I cannot give you my whole heart until I know the universe will not tear you away from me. I need to be sure we will grow old together."

"Does that mean you wish to end our courtship?" Sin'ma asked, sadly.

"No," Bell'ka replied, emphatically. "Despite my words, my heart belongs to you, and while you are still breathing, I will not pursue another. However, until I am sure you will have a long life, I cannot exchange vows of commitment."

Sin'ma nodded. Her response was not what he had hoped for, but it could have been worse. "I understand. It would not be fair to you for us to join, only for me to die in war and leave you bereft. I also thank you for not expecting me to step away from my role in this war as an alternative."

"I would never dream of asking such a thing," she responded, with honest surprise. "You are our leader. You are the one our people look up to, whether you appreciate that or not. I could not ask you to step away from that simply for the sake of my libido."

Sin'ma laughed at her statement, and Bell'ka smiled coquettishly back at him. She then cocked her head and looked past Sin'ma. "It is the brother of the one who revived Tia," she whispered.

Sin'ma turned around to see Grelt settle at a table by himself, followed there by all the eyes of the other patrons in the restaurant. Gossip travelled far and fast on the station, so they all knew who had saved Tia, and so recognised his kin. Not only that, but he was a striking individual, and it was hard not to stare at him. He stood head and shoulders over most of the other races, and his blue and white striped skin, and mop of equally blue hair, made him stand out among, and above, the other restaurant goers. As Grelt sat down, he looked up, and caught Sin'ma's eye, making Sin'ma feel guilty for having been rubbernecking. He cringed slightly as the alien stood and made his way over to their table.

"Captain Sin'ma," he acknowledged politely, much to Sin'ma's relief.

"Grelt. How is your brother?"

"He...heals...fast," Grelt answered, in faltering Human.

"I am glad to hear it." Indeed, that news had been the last thing Sin'ma had read before contacting Bell'ka. According to the medics tending to Ressen, his wounds had noticeably healed in the time he'd been gone to visit Tia. This, after a long time being open and oozing as he lay on his death bed. Something Tia had done had triggered his body into repairing itself. "What can I do for you?" Sin'ma asked the alien.

"I ask something?" Grelt then took in their half-eaten desserts and became embarrassed. "Sorry. You eat. I come back."

"No, it is fine. Go ahead," Sin'ma answered. The latter half of the day had improved his mood, and despite being on a date he was in good enough humour to not shoo Grelt away, especially as his brother had saved Tia.

"The war. You...many...fighters?"

"Some," Sin'ma answered, slowly, "but not enough."

Grelt seemed to dwell on this a moment before continuing. "I join?"

Both Sin'ma and Bell'ka looked at him slightly stunned. "Really?" Sin'ma finally managed.

"I see Alliance kill world. Maybe...one day...my world. I good pilot. You few pilots. I fly for you. Save worlds."

"Well, the GR is definitely in need of good pilots," Sin'ma confirmed. "If you truly want to help, we will not say no. However, you should think on this more. You are welcome to stay here, but your brother may want to go home once healed. I think it would be wise to discuss your desire with him first before signing on."

"You right...I wait.... But I think yes." Grelt gave Bell'ka a polite nod, then Sin'ma, before heading back to his table in deep thought.

"Another to our ranks," Bell'ka said, in a hushed tone. "It seems the more the Alliance tries to terrorise the races, the more they flock to us."

"Agreed. And it is not just those that have been directly affected by the Alliance. The union of races during the battle for Ciberia, and now Grelt, shows how species far beyond the Alliance's reach are willing to take up arms to protect their future. Soon it will be the entire rest of the galaxy against the Alliance."

"Do you think the GR will achieve that?"

"It is a dream I intend to make a reality." Sin'ma answered, with utter conviction. Bell'ka gave him a look of awe, a look that Sin'ma enjoyed immensely.

Chapter 13 - Leo

L eo lay in bed, spooned up behind Pra'cha, his free hand absent-mindedly cupping one of her four breasts. She was fast asleep; her calm, rhythmic breathing giving no indication that she was aware of Leo's presence, or even his hand. Leo didn't mind. He wasn't in an amorous mood, which surprised him. He had expected, on finally returning to his matrimonial bed after such a long time away from his mate, that no force in the universe would have been able to stop him ravishing her. Instead, he had showered, they had climbed into bed together, and the moment his head had touched the pillow, it had been lights out. He remembered kissing her, and was certainly physically ready for more, but his brain had other plans. After his stressful stint of watching over Tia, it seemed his subconscious had decided the best thing for him was a well-earned sleep, and so he found himself, thirteen hours later, wide awake.

However, he had no intention of waking Pra'cha. Rather, he happily laid against her, feeling her soft fur brush against his chest and stomach, as her body moved to her breaths. Her warm scent calmed his frazzled nerves, and his mind drifted off to what he should do with the rest of his day. Command had, unsurprisingly, given him several days holiday to recuperate. Pra'cha too had time off, in lieu of having returned from battle, but with everything that had been going on, she had delayed her down time until Leo was free of his self-imposed duty. Finally, after months of being apart, they were back to where they'd left off; a newly wedded couple celebrating their first days of matrimony.

Leo rolled onto his back and stretched his arms into the air. His silver bangle, the Zerren version of a wedding ring, slipped down his arm, and a lot further than it used to. Despite Pra'cha's best efforts, he had not been eating as much as he needed. On cue, his stomach gave a confirming gurgle. Leo knew a sign when he heard it and slipped out of bed to do something about it.

An hour later, Pra'cha walked into a kitchen that was smokier than it should have been, the fire alarm having woken her. Leo, frantically waving a towel at the sensor, gave her an embarrassed grin, while simultaneously trying to convince the security personnel on the intercom that the space station was not in imminent danger of blowing up. Pra'cha rolled her eyes, walked over to the environmental control panel situated on the far wall, and turned on the extractor fan. The smoke cleared, the alarm silenced, and order was once more restored.

"What would you do without me?" She asked an abashed Leo.

"Probably accidentally destroy the galaxy," Leo answered. "Sorry, I didn't mean to wake you, at least not yet. I wanted to get our honeymoon started by serving you breakfast in bed."

Pra'cha eyed his blackened attempt at scrambled eggs with suspicion. "Is a honeymoon a form of punishment?"

"No...honestly!" He grabbed the pan and began scraping its stubborn contents into the recycling shoot.

Pra'cha came around to his side of the kitchen, wrapped her arms around his waist, and gave him a light kiss on the cheek. "I am joking," she told him.

"I know." He gave up and threw the pan in the sink with its equally dirty comrades. He turned around in Pra'cha's arms to face her, circling her own waist with his arms. "We've been apart for so long, and I just wanted to bring a semblance of normality back to our life before the universe decides to go cock-eyed again."

Pra'cha smiled. "So, about this honeymoon? All I have learnt so far is that breakfast is important. What else happens?"

"Well, a honeymoon is a sort of vacation newly-wed Humans take to celebrate their marriage. In the olden days it used to be about intimacy and seclusion, these days it seems to be about taking the most expensive and elaborate holiday possible."

"I have just returned from a lengthy trip, so I can do without travelling off to somewhere else, but I like the idea of seclusion and intimacy." Pra'cha gave Leo a cheeky wink. "How about I order breakfast up from one of the bakeries on board, and we can go about starting our honeymoon?"

Leo recognised the spark in her eyes and grinned widely. He pulled her close to him and gave her a passionate kiss. "Sounds ideal," he said, on coming up for air.

*****

Their honeymoon had been going well. True to tradition, other than the guy that had delivered their first breakfast, Leo hadn't laid eyes on anyone else but Pra'cha, and they had so far spent three days sequestered away in their shared quarters, not even bothering themselves with clothes. It hadn't been all animalistic bonding though, and they'd been taking well-earned breaks to shower and refuel, but beyond that, they were finally becoming a couple. Separated from the day-to-day stress of their work, and the worrisome uncertainty of the oncoming war, they had slowly relaxed into a familiar rhythm.

Mealtimes had become less of a stop gap between enthusiastic bouts of lovemaking, and more of a time to chat about life. That evening, as Leo tucked into his dinner, Pra'cha chatted amiably about her plans for a second ceremony on Zerra. The idea being that Pra'cha's extended family could attend and see them bonded, seeing as they'd missed the eleventh-hour shotgun wedding. It was a conversation they'd had several times already, and Leo knew it would eventually turn to the banal topics of seating arrangements and menus.

But with Pra'cha's constant talk of wedding planning, Leo

was beginning to wonder whether his own family should attend, and if so, how he was going to discretely shoehorn them out of Alliance-held space. True, they were on the outskirts, and far away from the beating heart of the Alliance, but that didn't mean they weren't being kept an eye on. Big brother was still very much a thing, and Leo had no doubt that the Alliance was watching his parents and siblings even more than normal, what with him being a defector and an enemy of the state.

If he was honest, then he had to claim surprise at them having not already been rounded up and shoved into some penal colony to blackmail him back into the fold. *I guess with the GR giving them problems, it's not been at the forefront of their mind.* However, that could all change if Leo reached out to them. Up till then, his family would have plausible deniability on their side. They could claim that Leo had acted of his own accord, and that they disowned him and his actions. If he spoke to them, and they didn't instantly turn him in to the authorities, they would be charged as rebel collaborators, and could be sentenced to death.

Leo's stomach gave a lurch at that thought. It made him realise that his family needed to be taken out of harm's way, but that was easier said than done, and not just because he would be pulling them out of the clutches of the Alliance. The farm where they lived, where he had grown up, was their home, no matter its location. To his elderly parents, it was their entire world, and had taken up nearly every waking moment of their lives. Especially for his mother, who had never entered military service, and had spent her days, first with her own parents, then with the help of Leo and his siblings, keeping it ticking over in their father's absences. To simply walk away from that would be no easy feat for his parents. His brothers and sister were less tied to the place, but they were employees of the Alliance, and were doubtless being kept under close observation.

Leo gave a frustrated sigh, which made Pra'cha stop talking and look up from her own meal.

"That sounded like it had some weight behind it," she said, eyeing him with suspicion.

Leo flushed in embarrassment and wondered if he'd just interrupted her discussing something important about table setting colour themes. "I was just thinking about my family, and how much danger they're in," he confided.

Pra'cha's look instantly became one of sympathy. "When was the last time you heard from them?"

Leo cast his mind back. "It's been a couple of years now. I sent them a message shortly before the Alliance sent its soldiers to secure the station, and I got a communique back pretty much the day before everything kicked off, telling me to be careful. After that, there's been radio silence. I haven't dared contact them in case the Alliance uses them as a weapon against me. And they've not contacted me in return."

"Do you think it is because they are worried that doing so will endanger them, or do you worry that they have turned their backs on you?"

Leo took a minute to think. He didn't want Pra'cha to be right about the latter; however, the more he thought about it, the more he didn't think it was true. "They haven't disowned me," he said, with assuredness. "They were never big on the Alliance, and the more I look back on my life, the more I see the little clues. Propaganda stuff would go missing or get accidentally damaged. My eldest brother, Nathan, had to get a recruitment pamphlet from the neighbours, as our copy had 'accidentally' ended up in the recycling. My childhood disks, which I now realise were blatant brain washing, 'accidentally' fell in the fire. And whenever governmental agents came to visit us, me and my siblings were often unavailable to chat, being 'unfortunately' at the far end of our land doing 'farming stuff'."

"It sounds like your parents did everything they could to keep you out of the Alliance's clutches."

"Fat lot of good it did. My brothers and sister work for them, as did I."

"True, but it seems to me your parents, through their actions, prevented you all from becoming Alliance drones. No disrespect, but your position was minor, and so I think are theirs. You all became technicians, not soldiers. You may have joined their ranks, but you never became a cold-hearted murderer like so many others, and chances are, your brothers and sister are the same." Pra'cha gave him a supportive smile.

"Which basically has me circling back to my original worry of just how much danger they're in. The Alliance knows I'm a turncoat, and a high profile one at that." He gave his dinner an unenthusiastic prod, having lost his appetite several mouthfuls ago. "If the Alliance believes the rest of my family are poised to do likewise, it's something they can't let happen. They don't want people to start questioning the Alliance's leadership. Restless masses have the power to topple totalitarian regimes, which is something they'll want to nip in the bud ASAP."

"Have you spoken to Sin'ma and Ken'va about this?"

"No. It's something I've only recently started thinking about. I've been so caught up in chaos that it hasn't been until these last few days of peace that it's properly occurred to me."

Pra'cha nodded in understanding. "I expect you are not the only person to be thinking about this. There are many Humans aboard the station who chose to swear allegiance to us. I would imagine their families are in equal danger."

Pra'cha's words hit Leo harder than he was expecting. He had been so mired in his own worry, and for such a short amount of time, that it hadn't occurred to him his fellow Humans had probably been thinking the same thing, and for far longer. *Does Arron worry about this too? I can't imagine why not, yet he's never spoken of his fears. How many sleepless nights has he had because of his choice to stay and fight?*

His face must have mirrored the horror of his realisation, as Pra'cha had lent forward and taken his hand in hers. "I think it is time we address this problem," she said, turning into the pragmatic alien Leo was grateful to know and love.

He nodded mutely, not daring to speak, as he was feeling dangerously nauseated. He was also aware their brief honeymoon had just ended on one hell of a downer.

*****

Within a short space of time, Leo was seated in the captain's office, facing Sin'ma and Ken'va. However, to Leo it had felt like an eternity, as up until that point his days back at work overseeing the bridge crew had been accompanied by a constant, gnawing worry that had grown daily. In the interim, he'd spoken to a few of the Humans he knew, to get a feel of what their predicaments where. Unsurprisingly, Arron had been his first port of call, and his story had been the same as Leo's, in that the Alliance hadn't overly influenced his family. Mainly because, as fisherman, they'd spent substantial time out at sea away from the prying eyes of government agencies.

As Arron had said, "...as long as we brought the fish in, they were happy." He too had heard nothing from his family since the coup on the Scientia. "I just figured the Alliance were blocking communications," he had confided to Leo. "For all I know, they think I'm still some menial worker on an Alliance-run station and have no idea what's actually happened." If that were true, it wouldn't have surprised Leo. It was in the Alliance's best interest to keep everything on an even keel, and the fewer that knew, and the less they knew, the better. But that hadn't stopped Arron from worrying about his family as, like Leo, he knew full well the Alliance would happily use them against him if the need arose. "I may not believe in a god, but that doesn't stop me from praying that they're safely out at sea."

Leo's slightly lesser friend, Sebastian Wynn, a cleaner from the Munitions Department, had told a different story. He had grown up in the depths of the Orion Alliance, on one of Earth's oldest colonies. As he had come aboard the Scientia for its Zerren mission at the age of forty-one, he had spent a lot of years under the Alliance's corrupting influence. His elderly parents were clear indicators of that, and according to Sebastian, were staunch supporters of the Alliance. "I'm guessing I'm outta their will," he'd joked to Leo, but with a dark look in his eyes. "Not that I'm bothered mind. They weren't exactly what I'd describe as nice people...or parents." He had taken a long pause, leaving Leo to wonder if he was hinting at an abusive home-life. "They were the main reason why I chose to be a lowly cleaner on a space station, rather than use my enforced education in microbiology." He had raised a knowing eyebrow at Leo, and Leo had grasped the meaning behind it. A degree in microbiology usually meant a profitable career in biological warfare. "I think it's safe to say the Alliance won't be using them against me, and even if they try, I won't be biting. They can do what they want to them as far as I'm concerned."

The other Humans Leo had spoken to also seemed to divide themselves between the two camps. There were those who had grown up within moderate communities, had little dealings with the Alliance, and who worried daily about their families and friends. Then there were those who had been in the thick of things, and had then either, like Sebastian, chosen a different path to those around them, or else had, much like Walks and Lieutenant Commander Chavez, followed the herd until having an epiphany. Amongst the latter group, opinion was again divided between worrying about family, who may or may-not agree with Alliance rule, and those, like Sebastian, who didn't care in the least what happened to them.

For those who were worrying about kith and kin, things were at last progressing, and Leo was bringing the meeting to a start. "I asked you here to discuss what to do about the families of those Humans who have remained on the station." he said to the two Zerrens. "With the Alliance getting increasingly pissed off with us, there's a very real possibility that our loved ones will be used as bartering chips, threats against us, or as Human shields."

Sin'ma and Ken'va nodded in understanding.

"To be honest, it is not just your families that we have to

consider," Ken'va said. "The situation is shifting within Alliance space, thanks in part to our victory at Ciberia, and what I am about to tell must go no further than this room, at least for now." There were gestures of the affirmative. "I have received word of Humans, as well as other individuals from more moderate Alliance races, usually from outlying colonies, crossing over border space, or reaching out to non-colonised alien worlds, looking for asylum. It would appear many are losing their taste for the Alliance, its methods, and what it stands for."

"This is news to me," Sin'ma said, indignantly.

"I mean no offence, but that is as it should be," Ken'va answered, in a placating tone. "If these exoduses, or desire to do the same, became common knowledge, any mass defection would be ended as soon as it had begun. We need those who wish to change sides to know that we, as the Humans put it, have their backs. If we can get them out as surreptitiously as possible, all the better. We need them to know that escape is a valid option, and that they can trust us to help them."

"Those high up in the Alliance are not going to like this," Sin'ma said, sounding worried.

"Agreed. Which is why I have stayed silent on the matter until now," Ken'va confirmed. "It is certain that when they discover these uprisings and desertions, they will go about eradicating the treasonous behaviour the best way they know how. They will choose decisive and brutal action as a way of deterring other would-be deserters. The longer we stay under their radar the better."

"How many have come over?" Leo asked.

"My sources have it at a few hundred people. Most have their feet already on safe ground, having come with no warning. There have been less in the way of initial verbal requests, I expect because they are afraid their communications will be intercepted."

"And just who are your sources," Sin'ma asked, suspiciously. "As far as I was aware, we had no spies within the Alliance."

"We do not. No, these are…I suppose you would call them missionaries."

"How can you have missionaries with no religion?" Leo put in.

"That is why I regret using the term," Ken'va replied. "They are more like spiritual missionaries, and less like the religious recruiters you may know of. Members of my order have travelled far and wide over the centuries, providing spiritual guidance and impartial voices to troubled races, much like I do now aboard this station. They have bases of operations on many alien worlds, several of which border Alliance space. It is they who have heard the messages, as often the planet's government comes to them looking for advice on how to handle the situation."

"What kind of mix are we looking at?" Sin'ma asked, seemingly satisfied with Ken'va's explanation.

"Mostly Humans, but there have been a few Liktrarths, Espakelings, and Galays appearing. This is by no means a complete list of course. It changes weekly, and there are probably those we do not know about because they have headed towards less communicative worlds."

"Any Humans from Demeter Nine," Leo asked, hopefully. "That's where my family are from." *Could they have already left? Is that why I've heard nothing from them in so long?* He didn't want to dare hope, but he couldn't help it.

Ken'va took a moment to consult his data pad, but to Leo's disappointment, he shook his head. "I am sorry, but no."

"Figures," Leo said, sadly. "Although my world is on the outskirts of Alliance space, it's a long way from a free world. They'd need a good vessel to make that crossing, which is something a farming colony simply doesn't have. Plus, the planet's monitored by a defence grid, so anyone leaving would likely be discovered. Even if they somehow managed to get past that, then they'd definitely get found out when they activated the Alliance-run jumpgate." He gave a frustrated sigh.

"Have heart," Ken'va said, trying to reassure him. "We will

do everything we can to aid your family, as well as anyone else who is looking to escape to freedom."

"So just how do we go about dealing with this situation?" Sin'ma asked.

"The way I see things, our plan of action must be two-fold," Ken'va replied. "First, to those who need it, we must help them flee their world. Secondly, once that is done, and for those who have already found their own way off, we need to come up with an amnesty, and a safe place for them among the free races."

"Not everyone's going to like that," Leo reasoned. "I expect a lot of the free races will be mistrustful of Alliance races. I know I am."

"With good reason," Ken'va said, pragmatically. "There will be resentment towards them because of history, and suspicion that they are nothing more than infiltrators, sent to dismantle the rebellion from the inside out. There may be those among the deserters who have committed, or helped to commit atrocities, but who have had a genuine change of heart, and it will be up to us, as leaders of the GR, to help quell any fears regarding the presence of these refugees."

"And to make sure the deserters are what they claim to be," Sin'ma added, tersely.

Ken'va gave the young captain a warning glance. "We cannot afford to welcome them with accusations. If we do that, they will see us as no better than the Alliance and may choose to stay and continue aiding our enemy. We must be sensible about this. We will welcome them, but we will also keep a close eye on them, until we know for sure they can be trusted. As I speak, we have aboard this station men and women who took lives in the name of Orion Alliance glory, and yet they have cast off their old lives, and have begun anew here, so why not on other worlds?"

Sin'ma didn't seem entirely convinced. "It would be easier if Tia could scan them and tell us yes or no, like she did with the Humans aboard this station."

"I hardly think she will want to spend her time planet-hopping to scan thousands of asylum-seekers, not with war breathing down our necks. No, this is our responsibility, and we, and by that I mean the GR, will provide the solutions."

"This is going to be dangerous, not to mention a logistical nightmare," Sin'ma muttered.

Leo began to wonder whether Sin'ma's heart was still in the battle. *He seems dissatisfied with the whole notion of Alliance refugees. Considering what we're up against, I'd want as many people on our side as possible. Or is he just having a tough time trusting ex-Alliance races? Considering what nearly happened to his people, can I blame him?*

"You have managed to achieve more with worse odds," Ken'va countered.

"True," Sin'ma answered, in a conciliatory tone. "But while I agree that we must provide them with safe passage, we cannot afford to tie up our battle fleet with chaperoning refugees. If we had more battleships of our own, this would not be as big a problem, but with their creation put on hold until we can figure out their engines, we have nothing."

"With Ciberia secured, can we not ask their government to lend us their fleet to help?" postulated Leo. "I doubt the Alliance will be looking to attack them again, at least not straight after such a huge loss."

"It is a possibility," Ken'va said, mulling over his idea, "but they are some distance away from the planets in question. They are good vessels for long distance travel, but they are not the best for an incursion into Alliance space, they would be in trouble if they came up against an Alliance battleship. We won at Ciberia through a combination of stronger ships from other races, and the presence of Tia, Jarell, and the Tartarus. Alone, they would have been annihilated."

"Perhaps going big is not the answer," Leo stated, having a brain wave. "Perhaps what we need is small and fast vessels; all the better to fly under the radar, and to outmanoeuvre bigger vessels."

"Certainly, several races utilise such vessels," Sin'ma said, sounding a little brighter as the prospect of an answer to their predicament came into view. "They would not be able to carry many people at a time, but maybe there lies the answer. We need to rescue them in secret, like you said, so the method of going quickly in, gathering a few defectors, and getting out as fast as possible, could be the best way."

Leo sat on the edge of his seat as Ken'va considered his and Sin'ma's idea. "I can think of no better plan," the old priest eventually said.

"In that case," Sin'ma said, becoming authoritative once more, "Leo, I want you to review the information Ken'va has regarding the defectors. Locate their planets, and determine the best races to help them, considering planetary proximity, and vessel type and availability. However, as Ken'va suggests, we will keep this between ourselves until we have a valid plan...that includes keeping spouses in the dark." He gave Leo a look.

Despite the dread of having to keep a secret from Pra'cha, Leo nodded eagerly, excited at finally being able to be start the process of rescuing his family.

Chapter 14 - Walks

Walks wasn't sure what to make of the last week. It had been exhausting, that was a given, but beyond that, it had been extremely stressful, not to mention unnerving. Everything had been going south anyway, what with Shar's arrest, and a certain alien's attempted demands on his time, but then along had come a walking corpse. It was at this point his last frayed nerve had begun rapidly unravelling, and he was finally taking a much-needed day off before his brain completely broke. There were the other problems he had to deal with, like the issue with Shar, and the interfering busybody Kiskin and its insufferable aide, but they could wait while he regained what little of his sanity remained. I'm too old for all this weird shit, he lamented, rubbing the greying stubble on his chin by way of conformation.

How his subordinates took everything in their stride was beyond him. He had been grovelling an apology to the newly captured Shar when the message had come in that Tia had gone on a rampage and had holed herself up in the arboretum. In the time it took for the expletives to leave his mouth, Lieutenant Val'ka had organised extra security to cordon off the arboretum, Aben's murder scene, and the two large holes Tia had made in the station's sides. Unfortunately, that cordon hadn't included Walks, and he was left trying to avoid Ambassador Kiskin's ongoing and increasingly desperate push for Shar's trial.

The creature was relentless in its demands, but despite the announcement that Shar was a mass murdering soldier from a bygone age, Walks was reluctant to agree to providing any help. Top of the reasons why, was that Shar had been, and technically still was, his friend. When the Alliance had come to take the station, Shar could've seen Walks as an enemy. At the time, Walks was on the Alliance's payroll, and had been in front line battles, killing in their name. But instead, Shar had taken what could've been a dangerous chance, and had offered Walks the opportunity to fight by his side, giving him a chance at redemption. Walks had accepted, along with the pain that had come with it, namely a busted-up shoulder.

The other reason for his reluctance was Tia. Despite her having been otherwise engaged, Walks had been disinclined to step over her, and make a decision that affected one of her men to the point of death. As well as feeling loyal to Shar, he felt a certain sense of loyalty to Tia, despite knowing her less well than the sentient lizard. She had allowed Walks to remain on the Scientia, and had given him a respectable job, even though it tested his resolve at every available opportunity. He also took comfort in the fact that it seemed Captain Sin'ma was also being less than co-operative with Kiskin. As yet, Walks had laid no official charges against Shar, no date had been set for his trial, and no pressure had come from up high to do otherwise. Walks took Sin'ma's lack of haranguing as a sign that firstly, there was no rush over Shar, so secondly, he was welcome to take some R-and-R.

Time off, though needed, was not something Walks was accustomed to, and he was struggling to make beneficial use of it. Rather than the calming sanctuary it should have been, his quarters were starting to make him feel claustrophobic, despite its roomy nature. However, he didn't dare leave, because he knew that, as soon as he stepped outside the officer's area, Kiskin would be upon him. The Ambassador had an uncanny knack for homing in on him, and Walks had his suspicions that the alien's aide, Wrymiesk, was behind it. He'd seen it a few times, loitering along the thoroughfare, staring intently at people minding their own business as they ate lunch outside a café, or walked past it in blissful ignorance. Once, Walks had seen it before it had seen him, but despite being hidden behind a large, potted fern, the creature's head had nearly done a one-eighty to stare at the exact spotted where he'd been secreted. If Walks had entertained any doubts, he'd had none after that moment. *That little fucker is a telepath,* he'd growled.

It also seemed, just as he was watching Shar's back, an unlikely angel was watching his. Several times while doing rounds, he'd received a private message on his communicator telling him that either Kiskin or Wrymiesk was on the prowl, and to extract himself from the area post-haste. It had turned out the originator of those messages was Talon. It seemed the barman's questionable, and oft overlooked by Walks, dealings with ne'er-do-wells had helped him develop quite a network of people owing him a favour, and those favours had been called in. Wrymiesk may have had eyes on Walks, but Talon had many more pairs of eyes on Wrymiesk. With a quick call, Walks could be down a service corridor before the spy came within reading distance, or the ambassador came within complaining distance.

Unsurprisingly, Walks hadn't wanted to spend his day off playing hide-and-seek, so he was stuck with being surrounded by his ever-familiar apartment whose walls seemed to be encroaching in on him a bit more every day. Despite having lived in it for well over a year, it was sparsely filled; a sign of what little time he spent in it. A small, purple, Zerren dwarf succulent sat on his coffee table, adding a dash of colour to the backdrop of Alliance-regulation white-grey paint that adorned the walls of his home. It had been a recent impulse buy from the scientists at the arboretum, and had become his low-maintenance companion, with the occasional spritzing of water its only real need. Next to the plant were a couple of well-worn, second-hand Zerren novels, which he was trying to get through with the help of a translator app on his datapad. He had hoped reading would be his meditation, but he was having trouble concentrating on the stories. He couldn't decide whether it was because he was used to focusing on other, more important things, or whether it was because the narratives within the pages were just that bad.

An empty brandy bottle sat on the countertop of the adjoining kitchenette. It had been his most recent last alcoholic beverage, but this time its presence was a more promising sight. After rinsing it, Walks had started to fill it up with alien coins: loose change he'd been carrying, dropped coins he'd found around the station, or the contents of a criminal's pockets never reclaimed. His underlings had then got wind of his collection and would often turn up for work with a new offering they'd come across. Seeing all the different currency had made Walks grasp just how metropolitan the station had become since Zerra had claimed it. New races were always turning up, and some passed through, while others stayed. Refugees, businessmen, travellers, even, weirdly, holidaymakers, eager to check out the now famous Scientia. And with the extra foot traffic came extra criminals, all keen to make an illegal buck or two. Still, Walks couldn't grumble too much, as their presence kept him in a wage and comfy officers' quarters.

Comfy though his quarters may have been, it was occupied by a bachelor, confirmed by the messy pile of clothes sat in a corner, still waiting to be laundered. The only item not amongst them was his uniform's jacket, thrown over the back of a chair, and with its OA insignia crudely unstitched. The Zerrens had offered him a new uniform, devoid of any reminder of the Alliance, but Walks had felt oddly uncomfortable in it. Despite his old jacket marking him out as an ex-Alliance man, he felt an unplaced level of attachment to it, perhaps because it had weathered so many storms with him. It had been his jacket on the Battleship Vallentia, when as its commander, he'd baulked at slaughtering the May!ens. It had survived the removal of its stripes, just as he had, and it had kept him warm in the Munitions Department, as he had gained the begrudging friendship of Shar. Then it had been burnt and patched up, just like him, on being shot by a colleague and avid Alliance supporter. Bruised, battered, and wrinkled, it displayed the stripes of a lieutenant commander. Walks was the jacket, and the jacket was Walks, their surfaces showing their resilience to the tests of time.

The only well-cleaned and maintained thing in the whole place was Walks' sidearm, which sat beside his knee on the coffee table, and it was this object he carefully reached for as the intercom for his door buzzed. Walks eyed the panel with suspicion. His lieutenants, The Zerren, Val'ka, and the Ting, Tarl Aldarer, were both under orders not to disturb him unless a dire, station-threatening catastrophe was about to hit. There was always the possibility that this was the case, but then they would have called him on his communicator, as opposed to politely ringing his bell.

"It better not be that blasted Kiskin trespassing," he muttered to himself, as he levered his body out of his chair, and headed over to the intercom. "Yes?" he barked into it.

"Well that's polite," came a familiar sardonic voice.

"Talon?" Walks opened the door, and carefully stuck his head out, ensuring the man was alone.

"Kiskin is back to bending the captain's furry ear. I guess Tia's awakening has got it spooked. And its aide managed to skitter as far the main offices," Talon added, reading Walks' face. "Though, from what I've heard, it's supposed to be confined to quarters, so it's skating on some seriously thin ice with Sin'ma. I'm guessing that's why it's reluctant to follow me into a restricted area."

Walks grunted in answer, and let Talon enter. "I thought it had diplomatic immunity and could go where it wanted," Walks said, jabbing a thumb to his coffee machine, which had been percolating since he'd risen that morning.

Talon gave a nod at the proffered drink. "What constitutes Alliance diplomatic immunity is not the same as Zerren diplomatic immunity. The Zerrens are less tolerant of individuals pushing their luck, and in Wrymiesk's case, pushing its luck is putting it mildly, seeing as it's still out and about. Though it does seem to be on a bit of a shorter leash now."

"Any chance we can hang it with it?" Walks asked, without much mirth, as he poured two mugs of steaming coffee.

"If only," Talon sighed, theatrically, leaning against the breakfast bar that separated the lounge from the kitchenette, and accepting the proffered mug.

"So, to what do I owe this visit?"

"Shar," Talon stated. "I think I've found Kiskin's Achilles heel in the case."

"What is it?" Walks asked, leaning across the counter, desperate for news that would help bring the whole sorry situation to an end.

However, Talon was not about to be forthcoming. "The details I can't tell you, because if Kiskin or Wrymiesk find out, that'll give them the advantage when it comes to arguing the toss. As it stands, I, Kan and Shar know what it's about, and that's the way it's going to have to stay. No offence to you, it's just that, thanks to Tia, our minds are less easy to access than most."

"Wrymiesk," Walks said, with a snarl. Talon nodded in confirmation.

"Fair enough. But you couldn't have just called to deliver this cryptic message?"

"When you dabble in the business realm that I do, you tend to get overly suspicious and cautious."

Walks knew full well what that business was. Talon was a dealer in contraband, artefacts, and weapons. In Walks' mind, Talon should have been rotting in a jail somewhere, but again, his services, and boss, made that a minefield Walks was disinclined to cross. During Talon's years on the station, he had slowly been accumulating an arsenal in his bar, down in the wheel of the Scientia V. An arsenal that had played no small part in helping the rebels secure the station from the Alliance's soldiers. Even after the battle, Talon's questionable services had been needed, and he brought in weapons and equipment to replace those from sources cut off by the Alliance. It was why he'd been placed under Shar's watchful eye in Munitions, despite being an out and proud criminal. And, of course, there was the fact that the person holding his reins and making sure he didn't step too far over the line was Tia. "You afraid your lines are being tapped?" Walks asked, with a raised eyebrow.

Talon swirled the coffee in his mug, and watched it slosh around. "Afraid, no, healthily wary, yes."

Walks frowned. "Wait, if I know that you know something, doesn't that mean Kiskin will soon know that you know something?"

"Oh yes."

"And...."

"Doesn't hurt to rattle the cage a bit."

Walks shook his head, unconvinced. "So, you've come here to turn me into bait." Talon grinned in answer. "Well, if it helps put that thing on the back foot, or whatever the hell those things are that it skitters around on, so much the better. I'd planned on sending Tia a message today to see if she's up to receiving visitors again, and what her plans are for dealing with this whole Shar business, so you want me to tell her you may have a one-up?"

"Wouldn't hurt. As far as I can tell." he tapped the side of his head in a conspiratorial way, "she's compos mentis, she just hasn't actively reached out to us yet. And although Kan's back at his desk at work, he's still been researching legal precedence and possible optional sentencing during quiet moments. Who knew the guy could read? He seems to think Shar should be bound by Zerren law as he's in Zerren space, and as it stands, Kiskin hasn't made a formal request for extradition. As far as its demands go, it wants the trial here, probably because it realises demanding a trial elsewhere is going to be met with an emphatic no. That, and moving Shar will just end in death and destruction. He's a slippery bastard when he chooses to be. Post-trial I expect Kiskin'll want to use one of our airlocks." For a seen-it-all criminal, Talon gave a grimace at that comment. "But other than Shar being tried here, Kan's not come up with much else. As it is, Zerra's history lacks the influence of a mass-murdering sadist who helped annihilated an entire race. Iron-ically, it seems the presence of the Karee averted that stage of their history. No genocidal psycho, no precedence. Still, you can't fault the man for trying, especially as he and Shar aren't exactly bosom pals. As for me, I've got plenty going on keeping your back watched." He gave Walks a wink.

"Thanks for that by the way."

Talon shrugged his thanks away. "It's nothing. Though, per-haps, in the future, should I need a blind eye turned my way, you'll be obliging."

And there it was, the real reason why Talon had seemingly been so selfless in his helping of Walks. He gave a thin smile. *Should've guessed it,* he thought, shaking his head in exasper-ation. "So, you got something big planned?" he asked, casually.

"No, no. It's just good to get something in the bag, just in case."

Walks couldn't believe Talon's audacity. "Just an FYI," he growled, "I'm always turning a blind eye to you. If anything, you're paying me back." This was true, and there was no two ways about it. Talon had taken down the security cameras in his bar, and Walks had not pursued it. His bar played host to a never-ending line of dodgy clientele that came and went at all hours, and Walks had never questioned them. The occasional reports of late-night cargo movements, orchestrated by Talon, had turned up on his desk, and Walks had never followed up on them. He simply went by the belief that whatever Talon was doing, it was part of being under Tia's command, and should the worse happen, she would deal with it. *Talon may be unread-able by Wrymiesk, but Tia could crack his psyche open like a rotten egg.*

Talon gave another shrug. "Well, whatever. I'm easy either way." He straightened up to leave. "Just an FYI to you, you're still welcome in my bar any time, and I have the policy of not allowing backstabbing ancient beings over my threshold."

"Won't me being their scare off half your business?" Walks asked, with a wry smile.

"I can cope with the occasional low-income night," Talon replied, breezily. "Besides, they know as well as I that if it's after your hours, you can't arrest them, uniform or no. It's Zerren law." He swigged back the remains of his coffee and headed out the door.

Nothing to stop me calling in one of my lieutenants, Walks mused, watching him leave.

A few minutes later, Walks got a message on his communicator: The bug has left the building.

He took stock of his overly familiar surroundings. The blast of marginally fresher air from the corridor outside, on Talon's departure, had made him realise just how fusty and caffeine-infused the atmosphere inside his dwelling was. *Well, time to stretch my legs, and see how long it takes before the cage gets rattled.*

*****

Walks took a gentle stroll around the wheel to the arboretum; his plan being to have a pre-dinner wander before heading down to the wheel of the Scientia III to look for food along the thoroughfare. His slow steps also let him listen out for the skittering of tiny, pointed, carapaced legs that would indicate Kiskin or Wrymiesk making a beeline for him. However, it seemed whatever new ear-bashing the ambassador had received from Sin'ma had caused it, and its be-winged aide, to skulk back to their temporary quarters, and Walks got to meander the gravel paths of the arboretum unmolested.

With all the changes that had been going on throughout the station, Walks found comfort in seeing the arboretum remained unconcerned by it all. Fresh staff had boarded, people had been promoted, new and unusual races had come aboard, and a rampaging beast had, until a week before, nested amongst the plants to mourn over the body of her fallen comrade. And yet, despite all the comings, goings, and upheavals, the plants still grew, their leaves still embraced the

light, and the insects still gambled about, following their predictable instincts and schedules. Purple and turquoise plants
wafted to their own breeze, and pollinators rode the eddies of
the leaves, sometimes to alight on a large bloom, other times to
become the victim of a more veracious cousin. The arboretum
held within it a tiny civilisation, unperturbed by the goings-
on of the giant sentient creatures that occasionally invaded its
space. Indeed, Walks became a stopping-off point for several
tired creatures, who no doubt saw him as nothing more than a
walking tree. He brushed them away and watched as they flittered off to find a slightly more accommodating perch.

He passed some labs, the scientists within giving him a
polite nod on seeing him. Walks stuck his head through the
door. "Everything good guys? No missing equipment or samples I need to be made aware of?" Ordinarily, such trivial things
would be dealt with by his subordinates, or internally by the
scientists themselves, but the more Walks had to keep him occupied, the longer he could stay out of Kiskin's clutches.

The Zerren scientist closest to him shook his head. "Unfortunately, no, but tomorrow is another day." The tone he used
seemed to imply that something was due to go inexplicably
missing, meaning Walks was going to be preoccupied with
chasing down leads.

"Did you ever find those mould spores?" Walks asked, casually.

"Oh yes, sorry, forgot to tell you. We found them two days
ago in the wrong fridge. Seems they had been mislabelled and
misplaced. Apologies for not telling you sooner, and for keeping you from other more important things." Though the scientist talking was keeping a marginally straight face, several
of his colleagues were failing to do likewise, and had resorted
to staring hard down their microscopes in a bid to hide their
mirth.

"No trouble." Walks answered, smiling amiably. "I look forward to writing up the paperwork regarding their recovery."
A loud snort came from a Toch who had his head buried in a

fridge.

Walks acted like he hadn't heard the noise. He headed off again, whilst feigning ignorance of the chatter that was wafting out of the lab as the scientists went about figuring out what was suitable for accidentally losing next. Walks grinned to himself. News had travelled fast within the Scientia, and despite no official word being made about the whys of Kiskin's arrival, or the arrest of Shar, the ins and outs of it were well-known amongst the station's residents. Just as tool use was universal amongst the sentient races aboard, it seemed so too was gossiping, and with the rapidly shared news came the knowledge that one of the individuals standing between Shar's trial and execution was Walks.

If Kiskin had expected an easy time of things, then she had not bothered to read the room, and the space station was one hell of a room, full of several thousand independently thinking, calculating, stubborn people. Ordinarily, the announcement that an individual had nearly single-handedly caused the extinction of a species would have been met with revile, after all, their foe, the Alliance, was guilty of doing just that, but these were no ordinary times. Something Walks' aching brain was all too aware of. Shar may have eradicated a race in a bygone time, but that'd had no direct effect on the species aboard the station, especially the Zerrens.

The Zerrens, who were now the main race aboard the Scientia, and who occupied key roles within the staff, including its captaincy, knew several things to be true. Shar had been one of the main players in liberating the station from the Alliance, and in so doing, had directly helped save the lives of the Zerrens on board, and indirectly, those on the planet below them. Their gratitude to him for that was no small thing. Further, Shar was a soldier of Tia, whom many regarded as a guiding light in a time of war, and when she had gone missing, he had been part of the mission to find her and bring her home. Which he had achieved, bringing home not only Tia, but a Karee version of Tia. In the eyes of many, Shar had turned up on Zerra's doorstep with a god in tow. These were no mere trifling opinions. Thanks to his Zerren lieutenant, Walks knew at least one, if not all these developments, had hit home with every Zerren aboard the station. So, with Shar in danger, they had been doing whatever they could to delay the inevitable.

So, although none of the individuals working within the arboretum had any ties to Walks, they had decided to play their part in keeping him otherwise engaged, and thus away from Kiskin. They had not been alone in this endeavour. Copper wiring had been reported missing by engineers, shipments of canned goods by restaurant owners, and in one instance, an entire shuttle load of luxury toilet roll had mysteriously vanished: six thousand rolls worth. Occasionally, the thefts had been real, but most had simply been 'misplaced' or 'mislabelled' things that had turned up a few days later, safe, a few feet away from where they should've been.

Of course, Walks had played his part by stretching the truth of their importance. The copper wiring? A bomb alert in the making. The canned goods? A mass poisoning scare involving senior staff. The toilet rolls had been less easy to expand on, but a tall tale of black-market criminal cartels specialising in luxury stolen goods had certainly spiced up the file. Plus, it had required his investigative expertise out in the field, and seclusion in his office to write up the detailed and lengthy report.

As Walks mulled his next huge white lie, his footsteps brought him full circle around the arboretum, and with his hunger fully awakened, he decided to search out a non-home-cooked meal. Especially as a home-cooked meal for him constituted a reconstituted ready-meal of one of three flavours: rice with a slightly spicy tomato sauce, pasta with a different slightly spicy tomato sauce, or something loosely described as a roast dinner.

His trip to find food was near the reverse of the one he'd taken in escorting the alien Ressen from Tia's quarters to Tia, but rather than the service elevator he had used for the last stretch of Ressen's journey, he located the public lift that would take him down the Scientia II's spoke to the hub of the wheel. Once in the hub, he boarded the same hub shuttle to the one that had brought him up from the hub of the Scientia III. However, once in the Scientia III's hub, he made a slow trip to a spoke lift that would bring him out at the thoroughfare, rather than the one that ended near Tia's quarters.

When Walks finally arrived at the thoroughfare it was early evening, and the area was still bustling. It was the main shopping and recreation area of the station, and it consisted of one long, street-like corridor, which ran around a substantial part of the Scientia III's wheel; the lower staff and visitor quarters taking up the rest. The thoroughfare was so long it had its own tram line, which ran the entirety of its length, complete with stopping-off points. Usually though people just jumped off the slow-moving vehicle and headed off to their desired location at a bit of an enforced jog.

The street was packed with cafés, restaurants, pubs, cinemas, gyms, and general stores, run by all manner of races. In just one evening, a person could eat a three-course Pann meal, grab some Liverden sweets from a speciality store, see a subtitled Toch movie, and finish the night off at a Zerrenrun bar hosting a Ciberian band. Walks didn't think there was any other place like it in the galaxy. Beyond the official built-in store spaces were the little stalls, either set up by traders giving it a go, and who were trying to work their way up to a more permanent place, or by those who were just passing through, and colourful frayed awnings sheltered jewellery, strange idols, fortune-tellers, and dubious-looking snacks.

There were other entrepreneurs dotted about the place in the form of buskers, and individuals, playing weirdly shaped instruments, competed against each other, and filled the air with a discord of sounds that mingled with hundreds of alien voices to create a chaotic soundscape. Each musician, despite their differing visages and instruments, had adopted the universal call-sign of the busker, in the form of a collection pot before them. Glass jars, glass tankards, a turban, an instrument case, an odd shoe, each stood before its owner, filled sparingly with a collection of coins, tokens, and semi-precious gems.

Walks nodded to a couple of his lieutenants, who were trying to get the back end of one of the ramshackle stalls to be a safe distance from the tram line. They were doing the lifting and moving, one at each side of the small, rickety structure, while its owner, a blue and green-skinned androgynous Xalek, sat atop its UV heater, and harangued them in its mother tongue, while its striped prehensile tail kept a firm grip on its cash box. It was evidently more annoyed at losing selling time than by the fact that its whole stall could be taken out by a misplaced elbow at an open window of the tram.

Walks rolled his eyes at the scene, one he'd seen all too often, and skirted on by, while keeping an eye out for a decent looking eatery. Because the Humans were now less represented on the station, there was a shortage of good places to find Human-only food, but that didn't mean there wasn't food Walks could eat. The Panns specialised in salads; the Liverdens, curry; and the Ciberians, steak, if you didn't think too much about where it had come from. However, Walks missed the Human touch, whatever that meant. Day in and day out he saw strange, alien faces, which still thrilled him, but also left him feeling a little disconnected. He missed having casual conversations with familiar colleagues based around Human TV shows, films, and sporting events.

Walks found it strange to think that, even as the galaxy was at the brink of a full-blown war, these almost trivial, day-to-day things still occurred. Back on New Earth, generic comedies were still being written, action-packed cinematic treats were still being shot, age-old sporting rivalries were still being bashed out, and lame celebrities were still doing stupid stuff in the name of news headlines. The planet may have been the base of operations for a questionable and all-ruling government, but it was tucked safely away in the centre of Alliance territory. What went on at its borders had a negligible effect on those going to work, or raising a family, so long as they didn't question the Government's methods and drives too vociferously. In turn, chances were, the general populous didn't even have a clue as to what they were heading towards. The Government chose its words carefully, buried documents thoroughly, and silenced the outspoken quickly. And those that did have the wherewithal to speak-up, no matter how briefly, were often seen as unpatriotic crackpots and conspiracy theorists, fit only for a moment's derision.

But that didn't help Walks' dilemma. Despite being a man on the right (or wrong, depending on who you spoke to) side, and free of Alliance suppression, he missed Human cooking. Though if he were honest about it, the alien foods he could buy were like Human food, and the typical meals he was thinking of, like fry-ups, and steak and chips, weren't exactly culinarily exciting. Yet he was driven by the odd sense of homesickness, and the lack of, for want of a better word, the ordinary. It was a feeling that occasionally crept up on him, and it drove him to seek out his own kind, if just for a few hours.

He passed by the Ead'ell Marr Café, hoping to catch a glimpse of the widow Matthews, and to ask her how she was doing, and how her child was, but the woman appeared not to be at work. Abandoning that option, he carried on walking for a good ten minutes, his stomach getting more disgruntled at each step, until he came across a buzzing neon sign that proclaimed the store behind it to be a diner. Indeed, its name was just that, Diner, and underneath the sign was a small banner proclaiming it to be newly opened.

Walks took his time running his eye over the menu in the window, while surreptitiously looking beyond it to scope the interior's decency. The foods were listed in Human language, and to Walks' relief, mostly listed meals he recognised; burgers, omelettes, and pancakes to name a few, the reading of which made his stomach gurgle appreciatively.

What's more, at first inspection the place seemed clean, albeit a tad garish. The floor was a mix of large black and white tiles, which was a motif that was continued in a strip along the eggshell blue walls. The seating consisted of bright red couches and chairs, set around equally red lacquered tables, and the walls sported all manner of, what Walks could only think to call, random tat. It was certainly distinctive and hinted at the possibility of better food than the cheap aluminium chairs and tables of the Ead'ell Marr Café did.

He stepped inside, and was hit by warmth, and the smell of grease and sugar. Despite it being newly opened, it lacked clientele, and only a couple of tables were occupied, both by alien races. Two Ciberians, a mated pair judging by their disproportionate horn sizes, sat on opposite couches, and were tucking into steaks. Meanwhile, a family of Maisak, the offspring wearing the same regal-looking, brocaded tops and trousers as their parents, were crowded around a small table, sucking on large cups holding chemical-pink liquid.

A Zerren quickly came over to Walks. "I am Caz'may, and I will be your waitress today," it announced, breezily, its pitch of voice indicating it was a female. She was decked out in a body-covering red and white pinstriped top and trousers, over which she sported a small white frilly apron. The obligatory hood of her species completed her outfit, atop which was sewn a daft looking little triangular white hat.

Walks gaped at her and the surroundings, as he followed in her wake towards an unoccupied booth. As he made himself comfortable on a plastic couch, she smiled broadly, and handed him a sheet menu, before heading off behind the counter. Walks cast his eyes around, unsure of what to make of the place. The stuff tacked onto the walls seemed not in keeping with an eating establishment, at least not any he'd ever been in. Several posters were dotted around, capturing various alien singers in action poses. In one corner was stuck a mass of black plastic discs with colourful centres, the significance of which Walks was at a loss to explain, and above his head was glued a gaggle of toy Zerren automobiles.

Walks looked over to the waitress, who was occupied with polishing a shiny chrome machine. Behind her was a window

to the kitchen, where he glimpsed, with more than a little relief, a Human chef. He looked back to the menu, which like
the outside menu was all in Human, but also included pictures
of some of the different meal options. There were the Human
foods he recognised, as well as some highlighted alien special-
ities. There were also a few things he didn't know. *The fuck is a
hot dog?* he wondered, desperately hoping it wasn't a Ciberian
dish, though no animal calls could be heard coming from the
kitchen. After some browsing, he decided to eat one of the pic-
tured Human meals, with the idea that at least then he knew
what he was in for. He gave a heads-up nod to the waitress,
who came over, pen and pad in hand.

"What can I get you love?" she asked, completely throwing
Walks with her use of over-familiarity. Zerrens barely ever
called a spouse love in public, let alone a stranger in casual
conversation.

"Uh.... I'll have a double cheeseburger, fries, and a coffee...
and what the hell is this place?" All the eateries Walks had been
in, no matter the race, had been mute affairs, usually decked
out with cream walls, and white clothed tables and chairs. If
there was colour, then it would come in the form of a potted
plant or two, or a calming painting, or perhaps a fancy dining
set in one of the posher establishments. The Ead'ell Marr Café
did colour, but that had come about accidentally from its jum-
ble of mismatched mugs. It almost felt as though the proprietors didn't want anything to detract from the food, though in
some cases, the food served needed some serious distraction
from. The Diner was a whole new experience for Walks.

Caz'may jerked her head back to where the chef was. "He
said it is what is called a fifties' diner," she said, making sure to
enunciate the last two words, while sounding a little unsure.
"Would you like a fried egg on that burger?"

Walks was about to say no, thinking the grease from the
fried meat and potatoes would be more than enough, but then
he wondered when he'd next get the chance for a proper meal.
He gave a shrug, "why not?" Caz'may gave a slightly panicked

look, and he suspected his rhetorical question had gone over her head. "Sorry, I mean, yes please," he clarified, giving her a smile.

She beamed back, scribbled on her pad, and headed round the counter to bang on the window to get the chef's attention. He slid the window open, took the proffered slip of paper, and caught sight of Walks. He gave a nod of recognition, before slamming the window shut, no doubt to make Walks' meal. Caz'may fiddled about with one of the diner's chrome contraptions, and soon Walks heard the familiar sound of peculating coffee.

The resulting brew was pleasant enough, and after a surprisingly short wait, Walks was tucking into his meal, once again brought to him by Caz'may. The burger and fries weren't going to gain rave reviews, but they were tasty, not too greasy, and had a palate Walks recognised.

He had barely finished his last mouthful when Caz'may came and tidied his plate away. "Would you like a desert?" she asked.

Walks decided to push his luck at being undisturbed by Kiskin for a bit longer. "Sure, what do you suggest?"

"The apple pie is good. Though, to be honest, it is made from Zerren sea fruit rather than apples. But chef says it is authentic tasting. I like it," she added, hurriedly, catching Walks' unsure expression.

Walks gave it a shot, and was presented with a slice of warm pie, topped with cream (animal origin unknown) and which contained an excessively sweet-tasting yellow filling. Walks had to agree with Caz'may in liking it, despite the Zerren origin of its ingredients. *But then,* he rationalised, *where are any of these cafés going to get bona fide Human ingredients from?* Finishing off his coffee, he gestured for the bill. He thought for a second Caz'may hadn't understood him, as she banged on the kitchen window again, and exchanged words with the chef.

All became clear when the man himself appeared from a side door, and came over to the table, wiping his hands on his apron as he did so. "Consider your meal on the house," he said, giving a broad smile. "Law enforcement get to eat free here."

"What is here even?" Walks asked, gesticulating at his surroundings.

The chef gave a hearty laugh. He was a big meaty man, with dark hair hidden under a hair net, light brown eyes, and a healthy amount of fuzz on his square jaw. He plopped himself down heavily on the couch opposite Walks and put over a large hand to shake. I'm Javin Fetter, and this here is my fifties inspired diner."

"Your waitress said the same thing. I've never seen any place like it."

"Hardly surprising. This was all the rage in nineteen-fifties America, back on Old Earth when it was still habitable."

"How the hell did you even come up with something like this?"

"I wanted to do something different. A new place, a new opportunity, so why not? All the other places were boring affairs, and I wanted to catch people's eyes. I did a bit of searching and found some old photos of these types of diners. 'Course, I had to employ a bit of artistic licence. Couldn't exactly order reprints of ancient posters lost to the sands of time, so I had to make do with what I could find in alien stores. Same goes for the lack of actual Human car parts from the era."

"And what about those?" Walks asked, pointing at the black discs glued to the wall.

"They're what were called vinny-ell records." It was clear by the way Javin spoke, that he was genuinely enthusiastic about what he'd discovered. "Far as I can tell, they were primitive music storage devices. They were played in a thing called a Juke's Box. Them things stuck on the wall are just plastic knockoffs, no vinny-ell records exist anymore, but I've got a guy on Zerra trying to make a music system that looks like a proper Juke's Box. It's all bright and gold and is going to look pretty sweet in the corner over there." He gave an excited, almost child-like smile at that.

While Javin was raving about his historical research, Walks was trying desperately to place the man's face. Those Humans that were permanently resident on the station he knew, and those that passed through he kept a close eye on, just in case they were up to no good. But that didn't mean the occasional Human hadn't slipped through the net, either shielded by the confusion of the early days of the station's emancipation or smuggled in by individuals unknown. The death of Aben had exposed the slightly too lax nature of security, and it had since been cranked up, with large crates being thoroughly examined by the end of a plasma rifle. Therefore, Walks was certain he'd never seen the man seated opposite him before.

He gave up trying to recall the man's details. "I don't mean to be rude, but how did you end up on the station?"

"I came up from Zerra," Javin stated, then he gave a sigh, losing his air of joviality. "Truth is, until a few years ago, I was based on Maylar." Walks audibly sucked in his breath. Javin nodded his head in understanding, then casually dropped a bombshell. "I was one of the cooks aboard the Hawk." His words made Walks unconsciously reach for his gun hidden under his jacket. Javin picked up on his movement. "You don't need to blast me into oblivion," he said, trying to assuage the panic that was going on in the back of Walks' mind. "You're not the only one who left their past there."

"I don't get it, how the hell did you end up on Zerra from Maylar?" Walks had left the May!ar star system demoted, and with a steel-capped boot well and truly connecting to his backside. He had refused a direct command to lay waste to those fleeing for their lives behind the May!en's front line. The captain of the Hawk hadn't been so reticent and had slaughtered without compunction. Despite the forgiveness of one May!en, the guilt of his failure to save lives, while having taken those of the May!en soldiers trying to protect them, still haunted Walks.

"I guess because of you," Javin said, looking Walks direct in the eyes. "What you did became common knowledge on both your old command and my ship. Mainly because we, as my old captain said, had to clean up your mess."

Walks winced. "My mess was trying to save the lives of innocent civilians," he growled.

"Oh, I understand that now. Took me a while, but I got there in the end." Javin leant back in his seat and folded his large arms across his barrel chest. "After we secured Maylar, I decided to stay planet-side, as I'd had enough of being cooped up on that damn battleship, so I turned my hand to feeding the ground infantries instead. Thing is, being on the planet meant my path crossed with the Maylen. Learnt some of their cooking too, mainly 'cause I had to figure out how the hell to feed the troops on what the planet produced. And so, of course, I also got to see the planet for myself. Got to see a bit of how they'd lived until we'd..." he pulled a face, "...subjugated them. It slowly dawned on me why you did what you did. The Maylens I met were decent people, despite the shit we'd put them through. They weren't some blood-crazed enemy we had to subdue. They were like you and me; just people trying to make a life and trying to protect their loved ones against a far superior force that saw them as no better than cattle."

"So, what made you come to Zerra? Surely you knew the same thing was supposed to happen on her."

Javin shrugged. "Humanity...perhaps...if that's still a thing. I couldn't free Maylar, but I could make life better for the slaves that worked with us in the kitchen or did other menial duties. A few of the guys I worked with came around to my way of thinking, especially once they'd got on first name terms with the captives. They weren't front line, so I guess they didn't have the same bloodlust. Of course, we didn't play nice in earshot of the soldiers and the upper crust, but we could make their slice of hell a little better the rest of the time. We shared our meals with them, gave them access to our medical supplies if they needed, and hopefully treated them with a bit of decency. When I heard rumours that the Alliance was going to make its move on Zerra, I hopped on a passing freighter. I told them

I wanted a change of scenery again, when really, I had the idea of bringing a bit of humanity to future Zerren captives. I made planet fall, and one week later the Alliance got their asses wooped." He gave a smile. "Saw the explosions from the surface. The looks on the faces of the Humans when the news came in that it'd been the Alliance's ships getting blasted and not the station, and that the other battleships had turned tail, ho boy."

"I'm guessing they were a little rattled."

Javin chuckled. "To put it mildly. Dude wearing fatigues in my café looked at me, couldn't believe what he'd heard. Said, "We've lost Zerra," then looked at the Zerrens sat around, all just as surprised as he was. I could see what was going on in his head before he'd even said the words. He was going to take as many as he could before the Zerren authorities came for him. He reached for his sidearm; I broke his neck." Javin cracked his big knuckles to highlight the point. "After that, there was no question about me being allowed to stay. Even got a little medal." He patted his t-shirt to indicate he still wore it under his apron.

"It never really occurred to me that shit might've gone down on Zerra herself," Walks muttered. He had witnessed first-hand the chaos that had gone on in the station, both during the battle, and during the subsequent clean-up of questionable Alliance sympathisers. It had taken many days to wheedle them all out, even with Tia leading the charge, but there had also been light infantry stationed around Zerra; however, the Zerrens planet-side had been on their own when it had come to separating the wheat from the genocidal chaff.

"Oh, there were several pitched battles, but at the end of the day the Zerrens outnumbered the Alliance, and when the news came through that some ancient overlords had gotten themselves into the mix, they became nigh on unstoppable. Most of those who survived got shipped off with your guys. Those that got to stay, like me, were because of word-of-mouth testimonials from fellow Zerrens."

"I'm guessing only a handful of Humans remained then."

"If that. And those that have stayed are still treated with a fair amount of distrust, though honestly, it's hardly surprising. That judgement is the main reason I came up here. I mean, those I could call friends treated me nicely, and I ain't got a bad word to say about them. But walking out in public, being whispered about, and pointed at...," Javin gave a grimace. "They like to think themselves a tolerant race, but they can be right jackasses at times to people who don't fit in." Walks gave a sympathetic nod. "Anyway, I figured as there were more Humans up here, the judgemental attitude might be a little less."

"And is it?" Walks asked, glancing over at Caz'may, who was busy cleaning up the plates and glasses of the long-gone Ciberians and Maisak family.

Javin followed Walks' gaze. "Haven't had cause to complain so far. She's a hard-working lass and has always come across as genuinely polite. Same goes for the other Zerren who works for me."

"So, what pass did you use to get access to the station?" Walks asked, still wondering how he'd not come to know about the man sooner. Although their histories had crossed in an unpleasant way, Javin came across as a decent guy, and if anything, Walks was just disappointed that he'd not met him sooner. He was convivial, a plain talker, and seemed to be on Walks' wavelength. He also appeared to be about the same age as him, though a little less grey and haggard.

Javin grinned, "Back to being detective hey? Figured from the way you reacted you hadn't known I was here. Basically, after everything had calmed down, I relinquished my Alliance pass, and was given a Zerren one in its place. I also got papers from the local, I guess mayor, regarding my deeds and award so there'd be fewer questions about my background. I may not have pulled any triggers, but I was on a vessel that sure as hell did, and I don't need people knowing that, as I'm sure you'll understand." Walks did indeed. "Also, it kinda helped that I turned up the same time as your leader went bat shit crazy. I was hurried through before the station went into lockdown. So ends the ballad, thus far, of Javin Fetter."

"So, you're planning to stay here then?"

"Hopefully," he shrugged, "though who knows when I'll next get itchy feet. In the meantime, I intend to add a bit of colour to people's dining experience. Who knows, maybe it'll catch on."

Walks wasn't sure he was ready for a mass of restaurants and cafés done up in the same way. The Diner's uniqueness made it tolerable, whereas a dozen or more copycats would lead to the thoroughfare becoming tackier. However, he hadn't failed to notice that the thoroughfare had already begun taking on the feel of an exotic bazaar, which was slowly eradicating the sterile environment it had been under the Alliance.

Javin caught his expression of dubiousness. "Colourful eateries used to be all the rage on Old Earth. I know, 'cause I saw loads of pictures before I decided on this design. There were plush restaurants, and curry houses done out in silk drapes and bright colours, with ancient deities dotted about. Who wouldn't want to walk into a Liverden curry house done up like that? And did you know the colour red was thought to make Humans hungry, so loads of places had red walls and hangings?" He was starting his enthusiastic ramblings again.

Walks looked around at the red plastic tables and seating, then remembered caving to the offer of a fried egg and a dessert. *Damn, he knows his stuff.* He caught the time on a large clock on the wall and saw the evening had rapidly got away from him, and that he had an early start the next day filled with avoiding Kiskin. "Well," he said, giving a stretch, "I wish you all the best with your endeavour." He got up to leave.

Javin followed suit, proffering his large hand for Walks to shake goodbye. "Feel free to drop in any time," he said, as Walks obliged to his gesture. "Food will always be on the house for you and your staff. Top brass can pay though. They sure as hell earn enough." He gave a knowing wink.

"I'll let them know," *I wonder what Val'ka and Tarl will make of this place,* he thought, as he left. *I can just imagine those two loving its quirkiness.* He'd never had a local unless he counted the Bar. But then the Bar was just a means of escape, and a place to drown his sorrows in relative peace, and as he was off the sauce, at least for the time being, the Bar didn't seem ideal anymore. The Diner, despite its overly kitsch nature, was bright and cheery, had decent food, and despite Javin's past, he seemed a nice sort. More importantly, he was Human, with a similar past to Walks. *Could there be a friendship there?* he wondered, striking off for home, and he found himself debating what sports teams Javin might support, and if he'd watched any of the Human shows that were still available from the Scientia's databank. He got so engrossed in his happy thoughts that he didn't hear the clicks behind him.

"Lieutenant Commander Walker!"

Too late, Walks remembered he'd left his communicator on his kitchen worktop. If anyone had seen Kiskin coming, their warnings had gone unread. *Shit!* "Ambassador Kiskin." He turned around to find himself face to face with the permanently disgruntled alien, and its ever-annoying aide. "Wrymiesk," he added, trying to sound as pleasant as possible through his clenched jaw.

"You have been ignoring my request for an audience," Kiskin stated, before Walks could get out any more faux pleasantries.

"I have been extremely busy," Walks lied, hoping Wrymiesk didn't pick up on it. "And you've been ignoring the captain's request to keep that thing under lock and key," he said, pointing at the self-same creature.

"And you have been extremely busy avoiding me," Kiskin countered, ignoring Walks' statement about its aide, which only increased his irritability towards them both. "I will not tolerate it anymore. Shar must be officially charged, and his trial begun straight away."

"The man's not going anywhere," Walks snapped. "Considering his history, I'm sure if he was going to escape, he would have done so already. Rest assured, charges and date will be laid as soon as possible. In fact, I have an appointment with Tia tomorrow, so we'll be able to discuss details." This was partly true. He'd emailed her before leaving his quarters, requesting an audience, but had yet to get a reply, which he didn't find surprising given the circumstances. However, considering the subject line, and what Talon had said about her being of sound mind, he doubted she'd say no.

The reaction of Kiskin to Walks' announcement was marked. Her cream-coloured carapace flushed purple. "You are free now," she said, with more than a hint of aggravation. "Why can't you do the orders now?"

"Because I need to consult with Tia," Walks told her, slowly, as one might do to someone who wasn't too fast on the uptake. "He is under her charge, so she should be kept fully in the loop."

"Tia's involvement with the creature is irrelevant. He must be held accountable for his actions without further delay."

Somebody's flustered now she knows the queen is awake, Walks noted, with satisfaction. "I disagree," he said. Kiskin acted like she'd been slapped in the face. The creature was evidently not used to not getting its own way, and on the Scientia, she was hitting a lot of brick walls in the form of contrary senior staff. "And as I'm Head of Security aboard this station what I say carries weight. All involved parties will get to have their say. There are protocols to be followed, otherwise, it won't be a fair trial and punishment. This is a Zerren station, and as such, Zerren laws must be followed." *Thank you, Kan.* Kiskin, flushed even further. Her aide, who'd so far been quiet, said something to Kiskin in its own language, while keeping an eye on Walks. *Here we go.* He tried to keep his face as expressionless as possible.

Kiskin's head whipped back to Walks. "I demand the trial date be set immediately!" Kiskin's cool had been well and truly lost. Wrymiesk may have spoken to her in a useless attempt to conceal the fact that it was a telepath, but Kiskin's reaction was enough to make Walks not buy it any more than he already did. They knew that he knew that Talon knew...something, and Talon had called it; Kiskin was rattled.

"No," Walks stated, simply. "We'll be in touch. Oh, and if I see that creature on the loose again, I will arrest it," he stated, with considerable bravado. And with that, he turned, gave a self-satisfied grin, and strode off.

Chapter 15 - Tia

After shrinking down to a more manageable size, so she could retire, unnoticed, to her quarters, it had taken Tia barely a day to regain her 'normal' form, but since then, she had remained in her quarters. Battles and madness had taken their toll, and she had been unnaturally exhausted, and mentally unprepared to face the outside world. However, she hadn't returned to her vessel to heal as she normally would, as she just hadn't been in the right frame of mind. That, and she had wanted to put it off for as long as possible. She had no idea what Morrígan had planned for her, or what it would say to her, and she was in no rush to find out. Instead, she was recuperating the old-fashioned way, with a mug of Liverden hot-bean, and for the first time in ages, a movie, but as her mind was going ninety to the dozen, it was just noise in the background.

There were other things she was putting off too. Firstly, there was Aben. Tears stung her eyes as she reflected on the mess she'd made, and the stress she'd caused. *Brave Leo, watching over me as Aben's body rotted away beneath my wings.* She gave out a long sigh and took another sip of the chocolate-tasting beverage. After she had been roused from the darkness of her mind, she had moved away from Aben's resting place, barely able to bear witness to what she'd done. Rather, Leo had taken charge, reminding her, once again, why she had been right to put her faith in his abilities. He had called for a Pann nurse to escort the burnt alien back to the Medicentre, this time by a gurney, and not by foot. They, in turn, had called for someone to do what had needed to be done for weeks, and remove Aben's body to the morgue to await interment.

Tia still had no idea what she planned to do with his body and had been doing her best not to dwell on it. It didn't seem right to her to take him back to his homeworld. The planet hadn't been his species' place of conception, rather, the Karee had dumped his race on it, and had let them get on with it. Multiply or die, they hadn't cared. But to Tia, Aben had become much more than an afterthought. He had become a child of the stars, an explorer, and her faithful companion. As far as she was concerned, he deserved much more than a hole in the dirt on some random planet.

Thankfully, there were other more pressing matters that required her attention. Her trusted soldier, Shar, had been incarcerated at the bequest of Ambassador Kiskin. In Aben's absence, Kan had stepped up to the plate to be Shar's attorney. A move that had surprised Tia, because as far as she was aware, the two males still despised each other. *It feels as though each time I blink; the galaxy does a one-eighty.* However, Kan had achieved the little he could, and she knew she had to take up the gauntlet to save Shar's life, and quickly, but she was still mired in the after-effects of her blackout. She knew the answers would fall into place once she rejoined her mind fully to Morrígan and let the knowledge flow, but that brought her back to doing the things she was putting off. *At some point I'm just going to have to stop wallowing in self-pity, get a grip, and be the person I'm supposed to be,* she lamented.

There was also the issue of a murderer being on the station, the one who had taken Aben from her. Tia could be a forgiving person, *universe knows I put up with enough indiscretions from my crew,* but when she caught the killer, there would be no forgiveness. She wouldn't even give them the luxury of being one of her servant soldiers. Whoever it was could expect a very violent, prolonged, and excruciating end. The station had been locked down when Aben's death had become known, and it was still a case of no one in and no one out. Now that Tia had regained her sanity, it was only a matter of time until the perpetrator was found. *Enjoy what few hours you have left,* she thought, with considerable venom.

Lastly, there was the issue surrounding the mangled object sat on her coffee table. It was the covert surveillance device Leo had managed to nail with a stone. It looked harmless enough, but Tia knew it could have been sending all kinds of information back to its controller. *No doubt the Orion Alliance. Maybe even by way of the same bastard who killed Aben.* There was a silver lining to that cloud. A thorough search of the arboretum had failed to find another device. *With any luck, whoever was at the receiving end has no idea I'm whole again. Even if it was Aben's killer, it's doubtful he was the final destination of the intel, and with the station on lockdown, he can't get word out that I'm not still crazy. Advantage rebels; for a little while at least.*

A movement at the corner of her mind brought her out of her malaise a second before the intercom to her quarters buzzed. She sensed who was outside the door, and despite not being in the mood to acknowledge anybody, let alone speak to a person, she allowed them to come in. A world-weary man entered as she stood up to great him, and despite the discomfort he radiated from being in her looming presence, he acknowledged her with politeness.

"Tia."

"Walks." She waved him to a seat beside her and sat herself down again. "You wanted to talk to me about Shar's case," she said. Walks' message to her had been brief, just a concise note that things needed to be discussed ASAP, so despite her disinclination towards company, she had accepted his request for a meeting.

The man sighed, but not out loud, rather, his shoulders gave him away. "Look. I know you've just been through a lot, and I know full well it's not my place to rush you, but that damn alien Kiskin has got wind of your re-awakening, and it's getting harder to fob it off. It wants blood, Shar's blood, and I think it's freaking out at the prospect of losing its case. Especially as Talon's dug up dirt on it. It's been pressing for its day in court, and it's getting harder to find excuses to stall the inevitable."

Tia looked at Walks confused. "Talon's managed to find out something about her?" *How?* She wondered to herself. *Even I don't know who or what she is.*

Hindsight was a wonderful thing, and had Tia known she was going to go insane shortly after her first meeting with the alien, she would have done a proper scan of her there and then. As it was, she had been pre-occupied with reassuring Shar, before going scorpiad hunting, with a mind for doing an in-depth scan later. Something that, unsurprisingly, had yet to happen. Nevertheless, at the time, she had still been linked with her vessel, and as she had gazed upon Kiskin, her vessel could have thrown some information her way, yet it had stayed resolutely silent. *There's Morrigan holding more secrets from me.*

"Yes, though I'm not sure what," Walks was saying, "as he, Kan and Shar have been keeping the intel close to their chests. But now Kiskin knows that they know something."

Tia gave an involuntary growl. "Bet you anything she's been trying to read their minds without consent."

"Actually, it was her aide, and it was me it read, though that was Talon's plan." Tia raised a questioning eyebrow. "It looks like the love child of Kiskin and a giant bug. It even has wings, though nothing as impressive as yours, and it's been skittering around in places it's not supposed to, giving the excuse of diplomatic immunity. It goes by the name of Wrymiesk, and if you ask me, it needs to meet a large boot, sharpish."

Despite her depressive mood, Tia laughed. Then she grew sombre again. "You've had a lot dumped on your shoulders recently, and let's face it, it's all my fault. I'm sorry."

Walks shrugged. "Comes with the territory, especially with you in it, though if I'd known that, I may not have been so quick to accept the position."

Tia gave a sad smile. "Well, it's only right I should start easing your burden. Tell Kiskin she can have her day, though not in court. She will get to deal with me personally, which is something I'm sure she'll enjoy no end." She gave a grim smile at the idea. "In the meantime, I will get Kan or Talon to come and impart their wisdom on me, and then I will stop finding excuses to stall the inevitable." Walks gave a bemused look. "Karee business," she said, by way of an explanation.

Walks gave a nod of understanding, though Tia knew he could have no idea as to what she meant. She felt something niggling at the man, something he seemed disinclined to mention. He caught her penetrating stare, and she cocked her head to one side, in a gesture that she hoped would get him to disclose what was on his mind, before she forgot herself and transgressed into his thoughts.

Her quizzical look, coupled with the knowledge that she was a telepath, achieved the inevitable, and loosened Walks' tongue. "I'm sorry," he blurted out, "something that I seem to be say a lot these days," he added.

"Sorry? For what?" Tia asked. She knew the man had a tenuous grasp on his ability to do his job, but as far as she was aware, he'd never felt the need to apologise for the demons running around inside of him."

"For not finding the scorpiad sooner. If I had done my job better, less good people would be dead, Aben would be alive, and you wouldn't have gone crazy," he explained.

Tia shook her head. "Believe me when I say that what happened was not your fault. The scorpiad started off as a man, and it had the help of a telepath, and a station with too many hiding places. And even if you had discovered the man, or creature, sooner, chances are you'd be dead too, as would a lot more people. From what Chione tells me, you curtailed its stride, and that was no bad thing. Certainly, don't blame yourself for Aben's death. Believe me, I'm blaming myself enough for two as it is. Nor could you have done anything more regarding the wasteful deaths of the others. What happened, happened, and now we have to make the best of a crappy situation."

Walks looked glum but nodded in agreement. He left, giving an unconvinced utterance of thanks, and went firstly to find one of her men, then to give Kiskin the good news. Though Tia hoped Kiskin wouldn't remain the least bit jovial once she'd finished with the self-righteous alien.

The quietest of footfalls turned her head, as Chione enter the room. "Good morning," she said, as the cat gave an expansive yawn and stretch.

"Same to you," he answered. "I take it the weight of the galaxy is still resting squarely on the lieutenant commander's shoulders."

Tia winced. "He blames himself for Aben's death, for everything that lead to it, and everything that happened thereafter. Though when it comes to scorpiads, I think we both know none of this was remotely his fault."

"Agreed," Chione answered, taking a seat, and giving himself a cursory groom. After a moment he looked up to find Tia watching him. "And what about you? How are you feeling after all this?" he asked, cocking his head to one side, his pupils big and black in the low light of Tia's quarters.

Tia shrugged. "As well as can be expected. My mind's a muddle of clashing thoughts and emotions. Being a scorpiad had its advantages. There was nothing in my mind, just empty primal urges. Then Ressen roused me, and everything came crashing back in like a tsunami. It's taking a while to put everything back to where it was."

Chione gave a nod of understanding and went quiet. Tia could feel awkwardness radiating off her friend. There was a worry consuming him, and she waited patiently as he found the courage to voice the question he clearly didn't want to know the answer to.

"I have to ask; what of the other scorpiad? Did you know him?"

Tia knew why Chione was asking about the creature. Though he wasn't saying his reasons outright, he was wondering if it had been one of the creatures he had attended to when he oversaw the original project that had created them. But Tia was cautious, if the scorpiad had been of Chione's making, then there was no doubt the man behind the cat would be consumed even further by guilt. The creature's waylaying of her had meant Aben's death, and if there was one person who had been closer to the alien than she, it was Chione.

However, Tia had seen the creature's true face. It had belonged to a man, free to walk the station unencumbered, not some rabid beast, at least not to begin with. She remembered his deep eyes, close-shaven hair, and cruel mouth. "No, I didn't know him," she assured Chione, and she felt the weight lift off him at her words. "He was a Human male, that I know, but more importantly, he was Human when he first arrived on the station. He may have been smuggled on, he may have stepped on, but either way, he was not an old creation. Even if I could recall the faces of the others, I have no doubt he would not be amongst them."

"The Alliance are making scorpiads again," Chione uttered, with a sigh. "How much do you think Mister Ward and his telepath clones are mixed up in all this?"

"Considering he seems to dog my every move; I'm willing to bet a lot." Certainly, the man, or rather men, seemed to be everywhere Tia didn't want them to be. It had been a Mister Ward that had originally appeared on the station to question the Alliance personal about their loyalty. It had been another Mister Ward that had found his way on to the dead world to make a grab for the orb and had tried to blow her and her men up. And it had been a Mister Ward that had been at the other end of the scorpiads leash. Whoever was the original Mister Ward, if indeed he was a willing participant in what was going on, he was starting to get on Tia's last nerve. "If there's one group of people who see themselves as far above the rabble of the Orion Alliance it's the telepaths," Tia said. "Ergo, if there's one group who'd see the need to recreate the scorpiads, it would be the telepaths. Maybe they're playing another long game alone, and have need of the creatures, or perhaps the Alliance is fully in on their creation. What happened long ago with me curtailed their creation, that's for sure, but once the

Alliance figured out what my background was, it's not too far-fetched to assume they've decided to try again, and fight fire with fire. Either way, it didn't work, so with any luck all those concerned will think twice before trotting any more of those bastardised things out."

"I hope you're right," Chione answered, still sounding unhappy.

"Look, what you did in the past had unintended consequences. It led to deaths, some much closer to home than others." Tia felt Chione shiver inwardly at her words, as the image of his lost family members flickered into his thoughts. "However, what you did also led to me. Not to sound narcissistic, but me being here is no small, unimportant thing. I know you have regrets, and I know you're paying a terrible price for what you did. But also take heart in the fact that the free and oppressed people of this galaxy have a chance at better future, because of me. You set a ball rolling that's been gaining speed for centuries, but look not to where it came from, but to where it's going."

"I guess," Chione said.

Tia reached out a hand and stroked the feline's soft white fur. Ordinarily, the man behind the whiskers wasn't an enthusiastic fan of Human-pet interactions, but this time he made no move to escape her touch, choosing to take comfort in Tia's gesture. She wanted to say more to her friend; about how everything would be okay, no matter what, but even she wasn't sure just how bright the future would be. There was no denying that her presence had helped bolster the rebel races into forming alliances against the enemy, and that her presence in battle had helped stop the impending slaughter of the Ciberians. Unfortunately, she had no idea if her continued presence would help the rebels win the entire struggle. The Orion Alliance was strong in numbers, organised, well-armed, and had the support of an unknown and dangerous race. She tried to stay confident for everyone, to ensure they kept their eyes on the prize of a free future, but in private she worried that everything she was doing would be in vain against the far superior force.

And then there had been the statue of her, labelling her as the goddess of death. It was an image she couldn't shake, or a connotation she could ignore. Ever since she had laid eyes on it, there had been a nagging feeling in the back of her head that everything she was trying to do would come to nought. That she would be the death of those self-same races she was trying to lead to freedom. "Food?" Tia asked after a moment, just as much to distract her from her own dark thoughts as Chione from his. Chione nodded his head, the cat in him finally perking up.

*****

It was shortly past lunch time when one of Tia's men finally arrived. A mental hail from her had brought Kan to her door to tell her what he'd learnt from Talon. The man looked as exhausted as Tia felt, but he still managed a big smile of relief when he clapped eyes on her, and his relief at seeing her 'normal' was unmistakeable. He and Tia shared a look that spoke of memories between them, and despite being a galaxy-weary mercenary, he looked as if the thing he wanted to do most in the world was hug her. Instead, he kept a respectful distance from his leader.

Tia, on the other hand, had been on a roller-coaster ride of emotions, and had no intention of keeping with what little protocol she had. She scooped the big man into a bear hug, much to his surprise, and they stood for several moments, arms encircling each other, absorbing reassurance from each other. She felt his heartbeat, quickening against her chest, and as she inhaled his musky scent, she could feel her own heart and stomach twist amid conflicting thoughts and desires. She broke away, and held him at arm's length, giving him an appreciative smile. "Oh, I've missed you," she told him.

"Likewise," Kan responded, "and believe me, I'm not the

only one. Shar was climbing the walls waiting for you to snap out of it. Now he can't stop smiling, which is unnerving the prison guards no end."

Tia laughed, knowing how the reptile's fang-filled grin was disconcerting at the best of times. "In that regard, time waits for no man, or alien. You have information regarding Kiskin?"

"Yes." And so Kan explained to Tia what Talon had discovered about the alien's species being featured on the disc with the Karee orb.

Tia nodded at his words. "He's right, I remember the images, and I can't ignore their likeness."

"What does Morrígan tell you?" Kan asked, innocently.

Tia flinched at his words. "I haven't reconnected with her yet," she said, with considerable guilt. "I haven't been in the right frame of mind, but that has to change, for Shar's sake."

Kan brushed away her guilt. "I don't blame you one bit," he said. "You've been to hell and back. If I were in your shoes, I'd be taking time to get my shit together too. But don't forget you have us. We may not be powerful Karee, or touchy-feely psychiatrists, but we've got your back, for however long that may be."

Tia gave him a look of intense gratitude. "I know, and I thank the universe each day for you all. I'll admit, not so much at the beginning," she gave Kan a wink, "but now I wouldn't be without any of you."

Kan gave a nod of understanding. "Well, I won't keep you from the important things." Tia knew what he was alluding to, and a slight knot formed in her stomach. Kan left without further word, leaving Tia to the silence of her room. She sank back in her chair and released an audible groan of resignation. Then she did what she had put off doing for so long and opened her mind to Morrígan.

Morrígan, her giant spaceship, an alien creature that could traverse space, and with the right experience, time, and who had come into being with a wealth of instinctual knowledge, weaved its mind with Tia's. In so doing, it gave Tia access to the billions of years of information the Karee had accumulated before Morrígan's conception as an egg and interment deep within a newly forming planet.

However, with the information came Morrígan herself. She was an ancient, other-worldly creature, of energy and wisdom, and Tia felt like a guilty schoolchild in her presence, waiting for the inevitable stern telling off over losing her marbles. She braced herself for the expected berating over the fact that she should have been stronger of mind, and that she should have resisted her feral scorpiad urges, but the lecture never came. Instead, Morrígan wrapped herself around Tia like a warm blanket, and radiated comfort and understanding. *"Strength comes through time and experience,"* it told her, *"and when the time comes, you will be ready."*

Tia wished she had as much confidence. Her experiences thus far had either been victories through dumb luck, or mitigated disasters. *Will that 'time' be a moment just down the road, or hundreds of years in the future?* Tia wondered. *The rebels certainly can't wait centuries for me to master myself.*

Morrígan was monitoring Tia's internal dialogue. *"One step at a time,"* she said, albeit unhelpfully as far as Tia was concerned. *"You have more pressing concerns, yes?"*

"I have a man in trouble, and if I'm to help him, I need to know about Kiskin's race, those who inhabited the dead world all those centuries ago, so no holding back on the information." Gaining knowledge through her and Morrígan's shared consciousness was now nothing more than an instinctual act for Tia. She simply brought to the forefront of her mind the image of Kiskin, and the rust-red planet that had once been her species' home, and all the rest fell into place. It was as if the information had always been there and had simply required the firing of a couple of synapses to bring it into focus. Though as Morrígan often withheld information from Tia, there was always the chance that had it not been for her present dire need, she would have drawn a blank. But Morrígan seemed to understand when its own caution needed to give way to necessity.

Although Morrígan's innate knowledge ended long before

the dawn of Kiskin's people, she certainly wasn't lacking information. A little she had absorbed from her time within the planet, surrounded by Kiskin's race, but most of what she knew she had gleaned from Jarell, and the reason for her earlier silence on the subject became apparent. They were one of the few races whose details weren't divulged outside of the Inner Sanctum. They were an ancient and advanced race, and the Inner Sanctum held them in some prestige. Even going so far as earmarking them as a race that could follow a similar evolutionary process as them; to became creatures of space. However, the fact that Morrígan now had information on them also buoyed Tia. She now knew the other rogue Karee vessel was happy to share its knowledge with Morrígan, and hence, her, and it meant that most of what the Karee knew was finally within her grasp. Naturally, Jarell could decide not to provide certain intel, but as it seemed prepared to help in Shar's case, it bode well for the future.

Ambassador Kiskin had already identified itself as Skari, but what that meant was finally clear. The Skari were a sect, formally entitled the Elders of Skari, and they were the governing body of Kiskin's race; the Ethtas. Their old home planet, and Morrígan's resting place, had been called Qualter, but had subsequently been christened the Dead World by Tia and her men, simply because that's what it was. Its dirt had been rust and broken-down plastics, the rain, acidic, and the surface had been littered with the barely discernible remains of buildings. No life, certainly no complex life, had been present beyond Tia, her crew, and the Alliance landing party that had followed in their wake.

Morrígan then filled in some gaps, either through educated guess work, or from what she'd learnt from Tartarus, who had kept an ear on Tia's crew's discussions. The Ethtas had driven their planet to wrack and ruin. Industrialisation had trumped common sense, and a runaway greenhouse effect, along with acid rain, had stripped the planet of life, and had forced the Ethtas underground. Ideas that Morrígan further confirmed, through communications with Jarell. In their underground fortress, the Ethtas had come together, created interstellar arks, and had relocated to a new planet, Koron, in the system of Zooquar.

However, Morrígan's knowledge didn't answer the question of why she had been left as an egg inside the planet. Either Jarell didn't know or wasn't playing ball. *There's no denying Talon's reasoning that the survival of the Ethtas was as a direct result of the egg's existence,* Tia reflected. *Chances are, had the Ethtas not uncovered it and used it to power their immense subterranean city, the species would have become extinct long before they'd managed to figure out how to build their arks. Morrígan sustained the species, allowing it to thrive and remain biologically viable.* This made Tia wonder if the Karee had foreseen the Ethtas' downfall. She knew the Karee could predict the future by studying probability. *It wouldn't surprise me if they figured the Ethtas would end up going down a bad road like most advancing races and put the egg there as a backup plan. Which makes me wonder what other hands did they give? Did they surreptitiously provide the knowledge to build the arks, just in case?*

That was a question for a different day. Tia had found out all she needed, along with another juicy titbit, and it all confirmed Talon and Kan's reasoning. The Karee and the Ethtas were linked, and now the Karee were using the Ethtas as puppets in a move designed to sever Shar from her side. A soldier who had been instrumental in yanking the station from out the Alliance's clutches, while saving countless Zerren lives in the process. A species who was the Karee's last protected race. The facts were not going to sit well with Kiskin, or the Zerren government. The Zerrens were highly unlikely to sanction Shar's execution with the facts at hand, and Kiskin was unlikely to fight their decision, as that would mean going toe to toe with the Karee. The Karee wouldn't fight the Zerrens, as they were their legacy, and they had chosen to protect them, so fighting them wouldn't cast the Karee in a good light. Conversely, they wouldn't want to be seen fighting the Ethtas, as that would make them seem nothing more than arseholes in the eyes of the Zerrens. Moreover, they'd already played the arsehole card by threatening to leave Zerren space undefended, despite Kiskin's proclamation that their response was purely an exaggeration to make a point, and Tia knew the Karee wouldn't try that threat again. At least not straight away. They wouldn't want to be seen as nothing more than stroppy aliens, and if there was one thing the Karee truly cared about, it was their lordly image.

So, this is the kind of political wrangling Aben used to enjoy, Tia thought, her head spinning. *The only thing it does is tie my brain in knots.* Yet the toing and froing over what Kiskin and the Karee would and wouldn't do left a nagging feeling with her. She couldn't understand how the Karee thought they'd win this gambit. *Did they just assume my ignorance, and that I wouldn't be able to untangle their thought processes, or did they just put their hopes in me running away with Shar at the first sign of trouble? Do they honestly not know me, or have I grown as a person to such an extent that they can't confidently predict what I'll do?* Indeed, Jarell had told Tia that, since becoming Karee, she'd blinded them to their own future due to her own unpredictability, but Tia had to admit, she didn't think she was **that** unpredictable. *They do just seem to see me as some mindless monstrosity that acts rather than thinks.* That realisation made Tia seethe. *They are such an arrogant, self-absorbed, over-confident race.*

Morrígan chimed into her thoughts. *"The Karee are billions of years old. They have seen everything and have done everything. With that realisation comes a great amount of conceitedness."*

"You're not wrong," Tia answered. *"But there's an old Earth saying: The bigger they are, the harder they fall. Someone needs to remind them of that."*

"They will learn the truth of that one day," Morrígan replied, earnestly. *"For now, their resolve will be tested, and you shall be the one that tests them."*

And so begins my second war, Tia grumbled.

****

"Do you wish me to reiterate my points?" Tia asked, scrutinising Kiskin for any change in her expression. The Ambassador was stood opposite her, its mood one of indignation. Its servant creature, Wrymiesk, was indeed a telepath, and as such, a creature expertly bred to be able to read different alien races. It had tried to read Tia's mind the moment she had entered the Security Department, presumably hoping to take her unaware. It was regretting its decision and was nursing a major migraine courtesy of a mental right-hook from Tia. It was stood in a corner, its eyes shut, and its thin blue lips trembling.

The two Ethtas were not the only individuals in the office, there were three other people listening intently as Tia tersely addressed the aliens. Shar was present to witness the outcome of a conversation that affected his life. His four hands were once more handcuffed, a sight that made Tia rankle; however, she said nothing, as she knew the second member of the group, Walks, was only doing his job. He was stood beside her mercenary, but his weapons were safely holstered, and he gave off an air of remorse and hope; hope that Tia could get his friend Shar out of his current predicament.

As she spoke to Kiskin, Tia made sure she was coming across as a force majeure, backing up her words with a visual display. Her wings were outstretched, her long tail thrashed and rattled of its own accord, and her eyes had become brightly shining blue stars. She was also boosting her display for the benefit of the two Ethtas' eyes only. She had recalled that the signs in the Dead World's subterranean city had been created using bacteria that emitted heat, and only those with the ability to see infrared could make them out. With that in mind, she was expertly circulating heat through her wings, creating a dizzying display of patterns that Kiskin was sure to find distracting, or at least extremely annoying. Indeed, Kiskin, despite her indignation, had lost her earlier air of confidence, and was looking increasingly agitated. She had clearly been preparing for an encounter with a slightly dumb A'daree soldier, with the powers of a Karee, not a full-fledged and irate Karee who was more than capable of unravelling deceit.

Tia had declared the facts as she saw them, and by Kiskin's lack of protestations, she knew she had her bang to rights. Kiskin was a pawn of the Karee, accepting the task by way of payment for her species continued existence thanks to Morrígan. There was subsequently no denial over the fact that the charges against Shar were being brought by the Karee, and not the Ethtas, and as the Karee had already sentenced Shar, by putting him in servitude under Tia's command, neither Kiskin, nor the Karee, could change that. At least not without opening a huge can of worms.

At one point, Tia had sensed Kiskin was about to do what she had predicted and try to bring the Zerrens into the fray by suggesting that they should consider Shar's death sentence. Tia had cut her off before she could get the words out. She had reiterated how the Zerrens on the station had been saved because of Shar's actions, and that many saw him as a true hero, while others still considered Tia to be a goddess, and had no intention of rallying against what they saw as a divine force. Such ideology was enough for them to not want to interfere with Shar's punishment; not now, or ever. Sin'ma, the third member of the opposing group, and who had been stood warily off to the side, had nodded in agreement.

Kiskin could do nothing but admit defeat. "You realise this play makes you an enemy of us and the Karee," she announced.

Tia shrugged. "I've been an enemy of the Karee since they brought me into their fold, even more so now I am their equal. They couldn't stand me when I was the monster they needed to do their dirty work, and they loath me now for being able to stand up to them, mentally and physically. As for you," she glared pointedly at Kiskin, "you are a cowed pawn of the Karee, and I have nothing but contempt for you." Then, as the coup de grâce, she revealed the other bit of information Jarell had provided to Morrígan. "Your race knew about the Skarren-Verek war but chose not to involve themselves in it. Now you have the audacity to come here and throw charges about? Too little, too late. Shar may have been indirectly responsible for all those deaths, through his orders, but your species is just as culpable by its inaction. Shar has been sentenced and is carrying out his punishment. What about you?"

Tia, through her mental fact-finding mission with Morrígan, had learnt that the Ethtas had known all about the war. They even had tomes written about it. The Skarren-Verek war had happened long after the Ethtas had developed interstellar travel, and their second planet wasn't that far away from the remains of the Skarren and Verek systems. They had been in a prime position to help and mediate. Instead, they had sat back, watched two races burn each other to the ground, and had smugly congratulated themselves at having evolved beyond war. Tia wanted very much to punch Kiskin so hard her ancestors would feel it.

"Your species' inactions led to the deaths of billions of Verek **and** Skarrens. By that standing, your elders should join Shar in the airlock, if not precede him. Or..." she stared hard at Kiskin, "...perhaps the closest example of the race to hand would set a shining example to future generations." She didn't feel like mentioning that out of the two of them, Shar would survive his unprotected space walk through a combination of an intercepting Tartarus, and Shar's bolstered healing ability. "Tell me I wouldn't dare.... Go on!"

Kiskin pursed her lips but couldn't find a suitable comeback. Tia could sense the rage building up in the alien. "So be it," was her eventual response. "As far as this war with the Orion Alliance goes, our help will not be forthcoming."

"I wouldn't have it any other way," Tia retorted. Although her comment sounded petulant, it was measured and true. She wanted the races to be able to stand up to warmongers as a united front, without the help of high and mighty races. That way they, and their future progeny, wouldn't be answerable to a higher force, such as the Ethtas were to the Karee. It was Tia's hope that eventually, the Zerrens too would be able to stand on their own, without Karee interference. She just had her fingers crossed that that time came before the Karee decided, "To hell with it," and disappeared off somewhere else.

"In that case, we will leave," Kiskin announced.

"I am afraid not," Sin'ma stated, breaking his silence. "There has been a murder of a high-ranking member of staff, and the station is locked down until the culprit is apprehended."

Kiskin's head whipped round to face the Zerren. "I don't see how that should prevent us from leaving."

"No allowances, no privileges." Sin'ma responded, with a slightly malicious glint in his eye.

Tia took note of the exchange and sensed a change in Sin'ma demeanour. *He's more combative, which is a troubling turn around. It looks like his actions on the Vengeance are still affecting his mind.* Kiskin looked to Tia, expecting the Karee to overrule the lesser race, but Tia didn't share its mentality. "Sin'ma is the captain of this station, and as such, his rules are **the** rules. Your quarters are comfy, and there's plenty with which to occupy your time along the thoroughfare. Think of it as a holiday." Kiskin glared at Tia, but she just returned the look with an amiable smile. Then she turned to the still-cowering Wrymiesk. "Be warned, I have a mental lock on you now, and if I sense you trespassing in people's minds unasked, I will turn your brain to liquid." Wrymiesk shook noticeably, and despite its chestnut brown carapace, it managed to pale. It nodded carefully, its pounding migraine making it wince as it did so. "Good. You are both dismissed."

Tia could feel Kiskin rankle at being sent packing by someone whom she still saw as little more than a glorified grunt. However, the fact that the grunt was also Karee, made the self-preservation part of her brain kick in. But, as she scuttled out, she still managed a parting shot at Tia. "Those in the shadow of the goddess of war shouldn't be so quick to dispel us." Wrymiesk slowly and methodically followed behind, without uttering a word.

Tia didn't show it, but the words unnerved her. The statue came into being, without a doubt, before Kiskin's time. *Someone's been doing their research on me, that's aggravating.* She pulled herself together, and finally gave Shar and Walks eye contact. Shar was beaming. Walks looked like his legs were about to give way. The old man released Shar's hands from his cuffs, then sat heavily on a nearby chair.

"Told you she wouldn't let me die," Shar told Walks. "She likes having me around too much to let that happen." He gave Tia an expansive grin.

"It's from death's door to lecherous in thirty seconds flat with you," Tia remarked, giving him a smirk back.

"Honestly, I don't know how you two can walk through hell, come out the other side, and shrug it off like it was a mild inconvenience," Walks lamented, wearily.

"We've had years of practice," Shar answered, patting his friend on his unburnt shoulder.

"Although, these days, it's getting a bit more routine than I'd like," Tia added. "Honestly, we may be resilient, but jumping from one nightmare to another is not the best way to live your life, even if it is easy."

"Agreed," Shar said. "Speaking of which, I've had a hell of a time of late, and I'm in need of a smoke and a strong drink, or twelve." He looked to Walks and Tia. "Care to join me?"

Tia felt Walks' mind recoil at the mention of alcohol. *Looks like he's trying sobriety again. Good for him.*

"Make mine alcohol-free, and I'm in," the man said, with a noticeable sigh.

Shar nodded, choosing not to push the issue. "Trust me, most of what Talon has on tap is so diluted it's got less percentage and taste than pond water," he said, with an eye roll. He turned to Tia. "You?"

"You know I usually jump at the chance to join you in a drink, but I have other matters to attend to. Another time?"

Shar looked put out but took her answer at face value. "I'll hold you to that," he told her, before heading out the office with Walks in his wake.

Tia turned to the silent Sin'ma. "Thank you for your patience in all of this. I know it wasn't easy."

"Irritating was probably the word I would use," he answered. "To be honest, if it was not for Lieutenant Commander Walks' tireless efforts in waylaying that creature, things may have ended before you had awakened."

"So, you have fewer misgivings about my choice of Security chief?" she asked, while giving him a sideways glance. She sensed Sin'ma flush under his fur. She knew he'd had reservations over Walks' appointment since the beginning, even though he had kept those worries to himself in her presence. Yet she didn't begrudge him his concerns. Walks was an alcoholic who tipped alarmingly between sobriety and all out mess, and she knew that as well as anyone, but beyond that, Walks was a good and a trustworthy man. A rarity amongst the Alliance's top men. He had his demons, but Tia knew he had the strength to fight them, just as he had the Alliance's control.

"I admit I do question his placement," Sin'ma conceded, "but it is times like these that I see why you chose him." He paused for a moment. "What did that creature mean by the goddess of war?"

Tia swore internally. The last thing she wanted was a leader of the GR to doubt her, especially when she did enough of that herself. The trouble was, she wasn't sure how to spin a giant effigy of her, declaring her as the Harbinger of Death, in a positive light. "There was a statue carved of me on Kiskin's old homeworld, proclaiming that I would bring war and death." Sin'ma's eyes went wide. "However," she added, quickly, before he had time to entertain bad thoughts. "It fails to consider whether I am of a mind to fulfil its proclamation, and if so, who I will wage that proclamation against. As far as I'm concerned, I may be in the middle of war, but my sights are set fully on the Alliance." She could tell Sin'ma wasn't happy at this news. "You have your doubts?"

Sin'ma's fur almost blanched under her cold stare. "Do you think you can control the direction of such a prophecy?" he asked, in a small voice.

"Do you think I would turn against you?"

"No, but your actions have already indirectly caused the death of those who lost their lives at the battle of Ciberia. Who knows how many more will perish as we try to win this battle." His voice was still quiet, but it contained defiance, and the maliciousness he'd shown Kiskin was still bubbling under the surface.

Tia bristled. "Would you prefer it if I'd never been here? Do you think you'd be better off? What exactly do you think would have happened the day the Alliance made to claim the Scientia, and I hadn't been placed here by the Karee? I'll tell you what would've happened; nothing. There would have been no battle over the station, at least not one that would've been victorious. The Alliance would've claimed the station, along with the right to enslave your race, and then it would have been a short hop skip and a jump to Ciberia, where they would've done likewise." She could feel Sin'ma begin to quail under her tirade, his earlier defiance towards her rapidly evaporating. "You may not have had the capacity to fight back, and that would be your race's saving grace, but the Ciberians would fight back, no question, and it would be nothing short of wholesale slaughter. If I hadn't been thrown into the mix, then right now we'd be looking at a subjugated race, and a nigh-on extinct race. Is that what you'd prefer to a questionable prophecy that makes no mention of target or time-frame?"

"No," he said.

"It is an unfortunate fact that wars have casualties, and no matter how good I am, this battle towards freedom will leave bodies in its wake. But they will be a damn site fewer than if I leave you, and the other races, to face the Alliance alone. You'd do well to remember that." Sin'ma gave a quiet nod. "I'm sure I don't have to add that the discussion regarding the statue goes no further that this room." Another nod, and he hurriedly took his leave of her, distinctly uncomfortable at having revealed himself to be sceptical of her choices, and her.

There was also the problem of Walks having heard Kiskin's shot. But Tia had a better read on the man. Chances were, if he had any questions, they'd be directed at Shar, and Tia, knowing the two men, knew Shar would tell him to drop it, and that Walks would comply without further question.

Tia stood alone in the office. She didn't like having to lose her temper, especially at someone she knew to be a smart and capable leader. It was obvious to her that Sin'ma was still dealing with his own internal struggle, and Tia could only hope it didn't take him to too many dark places. She let her mind play over her to-do list as she tried to calm down and began ticking things off. *I've saved Shar; that's one thing done. Now it's time to close off Aben's chapter and lay him to rest. Then I'll go about finding the bastard who murdered him.*

Chapter 16 - Ressen

Ressen was back in the infirmary and had acclimatised to the hustle and bustle around him, which was now just background noise to him. He was taking in food, and though it was no more than protein mush infused with vitamins, he was doing it properly, with his mouth, and with each bite he could feel himself getting stronger. The biggest change however was what once had been blistered and open wounds was now discernible skin. He looked down at himself, checking to see it was still as it should be, and was content to see the blue and white stripes of his species once more wrapped around his body. And though his new flesh was still sensitive, a casual brush didn't leave him reeling in agony; consequently, his medication had been reduced, and he was feeling clear-headed and almost like his old self. Further, the strange guiding force was no longer present in the corner of his mind, so when he slept, he slept deeply, without feeling as though he were being watched.

His rapid recovery had come at the touch of Tia. As her blood had mingled with his, he'd felt a warm sensation sweep through his whole body. It was as if his insides had been wrapped snugly in a fleece blanket of the kind his mother used to swaddle his brother and him in when they were young. The pain that had surged through his body as he'd sat heavily down, after his body had finally given up following its horrific journey, had been washed away, and he'd felt unusually happy and giddy. Then he'd passed out.

He had awoken to find the wrappings had been removed from his body, and the incessantly beeping machines had been taken for those who were in more need of them. He was even expected to take toilet trips under his own steam. Then, having been declared relatively fit, he was allowed visitors.

First came an emotional reunion with his brother who, as he had hoped, had been fixing their ship and not, as he had feared, had scarpered. Ressen couldn't put into words how elated he felt on seeing his brother's beaming face. Although all those around him were courteous and friendly, communicating was still a struggle for Ressen, and it was causing him to feel isolated. Grelt had been busy in that regard, helping to provide a translation database, but it was a slow process, as their language was a difficult one for direct phrase to phrase translation, so being able to talk freely and easily with his brother helped dispel some of Ressen's depression, and they'd talked and joked, though at times Ressen felt his brother was a little distracted. Even so, Grelt had listened with wide eyes, and sympathetic murmurs, as Ressen had tried to explain what he'd been through; the visits from the disembodied Emma, his journey to find the necklace, and his ultimate meeting with Tia, all of which had left him feeling disquieted and out of sorts.

Grelt had his own story to tell; the one of rescuing Ressen from the explosion in the cockpit. He had doused his brother with water to put out the flames just in time, only to have the ship's generators die on him. It had been at that moment when a strange blue ship had uncloaked right above them, locked onto their vessel, and had headed full speed to the station, where waiting medics had rushed Ressen to the Medicentre.

Shortly after Grelt's visit, Ressen had received a second, surprise visitor. One of the Filteth refugees had stopped by, the new matriarch of their clan. Ressen had recognised her face but didn't know her name. He had only ever seen her in passing during his smuggling visits, and all he knew of her was that she had been a baker amongst her tribe. She had looked totally different to when Ressen had last seen her. Then she had been subdued and frightened, wrapped in soiled clothes, and clutching the arm of her mate. Both had been crying at the destruction of their world, and the loss of those they'd known. Stood at the end of his hospital bed was the female he remembered getting glimpses of, yet more so. Her long robes were clean, her shell jewellery was polished, and her light brown skin was freshly washed. But more than that, she had gained the regal poise of a leader. Her small brown eyes had held within them a sense of solemnness, and her heavy brow ridge seemed to no longer make her look primitive, rather, it had given her a look of deep concentration. With the help of a struggling translator, she had heaped praise and thanks onto Ressen for saving those few people he had. Her words had humbled Ressen but had added to his wretchedness. His biggest regret was that he hadn't been able to save more, but the matriarch was having none of it. As far as she was concerned, he had given her species the gift of a second chance, something the Alliance had afforded few races. She had told him, plainly, that he should be happy in the knowledge that her kind hadn't been made extinct, and that they were being taken somewhere safe. She hadn't elaborated on where, so all Ressen could do was wish her and her people a safe trip and a long future. As he watched her disappear across the ward he had realised, with a pang of guilt, he still hadn't learnt her name.

****

Shortly after the matriarch's visit, Ressen had the visitor he was both waiting for and fearing. Tia came. As she entered the ward, she gave the staff a courteous nod, and they responded in kind, with big-eyed apprehension. It was a different Tia to the one he'd first laid eyes on. The monster was almost, but not entirely, gone, being replaced in parts by what he recognised as Emma. Thankfully, the entire package had shrunk down to a less terrifying size, and though she wore a cloak of wings, a crown of horns, and a scary looking tail, she was no taller than Ressen. However, it appeared she and Ressen were exceptions when it came to height, and they both towered over the medics by equal measure. Going by the side-glances Tia received from the medical staff, Ressen figured he wasn't the only one who looked at her with a sense of overwhelming awe.

Once at his bedside, she grabbed a chair, and with some awkwardness, tried to settle herself into it, while appearing to tussle with a tail that seemed to want to go its own way. Ressen couldn't help but notice the three huge barbs at the end of it and wondered what they were used for.

Emma's face shone through the adornments of Tia and was as Ressen remembered from his dreams. Long blonde hair framed a gentle Human face with blue eyes, and a mouth that sported, on occasion, a slightly crooked smile. Her arms, which had once been blackened scales and huge talons, were now fair skinned, though Ressen noticed there were fine silver lines criss-crossing her flesh.

"So, we meet properly at last," Tia said, with Emma's voice.

Ressen understood her words completely, which surprised him, but he had the feeling all was not as it appeared. It was as if the words coming from her mouth, and the ones landing in his brain, were different. There was a slightly visual, fuzzy dis-jointedness between her mouth and his ears.

"You are correct," Tia responded, answering what he believed to be private thoughts. "I speak my own language, and you hear it as yours. I'm a telepath," she said, by way of an explanation.

Ressen decided to try it the other way around "A telepath?" he asked, in his own words. "I thought they were mythical creatures, like hoobies and scrives?"

Tia pulled a face. "I have no idea what they are, but I can assure you I am very real."

"Well, a hoobie was a little creature with wings that stole food, and scrives lived in the water and stole sailors," Ressen explained, feeling a little foolish as he did so. *Gods, did I just say all that? Why would someone like her care about childish fantasies?* He mentally rolled his eyes.

Tia simply nodded in polite comprehension. "So, kind of like fairies and mermaids in Human mythology. Interesting the parallels that come up between races." She looked at him directly. "You have questions."

Ressen wasn't sure if she was asking, or making a statement of fact, either way, he had them in spades. "Gods yes!" he answered, "but where do I start?"

Tia gave a little shrug. "Anywhere you like. I have the time if you have the energy."

The barrage came. "Who are you…? What are you…? What was Emma, and how did she get in my mind…? Oh, and what the hell was the whole necklace thing about, and just who made me get it…?" He took in a needed breath.

The quirky smile came to Tia's lips again. "I am Tia, and I am Karee. I know that means nothing to you, and that's fine. Just know that the Karee are a race that are powerful, ancient, and way beyond conceited. Luckily for most, I only tick the first of those categories. As for Emma? Well, she was an earlier incarnation of me, and there were a couple of others between her and me. However, she was simply Human and simply good, and she is still much a part of me. She's the part that laughs at silly movies, craves chocolate, and blushes around attractive guys." Ressen smiled broadly at that. "She's also the part of me that drives me to do the things I do; to not stand aimlessly by when others are in need, and to not see myself above those who are less 'developed'."

"She's your soul," Ressen put in, remembering Emma's words.

"I call in conscience, you could call is soul, but yes, very much so. As for the necklace, well that is a more awkward thing to explain. A while ago, before becoming Karee, I went on a journey to a dying world to find an artefact. Something in my gut warned me there was trouble ahead, and I would do well to have a backup plan if things went awry, hence the necklace. How well do you know computers?" she randomly asked him.

"Well enough. They crash more often than is decent."

Tia laughed. "True enough. Well, that necklace was my version of a backup disc in case I crashed. Being in proximity to it...rebooted me, for want of a better description. It contained some of my essence, a portion of my soul if you will, and it broke down the walls I had built to banish Emma to a dark corner, and it brought us back together, allowing me to regain my sanity. As for who guided your steps, I think that was the combined forces of what was left of Emma somehow finding a way inside your mind, and Morrígan."

"Who's Morrígan?"

"My ship. My sentient ship. The one that brought you and your vessel to the station."

"Oh." Grelt's description of the strange blue craft came to mind.

"Yes, that one," Tia confirmed, again answering his unspoken thoughts.

"In that case, I owe you a debt of gratitude for rescuing me, and for healing me."

"Believe me," Tia answered, "your debt is more than paid. You saved me, and the people on this station from me. I believe we are at an equal standing, and I believe that is why I, unconsciously, and Morrígan, consciously, chose you. Of all the people on this station, we were in the most need of help, and we helped each other. I guess you could call it karmic balance."

Ressen wasn't sure what to say. Someone he didn't know had given him a second chance at life, and that someone appeared to be a bit of a bigshot. He couldn't get his head around the fact that he didn't owe her anything. He could understand why, he had brought her back from madness, but it still didn't seem right to him somehow. "So, where do I go from here?" he asked, still feeling confused.

"That is up to you, but I think you should speak to your brother again before making any definitive choices?"

"Why?"

"That is for him to say, not me," was Tia's cryptic response, "but for now, rest and heal. You still have a way to go before you're back to full strength."

With that, she left, leaving Ressen with a worried feeling in the pit of his stomach. *What has Grelt agreed to now?*

****

Grelt's next visit was the day after Tia's. He caught the expression on Ressen's face and immediately looked guilty. "So? You have something to tell me?" Ressen enquired.

"Before you get mad, let me explain," Grelt gabbled. "I'm not downplaying anything you've done recently, believe me, but other than your supernatural walkabout, you've been cocooned in here." Grelt gestured around him at the recuperation ward. "I've been out there, surrounded by good, and battle-weary people. There's been a war simmering against the Orion Alliance for centuries, and now it's on the verge of blowing up into all-out conflict, and the people leading the charge against it are struggling to meet the challenge. Having seen what the Alliance is capable of first-hand...I offered my services."

Ressen stared at him wide-eyed. The reason for Grelt's earlier distractedness was finally becoming clear. "To do what?" he pressed.

"Pilot vessels. I'm a good pilot, even you can't deny that, and a lot of the rebels' original pilots died protecting their own worlds, so they have need of people like me."

"You are seriously volunteering to go on the front line?"

Grelt looked downcast. "Are you mad?"

Ressen wasn't sure what he was. His young brother had always been impetuous, and the way he'd behaved in the past could well have seen him become a criminal, and not for long, as his impetuousness would have seen him get caught, or worse. And though Grelt had never been one to run from a fight, he certainly had never been one to run into one, given the choice. His volunteering to join the rebels was a side of Grelt that Ressen hadn't known was there, and with the mixture of brotherly concern, and outright panic for his safety, was undeniable pride. "You are wrong about one thing, you are an exceptional pilot, and the rebels should be honoured to have you. And no, I'm not mad. Gravely concerned as only a loving brother can be, but I won't tell you not to do this, because I know you, and you never listen to a word I say." He gave his brother a supportive smile.

"Thanks, but that does mean you'll need to find a different way to get home."

"We shall see," Ressen said, non-committally, while thinking about his earlier visitor, "but there's no rush."

Chapter 17 - Tia

The official gathering in the arboretum was small and congregated near a tree that had been kindly planted by the station's botanists in memoriam of those lost to the scorpiad. A small, unobtrusive bronze plaque, attached to its trunk, listed the names of Carl Matthews, Mee-Ine, fellow scientist Zen'nath, and Aben. Its turquoise leaves were tipped with gold, and they rustled gently in the arboretum's ceaseless breeze. To Tia, the scientists had chosen well, and she found the tree a fitting epitaph to those who'd passed.

She was stood, surrounded by those she loosely described as family and friends: Shar, Kan, Talon, Tay and Bal. Amongst them were her colleagues and acquaintances: Sin'ma and Bel'ka, Leo and Pra'cha, and Ken'va. At a polite distance stood Walks and his close lieutenants, and hidden amongst the bushes, Tia could sense the warm familiar presence of Chione, Aben's truest friend. Curious onlookers dotted the paths, but they didn't intrude into the main group.

All heads were looking up. Looking through the huge glass windows that topped the arboretum. The panes were there to let the life-giving rays of Zerra's sun through to the plants, but now they were to be a viewing platform to what was about to happen. Stars dotted a black sky that wasn't filled with the planet or sun, but they were a mere smattering compared to what made up the galaxy. Most of the stars struggled to be visible against the overpowering sunlight, as well as against the arboretum's own lamps, which were there to give a much-needed UV boost to plant and station inhabitant alike. However, Tia, wasn't so blinded, and she changed her visual perception so, unlike the other people around her, she could see all the stars. Before her were a mass of lights of all manner of wavelengths, and blue and white giants, yellow normals, and red dwarfs filled the dark void.

Then came what the throng had been waiting for. A new, moving star, had joined the tableau of lights. It was a small, pastel green pod, and Aben's final resting place. It was painted to match his skin tone and had a small engine with enough fuel to push it on a terminal trajectory into the heart of Zerra's sun. As it made its way out into space, two crafts uncloaked abreast of it. One was a vessel of deep purple, the other, turquoise. The mottled patterns on their surfaces shifted hypnotically, and their sides undulated as they kept pace with the tiny craft. It was Jarell and Morrígan, and they were to be Aben's funeral procession, making sure the little alien reached his destination unscathed. Also, if Tia shifted her vision slightly, she could make out another vessel following at a distance. It was a large, cumbersome-looking vessel of grey metal plating, some of which was turning rusty. It was Tartarus, and Tia knew the rest of her 'family' were attending Aben's last journey from the safety of the old, slightly sentient ship.

She gave a silent sigh as she watched the procession get smaller. Chione, her and Aben's feline companion, radiated sadness from his hiding place. Tia reached out her mind to him, and gave him a mental hug, much like Morrígan had given her when they had rejoined. *"I'm going to miss him,"* the cat told her. *"Who else is going to take me on journeys to give me a holiday?"*

Tia had no answer for him. She didn't even know how she was going to cope in Aben's absence. He may have seemed like an ineffectual creature to many, but those who had known him had quickly become aware of his intelligence, and his gift for discourse and data. Tia wasn't so blessed. The Karee had moulded her to be a soldier, an entity of action and few words. She had saved Shar through the unravelling of deceit, but she'd had help from several quarters, namely Talon and Kan, and Jarell and Morrígan. To do something like that daily, much as Aben did when dealing with head-butting bureaucrats, seemed implausible to Tia. She could only hope Ken'va and Sin'ma could fill the surprisingly big hole left by Aben. *"I'm sure the universe will send someone your way when the time is right,"* she said to Chione.

"You're starting to sound like a cryptic Karee," Chione responded, with an audible, to her ears, sniff.

"The Karee only say wishy-washy things like that because they can't come up with a more useful answer. I like to think I'm more helpful than that." She sensed Chione smile inwardly at her comment, though he remained mired in his sorrow.

A polite cough caught Tia's attention, and she looked down to realise she was the only one who had still been looking up; the average entities around her having long since lost sight of the coffin pod and its vanguard. "Sorry, it's hard to say goodbye," she said, trying to brush it away. Everyone else nodded politely in understanding.

Talon clapped his hands together and addressed the assembled throng. "It's an old Earth custom to commemorate the passing of a friend through eating, drinking, and reminiscing, so for tonight only, all food and drink at the Bar are on the house. Though for some," he looked pointedly at Shar, "there will be a drink minimum, otherwise I'll end up out of business." Tia's men laughed heartily, Leo smiled in understanding, however the four Zerrens looked slightly perturbed by the sound of merriment, as they were used to funerals being sombre affairs. Talon caught on to their expressions. "Facing sadness with a smile and fond memories makes healing easier."

"Though we will understand if you wish to forgo this part of our mourning process," Tia added. Although her men had all known Aben well enough, the likes of the Zerrens had only socialised with him through business. If Tia was honest, she wasn't sure she wanted them at the wake. She knew they were sure to come out of politeness but feared their awkward presence would make the atmosphere uncomfortable, especially to an entity like her who could pick up on people's thoughts and emotions.

"I am sure I speak for my colleagues when I say Aben will be just as missed by us as by his closest compatriots," Ken'va stated. "We may not have known him as keenly, but he was an important part of our lives. He was unassuming, yet intelligent, and much of what we have achieved with the GR could not have been done without him. I, for one, would like to mark his passing in a way he would appreciate." The three other Zerrens nodded in agreement.

Tia bowed her head, partly in thanks, but mostly to hide the tears that were threatening her eyes once again. "Thank you. We will be honoured to have you join us." She meant it too.

****

A few hours later, the wake was in full swing. Talon had resumed his post of barkeep and was ensuring everyone got plied with drinks and snacks, and his newly deputised staff, Tay and Bal, twin sisters who were, according to the emotions emanating between the trio, both his concubines, travelled around the space carrying trays laden with glasses of amber whisky, and bowls of purple nuts. As she watched them, Tia mulled over the implications of some her people being in a semi-incestuous ménage à trois. Certainly, relationships and hook-ups happened amongst her soldiers, and she was no stranger to them either. And the fact that her crew abounded with aliens meant such dalliances could be exotic affairs, and oft questionable in the eyes of most Humans, hence she had little recourse to argue against incest. But the fact that she had given into temptation at times also meant she was no stranger to the problems that happened when things went tits-up, and she had needed to beat Shar into submission after her fling with Kan had caused him to get overly territorial on her. Considering she had brought the sisters to heel after they had gone around incinerating men during their time as prostitutes, the future for Talon, if he wasn't careful, could very easily be crispy. *I hope he knows he's literally playing with fire,* Tia thought, as she pulled her gaze away from the fire twins, to cast her eye around the rest of the throng.

People had split into their respective groups. Tia's soldiers were in a corner, laughing raucously, and playing darts, albeit with large knives, and a pall of smoke hung about them from the copious cigars and roll-ups that were being smoked. *I guess Talon's unplugged the smoke detectors as well as the security cameras.* Tia rolled her eyes. *As if this place needs to become any more of a death trap.* She just hoped the sensors in the munitions bay didn't get wind of the smoke, otherwise they were going to be in for a long night if the emergency fire procedures kicked in, and the blast doors slammed down.

The Scientia's staff were gathered a safe distance from her men, and were more sombre in their interactions, choosing to talk quietly about the day-to-day goings-on of work and home life. Tia noticed that Sin'ma and Bel'ka stood as close together as Leo and his mate Pra'cha did. She smiled to herself, as she let her mind brush over the couple, and found Sin'ma to be calm and collected in Bell'ka's presence. *Hopefully, she will sooth his turmoil,* she thought, remembering Sin'ma's earlier, contentious behaviour. Walks seemed to be torn between standing politely with his colleagues, and rebuilding his friendship with Shar, and Tia watched him traipse backwards and forwards between the two groups, looking like a fish out of water in both. Shar eventually caught him in a friendly shoulder hug, and Walks was forced to stay and observe the violent darts match.

Amongst it all, Tia was where she usually ended up, sat on her own, watching the scene, while nursing a drink. She didn't mind too much, but she had to admit, she did feel left out of the camaraderie. Chione was curled up on a seat beside her, though due to his feline nature, he was fast asleep. A calm had finally come to those around her, and the terror her brief transformation had caused had noticeably diminished. The capture of the Vengeance, and the building of the Zerren battleships, was filling people with a sense of confidence, bolstered by the fact that the rebels had two Karee vessels and Tia on their side.

Tia caught Shar's eye, and he gave her a friendly nod. *"Try not to impale anybody,"* she told him, eliciting a smile in return, then she stood, scooped up her slumbering cat, and wandered away from the revelry. She made it back to her quarters without interruption, placed Chione carefully on her bed, then settled herself in a chair in her lounge. She closed her eyes, took a couple of cleansing breaths, opened her mind, and let it envelop the station.

For Tia, sensing minds on the Scientia was like looking up at the stars through the arboretum's window. Normally she was only aware of a few bright individuals, namely her crew, and the select few she chose to keep tabs on, like Leo and Sin'ma. However, when she changed her perspective, all became clear to her, and it was like looking at the full star spectrum of the galaxy. Her soldiers were like the blue giants and shone the most vivid in her mind. The primitive creatures were like the red dwarfs, harder to spot, but much more plentiful. They were the Zerren cats and vermin patrolling the stores, the fish and insects clustered in the arboretum, and the random pets that graced peoples' quarters. Then there was everybody else, and they filled the void like yellow, homely suns. She studied the scene. Some dots remained stationary, as their owners slumbered in their quarters, while others completed strange orbits, as people went about their evening. Tia studied each one as carefully as an astronomer studies the night sky, looking for one specific light that was giving off a particular signal. The astronomer may have been looking for signs of an elusive pulsar, Tia was looking for signs of an elusive killer. Aben's murderer. She was looking for a light that revealed its owner's corruption.

She was not alone in her search though, and for one last time, from beyond the grave, Aben guided her. He had already been dead when she had found him, but before the moment his last breath had left his body, he had cried out; cried out for her. His mind, his final thought, had hit her like a sledgehammer, setting about a chain reaction that had pushed her towards the madness that would consume her on finding his lifeless body. But in that desperate cry had come more than words. There had been feelings; pain, fear, hopelessness, but also a fleeting image, one of a man with hatred in his eyes. It had been all too brief, providing nothing more than a blurry photo of a murder caught in the act, but it was there. And along with that mugshot was a mental imprint of the man Aben had subconsciously picked up on, thanks to the manipulation Tia had performed on him to let them become linked at times of need. It was these imprints, burned into Tia's mind, that she used to home in on her target.

The act of searching took mere seconds. She found the star she was looking for. Its owner was holed up in one of the cheap hotels on the thoroughfare that supplied temporary room and board to travellers passing through. With the station locked down, they had been raking in the money, and now Tia was going to make an unwelcome visit to an exceedingly unwelcome customer. She closed her mind to the rest of the station, rose, and headed back out into the chaos of the Scientia.

****

Tia made her way slowly down the thoroughfare, only dimly aware of the businesses and their attending hubbub. Despite it being late in the evening, patrons flocked, music played, and the aromas of food and people wafted past her. Normally, most citizens chose not to engage with her, preferring to give her a cautionary glance and a wide birth; however, her current mission didn't need someone drawing attention to her, so to ensure privacy, she put up a telepathic wall around her, to shield her presence from even the most determined onlooker.

Tia soon found herself before the entrance of a hotel, and

a quick scan confirmed her target hadn't moved from his original position. The hotel itself was a nondescript affair. Its façade was painted the same standard grey the Alliance had seemed too fond of, so outwardly it looked like the entrance to any living quarters, except that it was nestled between two shops. But its grey fronting hid the fact that it was a multi-story structure, and whereas the shops filled their extra rooms with consumables, the hotel filled its' with people. A plaque next to the intercom proclaimed that it offered nightly rooms, with ensuite sink and toilet, plus a basic breakfast, at a medium price.

The owners, an elderly Zerren couple, gave a start when Tia entered the foyer, having let her in after nothing more than a press of the intercom button. She asked them for a room key and told them to wait in their back quarters. They handed over the card, and promptly disappeared without questions.

Tia ascended the staircase and walked straight up to the door. There she stopped, and for a heartbeat she let the world before her dissolve, so she could see, unhindered, into the lair of the beast. Her prey was lying, oblivious, on his single bed, reading a datapad, and Tia wondered for a moment if he was re-watching the bug's feed. The techs on board had given the device a thorough examination and had concluded that it couldn't broadcast its data far, though what that data was, was unknown, as Leo had snapped its memory chip in two. One thing was for sure, the bug had needed a middleman to relay what it had learnt, and that man was highly likely to be the one Tia was presently studying. On the nightstand beside him was a small plasma pistol. Tia had no doubt it was the same weapon that had taken Aben from her.

She contemplated her next move. She had the option of bursting through the door in a mass of flying shrapnel and madness, but decided against it, as that would probably kill her target, and undoubtedly ruin the walls of the room. She was furious, but she didn't want to upset the innocent hoteliers, or the people in the adjoining rooms. This left her with the choice of either mentally incapacitating the man, then entering, or knocking and seeing what would happen. She made to knock, but caught herself, questioning the outcome should the man start firing wildly with his weapon, so she went with her remaining choice instead, and she reached out with her mind, found the sweet spot, and pushed. The man blacked out, his arm dropping the datapad as his muscles instantly relaxed. Satisfied, Tia keyed the door open.

With the man out cold, Tia could take her time, and with skilled precision born from a lifetime of doing the Karee's dirty work, she dissected the man's mind. Methodically, she introduced keywords, ideas, and imagery into his unconscious thoughts, and read what memories they triggered. What her manipulation revealed was that he was a soldier of the Alliance, his orders coming from a yet unknown player named Imahu, a Fleet Admiral. She saw an image of the man, a cycloptic, green-blooded, skeletal creature who walked on hooves, and who had pincers for hands, and recognised his race as Tolphamicun. Her knowledge told her the Tolphamicun were an old and brutal race, and a perfect fit for the Alliance. She pushed deeper into the prone man's memories but gleaned little else. Imahu alluded to his orders coming from higher up, but her assailant had no idea who that was. Tia wondered briefly if that meant the Alliance's Human telepaths, or the Collective Consciousness as they so narcissistically liked to call themselves. *Wouldn't put it past Mr Ward to be further involved in this somehow,* she grumbled, taking a moment to dwell on the annoying telepath's seemingly unending supply of clones. In all, what her probing had unearthed boiled down to the man having been sent onto the station to take out one of her own, in a bid to shake the foundations of the GR. However, just like the scorpiad plan, it had failed, and now the murderer was Tia's unsuspecting plaything.

Her original plan changed. She had thought long and hard about what she would do once she finally caught up to him. From blowing him to smithereens, to taking him apart, piece by piece on the cellular level, until nothing remained, all her plans had culminated in his painful death. But having investigated his mind, Tia appreciated she had to put her selfish desires to one side. She needed him alive. She carefully removed his weapon from the nightstand and put her face close to his. "Wake up."

The man woke with a start, and Tia found herself staring into a pair of panic-stricken brown eyes, as he instantly grasped the trouble he was in. She felt his arm surreptitiously try to move to his nightstand and tutted in response. "Do you honestly think I'd be foolish enough to leave your weapon within arm's reach?" she asked. "This isn't my first capture... and torture."

The last word caused an instant freeze in the man, and he barely dared to breathe. His heart, however, was beating nineteen to the dozen. He eventually pulled himself together enough to respond. "I'm sure you've already taken all the information you need from me. I doubt there's any need for torture." His voice was hoarse, and his breath smelt strongly of too much cheap food and not enough toothpaste. Tia tried to not let her disgust show.

"Indeed," she confirmed, "you are Hanno Delao, a hitman who prides himself on getting the deed done with the minimum of fuss and no detection. Your handler is one Fleet Admiral Imahu, who commanded you to help spy on me, as well as take out at least one of my men. Congratulations, job done. You installed your little drone in the arboretum and murdered my good friend Aben. Unfortunately for you, the drone has been destroyed, and you have elicited the wrath of a creature that can take you apart cell by cell, while enjoying it." Tia gave him her best unpleasant smile.

The man who was Hanno shrank a little further into his bed. "Killing me won't do you any good," he reasoned. "There will be others sent to make your life hell. Fleet Admiral Imahu was already making plans to mass a force of spies and assassins when I left. Chances are, they're already planning on how to infiltrate the station and deciding what havoc they'll cause. Once the embargo is lifted, they'll be in, just like I was."

Tia knew he wasn't wrong, yet she couldn't spend every minute of her days monitoring the station. There were strategies to plan, battles to win, and sleep to be had. There was also the problem that she, and the Scientia, may not be the only targets. Alliance spies could infiltrate other strategic areas, such as Zerra, or other outlying worlds. *That is if they haven't already. We are at a distinct disadvantage when it comes to figuring out what the hell the Alliance are up to. A lack of our own spies within their ranks could lead to problems in the future.* She looked down at the prone man and smiled. "You make a valid point," she said to Hanno. "It would help if we knew who we were looking for."

"Don't look at me," Hanno replied, "I don't know who's being sent, and it's doubtful I'd know their faces even if I saw them. It's not like we hang out together."

"True," Tia said, sweetly, "but you could help give me a heads-up."

Hanno snorted in derision. "As if I'd do that for you. I wouldn't agree to help even under the threat of torture."

"As if you'd have a choice," Tia answered. The feigned sweetness gone from her voice. Realisation slowly dawned on the man's pale face. "That's right, I'm the incredibly powerful telepath, and you're the feeble-minded murderer who owes me his life. What better way to repay me than by being my little informant within the halls of the Alliance?"

She could feel the protestations forming in his mind; *"You can't do this, I won't let you do this,"* but the words never made it past his lips. He knew they were useless phrases. Tia could do it, and there was nothing he could do to stop her. She took hold of Hanno's mind, and set to work bending him to her command, as his body sagged in submission.

Chapter 18 - Sin'ma

The three heads of the Galactic Revolutionists sat around Sin'ma's table. As there was a moment of stability, he, Ken'va, and Tia had convened to discuss the future of the GR and iron out issues. Sin'ma had only one important request, but was waiting until the right moment, as Tia and Ken'va were reaffirming their old friendship.

"How does it feel, being a Karee now?" Ken'va was asking her, his voice tinged with awe.

Tia shrugged. "It's hard to put into words," she answered. "I am aware of so much more around me and within me. It feels as though at any moment I will lose control and set myself on fire."

Sin'ma arched his eyes. "Please do not," he put in. "You have already caused two blow-outs, and scared a good portion of the population here, I do not need you incinerating the station as well." Ken'va shot him a warning look, but Sin'ma brushed it away. "I did not mean for that to sound disrespectful. It has been a trying time for all of us, including yourself. I was trying to be light-hearted."

Tia seemed nonplussed. "I am not insulted, at present. Just be aware there is a fine line between personal ribbing and insulting. Not everyone is telepathically able to tell which you are projecting." She gave Sin'ma a look that made him feel uncomfortable.

"What of Ambassador Kiskin," Ken'va interjected, trying to rapidly change the subject.

"She departed in the early hours of today, barely a minute

after the station was declared no longer locked-down," Sin'ma confirmed. Then to Tia, "Speaking of which, why did you request the re-opening of the station? What of Aben's killer?"

"He has been dealt with," was her response. Sin'ma didn't like the sound of that. Tia got wind of his expression. "I know what you're thinking, and no, I didn't dissolve him. I know you and Ken'va have bemoaned our own lack of spies within the Alliance, and so I took the opportunity to recruit one, albeit against his wishes."

"Do you think he will be of any use?" Ken'va asked.

"He was sent by someone high up the Alliance's rank, Fleet Admiral Imahu to be exact, and he looks to have a good connection with the admiral, so chances are he will be able to provide further information on their plans. Indeed, he's already told me that more are on their way."

"More spies?" Sin'ma asked, aghast.

"Spies, infiltrators, probably assassins too. Unfortunately, he couldn't supply details about them. He was kept out of the loop as to who they were and what their goal will be, no doubt in case he was caught. Another reason why I sent him off to gather intel."

"This is a rather disturbing turn of events," Ken'va said.

"There is one positive in all this," Tia added. "Thanks to Leo's flick of the wrist, the information that bug collected didn't come to much. The device was placed in the Arboretum to monitor me, as it was a convenient place I was known to frequent. Fortunately for me, when it was placed, I was out gallivanting about the galaxy becoming Karee. And the rest of it. Well…." She didn't need to elaborate. "Who originally placed it is up for debate. Considering neither the Ward clone, nor this latest reprobate, had keen memories of placing the device, my money's on the Scorpiad while it was still in Human form. Either way, the Alliance hasn't gained much in the way of critical information, other than what happened recently. And thanks to the communications lockdown, any spies already in transit probably don't know I'm back to full strength…or even that I'm now Karee."

"And those spies could be anyone, and anywhere, with the sole purpose of dismantling the GR," Ken'va muttered.

"All the more reason why we should always be on our guard." Tia pointed out. "We are at war, and we shouldn't forget that. Carelessness can cost lives. Any stranger coming within our midst should be scrutinised."

"Like those two aliens, Ressen and Grelt." Sin'ma pointed out. "Grelt has chosen to join the GR, what if he is a spy."

Tia shook he head. "Don't worry about them. They are as they seem; two creatures finding themselves in the wrong place at the wrong time. Or right if you ask the Filteth. Grelt's desire to join the GR is genuine, and as a pilot, he will make a good addition. The more ships we can man the better."

Sin'ma saw his opportunity. "Talking of which, we have a big issue regarding the creation of our own battleships." He saw Ken'va's head nod in agreement.

"Go on," pressed Tia.

"Pra'cha and her team have deciphered the shielding schematics, and we know what needs to be done to create our own jump engine shielding, the problem lies not with the shielding, but with the engines themselves. They use a different sort of crystal compared to earlier Alliance vessels, and we are lacking our own source. It appears they are of a type seeded with impurities from ancient supernovae. We have no idea where to start looking for these crystals, or rather, we could have a clearer idea of their location, but it would take us too long to scan the galaxy and calculate possible positions. We are talking years, even decades, even with the joint insight of astronomers from multiple worlds. We also believe that is why the Alliance destroyed the Filteth's world, because it contained a large supply."

Tia pulled a face that showed she was unhappy with this news. "So, you have a suggestion, or a request?" she asked.

"Yes," stated Ken'va. "The supernovae existed briefly during the dawn of our galaxy, and searching for their remnants would be, as Sin'ma stated, a long and arduous task. It would be easier if we had some old, local knowledge to point us in the correct direction. Would Jarell or your own vessel have knowledge of these past events?"

Tia stayed quiet for a while, and Sin'ma wondered if she was conversing with the vessels. Eventually she gave a nod. "Jarell's knowledge is extensive about the formation of this galaxy, and what Morrígan is lacking, Jarell can share. If you provide me with the elemental breakdown of the crystals, I can get them looking for likely planets. They can even retrieve samples and would go about it in a much more respectful manner than the Alliance."

As Sin'ma handed Tia the information, he asked her something that had been niggling him. "How come your vessel or Jarell did not pick up on the shielding sooner? And how come they did not know how they were made?"

Tia gave him a look that seemed to hint at her being irritated by his constant questioning of her abilities, or that of her cohorts. "In answer to your first question," she said, in a voice that gave no hint of backup to her expression, "the shields weren't activated until the last minute. It's conceivable the shielding interferes with a ship's ability to enter hyperspace, and it may even cause problems travelling long distances through hyperspace. That, and the Alliance no doubt didn't want us to know they had them. As to the second. The reason neither Jarell nor Morrígan knew no more than you is simply because they had never come across the shielding. When faced with the unknown, they are in the same position as any one of us and must learn. Certainly, they already have a lot more knowledge, and can learn a lot faster, but still, they have to gain the facts before they can propose an answer."

Ken'va spoke up, concern tingeing his voice. "Who will protect us while the vessels are gone? Knowing there is usually a Karee vessel stationed close by provides a sense of security; to all of us." Sin'ma agreed with his sentiment, he also didn't like the idea of the station, and his home planet, being undefended.

"Tartarus can remain," Tia assured them, as she scrolled through the crystal data. "It may not be as sleek and intimidating as a Karee vessel, but it can stand up to any interlopers long enough for the Karee cavalry to come. Though I doubt we need to worry about any big incursions from the Alliance, it's the small, sneaky ones we need to keep an eye out for."

"Like spies," Sin'ma said, understanding her meaning. Tia nodded in agreement. "How soon do you think your ships can head off? I do not want to sound demanding," he quickly added, in a bid to mollify the unspoken tension between them, "but the sooner they can get some crystals, the sooner we can start preparing them for use in the engines."

Tia looked up from the datapad and gave a little smile. "They've already gone."

Chapter 19 - Shar

Shar was sat idly in his captain's chair back on Tartarus, his feet resting on its arms, while overseeing the bridge crew. He didn't need to be there, he didn't even need to be in the captain's chambers on board for that matter, as the crew aboard the old ship were more than capable of running things in his absence. Rather, it was a visit for his well-being.

After his release from confinement, he had felt the need to surround himself with his crew. It was mostly to reassert his dominance after it had been shredded by his enforced incarceration at the pincers of Ambassador Kiskin. But a small part of him had also needed to feel the proximity of people he knew, trusted, and who were friends. He would never admit it, but he had needed comforting, and for a creature who wasn't big on emotional displays, being in familiar surroundings was the best way of achieving it.

To save face, he'd thrown out the lie that he was ensuring everything was working efficiently, since Tartarus had become the primary guard of the Scientia. Much like Tia, he didn't expect any problems from the Alliance, such as another vanguard of battleships, but he also agreed that a show of strength helped put those ideas out of any would-be interloper's mind. Tartarus was a solid ship, and it had the benefit of being loaded with Karee technology, so it could stand up to a fair amount of punishment and return the favour with a few added surprises.

However, as everyone around him was so efficient, his input wasn't needed, and he was left with nothing else to do but peruse his datapad. His first distraction had been the department he'd been put in charge of, but hadn't spent much time in, thanks to the universe throwing a missing compatriot and a war his way. Therefore, he'd got up to speed with business in Munitions, and fired off multiple commands to his reluctant underling Talon, much to Talon's chagrin if his responses had been anything to go by. That entertaining chore had dissipated once Talon and his team had got things in hand, so Shar had been left with no other option than to read the station's information bulletins, GR updates, and what passed for Zerren local news reports. He was even beginning to contemplate downloading one of the many novels held in Tartarus' database. *This is not what being a captain used to mean,* he reminisced. *When I was a leader, I barely had time to think, let alone read local gossip. My days were filled with planning incursions, taking stock of infantry movements, and prising information out of enemy combatants. I know we're supposed to be at war, and moments of peace are supposed to be good, but gods I'm bored!*

Ensign Uree Gelken, the reptilian-like Xalek, who had been quietly manning an array of sensors, gave a grunt of what Shar took for either confusion or surprise. He looked over at the ensign, who was busy typing on zir console's screen. "You care to enlighten me ensign?" Shar asked.

Uree looked up, a quizzical expression on zir blue and green mottled face. "Tartarus has alerted me to something strange," zie responded. "The rogue world discovered recently has change its course."

"How is that possible?" asked Shar, straightening upright in his seat, and placing his feet back on the floor. "Did it encounter another body?"

Uree shook zir head, making zir crest of blue feathers waft about. "As far as Tartarus can tell, there was nothing in its vicinity, at least not anything big enough to be detectable by its scanners. My understanding in physics may be lacking, but I doubt a small meteor or comet would have been enough to cause the shift seen here."

"This can't be good. Can Tartarus figure out its new course?"

Ensign Uree returned zir attention to the console screen to confer with the ship's big brain. After a couple of minutes, zie gave an answer. "Its new trajectory brings it through the Zerren solar system, within gravitational range of the furthest most planet."

Shar didn't like the sound of that one bit. "Why does this seem like something the Alliance is behind?" he asked the bridge in general.

"If for destruction, it convoluted plan," Ensign Harv-An, the communications officer, put in. "Any Karee vessel can destroy small world. Disaster stopped before even in range of Zerren system."

"She has a point," Uree said. "If whoever changed its course hoped to disturb this system's planets enough to somehow destroy Zerra, then it's an overreach with the Karee about. Plus, it's still several years away. Even if we couldn't get the Karee to blow it up, the Zerrens would be more than capable with this length of a warning."

"Agreed," Shar said, "which makes me wonder what their game is."

"Nothing says come visit me like rogue world taking sharp-angled course change," Harv-An postulated.

Shar nodded in agreement. "I guess someone's sending Tia a rather large come-hither." He thought back to his earlier comment of being bored. *I really should be careful what I wish for when the Sadirer universe is listening,* he reflected, too late. Not that he really believed in his race's quasi-religious idea that the universe was a self-aware entity, yet he couldn't help but feel his lack of faith was getting tested more with each passing month.

****

Shar made his way to Tia's quarters. With her host ship out searching the galaxy for the crystals so dearly needed for the GR's battleship engines, Tia had been forced to return to her old quarters. He could've sent her a message, but as the rogue world wasn't about to turn up in their backyard for a few years, he figured he could take the time to head over to the station to give her the news himself. And hopefully do so before the Zerren scientists got wind of its new course and panicked.

He absent-mindedly ambled along the thoroughfare, his acute senses making the environment more vibrant to him than for some other species. Then he ducked down a side corridor, and soon found himself in the regimental-looking quarters section. A sterile corridor curved away from him, broken at intervals by steel doorways that led into people's homes. Plaques by the doors gave a clue to their occupants. It was a world away from his quarters in the Scientia II. There, the higher ranks had their quarters, and the atmosphere reflected it, with less industrial looking walls, carpeted floors, and potted plants. Shar still didn't understand why Tia had never chosen a home among the higher-ups. Even after she had revealed herself to be an emissary for the Karee, and was therefore, in the minds of many Zerrens, virtually a goddess by association, she had never relinquished her old quarters. Shar on the other hand hadn't thought twice when given the opportunity to move.

His footsteps brought him to Tia's nondescript door, and he wondered for a moment if he should have called ahead in case she was off doing something else. *Nah, she knew I was heading her way the moment I set foot on the station,* he presumed, and he rang her door's intercom. The door opened the moment he released the button, and he stepped through into Tia's familiar abode.

Tia herself was sat, half curled up, on one of her chairs in the corner of the room that passed for a lounge. Around her was the usual chaotic mass of paper she seemed to accumulate when she sat in one place long enough. Though most things could be gleaned from a datapad, Tia preferred the tactile approach to reading, and Shar noted the fresh copies of documents, interspersed with the tell-tale yellowing paper of ancient texts and maps. She looked up from the paper she was reading and acknowledged Shar. He sat on the chair next to her, removing its occupying pile of documents as he did so. "Anything interesting?" he asked, nodding at her reading material.

Tia pulled an exasperated face. "To tell you the truth, no. This is the remains of what Aben was working on until…," she trailed off, and gave a small sigh. "Anyway, I told Ken'va I'd give it all a quick read through and figure out what needs to be kept, and what can be thrown away, before I hand the stuff over."

"I was just thinking about how much you like paper copies of things, I guess Aben was the same. Did he get that from you, or you from him?"

Tia gave a sad smile. "I guess we were similar in quite a few ways, despite being completely different creatures. Our sense of wonder, our desire for adventure, our need to prove ourselves…as well as both of us being minions of the Karee." She said the last bit with bitterness in her voice.

"Yes, but his life didn't end that way, and neither will yours," Shar reminded her. "He got to break free of their shackles because he came to work for you. You broke free because you became Karee, mostly because of Aben's actions."

"I guess. He figured out what the orb was, or at least what it needed…namely me. If he hadn't, when he threw it into the abyss on the dead world I wouldn't have jumped after it, instead considering it as lost to the Alliance as us. It's amazing how two seemingly opposite souls can be woven together, their futures dependent on each other." She went quiet and remained staring at the document still in her hand.

Shar felt slightly uncomfortable and ran his eyes round her room. Her kitchenette, and nook of an office, were as unchanged as when she had first arrived on the Scientia, under the guise of a Human botanist. "Why did you never accept a new place with the higher-ups?" Shar asked, trying to alleviate the silence. "I'm sure you were probably offered a better living space up there."

"You're right, they did. They offered me the place you now enjoy," she revealed, with a smile. "But as to why I didn't accept…. This place was my home for five long years, and to be honest, I was used to it. It is my unchanging sanctuary in a life inflicted with all too many changes. I know where I am. I know where everything is. And for a brief few minutes when I'm here, I can almost forget that I'm some crazy super-being with the future of the galaxy resting in her hands. That is until I knock something over with my damn tail or wings." She gave Shar a broad grin as she rolled her eyes in exasperation. Shar laughed, the tension of a moment ago now broken. "But I'm sure you didn't come here to discuss my living arrangements."

"Unfortunately, you are correct. Tartarus was keeping track of the rogue world spotted a while back, and it's suddenly changed direction and is heading our way."

Tia raised a questioning eyebrow. "Did something interfere with its course?"

"That's exactly what I first thought, but Tartarus says no. It looks like some unseen force caused it to do a forty-five-degree turn."

"This can't be good," Tia answered, mirroring Shar's earlier statement.

"Agreed. I mean, it's not going to enter the Zerren system any time soon, at least not at present. There was no discernible change in speed, so I doubt it's a direct attack, which begs the question…."

"What's the Alliance's end game?" Tia said, finishing his thought.

Shar nodded. "Harv-An thinks it's a big come-hither, and I'm inclined to agree with her. Nothing says come and investigate like a planet suddenly changing direction."

"You're probably both right, which makes me think there's one hell of a trap on it."

"So of course, you're not going to play into their hands, and will blow it up instead." Shar said, with a pointed look.

Tia's blue eyes gained a mischievous quality. "Well now,

they've gone to all this trouble to set a planet barrelling through space to get my attention. It would be remiss of me not to respond."

Shar gave an audible groan. "I'll get Tartarus ready to ship out," he said, making to get up.

"No!" Tia responded. Shar gave her a quizzical look. "We're both smart, and this probably really is what we expect it to be, i.e., a trap, so the last thing I want is to leave the Scientia undefended. Whoever's behind this may be hoping to draw any guarding vessels away from her. I doubt they know that Jarell and Morrígan are already elsewhere, and there's no way I'm going to risk leaving this station and Zerra undefended. If they launch a surprise attack in my absence, at least Tartarus has a chance of holding the fort until bigger help arrives."

"So, you're not going to recall your vessel?"

Again, Tia shook her head. "No. Its priority right now is to find crystals for the rebel battleships. I'll go it alone."

Shar didn't like her idea one bit, but he knew she was right about Tartarus having to stay. "Okay, may I suggest we find a smaller vessel and go together."

Tia leaned forward. "There will be no 'we' in this. I know you mean well, but you must appreciate your place is on Tartarus' bridge, just in case things go sideways. Of all the people I know, you are the best when it comes to leading an offence, if such a need arises. I will find another way to this planet."

Shar released a low growl. "I would like my thorough dislike of this plan to be on record," he stated. "Last time you decided to go it alone, you pretty much died, and then went missing for over half a year. I'm not sure I, or anyone else for that matter, wants to have to go through the stress of losing you again." He remembered the helplessness he'd felt as he and Kan had scoured the galaxy looking for her, and it was not the kind of emotion he wanted to have to deal with again so soon.

"True, but I came back stronger than ever."

"Even you can't believe the universe will keep things going in your favour. Eventually your luck will run out, and I don't want to be the person carving 'I told you so' on you coffin."

Tia gave him a sympathetic look. "I don't want that to be the case either, but you must understand that I'm no longer an A'daree. I'm Karee now, and a way more robust and capable creature than I ever was as one of their foot soldiers. Granted, I'm fallible, and my life is not truly eternal, but I have the power to take care of myself, and no offence, that power allows me to take better protection of me than you. If anyone should worry about carving epitaphs, it's me carving yours. I have already lost someone who was close to me," she added, in a whisper, "and I'm not sure I have the strength of mind right now to lose another, especially you of all people."

Shar felt awkward under her unwavering stare. He was an imbecile when it came to talking about feelings. He wanted to tell her how worried he was about her, despite her protestations that she could look after herself, and he desperately wanted to be able to put words to how he never wanted her to leave his side, or for him to leave hers. Yet whenever he tried to form the sentences in his brain, they came across as trite and stupid. In the end, he could only answer her with painful silence. He wondered if Tia was aware of his thoughts, though if she was, she didn't help him by bringing them up, and so important things were, as usual, left unsaid.

"Look after Tartarus, and do your duty by this station, and I promise you, I will come back."

"When?" he asked, tersely.

"A damn sight sooner than last time."

Chapter 20 - Tia

Tia read up on all the information that had been collated on the rogue world, which wasn't much. More pages of data were given over to the lists of numbers plotting its spectral analysis, and its trajectory through space, than the actual, decipherable summary itself. What the scientists at Zerra's Observatory Institute had concluded was that it was a cold lump of rock. That they knew for certain. They had speculated that it had the gravity of an average moon, thanks to its metal core, and that this self-same core was probably allowing the planet to retain some atmosphere. Indeed, observations by Tartarus seemed to back this up; however, Tia doubted a normal person could survive for long in such a thin atmosphere and would suffocate or freeze quickly if left exposed on its surface.

After familiarising herself with the data, she took time to mull over two important considerations. The first was how she was going to get there. This question didn't pose too much of a conundrum, as there were plenty of small vessels available to her, several of which were in Tartarus' hold, so she figured she wasn't going to be short of a ride, even if it meant piloting a ship herself.

The second question was more worrying and was concerned with what she'd find on the planet once she got there. She was certain it was some elaborate trap, but she was unsure of what kind of trap could ensnare a Karee. The Karee were ancient creatures, the oldest being billions of years old, and were more than capable of defending themselves, but despite evidence to the contrary, they were mortal. They could be killed, but the thing was, nobody had come close to having the ability, or the opportunity, to do so during the races' existence in the universe, and so modes of murder were uncommon knowledge. All Tia knew for certain was that it would take an inordinate amount of time and energy to do the deed. Of course, this was if it was a layman plotting her demise; Karee versus Karee was another matter entirely, and something she had experienced first-hand, having fought the black ships at Ciberia. They may not have been Karee, but they were eerily alike, and more than capable of holding their own against her, as well as hurting her. However, she had proven she was just as capable of retaliating, so she was not going to be an easy target for whoever was signalling to her using a planet.

Despite her faith in her abilities, Tia still experienced a twinge of worry, and she appreciated why Shar was so concerned for her well-being. She had a habit of reacting without thinking, as evidenced by her hair-brained leap into a pit after an orb, and Shar was fully aware of this. Yes, her reactive jump had culminated in a positive outcome, with her being reborn as a Karee, but it could just have easily ended up with her being splattered on the bottom of a deep pit. Tia knew she had to be smart about things, especially as she was going to be lacking any useful back up.

A fleeting movement in the corner of her eye made her turn round, as Chione exited her bedroom after a day spent snoozing on her bed. He gave an extensive stretch as he came, then jumped on the counter to indicate his desire for food.

"What? Bilge rats not good enough for you?" Tia asked, joking.

"When was the last time you ate rat?" Chione retorted. "Oh, that's right; never! No culinary experience, no opinion."

"Fair enough," Tia answered, heaving her bulk from her seat, and making her way to the kitchenette. She rooted around her freezer for some meat, and once found, set it to heat up in the oven. She leant against the cabinet as she waited, and absent-mindedly stroked Chione's head. The cat part purred.

"So, what's your plan regarding this planet heading our way?" He casually asked, as Tia went about putting the warmed meat in a bowl for him.

She gave a shrug. "What can I do but go there and see what's what?"

"You could blow it up," Chione said, between mouthfuls.

"Thanks for that idea...Shar...." She gave him an exasperated look. "But what if there's something important there I need to know, something that could be crucial for winning this war? I can't take the chance of missing out."

"Which is what they're probably hoping you'll think too."

"You think I don't know that. You don't think I've considered that I'm putting my head in the noose, yet again. I understand that this time I'm not going to come back bigger and better. Being Karee is as far as I can go up the evolutionary ladder...at least as far as I know, but there's a good chance I can come back with useful information."

"And what if what you're heading for is simply a giant bomb?"

"I won't go wearing my good pants." Chione gave her look that said he didn't think she was taking things seriously. In truth, Tia was taking things all too seriously, it was just that she needed to bring some lightness to the situation before her worry consumed her.

Chione finished licking his mouth, then went into grooming autopilot. He stopped for a moment. "Well, if Shar can't stop you from going, I doubt I'll have better luck, so please, invest in an automatic can opener...for my sake."

As it was, watching Chione eat was making Tia feel hungry. Normally she didn't need to eat, at least not much, as being Morrígan's symbiont was her main way of staying nourished. However, with her vessel gone, her stomach was starting to rumble, reminding her she needed to turn plant matter into energy. "Fine, I'll go get one now," she answered, deciding to kill two birds and grab a bite of lunch as well.

****

It was early evening on the station, and the thoroughfare was bustling with activity. Tia had a wealth of eateries to choose from, from Pann salad bars to Ciberian cafés offering the discerning carnivore a smorgasbord of meats. However, Tia was vegan, and had been from the moment she'd been given the gift of telepathy, so she opted for a newly opened Selden vegetarian restaurant. The Alliance had decimated the Selden population, and they were still picking themselves up off the floor, so any business opened by them was a welcomed step to recovery, and the locals aboard the Scientia had quickly become supportive patrons. Tia found the place packed, even though it was several weeks after their grand opening. It seemed everyone wanted to try out rare Selden cuisine.

It also helped that, as a species, the Seldens were easy on the eye. Grey-dappled white fur covered them from head to toe, over which they wore long, almost medieval-like robes, done out in pastel colours, and edged with intricate stitching. Atop their heads they had two, huge, velvety grey ears, and their large, doe eyes, were bright orange, and flecked with gold. Tia noticed that the clientele in the restaurant was disproportionately made up of those races that hankered after Seldens. Not that it made any difference, as Seldens didn't couple outside of their own race.

The maître d' spotted Tia peering through the open door, and quickly glided over to usher her in. Despite being wall-to-wall with customers, the maître d' managed to find Tia a small table off to the side, and with profuse bows, handed her a menu. Tia studied it, conscious of the fact that every eye and mind in the place was fixated on her. Fortunately, it was something she'd become accustomed to over the decades, and it no longer phased her. It also helped that she could switch her mind off to her surroundings, allowing her to exist in a mental vacuum of her own creating.

Just as she was narrowing down her choice, she picked up on a shift in collective focus, and peered over the top of her menu to see Ressen walk in. His appearance surprised her, as she had no idea he'd been discharged from the Medicentre. *I bet there's a message lurking in my spam filter about this*, she thought. She took in the form of the alien and was pleased to note he was free from the horrific burns that had covered him, and his fresh growth of skin seemed to gleam in the light. His hair had also grown back remarkably quickly, and he was sporting a healthy mop of blue hair that matched the blue of his skin's stripes. He was decked out in a regal-looking purple shirt, jacket, and pants. Gold trimming adorned the jacket and was matched by a gold belt buckle. A pair of heavy-duty black boots with shiny steel toecaps completed his wardrobe. Tia had to admit he cut a dashing figure, and the fact that he stood head and shoulders above everyone else certainly added to the overall effect. What she also noticed was that his clothes were hanging a little loosely on his body. His slightly lanky frame was in clear need of several decent non-hospital meals, which was probably what had drawn him to the restaurant. *His brother has probably given him rave reviews about this place*, Tia figured, knowing Grelt had barely ever been seen in the same eatery twice.

Ressen's dark blue, almond-shaped eyes, scanned the room nervously, and he seemed hesitant to enter with so many people watching him. Then he caught Tia's eye, and without thinking, she gestured to the one free seat opposite her. He quickly crossed the room, and sat down before her, giving a shy look as he did so. Tia noticed that his irises were barely visible dark slits, and for a second it was like looking into Aben's eyes. Then the illusion was lost as Ressen croaked, "Thank you," in a voice that was still suffering the after-effects of fire inhalation.

"No problem," she said, giving a smile that was a bit more enthusiastic than she would have liked. "So, how are you doing?" Again, she conveyed the words into his mind telepathically, so he could understand her.

"My skin is what it once was, and I feel my strength has nearly returned, yet my voice is still rough, and I am starving most of the time." He looked down at the menu that had been placed in his hand with notable confusion.

Tia took pity on the alien, knowing he could barely read a word of what was in front of him. "What do you like to eat?" she asked.

Ressen glanced up. "My father used to make this huge pan full of grains, beans and white meat, all cooked together in heavily seasoned broth. It was cheap and easy to make, but extremely tasty, and a full pan could feed at least eight. Or four if we were feeling particularly ravenous." He perked up at the memory.

Tia looked to her own culinary experience to try to find a dish close to what he was recalling. "Sounds to me like you were eating something akin to paella. The Seldens have something similar, though with more beans instead of meat. It's called tomall, and considering your appetite, you should find it ideal."

"Tomall," Ressen parroted, trying the word out for himself.

Tia gave him a nod of encouragement. "They'll probably be happy to add a couple of boiled eggs to it too, for an added protein boost."

"Sounds perfect," Ressen said, putting his menu down. All their talk about paella had got Tia salivating at the idea, and she decided that was what she wanted too, so when the waiter eventually came to the table, she ordered a tomall for each of them, and ensured Ressen got his extra eggs.

As they waited for their meal, they chatted lightly. As Ressen hadn't had much experience about the Scientia, other than what went on within the walls of the Medicentre, that is what their conversation revolved around. He waxed lyrical about the doctors and nurses, bemoaned the blandness of the hospital food, and asked Tia seemingly a hundred questions about the different races that staffed the ward; his enthusiasm to learn about the station's occupants amusing Tia.

Auditory relief came with their paella, and they ate their food in comfortable silence. When their dishes were cleared away, to be replaced by dessert menus, Tia noted a slight change in Ressen's mood. He seemed to be struggling internally with something, and it wasn't just the writing on the menu. "Are you okay?" she asked, not wanting to sound like she was prying.

"I was just thinking how nice this meal has been with company, but when I leave here, I don't know what I'll do with myself. I mean, now I've left the ward I can stay on my ship, at least for the time being, and with Grelt as company, but soon he'll soon be too consumed with the GR. Even now I barely see him, as he spends a lot of his time attending meetings with other ship captains. Please don't misunderstand me, I'm proud of my brother's decision, and I don't for a minute want to stop him from doing what he's doing, no matter how worried I am for him. It's just that I miss him, and I know it'll only get worse. I guess what I'm trying to say is that I'm lonely...and a little bored."

Tia nodded in understanding. "You've found yourself unwittingly in a strange place, knowing only one other, and you feel as though you've lost direction, and have no idea where to begin anew."

"Exactly."

"What can you do? What are you good at?"

"I'm a smuggler of off-world goods, and I know a bit about piloting a craft, though not as half as well as Grelt, and I know about electronics."

"Well, you set up your smuggling operation, and I would assume you needed to broker deals with the contraband providers, so I guess that makes you an entrepreneur with good public relations skills."

"Put like that, I guess people like me are plentiful on worlds, so job opportunities will be thin on the ground." Ressen was starting to look downcast.

"I don't recall men lining up to revive my soul when madness took me over. Believe me, you are a rarity. Even more so once I was revived."

"What do you mean?"

Tia lent close to him and spoke under her breath. "Not to sound indelicate, but I shared body fluids with you. Few people around here have been as privileged, which also puts you and I in an interesting position." Ressen looked at Tia with confusion, and she wondered for a moment whether she should continue with her explanation. "Come, walk with me," she said, as she waved away the service of the waiter who had come to see if they wanted dessert. She headed outside, passing a handful of Zerren currency to the maître d' to pay for their meal as she did so. The Selden didn't even count it. Ressen trailed out behind her, after being shooed away by the maître d', who didn't need his money; Tia having paid for both their meals.

Back out on the street, Tia kept pace with Ressen, who seemed to still be moving a little slow. *The people who work for me do so because they have done some great wrong,"* she began, using full telepathy for privacy's sake. *"Their sentences are to carry out my orders until they are deemed to have paid their karmic debt to the universe. For some, that is a dangerous job. They have found themselves many times on the front line and have often been injured because of it. When that happens, I heal them, the same why I healed you, and because of that, they, I, and now you, share a deeper blood bond. For them, it is a bond born of karma and of redemption, and it shackles them to me. But you have no crimes to answer for, at least nothing like what my men have done, so despite the blood bond, you are a free agent. Then again, under normal circumstances, you would be indebted to me for healing you, but as far as I'm concerned you already paid that debt in kind, by reviving me first. Therefore, if you choose, you can ignore the debt because it happened after the fact."*

"You mean, I could choose to enter your service, if I chose to ignore the fact that I healed you first?"

"Yes. In a roundabout way, I am offering you the possibility of working for me. It wouldn't be the karmic servitude my men

'enjoy'. Then again, considering what we do, it wouldn't be a leisurely ride either. You would run errands for me, help me out in situations, and even find yourself on the battlefield if the need dictates. Or you can choose the safer path, consider yourself paid up, walk away, and hopefully find a less dangerous calling."

Ressen went quiet, and Tia knew he was weighing up the pros and considerable cons of her offer, but she didn't stray into his thoughts, thereby allowing his deliberation to be a private affair. As they walked in silence, she guided their footsteps towards an electronics store, and once there, left him outside while she searched for an elusive hands-free tin-opener. When she came out, box in hand, she could tell by his demeanour that he had decided.

"I choose to come and work for you," he announced. "My brother has chosen to help with this war, and so should I."

"Fantastic," Tia said, feeling strangely glad. "Your first task is to get fully fit, because once you are, we will have a date with a planet."

Chapter 21 - Ressen

It had taken Ressen several weeks, plenty of hearty food, and a lot of time in the gym, to get back up to his fighting weight. His change in physique had given him a much-needed boost in confidence, and knowing he had a direction in life, thanks to Tia, also had him feeling good about his future. As well as improving his fitness, he had begun learning the common language of Human, and he and Grelt had spent what free overlapping evenings they had practising. Ressen was glad of his brother's help, as he felt less self-conscious as he stammered over the words. Nevertheless, despite his positive outlook, there was a vein of worry running through him. He was in a sector at war with a superior force, and there was no knowing when, or how, it would end.

Still, he had faith in Tia, more so after he'd spoken to some of her men. Surprisingly, despite being high-level criminals, and in never-ending servitude to Tia, they all spoke fondly of her. They assured Ressen that she would never put him in a situation that had him completely out of his depth, although she would push the boundaries of what he was capable of. Ressen therefore looked to his future with trepidation, but also a great deal of hope that he could do what was asked of him.

As the days had drawn on, he'd contemplated his future mission more. He knew the planet Tia had alluded to was the recently discovered wandering planet, which was a secret everyone on the station seemed to know about, and he wondered what terrors they'd find there. He had no idea whether she expected him to go down to the surface with her, and with the realisation that he may well be joining her, came a second one, which was he hadn't fired a weapon in ages, at least not since his military service days. Subsequently, along with his regular gym trips, he'd added visits to the firing range, and despite a shaky start, muscle memory meant he was soon shooting fast and true.

Feeling surer of his abilities as an escort, Ressen had begun thinking on whether a third member of the team was needed. He'd gone over scenarios in his head, which often led him to the same question: *If I'm down on the planet with Tia, who will man our craft?* As an answer, he could think of only one person he wanted for the job: *Grelt,* and on one of their coinciding evenings off, he put his thoughts to his brother.

"If trouble heads our way, and we need to make a fast entrance, or exit, I can think of none better than you to get us to safety," he said.

Grelt, who had been listening to Ressen intently as he'd explained his current position as Tia's helper, and their soon-to-be mission, tapped the arm of his seat as he thought. "I doubt she's taking you along for your piloting skills," he said, after a pause, giving his brother a friendly verbal jab, "we all know how poorly you did on your test flight exam."

Ressen winced. "Thank you for opening that old wound," he said, pulling a mock angry face. While his brother had excelled at manoeuvring a vessel at speed, Ressen had never got further than the simulator, having crashed his imaginary vessel on multiple occasions. Piloting a large transport ship through empty space was one thing; dodging holographic enemy fighters and computer-generated terrain had been another thing entirely. "If my bad flying ability is common knowledge, she's not going to want to use me as an escape plan, in which case, we'll need a better option...you."

"Well, we've not got any major skirmishes planned, at least for the time being, and helping Tia means helping the GR, so I guess offering my services would be the proper thing to do."

Ressen felt extremely relieved knowing his brother would be along for the ride. Although he trusted Tia, and felt unusually comfortable in her presence, she was still a stranger to him. Having someone along whom he knew and trusted implicitly made the mission seem marginally less overwhelming. "I'll let Tia know when I see her tomorrow."

"You've got another liaison with her?" Grelt asked, emphasising the word liaison with a salacious tone, whilst giving Ressen his best sly look.

"She's my boss," was his slightly lame reply, "so it's definitely not like that. We're meeting to discuss the mission."

"And where will you be having this meeting? In an office?"

Ressen paused, knowing his response was just going to fuel his brother's cheeky fire. "No…at a restaurant."

Grelt roared with mirth. "Totally a liaison," he announced, giving his brother a friendly punch on his shoulder.

Ressen sank a little in his seat from embarrassment. "As if anything like that is going on, or could even happen," he protested, but inside he was thinking, *Would it be so bad if I became her consort?*

****

Ressen and Tia's 'it's not a date it's a meeting' took place in a secluded corner of a Pann restaurant, away from prying eyes. Ressen, in a bid to try to project the 'not a date' vibe, wore the same clothes as he'd been wearing during their impromptu meal together, albeit all freshly laundered. However, when he clapped eyes on Tia, he again questioned what he thought he knew about what was going on. The previous time they'd met she'd been wearing an outfit that had seemed to be a cross between a dress and a priest's robe. It had been of a charcoal black, and Ressen would have referred to it as understated. That is if you ignored Tia's giant black wings protruding from the back of it, or her giant black tail trailing out from underneath its hem, or her giant crown of black horns. What Tia was wearing this time was less demure. It was still in the same vein as a dress-come-robe, complete with voluminous sleeves, and floor brushing hem, but its colour was vibrant red embroidered with black swirls. Also, its bodice was lower cut, and more fitted, and Ressen suddenly found himself uncomfortably aware of Tia's curves.

Unlike the Selden establishment, the Pann eatery was sparsely occupied, allowing the couple to talk a little more freely. As soon as they were seated, Ressen, in a bid to drown out his brother's insinuation that was still going around in his head, brought up the possibility of his involvement. "I think we should bring Grelt on this venture. If we must go down to the surface, we will need a third person managing our craft, and I trust Grelt with that task, absolutely."

"What does Grelt have to say about this?" Tia asked.

"He's eager to help. I think he wants to prove himself a capable asset to the GR, and this would be ideal for him to do that."

"He's a good pilot?"

"Oh yes, without a doubt, and much better than me, which is something he will no doubt tell you the first moment he gets."

Tia gave a little smile. "To be honest, I was expecting this. Grelt's piloting competency has been proven both through your escape from the Alliance, and the tests he's done while here, and I too have been thinking about our mission, and the need for a third. It didn't take much of a wild guess to think you would ask your brother to join us." Then she grew a little serious. "However, does he understand the possible dangers that lay ahead? Even I don't know what to expect once we get there."

"We spoke about it at length, but like you say, we don't know what we will find there. All I can say is, he's not going into this blindly."

Tia nodded her head slowly, convinced by Ressen's assurances regarding Grelt. "Fair enough, in which case, how's your vessel looking? It would make sense for Grelt to pilot us in a ship he's familiar with."

"Everything is nearly fixed. We're just waiting on some specially made micro-supercapacitors we had to order from Zerra for the weapons' upgrade, but they're due up in one of tomorrow's delivery pods. Once they've been put in place, we'll be ready to go, so I guess that means we can leave the day after tomorrow." Announcing the deadline gave Ressen a chill, and he concentrated on his menu to mask his anxiety. "I don't suppose they do tomall here?" he asked, trying to sound relaxed and convivial, but having his voice betray him by going up a pitch.

To his relief, Tia chose not to mention his obvious nervousness. "They do something similar, though it's a bit spicier than a Selden tomall." she said. "I can order that if you wish." Ressen nodded in confirmation, so when the Pann waiter arrived, Tia reeled off their orders, and the Pann left without need of any input from Ressen.

He stared down at the two-pronged fork sat beside his placemat, unsure of what else to say. Grelt's words, and mischievous expression, floated back into his brain. "You know, we could have said all this in an office," he said, still looking at his utensil.

"True, but as you'll be the one watching my back, I think it's better that we get to know each other away from forced formality. I need to know what makes you tick, how you react when you're out of your comfort zone, and any issues you may have that I need to watch out for."

"Oh," said Ressen, looking up; his voice betraying his disappointment before he thought to catch it.

Tia raised an eyebrow at him but didn't comment. Ressen was sure she was picking up on the embarrassment that was causing his insides to feel like they were being sucked into a giant black hole. In his youth, he had never been short of female companionship, he just hadn't been the best at reading the signs, and though the years had passed, the come-hithers still confused him as much as the get losts. The relationships he'd found himself in had usually been arrived at by accident, with him clueless until the last minute. He still remembered, with acute teenage awkwardness, the moment when his (in his eyes) platonic female friend had disrobed in front of him. Then there had been those he'd thought were interested in him, only to have it proven otherwise through a hard slap to the face, or worse. He'd often bemoaned to his brother that he wished he belonged to a species that actively advertised their interest in courtship. "Our females are too damn cryptic," he'd griped, much to Grelt's amusement. "What I wouldn't give for them to have a body part that changed colour when they were in the mood."

Ironically, when he finally managed to get out of Port Befuddled, it was all plain sailing. He could be suave, he could be romantic, and he took pride in being an attentive partner, who could sweep a female off her feet, and leave her begging for more. Trouble was, unless the female came with the words 'I'm yours' tattooed on her head, his abilities often went undiscovered by the opposite sex. Annoyingly, his brother had no problems with reading the invisible signs, and Ressen often dragged him along on female reconnaissance missions, just to make sure he wasn't heading for an involuntarily kicking. *I wish he was here now, then he could confirm this is anything but a liaison,* he thought, as he began second guessing everything Tia was saying and doing.

While he brooded in confusion, Tia received their meals with thanks, and Ressen quickly tucked into his spicy paella-like dish. Tia had opted for something different and was occupied with a mound of white spiral shaped things that was covered in a red sauce packed with chopped vegetables. "I'll have you know," Ressen said, between mouthfuls, in a bid to dispel his residual awkwardness, "that I'm good with a weapon. I was in my class' top five percent, both in class, and in field combat training."

"Good to know, though training is worlds away from being in the thick of real action."

As Tia's words faded, Ressen had a flashback to the moment that had started his journey. When the scary-looking alien ship had attacked the Filteth, and had been taking potshots at people, he had been rooted to the spot in fear and surprise. It had taken a shout from his brother to break the spell, allowing him to flee to safety. Ressen gulped, suddenly unsure if he was cut out for the task at hand.

Tia caught his expression and gave him a knowing look. "I am sure you have what it takes. If I thought you were a liability, you would not be coming."

"That's reassuring," Ressen answered, a tad sarcastically, "and easy for you to say. You're an indestructible super-being. I doubt fear weighs heavily on your mind. Why am I even coming on this mission?"

"First off, I am no indestructible super-being. I may not be easy to kill, but not easy doesn't mean impossible. The average race would be hard-pressed to curtail my stride, but older, nastier races may have more options at their disposal. This brings me to your second allegation, and in answer to that I argue that I do fear. I may not fear the races on this station, but I do fear the older races. There are beings in this galaxy who transcend space and time, and there are beings in this galaxy who are vile simply for the sake of it, or because they see those below them as no better than bacteria. They I fear because I don't fully know what they can do to me. I also fear for the people around me. Not to sound insulting, but you are delicate creatures, born of fragile flesh and limited lifespan, and easily trodden under foot by those who are stronger. And I worry each day for the races trying to protect their future from the Alliance, because they are woefully unprepared in comparison."

Ressen felt a little guilty over his words. He knew the legends and gossip surrounding Tia and had bought into them. He too saw her as something akin to a high and mighty goddess and a terrifying warrior, not least because he'd been on the receiving end of her powers, yet he was beginning to understand that the female before him was also a caring soul, who was just as fragile as the lesser species aboard the Scientia.

Tia wasn't finished though. "In answer to your final question, you are coming on this mission because of this...." From somewhere in her robes, she fished out a pendant. It was made up of a long chunky silver chain, from which dangled a tapered quartz-like crystal in marbled shades of purple and turquoise. Ressen, confused, took the proffered necklace.

"You remember the other necklace?" Tia asked, quietly. Ressen nodded. "Same deal. But I think this one would look better on you than me."

"I see," he said, her words making him feel slightly odd. "Wouldn't it make sense to keep it far away and safe?"

"No. The situation may arise where I need it quickly. You've proven yourself a valuable bearer once before, let's see if you can be so permanently." She took the pendant out of his un-protesting hand, stood up, and came around to his side of the table, where she went about fastening the chain around his neck.

Ressen could feel the eyes of everybody in the restaurant on him. He had no doubt there would be plenty of gossip after this as to the meaning of Tia giving him an item of jewellery. He knew that in a lot of cultures, the exchange of expensive goods went beyond just a polite hello. They meant something deeper, especially between members of the opposite sex, and Tia's action of placing it on him had probably spoken volumes to those watching. Tia done, he tucked the crystal safely under his shirt, and felt the coolness of the rock against his skin. Tia sat back down, unconcerned with the whispers that were raging. She gave him a satisfied smile.

Ressen felt totally out of his depth. He tried to push the feeling aside by embracing a different, bad feeling. "Just what are you expecting to find on the planet that warrants a backup disc?" he asked.

"Same thing I'm always expecting when I go into an un-known situation; trouble, and as they moved an entire world to say hello, I'm erring on the side of big trouble."

Ressen's confidence finally slipped. "I don't think I can do this," he told her, meekly.

"From what I've seen, you can do a hell of a lot more than

this," she answered, kindly. "You saved a species from extinction, you travelled nearly half-way across the galaxy to make sure those same survivors had a chance at life, and you braved pain, and the unknown, to save me. You think you can't do what's asked of you because you're doing just that...thinking. Yet when you're thrown into the thick of things, with no time to dwell on inevitable bad outcomes, you manage to achieve what's needed. You may have doubts over your ability to help me, but I don't."

"What if I'm attacked? Not thinking isn't exactly the best defence against a plasma charge to the chest."

The corner of Tia's mouth twitched. "You are somewhat more robust than you used to be," she answered, candidly. "My blood that healed you still runs through your veins. It's made your body more resilient, and it can, if needs be, help heal bad wounds, though it has its limits."

"So, if I get blown up, I'm on my own."

"Pretty much...so don't."

"I'll do my best," he said, before going about finishing off his meal. As he ate, it occurred to him that what Tia had said about his body's resilience was something he should have known, at least partially. Having spent a long time lying comatose on a hospital bed, his physique had suffered, and his muscles had wasted through lack of use. Once he'd signed on to be Tia's helper, he'd started hitting the gym in preparation. He had no desire to become as muscle-bound as some of her closer allies, but he knew he needed to reach an appropriate level of fitness. However, after all the times he'd been, it hadn't occurred to him, at least not until Tia had mentioned it, that he'd been lacking one of the main repercussions from working out, namely muscle fatigue.

He remembered back to his youth, when he'd started his military service, and the fitness trials his squad had been put through. Having never done anything similar before joining, the days after the gruelling obstacle courses had been pure torture, as every bone and muscle in his body had protested at having been used. His first night had been the worst, and he'd had to crawl back to his bunk on hands and knees, and he hadn't been the only one.

Yet after his first foray to one of the Scientia's gyms, he'd felt fine. He remembered thinking he hadn't done his exercises properly and had gone back the next day to push himself harder, only to again suffer no ill-effects the following day. After that, he'd never questioned his lack of fatigue. Now he understood why. His body could heal itself better and faster thanks to Tia and knowing this gave him a renewed boost. He had no intention of doing anything rash, but he knew if things went sideways, he wasn't going to be completely useless.

Having finished their main course, a Pann waiter came to clear away their plates. Ressen's eyes were drawn to the Pann. He recognised the race from his hospital wing, where they were the most prevalent species amongst the staff. They, like him, had dark blue skin, though unlike him, it was striped in dark grey. In contrast to some races aboard, their genders were hard to distinguish. They all had the same sized curved blue horns; had the same perfectly round, dark maroon eyes; and all wore the same kind of clothing, which was usually an embroidered silk tunic if they weren't wearing a uniform. Conversely, Ressen was certain Tia was a female of her species.

"Dessert?!" the waiter stated, shoving a piece of paper under Ressen's nose.

For once, Ressen recognised the phrase, and before Tia could answer for him, he said, "Yes." The waiter left without saying another word. Tia gave Ressen an approving smile. "I never can tell," Ressen said, as he scanned the menu desperately for something that looked vaguely recognisable, "whether they are asking me if I want something or stating that I will be having something. Grelt has the same problem."

Tia nodded. "They lack a sorely needed inflection when asking a question. It confuses most people, even those who understand the language well. It doesn't help that they can be blunt to the point of being obnoxious." She leant forward and whispered her last statement to Ressen, even though the Panns around them couldn't understand her use of his language.

"You're not wrong. I think most of the other people in my ward didn't enjoy their...what do you call it, oh yes, 'bedside manner'. I'm not ungrateful, far from it, they looked after me wonderfully, but there was a distinct difference in the way I was treated by them and say, a Maylen. A sponge bath from a Pann was more painful than having head-to-toe burns."

Tia roared with laughter and drew indignant looks from many of the patrons. "I can well believe that," she said, when she'd calmed down. She beamed at Ressen, and he shared her smile. For a moment, they shared a look. Ressen usually found extended eye contact a little disconcerting, especially from individuals he didn't know that well, yet the look he shared with Tia felt comfortable. His insides started to feel a tad warm, and he hurriedly went back to looking at his indecipherable dessert menu. Luckily, each choice came with a picture; something a lot of the restaurants seemed to do to help the multitude of different races figure out what was edible. His eyes were drawn to what looked like a pie, topped with small round berries of every colour of the rainbow, drizzled with a dark indigo sauce. His full stomach lied to him and told him he had plenty of space left for pie.

He pointed to the picture, and when the waiter returned, Tia ordered it for him, along with something for herself. That something turned out to be a large narrow glass filled with layers of more colourful fruit, interspersed with thickly whipped sauces in a range of pastel pinks and blues. Though he struggled, Ressen finished every bite of his dessert. It'd had a crunchy, neutral-flavoured base, and though the berries had been slightly tart, the sauce had been thick and sweet, complimenting the fruit nicely. Ressen gave a satisfied groan on swallowing the last mouthful. "Now I understand why Grelt goes to different restaurants all the time. There's so much to experience, and so little time to do it in. I hope I survive the mission, so I can come back and try your dessert next time."

"Oh, I think there's a very good chance of that happening," Tia said, reassuringly, and this time, Ressen believed her.

Chapter 22 - Grelt

Grelt stood nervously in the control room of his vessel as Tia ran her eyes around the cramped space. It was his first time being up close to her, and there was a lot more of her than he'd bargained on. Her height and appendages near filled the room, and Grelt cringed every time her wings or tail came too close to a fragile surface. An involuntary movement on her part could cause a major dent in the panelling, or worse, loosen the wiring behind it. Wiring that had taken the brothers an age to fix after the fire.

Ressen was watching too, but from the safety of the corridor. Grelt noted his expression, one of undisguised admiration, and he hoped his brother wasn't biting off more than he could chew on accepting his new position with Tia, as her, as Ressen had called it, 'Soul Carrier'. Grelt dared to glance away from Tia to his brother's chest, where he knew a crystal pendant was hidden away under his shirt. Ressen had explained the gift and his honoured position, the moment he had returned from their cosy meeting. Grelt had to admit he'd been a little awestruck. From the various meetings he'd been privy to on joining the GR, he was aware of the level of reverence a lot of the members gave Tia, even after her scary rampage. He had been swept up by that sentiment and had just as much esteem for her as the rest, though, at that moment, he wished she would kindly leave the control room before she unwittingly caused an accident.

Having satisfied herself with the state of repairs, Tia turned to Grelt. "So, how are we looking?" She spoke the words to him, and into his mind, simultaneously, much like she did with his language-impaired brother. Though handy, because it meant Grelt wasn't slowed down by having to translate what she was saying, the result of the process was a little disconcerting, as her mouth and the words didn't exactly match up, and it was like watching a film with badly dubbed audio.

"We're up and running one hundred percent," Grelt answered, in his own tongue. "More so, thanks to the upgraded components I've had from Zerra, and from the Engineering Department here. I've had the larder stocked, ordered extra fuel, and we have a back-up supply of crystals for the engines, just in case."

Tia nodded. "Would you like me to safely extricate myself from the control room now?" Her eyes twinkled mischievously.

Grelt swallowed a little hard, knowing he'd been a bit too free with his thoughts around her. "If you wouldn't mind," he answered, as apologetically as possible.

Tia deftly curved her tail around her, ducked her head down a fraction, and stepped out into the corridor. Neither her horns, tail, nor wings grazed the door frame on the way out. Grelt cringed guiltily, then saw his brother was trying, and failing, to suppress a big grin. He gave him a look of daggers…and swords.

"Well, the various departments have green lit you as good to go," Tia stated, ignoring the face pulling battle that was going on around her, "so I see no reason for any further delay. The sooner we leave, the sooner I can meet my next fate."

Grelt stopped trying to commit glowering homicide. "I'll contact the Scientia's bridge and get us queued for departure. I expect they'll be glad to get their docking bay back."

"You've certainly made things interesting for them," Tia replied, pragmatically.

"I'll show you your quarters, or what passes for them," Ressen piped up.

It was Grelt's turn to dole out a surreptitious smirk after Tia had turned her back. He watched the pair head off down the corridor, listening as Ressen apologised excessively for the lack of space that would greet her. As their voices faded, he turned back to the control panels, hailed the station's bridge staff, and with a greater grasp of the Human language than his brother, requested a window for departure. He recognised the voice of the crewmember who answered his hail. It was the Human, Arron.

"I can give you a slot in thirty minutes. Make sure your hatch is locked and remember to undock on thrusters alone. We don't want you inadvertently blasting a hole in the side of the station; we've had enough of them of late. We'll let you know when you're clear enough to engage main engines."

"Understood," Grelt responded. "I confirm hatch is locked. We are ready to leave."

"Good." There was a pause before Arron added, "You take care out there. I dread to think what you'll find on that planet."

You and me both, Grelt thought, as he cut the call, and sat back in his seat to watch the minutes count down to when he could disengage the docking hatch. After a while, he began busying his mind with the various readouts on his control panel, and he checked and double-checked that everything was within optimum parameters. He also gave their ship's newly installed weapons another once over. Not that he didn't trust the Zerrens to provide him with reliable armament, he just didn't want to dwell on the horrors that could be waiting for them on the cold and nondescript planet heading their way. Ships had been told to keep their distance, and those that had scanners with long-range capabilities had carried out preliminary surveys, but nothing untoward had shown up. Either there was absolutely nothing happening on its surface, and it was just a rocky ball that had been sent off its original trajectory, or there was plenty going on under some impressive cloaking technology. Grelt, unsurprisingly, prayed for the former, because if so, then the long-range threat the planet represented would be nullified later once Tia, or her vessel at least, paid it a proper visit. The other possibility was what was giving Grelt sleepless nights.

But as he kept reminding himself, he had chosen to go along on the mission. He could have handed the controls of his vessel over to another willing and competent pilot, or he could have simply refused his vessel altogether. However, his loyalty to his brother, and his determination to help the rebels, had overridden what little sensibility he had. Moreover, though he trusted Tia to have his brother's back, there was no guarantee she could save him if things went awry, and Grelt couldn't stomach the thought of his brother facing death on an alien world far away from his kin. They had been a team for many years, and though their paths had been separating, thanks to their different responsibilities, Grelt still felt those bonds strongly. He wondered if his brother did too since becoming distracted by the force of nature that was Tia.

A loud alarm chimed into his thoughts, telling him his thirty minutes of reflection time were up. He disengaged the ship's hatch from the station and passed the minimum amount of power possible to its thrusters to gently push it away from the station. A couple of shorter bursts, and they were silently sliding pass a gamut of bulky transporters, and small surface to ship vessels, all keenly waiting for their turn to dock. After a while, the swarm of smaller ships was replaced by the big guns; battleships of various races parked around the station, either to visit, or in the case of conquered races, as a means of protection. Grelt gazed out the cockpit's window as they passed by, marvelling at their size, and the amount of firepower that peppered their flanks. His world had a couple of destroyers, but they were old, on the verge of being decommissioned, and nowhere near as impressive.

Arron's voice broke through the intercom one last time. "You are now free to engage main engines. Good luck!"

Grelt brought up the pre-planned course Tia had given him, fed it into the autopilot, and let it do the rest. A moment later, he heard the engines power up, and the vessel lurched as it changed direction towards its first goal, the jumpgate on the edge of Zerra's system that would allow them to leave their region of space. Because of the placement of jumpgates, and the lack of jump engines on Grelt's ship, theirs wasn't a direct course. Rather, their route was taking them to a deserted mining system, beyond the wandering planet, at which point they would double back, under the power of normal engines, to catch up with the planet. Till then, all Grelt had to do was make sure everything ran smoothly, and that he and his fellow passengers stayed fed and watered.

Chapter 23 - Leo

Leo had been slowly formulating the plan Sin'ma had asked of him and had been finding suitable races to help ferry the desperate to safety. It had been like trying to do the worst jigsaw puzzle imaginable. The pieces were spread out across the galaxy, were quite often contentious, and those that were more amenable didn't always fit. Several candidates had vessels that would be ideal for the purpose, but they were, unsurprisingly, less than enthusiastic about taking them into Alliance space. Excuses ranged from not wanting to lose precious vessels on a suicide run, to not wanting to incur the wrath of the Alliance onto their own world if discovered. Leo had sympathised with their worries. His answer to that had been that as the races were on the edge of Alliance space, the Alliance would eventually come for them, so better to have Humans and other races on their side, bolstering their numbers, when the inevitable happened. After that, he'd had some begrudging confirmations, but there were still some holdouts, specifically near his family's world. As it was, they were well away from any rebel planet of note, meaning any small rescue vessel would have to use the Alliance-monitored jumpgates leading in and out of the system. An answer to the problem would be to use a large space-faring vessel that could create its own jumppoint, but that would lead to it being immediately detected, as like all Alliance systems, there were monitoring arrays and satellites all over the place. Leo had a problem, and after a month of methodically thinking himself into a corner, he decided his only choice was to break his promise to Ken'va and Sin'ma and ask for input from a higher source, his wife.

Over dinner, he explained the whole situation to Pra'cha, then the immediate problem as he saw it; that big or small, any ship entering the system of Demeter Nine would be seen, and repercussions would be forthcoming.

"Could a large vessel not ferry the smaller craft close enough using its own jump engines?" she asked. "This would allow it to bypass the jumpgates."

"I did think of that, and in several instances that's what's being planned, but only because the smaller rescue crafts can cope with long-haul flights, leaving the larger vessels out of range of the monitoring stations. Unfortunately, the Transersalans aren't that advanced, so they don't have any small craft that can make the distance from their world to Demeter Nine, nor do they have any large vessels capable of creating a jump point. Any race that does is nowhere near Demeter Nine. I mean, we could get another large ship to head that way, but the plan is we do this initial evacuation as simultaneously as possible. If we enter on multiple fronts, the Alliance will have a harder time quashing the escapees, as it will be sudden, and spread out. If I get a large vessel sent from a more distant colony, we run the risk of having to delay the whole thing while it travels there. Meaning there's a better chance of the Alliance uncovering what we're planning. Or we carry on with the planned evacuation, and my family's ship comes in late when the Alliance is on high alert. In which case, they could well take my family before the ship has had a chance to arrive at their planet."

Pra'cha pulled a face that showed she empathised with his predicament. She took a moment to have a forkful of salad, and a look of intense concentration passed across her face as she chewed. Swallowing, she asked, "Didn't you say your brothers worked at a jumpgate there?"

"Yes, they run maintenance for the entrance gate. Why... what are you thinking?"

"Say we got a small vessel to head through the gate, could they keep it under wraps somehow?"

"What, like fudge the readouts so it looks like an Alliance craft?"

"Possibly. I mean it is doable, tricky…very tricky, but doable, and it would get you in and out without tripping any alarms."

"I doubt they have the skill for that," Leo answered, glumly. "Yes, they're computer-savvy, but they mostly do hardware-fixing jobs, and relay software updates. They're certainly no Pra'cha-level hackers." He gave his wife a wink. "And even if they were, they'd be hard-pressed to do something like that on the down-low. Let's be honest, with me as their relative, they've probably got a higher-up surreptitiously breathing down their neck twenty-four-seven." Then it hit Leo like a bolt from the blue. "What am I thinking? We don't need to be thinking anywhere near those lines. Hell, why didn't I think of this sooner?" Pra'cha looked at him wide-eyed as he started gesticulating madly towards the bulkhead. "We have a whole damn ship full of Alliance vessels parked right outside!"

"The Victory." Pra'cha gave out a groan. "Of course, why did I not think of that?" She gave Leo a grin.

"See! I knew talking to you would help," he told her, beaming back.

"It was not my idea," Pra'cha said, abashed.

"No, but it woke some of my brain cells up. Now I just need to come up with a way to get one of those ships to Demeter Nine. And that'll be the easy part. Getting the pilot to convince my family that they're not an Alliance operative who's going to do terrible things to them because of me won't be easy. They're not going to trust some random alien, and they're certainly not going to trust some random alien in an Alliance ship."

Pra'cha stared hard at him. "Leo Jackson, I know how your mind works, and I know where this is going."

Leo tried to look innocently back. "What do you mean?"

"Say it," she told him.

"Say what?"

"Say it!"

Leo caved in. "Fine…. It looks like I'm going to have to go and save my family myself."

****

Leo had precious time to hatch his plan. While he was persuading command to let him go and trying to figure out the logistics of it all, the other races in the loop would already be preparing to mobilise. It left him scant time to get to his parents' planet, and in the end, he'd had to face facts; he just wasn't going to be able to get to them in time. Still, he did have one thing on his side. Although the first wave of rescues was to be simultaneous, there would be several stragglers after, bringing the Alliance's defences to task, and giving him the opportunity to slip in and out unchallenged. At least, that's what he hoped.

However, as he sat in the captain's office late the next day, explaining his paper-thin plan to Sin'ma and Ken'va, he could tell his audience was not convinced, and their responses were considerably less positive than Pra'cha's. She had simply rolled her eyes at his announcement but had known better than to try to dissuade him. In contrast, Sin'ma and Ken'va weren't enthused with seeing Leo, a young Human with barely any fighting experience, heading off into Alliance territory.

Sin'ma's counter plan was valid enough. "If their rescue is to be delayed, better we send experienced fighters to go and collect them."

Leo appreciated their rational. If the Alliance got wind of their plan, and made a grab for his family, better to get seasoned combat veterans to go to the rescue, as they would know how to deal with the situation. His counterargument was along the same lines. "If the Alliance are going to detain my family, and chances are they know this is a real possibility because of my defection, then they're not going to trust anyone. No matter how convincing they are when they say they're there to rescue them. The only person they're going to trust is me."

Ken'va let out a frustrated exhale. "You are determined to

do this." he stated.

"Yes, so I'll need one of the transporters or system-scouters from the Victory. They're two-seaters, with plenty of storage space in the back, and can do a good distance. I just need a larger vessel to drop me off as close as safely possible to one of the jumpgates that can connect to Demeter Nine's system. After that, I'll head to my home planet, grab my parents, and somehow pick up my brother and sisters on the ride out. Meantime, the larger vessel can tack over to the where the exit gate spits us out, and I'll rendezvous back with it."

Ken'va and Sin'ma exchanged looks. "And what if something goes wrong?" Sin'ma asked. "What if the Alliance is waiting for you and captures you, what then?"

Leo cringed. He didn't want to think about that.

"With all due respect," Ken'va put in, "you have little combat experience. If things go wrong, it is doubtful you will be able to turn the situation to your advantage."

"Sin'ma has just about as much experience as I have, and he captured an Alliance battleship," was Leo's slightly petulant response.

"Yes, but I had a bunch of Rolst assassins, an expert hacker, and a group of Human military personnel on my side. You would be alone."

"But...." Leo tried desperately to come up with something to help plead his case. His brain failed him.

"We have no intention of leaving your family stranded," Ken'va said, trying to reassure him. "Allow Sin'ma and I some time to talk. Perhaps we can come up with a better solution."

Leo could do nothing but trudge out of the captain's office and leave his family's fate in their hands. He didn't feel like heading back to his quarters, as he was feeling too disenchanted, and he needed to deal with his depressive mood. Instead, he decided to go to a place he hadn't been to in a long time, but that had been an all too regular haunt for him during the stressful time of the Alliance's occupation of the Scientia, and he headed down into the bowels of the station and made a beeline for the Bar.

****

Compared to the rest of the station, the Bar was not a wholesome place. No parents brought their offspring there for a family meal, nor did well-to-do couples stop there post-work for a quick drink. It was primarily graced by dodgy characters and run by an even dodgier one (when he wasn't wearing the cloak of respectability as second in command of the Munitions Department). Despite that, it had been Leo's place of solace until a respectable job of his own, coupled with a home life, had kept him away.

The Bar was dimly lit and lacked the security cameras that peppered the rest of the station. All the better for back-door dealings to go unnoticed. The mediocre lighting also kept patrons from noticing the grimy walls and floors, though as they were there primarily to drink, barter, and gamble, such things probably didn't bother them. Leo had long since learnt not to lean against the walls for fear of getting stuck. Initially, they had been nothing more than metal-plated blast-resistant walls; needed in case the Munitions Department nearby had an explosion. However, on being turned into the Bar by Talon, the walls had been coated with, for want of a better word by Leo, wallpaper. It was just a bunch of mismatched scraps of paper, rescued from the recycling plant and glued up with industrial adhesive, but time was already taking its toll, and in some places the paper had started to come off. Repair attempts had been made with further scraps, including magazine pages, which made for an eyesore of patchwork. Then there was the occasional surfeit of glue, resulting in unwary patrons leaving potions of clothes, or themselves, attached to the walls when getting up suddenly at the end of a night's heavy drinking. It was obvious that Talon had never been an interior decorator.

As it was the end of the day, the man himself had reclaimed his position as barman, though it seemed to be more of a symbolic role. The Gorlen barkeep, and the fire twins, Tay and Bal, seemed to be doing most of the work. The Gorlen was a scary-looking, white-scaled reptilian male, with intimidatingly clawed hands, a long tail, and big green eyes. The fire twins, while less intimidating to look at, were, to those who knew, way more dangerous than any Gorlen. They were feline-like, covered from the tips of their ears to their toes in orangey-red fur, and had ruby-red eyes. But that's were their relative cuteness ended, as each one held within their wrists glands that contained a cocktail of chemicals, which when released, caught alight in an exothermic reaction that could barbecue an unwary aggressor. Such was the mess they had made of the Alliance soldiers that had tried to gain control of the Scientia.

During his bachelor days, Leo had been fortunate enough to watch the sisters ply their questionable trade, when Talon had employed them as exotic dancers. However, since their mission aboard Tartarus to help protect Ciberia, they had been promoted to bar staff, *no doubt to help protect Talon's profit margin in his absence,* so gone were their diaphanous gowns, to be replaced by mundane attire and aprons.

Leo wandered over to the counter, to be greeted by a friendly head-nod from Talon. "Not seen you down here for a long time," Talon said, amiably.

"Not really had a reason to come," Leo said, grabbing a seat on a bar stool, "but I've been feeling a bit crap of late, and as this is the place I came when feeling that way when the Alliance was breathing down my neck, I figured what the hell."

Talon gave a grunt of understanding. "The usual then?" he asked, making a reach for the tap. Leo nodded, and watched as Talon grabbed a glass, and filled it up with an ale that Leo knew barely hit one percent in its alcohol content, despite being advertised otherwise. "So, what's eating you?" Talon enquired, as he handed the completely flat pint to Leo.

Leo gave a dejected sigh. "I need to go rescue my family, but Command are refusing to let me lead because I'm too inexperienced. They want to send a soldier, but I know my family, and they'll never trust them considering my traitor status with the Alliance."

"This about the mass rescue mission that's about to kick off?"

Leo looked aghast at Talon. "How the hell do you know about that?"

Talon gave a casual shrug by way of an answer. "Seems to me," he said, side-stepping Leo's question, "that you need to take an experienced fighter with you."

"Like anyone in the armed forces is going to want someone who's no better than a civilian tagging along. They'll see me as a liability and will spend more time making sure I stay alive than focusing on the mission."

"Well, how about someone who's not in any force, but is worth three or four soldiers all rolled into one, and will be perfectly happy to let you off the leash? Mainly 'cause he won't give a damn."

Leo eyed Talon suspiciously. "Who did you have in mind?" *Surely, he doesn't mean himself.* He took in Talon's scrawny form.

Talon read his expression. "I wasn't suggesting me you idiot. I'm not that suicidal." He gave a head-jerk towards the far corner of the room.

Leo turned around to see who he meant, and at once recognised the man. "Kan?" he hissed, under his breath.

"Why not? He's smart, he's battle-experienced, and he's a trained mercenary." Leo gave Talon a look that he hoped conveyed his scepticism. Talon continued. "Look. The guy knows you. He knows you've been up against the Alliance and managed to kill a fair few, so he's not going to be watching your back twenty-four-seven. Plus, he's an ex-merc who's done plenty of missions. He's made, literally, for your job."

Leo knew Talon was alluding to the fact that Kan was a genetically engineered Human, bred for battle, and the more he thought about it, the more he figured Talon was on to something. He grabbed his beer off the counter, slid off the stool, and headed over to Kan's table. The man was intimidating, both to look at and to talk to, and Leo had had more than enough experience of that when Kan had been his boss, back when he'd worked as an engineer. As he got close to his destination, the big-muscled man looked up, and fixed Leo with his bright green eyes. "Mind if I join you?" Leo asked, in a timid squeak.

Kan gestured to the chair opposite. "Go ahead," he said, in a voice made of gravel.

Leo sat meekly down, taking a shaky sip of beer to try to steady his nerves, while wishing his 'usual' was way stronger. "Um, I'm in a bind and need help," he began.

Kan sat back in his chair and regarded Leo from underneath a scrunched brow for what seemed like an age. "How so?"

Leo went about explaining his predicament yet again. Kan kept silent throughout, and when Leo had finished, and was taking another gulp of beer to restore his dry mouth, he still didn't speak. However, the corner of his mouth was turned up, as if he were in deep thought. Eventually, he spoke. "And what makes you think Sin'ma and Ken'va are more likely to approve this mission if I'm on board?"

It was a reasonable question. "It's my final shot. I'm hoping that your presence is enough to convince them, considering your history, and whom you work for." Leo didn't want to play the Tia card any more than Ken'va and Sin'ma did, but it was the only one he had. "If not, well...history has shown you're not averse to breaking the rules."

Kan arched his eyebrows so high at Leo's comment that he went slightly bug-eyed. Leo had to take another sip of his drink to hide his smile. "Let me get this straight, I'm either to be a bargaining chip or a thief in this little enterprise of yours?"

Leo shook his head vehemently. "No, it's nothing like that. Talon told me you'd be the best guy for the task, and I agree with him. You're a fighter, you're a good strategist, and you're bloody scary."

Kan gave a little grin of self-satisfaction. "Well, you're not wrong there." He gave Leo's request some more brain time, taking a couple of swigs of his own drink as he did so. "To be honest, I can't think of a valid reason to say no. It'll be nice to go on a mission again. As it is, my wits are getting dulled from being stuck behind a computer all day."

"So, you'll help?" Leo asked, eagerly.

Kan gave Leo his huge hand to shake. "I'm in," he responded, practically breaking Leo's fingers as they shook.

****

Even with Kan on board, it had not been easy to persuade Sin'ma and Ken'va to let him go on the rescue mission. They ummed and ahhed for over a day, which made Leo feel even more antsy. Kan had remained resolute in silence. Sin'ma tried to come up with reasons for the two not to leave. His suggestion of the Engineering Department needing Kan was swiftly brushed aside. It had managed to continue functioning in both Kan and Pra'cha's past absence, and as Kan was the only one going to be absent this time around, Engineering was, as far as he was concerned, in safe hands. Even Sin'ma had to grudgingly admit to that being true. Similarly, Leo's absence was a non-issue. The station hadn't ground to a halt while he had been watching over Tia, and it wouldn't do so again. The two parties had reached stalemate, and so, with clear reluctance, the two Zerrens had finally given Leo and Kan their blessing.

With nothing to hold them back, Leo and Kan rendezvoused at the Scientia I's docking hub to wait on the transporter that would take them across to the Victory, and to the system-scouter ship that would be their snug home for most of the mission.

When Leo arrived, Kan was already there, decked out in his combat gear, and with a large kitbag held against the deck by his foot. Leo too sported a large holdall, and inside were several cans of deodorant and dry-shampoo (toiletry facilities were going to be at a minimum), a datapad with plenty of reading and video material on it, dry-rations, and a change of clothes.

In addition, there was some fresh food that Pra'cha had packed for him, to see him through his first few days.

Pra'cha herself had come to wave off the two men. Kan had no-one present; still the eternal bachelor, and as they waited for the transport, they discussed their plans, checking and re-checking each detail.

"We'll head off through the jumpgate here, and come out near the Endier system, where we'll meet up with the Rotaiz-ian ship Qosec Three," Kan reiterated to Pra'cha. "The Rotaiz-ians having kindly agreed to help us in our endeavour. The Qosec Three has jump engines, so can get us quickly through hyperspace towards the Transersalan system of Parania, and as close as we can get to the Alliance jumpgate without trip-ping any alarms. Once there, we'll have to head through nor-mal space in the scouter until we reach the jumpgate that'll take us into Demeter Nine's system. Our exit comes out near to the other side of the Parania system, so we'll have to trek out to meet back up with the Qosec Three, who should be hiding somewhere out of scanner range."

"What are your supplies like?" Pra'cha asked, sounding con-cerned.

"Don't worry," Kan reassured her, "we'll have plenty. These scouters are well-equipped for extended missions, so there's plenty of dry-rations, medical supplies, back-up components, urine recycling, the works. It does mean there won't be much room to stretch our legs though, so we'll have to enjoy our short stint on the Qosec Three."

Pra'cha nodded, but still looked a little worried, and she took Leo's hand in hers, and held on tight while they counted down the minutes. Leo tried to keep her spirits buoyed but wasn't the best when it came to cheery small talk. "Now you know how I felt, seeing you go off on your hair-brained mis-sion," he told her.

Pra'cha gave him her best exasperated look. "At least I had backup."

"So do I, I've got Kan." He nodded in the big man's direction.

"He's one of Tia's men, you can't ask for better backup than that."

"Yes, I can, I can ask you to take more."

"There'd be no room to breathe in that scouter," Kan reminded her, matter-of-factly, "and I'm dammed if I'm spending another mission practically sat on Shar's lap. I may have got him out of trouble with that arrogant alien, but that doesn't mean I want to cosy up with him again. Your boy-husband on the other hand is quiet, doesn't take up much room, and has the decency to fear me." Kan gave Leo a wink.

Leo knew he was jesting to lift Pra'cha's mood, but he was also keenly aware Kan was correct on all three points. He began wondering how he was going to cope with being cooped up in a tiny vessel with a super-humanly strong killer. Shar and Kan's bouts of fisticuffs were legendary, and that was even with Tia in the vicinity. Tia may have brought her men under some semblance of control, but Leo wondered how controlled they were in her absence. He gave Pra'cha's hand another squeeze, more for his benefit than hers.

A clang from the other side of the airlock marked the arrival of the transporter. The little vessels were numerous and had a short turnaround time to prevent backlogging the bigger vessels, and each other, so Leo had until the airlock was given the green light and opened to say his last farewells. He swept Pra'cha up in a bear-hug and buried his face in the nape of her neck. In return, she lightly kissed the back of his head. They stood, immobile, until they heard the airlock door loudly clunk, indicating it was unlocked.

"Come on you love-birds, time to smooch and move," Kan told them, grabbing his bag.

Leo planted a kiss full on Pra'cha's lips. "I'll be fine," he said, as they broke away. "And just think, in a few weeks you'll get to meet my family. That'll be cool."

Pra'cha seemed to have more on her mind to say, no doubt consisting of her fears for Leo, and what problems his mission could hold, but she didn't manage to get any of that out.

Partly because she, like Leo, knew they were wasted words that would solve nothing, and partly because Kan had grabbed the back of Leo's collar, and was dragging him towards the open door to the transporter, and the maddeningly beckoning pilot.

Pra'cha grabbed Leo's bag, and threw it into his outstretched hands; unfortunately, the low gravity in the area meant it didn't quite do its expected arc, and Leo flinched as it nearly hit him in the face. "Take care…both of you," Pra'cha called after them, whilst giving her husband an apologetic look.

"Don't worry, I'll bring him back in one piece," Kan yelled, as he shoved Leo into the vessel before him.

Leo didn't have time to respond. By the time he'd regained his footing and turned around, Kan had already manually yanked the airlock shut. "The more time you witter, the harder it is to leave, trust me," Kan told him, pointing to a seat.

Leo numbly sat down as the transporter hummed to life, and he managed to buckle himself down before the last dregs of artificial gravity left them. There were no portholes to look out of, so he couldn't even watch the station disappear out of sight. The transporter gave a lurch, as the pilot pulsed the thrusters to pick up momentum, and Leo looked over at Kan, to find he had his holdall pinned to the floor with his feet and was leant back in his seat with his eyes closed, already dozing. Leo was still clutching his bag to his chest. He had the overwhelming desire to cry, but fought hard, and kept his emotions relatively in check. If Kan heard his loud sniffs, he had the decency to let them slide.

The journey to the Victory was swift, and within a couple of hours they had docked. Leo found he'd dozed off, as the transporter, thumping down on the deck, awoke him with a start.

Kan grunted and stretched. "Gotta keep moving," he muttered. Leo nodded in answer and hoisted his bag up. Kan led the way out of the airlock, and across the Victory's hangar, the artificial gravity created by the immense vessel making walking a lot easier than in the Scientia's docking hub.

Leo had never been on an Alliance battleship, having arrived at the Zerren system in one of the wheel sections of the Scientia, before the wheels had come together to form the space station. Therefore, what he saw within the battleship's hangar made him feel small, and very worried. An Alliance battleship was three times the size of the Scientia, and Leo knew each one was well-populated with vessels, and he even knew the average tally and types of ships. Each battleship contained within it hundreds of short-range scouters, terra-scouters for close planet work, system-scouters for space reconnaissance, and two-man fighters for attacking, as well as simple freighters and transporters. In the immense battleship, the rows of these smaller craft extended for kilometres ahead of him. Being surrounded by rank upon rank of shiny metal ships made him realise, once again, what kind of force the rebels were up against, and it didn't paint a pretty picture.

The atmosphere in the hangar was ice-cold, and had a metallic tang, and when Leo exhaled, his breath condensed before him. Kan, in his short-sleeved black leather vest, gave a noticeable shiver. "Time to press on, otherwise we're gonna turn into icicles," he said.

Leo, despite his trepidation, agreed, and picked up his speed as Kan strode in the direction of a gesticulating Zerren stood beside a squat vessel. "This it?" he asked, once they were in earshot.

The Zerren nodded vigorously. "It is all stocked, fuelled, checked, and ready to go," he announced.

Without dawdling, Leo and Kan secured their bags in the small hold and seated themselves at the scouter's controls. Leo then asked what he realised he should have asked a lot sooner. "Do you know how to pilot one of these?"

Kan looked at him with an audible eye-roll. "Some time to be asking me that." He said, with a voice dripping n sarcasm. "However, you're in luck. I piloted many a small ship in my day, and most of them were Human-Alliance built. That, and working in engineering means there're no surprises here." To

confirm his answer, he started pressing buttons and checking monitors. His methods worked, and the scouter began to
vibrate.

A siren started blaring outside the ship, telling any crew-
man to vacate the hangar, as its contents were about to be
exposed to the vacuum of space. A bang came next, followed
by a prolonged tremor, as the hangar bay doors began to open.
Leo craned his neck around to his left and could just make out
the huge steel doors opening through his little porthole. Kan
flicked a switch, and the metal plating covering the front of the
scouter was overlaid with a live video feed of the outside of the
craft. Once again, Leo was met with the ominous rows of space
craft, and he hoped they didn't meet an Alliance battleship on
their journey.

Kan took hold of the control stick, and with a few more button presses, got the scouter taxiing out of its rank. He curved
the vessel left, and Leo found himself looking out the open
door of the hangar, towards the star-lit void.

"Hold on to your breakfast," Kan announced.

Leo didn't have time to ask him what he meant, as a split-
second later, he was thrust against his seat, the g-forces winding him as the scouter rocketed out of the Victory's body. His
mission was a go.

Chapter 24 - Walks

Walks was back where he was supposed to be, in his office in Security. It was as he'd left it, a mess. Through his open door, the workings of the office beyond filtered into him. There was a constant, rapid, tap-tap-tap, as his lieutenants went about writing up reports; the melodious sound only broken by a constrained cough, or heart-jumping buzz of a communicator. The computers were, for the station, archaic, and the touchpads were smudged and scuffed. It didn't matter though, as his lieutenants were barely aware of their typing, used as they were to their daily grind of filling in forms and writing up details.

The warm musty smell of electronics intermingled with that of stale caffeine, to produce an odour that was as familiar as the sound of keystrokes. Walks had been hiding from Kiskin for months, and he'd missed the place. Those times he'd dared enter, it had been fly-by visits, led by the assurance of Val'ka to Kiskin's lack of presence, and he hadn't had the opportunity to soak in its familiarity.

Running his eyes over his emails, he caught site of one he'd not archived. It was a short, automated message, confirming Kiskin and Wrymiesk's departure off the station. On first opening it, he'd requested an additional tag from Command to alert him to when their ship had left Zerren space, and that confirmation was there too, just above it. *Good riddance!* It had been nearly a month since the Ethtas had scarpered, but despite their absence, they still had the power to aggravate his blood pressure when he accidentally thought about them. The email was there to remind him that they had successfully washed their hands of that belligerent race.

At first, there had been concern that Kiskin's departure would mark the end of the Karee's protection of Zerra, and people had spent a few days on tenterhooks, not knowing if the race still had their backs. However, these worries had been swiftly put to rest on the news that a Bardak cruiser had been taken out after it had blatantly put its foot over the line, perhaps they too thinking the Karee would leave, from whatever leaked information they'd been getting. However, it seemed whatever beef the Karee had with Tia didn't translate to bad blood towards the Zerrens. The Karee had already come across as churlish thanks to the whole Shar incident, and it seemed they didn't want to be the bolshy creatures many people saw them as, Walks included.

More than anything else, Walks was relieved that, despite being the one to have cuffed Shar, on several occasions, the lizard bore him no ill will. A shared drink in the Bar, followed by a hearty handshake, was all it had taken to put the miserable incident behind them. They were once more comrades in arms, and Walks was glad he hadn't lost Shar as a good friend. He took a moment to dwell on the absurdity of that idea. Shar had been responsible for the deaths of billions, yet Walks was having a tough time marrying that to his experience of the alien. Yes, he was strong, violent, and had no problem with killing, as his head count during the liberation of the Scientia indicated, yet he had always been good to Walks, and had even given him the chance to fight for freedom, when he so easily could have ended his life. In the end, Walks had come to a tenuous decision. He too had been responsible for countless deaths before his change of heart at May!ar and had found a second chance in fighting for the freedom of the GR races. And if he could be given that second chance, why not Shar?

Walks pulled his eyes from the computer screen and on to the pile of folders sat on his desk. A pile that never seemed to diminish in height, despite him having spent days working slowly through them. His staff had been as efficient as always in his absence, and the older folders sat on top, each bearing a label announcing the contents were for review only, after which, it could join its brethren in a box to be sent down to Zerra for archiving. Despite computers being able to do virtually anything, nobody fully trusted them, and hard copies hadn't been consigned to history just yet. Walks flipped through the folders. Amongst the backlog of his own questionable write-ups of missing toilet paper, and a vanished consignment of Liverden chillies (a painful tragedy averted), were other more important reports. They covered the arrests of several pick-pocketers, a couple of drunken assaults, and the attempted smuggling aboard of a cage of non-quarantined Ciberian Southern Island Valdens.

Aben and Shar's files were amongst them too, the wheels of bureaucracy and report stamping having finally sent them in his direction. Walks pulled them out first, so he could pay proper attention to them. Aben's file was short; his murder considered solved. Among the pages was his final pathology report, summarising that a close plasma shot to the stomach had resulted in his demise. The wound had been unmistakable, despite his advanced level of decomposition. He had been brutally murdered for the sole purpose of sending a message to Tia, and to the rest of the GR. Most likely along the lines of no matter what, they were no longer safe on the Station. In response, security had been stepped up, as another file showed, and inspections of passes and papers tightened, but nobody knew how effective it would be against determined assassins. Aben's murderer had been found, and Tia had made sure he would pay his debt. 'Helping with enquiries' was the final note for Hanno Delao. Shar's file was even more barren. The charges were noted, as was the fact that they had been dropped. No follow-up was needed, and the case was closed.

Walks took Aben and Shar's files and placed them in a separate envelope. Their files were not destined for Zerra, rather, they were to be sent to the Tartarus, to be received by whatever filing system they had aboard. I'd wager on a shredder,

Walks thought, with a silent snort, as he sealed the parcel and dumped it in his out tray. The rest of the files he glanced over, stamped as approved, and dumped them one by one into the box. By the time he'd finished, he was parched, and in desperate need of a coffee refill. He grabbed his mug, and was about to stand, when across his screen a red messaged flashed with the words: Amber Alert: Flagged Pass.

"The hell is this?" he shouted, watching the words blink away.

Val'ka's voice came back to him through the doorway. "We got Tech to set that up when you were away, as part of the increased security after Aben…." His voice had trailed off at the mention of Aben, but he recovered it quickly. "It means that someone has come aboard the station, and their pass has been quietly flagged as suspicious by some AI that cross-references data files, phrases, and keywords from our and other aliens' databases. Could be nothing. Could be we are about to be in a lot of trouble."

"Any way we can tell?"

Val'ka appeared in the doorway. "The warning is location and time-synced, so we can use the security cameras to find them."

"How long ago did the person enter the station?" asked Walks, as the pair of them went over to the computer that processed the security camera feeds.

"About an hour ago," Val'ka told him, as he found the feed from the camera pointing at passport control and entered the time in question.

"Great! That means if they're a problem, they've already got a head start on us," Walks grumbled, as they watched as, in Walks' opinion, a striking, young, and very Human woman showed her pass to the alien manning the check-in desk.

"Unfortunately, yes," Val'ka responded. "This AI system has a lot of people and information to deal with, and the station's computer system is not designed to run such a complex and data-intensive program, so an alert can take a while to appear."

He scrutinised his datapad. "It says here her name is Ralay, no last name, and she is employed by the Alliance as a freelance consultant." He looked to Walks for elaboration.

"She's pretty brazen to come aboard this station and flash that kind of pass," Walks said. "Terms like 'freelance' and 'consultant' usually mean they're employed to do unsavoury business...like murder."

"So, this would be one of those 'heap of trouble' deals?" Val'ka postulated.

"You are correct," came a female voice behind them, making the two men spin round. Walks reached instinctively for his weapon as he found himself face to face with the woman from the screen.

If anything, the woman who called herself Ralay appeared even more stunning than she had on the camera feed, and despite the danger she presented, Walks' stomach still did an involuntary flutter. The woman's ancestry had been lost in height, and though she was undeniably a woman of oriental descent, she stood at an atypical height of one-meter-seventy. Rather, her genes showed themselves in her face. She had pale skin, pitch black shoulder-length hair, a heart-shaped face, and dark narrow eyes. She wore a floor-length dress, which covered her from the neck down, along with both arms, and that seemed to be made from thin metal, complete with small rivets along the joins. A black hairband kept her hair from her eyes, and her lips were full, and painted dark red. Her movement was fluid, almost dance-like, and she wandered across the office as though she was permanently 'en pointe'.

"Please," she sniffed, as she watched Walks rapidly unsheathe his pistol, "if I were here to kill you, you would already be dead." Her voice, though soft, was as deadpan as her face.

Despite her reassurance, neither Walks nor Val'ka were taking any chances, and both gained their weapons, and pointed them unquestionably in her direction. "Who and what are you?" Walks asked her.

"You know who I am, I heard you say, but so be it. I am Ralay, and I am a freelance consultant with the Alliance."

"Assassin?"

"Yes."

Walks' jaw dropped at her frankness. "And I shouldn't shoot you right now because…?"

"Because without me, you will have no chance when it comes to locating the spies and murderers heading to, and whom are already on, this station."

"There are more already here?" Val'ka asked, in disbelief.

"By my reckoning, there are three already aboard, one on their way, and four planet side."

"From one shit storm to another," muttered Walks.

****

The Alliance assassin had begrudgingly yielded to a pat-down by Val'ka, while still looking down the business end of Walks' pistol. She had muttered darkly about being able to break Val'ka's neck should she so desire, continuing her air of 'I could've already killed you if I wanted to'. Even so, she had stayed stock still as the Zerren lieutenant had checked for hidden weaponry and toxins.

At a nod from Val'ka, Walks had holstered his weapon, with a begrudging nod of acceptance. The stand-off survived, Walks took the approach of moving their discussion to somewhere more inconspicuous, or at least somewhere where fewer questions would be asked by outsiders. So, shortly after giving Ralay directions, after which Walks had crossed his fingers he'd not done something stupid in letting her wander off, the three reunited at Talon's bar.

The man himself was not there, and his Gorlen counterpart was holding down the forte in his place. Walks ordered his usual, a glass of tepid water, as did Val'ka. As they made their way over to where Ralay was already seated, the young Zerren gave his glass and contents an unimpressed look and went about cleaning the rim of the glass with the sleeve of his jacket that he'd thrown on over his uniform to make himself marginally less conspicuous. Walks hadn't bothered with a jacket. He knew the place and the people all too well to not be phased by their presence, and vice versa.

Ralay too appeared to be drinking water, but the sharp smell of alcohol that hit Walks' nose when they got close enough told him it was a vodka of some description. The smell made his stomach turn. He wasn't sure if it were because he missed the taste of alcohol, or because he'd been off it for so long his body was rebelling at being in proximity to it. He tried to disguise any hint of revulsion on his face by taking a swig of his own, off-tasting drink.

Val'ka, mean time, was looking about him with an expression of disgusted interest on his face. "You never been in here?" Walks asked, as they claimed their chairs.

"Gods no!" the Zerren exclaimed, a fraction too loudly, eliciting a couple of marginal head-turns his way. "Why would I ever choose to come to a place like this?" He picked at something that was ground into the table, then, with a clear look of horror, though better of it, and quickly wiped his hand on his pants.

"It has its charms," Walks said, though even he had to admit those charms were tenuous. It had alcohol and an unquestioning clientele, and that was about it.

Ralay too seemed to be regarding the place with more than a little distaste. "I am surprised a place like this exists on this station," she muttered.

"This place came into existence the moment it became a fully operational station," Walks said.

"And the Alliance never questioned it?"

"No. But then there were several other glaring things they failed to question, and they all hearkened back to Tia."

"Ah yes, the alien woman. She has had quite the hand in subverting the Alliance's plans." Walks wasn't sure, but there might have been a hint of admiration in Ralay's voice.

"You know of her then?"

"Of course, why else would I be here? I take it, from the relaxed nature of the people aboard this station, that she has recovered."

Walks and Val'ka eyed her suspiciously. "Recovered and fully functioning," Walks said, in a warning tone. "What do you know of her predicament?"

"Only that another government shill was ordered here to send her and the rebels into turmoil, and all told, succeeded in driving her mad."

"It was a temporary wobble," Walks said, choosing not to go into the hows and whys of her resurrection. "And what do you know of the scorpiad attack?"

Ralay shrugged. "I know of no attack, or even what a scorpiad is."

Walks watched her for a moment, to see if he could tell if she was lying, but her face was a blank canvas. *Dammit, it's like trying to read polished marble.* Walks decided they'd had enough pleasantries. "I assume you were sent here to cause further strife."

"Yes."

"So why the hell then did you so blatantly come aboard, and why have you offered to help us instead?"

"I was blatant to add credence to my offer, and my offer comes because I have no more love for the Alliance than you do."

"Care to elaborate?"

"Must I?"

"Let's call in further credence," Walks said, folding his arms, and glaring at her.

Ralay stared back for several seconds before giving a resigned sighed. "Very well. If I must lay myself bare for the sake of trust, so be it. I am here for revenge," her voice, though one of an aggrieved killer, was disarmingly soft, and never ranged in pitch. If a person didn't listen to the words, they could have believed they were listening to a shy young girl discussing the weather, not a murderous woman out for blood.

"Revenge for whom?" Walks prompted.

"For my parents, and for me." As she spoke, she absent-mindedly steepled her fingers together, interlacing the tips of her deceptively delicate fingers together as she did so. Her voice gave away no trace of emotion, even as she told them of her parents' death at the hands of the Alliance. For what crime, no-one had ever told her, that was if such a crime existed. She still remembered vividly her parents' execution, even though she had been barely one year old at the time. She didn't know the faces of the men that had come to her house, knelt her parents down, and had blown them away. They had worn masks and had shot her parents through the back of their heads. In Ralay's mind, they had been cowards. But they hadn't killed her. Instead, they had taken her, and had moulded her for their own nefarious ends. Walks knew what the Alliance were capable of, and their questionable means of conscripting young fighters to their ranks, so the facts of Ralay's past didn't surprise Walks as much as they did Val'ka, whose face was a picture of dismay.

And now Ralay was at their door, wanting payback. She knew she would never get the revenge she so sorely wanted on the men who had carried out the deed. They were shadows from her past, and time may well have already taken them, or their act had been lost to history, so she would never find them. Knowing that had slowly burnt a hole in her soul and carrying out brutal Alliance orders had done nothing to quell the fire. The shifting of power in the rebels' favour had given her the opportunity she desired. It had provided her with the chance to turn her vengeance against those she knew had given the orders, the Alliance, and in so doing, she hoped to at least find personal peace.

However, despite having turned her ire against the Alliance, Ralay was not about to fly the GR flag. "This I do for me. I have no desire to entwine myself in your vain attempt at liberation," she concluded, bluntly.

Walks and Val'ka shared a look. "Good to know," Walks said,

not holding back on the sarcasm.

"You must understand, the Alliance are the better force. They have better ships, more ships, more men, and better backing."

"But you admit the balance of power had shifted in our favour?" Walks queried.

Ralay gave a half shrug. "For now, but compared to them, you are nothing more than an ant trying to take down a Tiger."

"Tigers are extinct now," came a familiar dry voice from behind them, "but I can find an ant, or at least something ant-like, in the arboretum. I think that nullifies that argument."

"You eavesdropping again Talon?" Walks asked, without turning around.

"Always." Talon came around to their table. He was still wearing his blue Munitions uniform shirt but held his barman's apron in his hand. Walks realised the day had gotten away from him again, and that working hours were over. Talon looked over at Ralay. "And who's this fresh-faced killer?" he casually asked.

For the first time since their meeting, Ralay displayed a brief flicker of emotion. Walks saw Talon had put her on the back foot. "What makes you think I'm a killer?" she asked, with finally a hint of suspicion in her voice.

"Sweetheart, I've seen that look and poise enough times to know. You take enough lives unchallenged, what lies behind the eyes decays, and the body carries itself as if it holds within it the unstoppable force of Death himself. You're no different."

Walks watched as the two sized each other up, and there was no doubt that Talon's presence discomforted Ralay. There seemed to be a silent tug of war going on between them, which finished with Ralay looking away, and paying excessive attention to her half-drunk drink. Talon gave the vaguest hint of a smile. Walks wasn't sure what had happened, but undeniably something had.

Walks never knew how to take Talon. On the surface, he came across as a bit of a vagabond. He was tall and lanky, though with a bit of muscle, and his general demeanour was scruffy, thanks to his day's old stubble, and messy, ear-length, mousy brown hair. His penchant for wearing ostentatious gold jewellery didn't help his overall look, and it tended to make his pale skin look even more sallow. But Walks had the feeling there was a hell of a lot more going on behind the man's pale grey eyes than it otherwise appeared. There was a cunning and intelligence there that was bordering on the wrong side of dangerous.

"So, what story has she brought you?" Talon asked, his eyes not straying from Ralay, even though he was now looking at her left ear.

Walks was still trying to make sense of Ralay's response, so Val'ka finally found the opportunity to chime in. "She alleges that there are more killers on the station, with others on their way, and several already planet side."

Talon took his words on board. "Wouldn't surprise me," he said. "There's no knowing who the Alliance have co-opted to carry out their dirty work. Every race has its bad seeds. We expect death to come at us from behind the mask of a Bardak or Human, but it could just as easily be a Beeden, or a Maisak, or a Ciberian."

"Have you heard anything?" Walks asked him, hoping that Talon's contacts were in the loop.

Talon shook his head. "Whoever they are, they're lying low, and not bringing attention to themselves. There's always fresh faces on this station now and trying to work out the snakes from the miscreants isn't as easy as it used to be."

"Why does this major shit always happen after Tia leaves?" Walks wondered out loud.

Talon cracked a smile. "The monsters certainly like to come out of the woodwork when she's not around." He turned back to Ralay. "So, Ralay..." *How the hell did he know her name?* "... how do you intend to help us deal with our infestation?"

Ralay, dared to return his stare. "I intend to hunt them down."

"Do you know who they are?" Val'ka asked.

She shook her head. "No, but I will know them when I see them."

Talon's right eyebrow raised the merest fraction, but he didn't say what Walks was thinking, which was: *Just how exactly will you know them on sight?* Walks had an off feeling about Ralay, and not just because she was an assassin. His gut had told him that Wrymiesk wasn't one hundred percent legitimate, and now he was getting the same vibe from Ralay. He'd been spot on about Wrymiesk, having figured out the creature to be a telepath, yet Talon didn't seem to be inclined to curtail Ralay's visit to the station. So, Walks listened to the other part of his gut, the one telling him, if in doubt, trust Talon, even though he was a reprobate of the highest order.

Walks mulled things over internally for a moment. "I'm not sure anybody, me included, will appreciate you running around the station, unattended, bumping people off, even if they are paid Alliance killers," he said. "Besides, I'm pretty sure the likes of the captain, and Tia, and me for that matter, would like to question them thoroughly. After that, it's anybody's game."

Ralay looked the tiniest bit put out by his statement. "What do you suggest?" she asked, coolly.

"You and me will go for a wander, and you can point out any likely suspects."

"As if they won't run when they see a uniform," she pointed out.

"As if they won't run when they see you," Talon added, from behind the bar, as he tied his apron up over his officer's uniform. "That is if they haven't already gone into hiding. You're hardly Miss Incognito going around dressed like that. Face it, no young woman, dressed in New Earth high fashion, would be seen dead either in the presence of a grizzled old git like him," he head-jerked in Walks' direction, which made him shoot Talon a 'what-the-fuck?' look, "or rummaging around the grotty back corridors of this station. If you're going hunting, you both need to dress down." Walks exchanged a glance with Ralay. *Dammit, Talon's right, we stand out like a pair of warning beacons.* "You could also probably do with hiring the services of someone who knows this station like the back of his paw."

Walks' head whipped round back to Talon. "Are you kidding me?" *He does believe Chione is just a cat, right?*

Talon gave a nonchalant shrug. "Aben was his friend. He'll be as invested in this hunt as you."

Walks stared hard at Talon, trying to read his poker face, but just as with Ralay, he came away empty-handed. *Dammit.* He knew that as far as Chione was aware, the only people alive who knew he could talk beyond Tia were himself and Leo, and they had both been sworn to secrecy over the matter.

"Who is it he's talking about?" Ralay asked, cautiously.

"Chione," Walks answered, not taking his eyes off Talon's blank expression.

"And he is?"

Walks sighed. "You'll find out soon enough."

****

"A cat?" Ralay was looking down at the snow-white fur ball that was Chione. He, in turn, was scrutinising her with his big green eyes. All semblance of her frosty demeanour had gone, to be replaced by unabashed incredulousness.

"Yep," Walks said, simply, as he shrugged on an old, battered jacket of his.

It was the day after their bar room meeting. Since then, Val'ka had secured Ralay a hotel room, and a change of attire, having spent the evening rummaging through the clothes left by departed Alliance personnel to find suitable garments. Subsequently, Ralay had turned up in the office that morning wearing the less conspicuous attire of faded jeans, scuffed trainers, a dark maroon jumper, and a tailored black jacket. Val'ka's ability to judge size had Walks a little impressed, and all the garments fitted Ralay perfectly, while at the same time disguising the weaponry Walks had regrettably provided for her to secrete on her person. However, the blandness of the clothes failed to disguise the person within them, and Walks could tell that her looks, and overall presence, meant she was still going to draw attention. Walks too had dressed down and gone were his security jacket and black pressed slacks. In their place, he wore black jeans, a threadbare brown t-shirt he'd discovered scrunched up at the bottom of his wardrobe, and his old faux-leather black jacket, which was as weathered as his face.

While Val'ka had been playing fashion designer, Walks had tracked down Chione to Tia's quarters, and had requested his services. Talon had been right; Chione didn't want to see anyone else he knew being callously murdered and had accepted without hesitation.

The question of why Talon had brought up Chione was one they had both questioned, and Chione had been adamant Talon didn't know his secret, despite all their years together on Tartarus. "I was always just a cat, albeit Tia's cat. In fairness, I came across as well-trained, and I was Aben's closest pet-slash-friend. I suppose it's no great leap to assume I would be of some help," Chione had postulated.

"Yes, but he specifically said I should hire you," Walks had countered. "That's not something you do unless you know intelligible help is forthcoming. Saying, 'good kitty, go find three assassins,' doesn't usually result in a lot of help, well-trained kitty or not."

Chione had given a confirming grunt, but the question had remained unresolved. *Yet another reason why I question everything about that man's existence,* Walks had grumbled to himself.

While Walks was happy to have gained the services of what was a sentient bloodhound, he wasn't completely happy with Chione leading point. He would have preferred Shar, as the big lizard would've added extra muscle and firepower to their hunt. However, he had quickly realised that much like a dressed-up Ralay, Shar would stick out like a sore thumb and send their targets running, especially as he was a known associate of Tia. There was also the fact that, though he may have been a long-time resident of the station, he didn't know its guts as well as a highly exploratory cat. Therefore, Walks had begrudgingly concluded that Shar's time was better spent focusing on captaining the Tartarus while the two Karee vessels, and Tia, were off doing their own things.

As Walks juggled his jacket and holster, in a bid to hide his gun, he watched the eyeballing between the assassin and the cat. It was just him, Ralay, and Chione in the office, so Chione was free to speak, but he had yet to utter a word. Walks had the distinct impression he was toying with her. Just when he thought he was going to have to explain things, Chione finally broke his silence. "You question my usefulness?"

Ralay's eyes went wide, and she made a noise like she'd swallowed her uvula. Walks tried to keep a straight face, remembering how gob-smacked he'd been when he'd first been faced with a talking cat. He had accepted the reality of the situation swiftly, as there had been no other explanations forthcoming, and he wondered if a similar argument-counter argument was running through Ralay's head.

She rallied some of her poise quickly. "You speak?" she said, quietly.

"Yes."

"How?"

"Long story short; was a Human scientist, got blown up by the Alliance, got rescued by Tia."

Chione's story, while concise, hid a lot of truths. Truths that Walks knew, and few others did. Chione had been at the forefront of creating the scorpiads; mindless soldier creatures created through the splicing of male Human and alien DNA. They were of the same creature that had been smuggled onto the station to kill and cause panic amongst the GR, and the same creature that Tia had been morphed into, many centuries before, through an ill-advised experimental tangent involving Human female DNA. But whereas the males had been used to quash rebellions on outlying worlds, the female could not be controlled. Tia had become a queen and a destroyer and had been left to run rampant until the Karee had brought an end to the unknown reign of terror she had pursued. For his part, the man that had become Chione had tried to make amends and find a way to bring down the scorpiads that still survived. The Alliance had got to him first, killing his family, and all but destroying him. Tia had transferred his mind from his broken body into that of his cat. The intricacies of Chione's history, Walks doubted Ralay would ever know, nor would she know the period behind Chione's sentence, as by all accounts, the cat was nearly as old as Tia, who was an inconceivable five hundred plus years old.

Ralay had regained her usual aloof air, having accepted the inconceivable truth that was Chione. "How do you intend to be of service to us?" she asked.

"I have been on this station since its arrival in this system. I know every dark corner, every suitably sized ventilation duct, and every shortcut. I know its smells and its sounds. I know this station better than the engineers who thought it into being, and the engineers who spend their days maintaining it. If you want to find something untoward, or someone questionable, I can tell you where it, or they, are likely to be, and whether something is amiss."

"Just remember our deal," put in Walks. "No putting yourself in harm's way. I really don't want to be on the receiving end of an angry Tia."

Chione nodded in confirmation. Although Walks had conceded to having such a handy ally in their hunt, he felt one-hundred percent responsible for the feline. Aben had been with Tia for a relatively short time, and his death had sent her off the rails, so there was no telling what affect the death of a friend of several centuries would have on her and Walks certainly didn't want to find out. Chione's part was to lead Ralay and Walks into promising territories, using his knowledge and his nose to let them know if anything was wrong, and then to get the hell out of there.

However, Talon's words were still in the back of Walks' mind, and an idea had formed that he was having a hard time getting over. It would be easy if all those preparing to cause havoc were like Ralay, namely Human, as Humans were rare, and questionable faces could easily be verified. But as Talon had pointed out, there was no guarantee who they were up against was Human. Amongst the allied species aboard the station could be bad apples with falsified papers, having come aboard under the guise of traders, entrepreneurs, or refugees. All said and done, Walks, Ralay and Chione had a tough road ahead of them.

With the knowledge that there may be another assassin on the way, and another three allegedly about to jump ship, Security was on even higher alert. "We're looking at red alert in the rear-view mirror with this one," Walks had explained to his, not completely understanding, alien security force. However, what they did understand was discretion, and as well as the checks at arrivals were the 'random' spot checks, the quiet scrutinising of hotel visitor logs, and the causal passing of an eye over café clientele.

A similar situation was happening planet side, with prominent members of government laying on extra security to watch their backs till such a time as Walks and Ralay could head down. It was all damage limitation, and Walks knew it wouldn't stop a determined assassin from getting aboard. Rather, it was a means to slow them down, hopefully long enough for him to nab them. Fortunately, Walks had one extra arrow in his bow compared to those on Zerra, and it wasn't Ralay or Chione. It was Talon. He had sent the word forth to his many eyes, and while Chione knew the dark and secretive places, those who answered to Talon knew the comings and goings of the station, even better than Walks and his security force. Any unusual activity, and Walks would be the first to know...after Talon that was.

"We ready?" Walks asked Ralay and Chione. They both nodded in confirmation. "Right then. We'll separate off and reconvene at Talon's Bar. After that, it's Chione's choice."

Ralay headed out, shortly followed in the opposite direction by Chione. Walks killed some time by flicking through security camera feeds, mildly hoping that someone would make an obvious run for it, but he remained disappointed. Alien faces, all looking thoroughly innocent, streamed past him on the screen. He swore with frustration.

"I thought you would have already left," came Val'ka's voice from behind him.

Walks stood up and stretched his back. "Just giving the others a head start," he explained.

"I see," his lieutenant said, placidly, as he took his seat behind his desk. "Anything I should know before you leave?"

Walks knew Val'ka understood the score, and what to do if things kicked off again. He was fast coming to terms with the fact that there was precious little new advice he could impart on the young Zerren. "Just keep on doing what you're doing," Walks said, lamely, before heading off to meet the others. *That little git's going to have my job before I know it,* he thought, wryly.

Chapter 25 - Chione

C hione took point, his nose testing the air, his ears swivelling to catch the faintest hint of something, or someone, lurking in the shadows. Behind him, Walks, and the woman known only to him as Ralay, followed; their tenseness with the situation and each other palpable. At least to Chione's acute feline senses.

Despite the danger presented by the hunt, Chione was glad Walks had come to him for help. He had spent too long wallowing in depression over the loss of his good friend Aben. Unlike Tia, who had shown her heartbreak only too clearly, Chione, being on the surface just a cat, hadn't been able to display such a level of anguish, but underneath his fur, his soul had shattered too. What may have seemed to some just a cat's disinclination to move, was really a Human disinclination to live. Chione had grown accustomed to having two close friends in the galaxy: Tia and Aben. For centuries, he'd been a comrade in paws to Tia, then, when Aben had come along to be Tia's aide, he had become an integral part of Chione's life too. He had often travelled with the little alien, as he had gone off to broker deals with other races at the behest of Tia. Chione had enjoyed those days. He may have gone as a spy, and to literally sniff out lies and deceit, but he had also enjoyed the change of scenery, and the chance to explore alien worlds. Just as he had once done, many times before, with Tia.

When Tia had vanished after everything had gone to hell on the dead world, he had been less pessimistic than most about what may have been happening to her. He had seen the woman's transformation from Human woman to alien warrior. And though others had fretted over her fate, he had held fast to the belief, backed up by experience, that she was merely going through a transition. And he had been ready to accept that transition, as he knew that while Tia's future lay down a path separate from his, he would journey on with his companion Aben.

Then Aben had been murdered, and Chione had found himself very much alone. Tia had spent a short amount of time in her quarters, but her true home lay within Morrígan. Consequently, Chione was no longer sure where he belonged. As a matter of routine, and to keep familiarity in a choke hold, he had remained in Tia's quarters, with Leo kindly popping by to help feed him, and to chat, yet Chione knew the arrangement couldn't stay that way for ever, especially as Leo had shipped out to rescue his family. Pra'cha had then filled the void, but as she didn't know he could speak, it hadn't had the same loneliness-busting impact. There was always the possibility of him returning to Tartarus, and interacting with the crew there, but he didn't feel the level of kinship with them that he'd had with Aben and Tia. He was at a theoretical crossroads and didn't know which way to go.

Chione noticed he'd increased his pace while he'd been thinking and stopped in his tracks. He turned back to Walks and Ralay to wait for them to catch up. The two Humans were the other's opposite. Ralay was young and elegant, and almost glided along with a sure, yet feminine gait. Walks looked hunched and tired. His greying dark hair was down round his ears and met his facial stubble, which was also getting unruly. He had considerable bags under his eyes, and occasionally he'd unconsciously rotate his left shoulder, as if his old battle wound still plagued him with discomfort. Chione felt a pang of pity for the man. The likes of Sin'ma and Ken'va carried the weight of the war on their shoulders, but never showed it, so as not to appear weak in the face of the enemy. With Walks, the weight was there for all to see, and he didn't seem ashamed over who saw it.

He caught Chione staring at him. "Anything?" He asked, brusquely.

Even at a distance, Chione caught the sharp smell of old coffee on his breath. A further odorous addition was the remains of his breakfast, which Chione figured had been egg-based, due to the sulphuric tinge that was interwoven with the caffeine aroma. In contrast, Ralay barely smelt of anything other than the base scent of a recently washed Human. There was a slight chemical smell emanating from her makeup, but nothing of a level that made him want to wrinkle his nose, unlike Walks.

"Nothing yet," he said, in answer to Walks' question, "but there's a specific place I want to go to first." He trotted off again.

The place he was heading was somewhere he'd avoided going, despite believing it to be all clear, at least up until he'd heard the news of the assassins having infiltrated the station. It was a location that filled him with dread whenever he thought about it. It was where the scorpiad had killed its last victim, the engineer Carl Matthews, and an area close to where Tia had eventually found the creature and killed it. Chione figured it to be the scorpiad's last hiding place. It, and its telepath handler, Mister Ward. Chione had never seen the creature, but he had unknowingly stumbled across its final act of murder. A Zerren cat running for its life, and a strange odour, had meant nothing to him until Aben had casually mentioned a crewmate's pet scorpions. Then it had all come crashing together. The wildcat had been running for its life, and the smell had been Carl Matthews dissolving into a pile of denatured cells. Chione shivered at the thought.

"You okay there?" came Walks' voice, tinged with concern. Chione stopped to look at him, questioningly. Walks nodded at his tail, which had involuntarily puffed up to thrice its usual size.

"Yes," Chione fibbed. "Just remembering what was once hunkered down here."

"Security never did find its hiding place," Walks said, pulling a grim expression in response to his own memories.

"Doesn't surprise me," Chione replied. "There are so many twists and turns down here, not to mention ventilation ducts, engineering tunnels, and loose siding. A determined person could hide down here forever."

"Not forever," Ralay said. "They would need to come out for food."

"Perhaps, perhaps not," Chione said. "The likes of the Munitions crew, and the part-time techs that come down here to check over the recycling plants, all have stashes of food lying about. They do it so they can eat without having to traipse over to one of the department's canteens, or back up to the thoroughfare. If someone can find a good hiding spot, they'll probably find the food too." As he said the words, he came up to the door that led into the main fluid recycling centre.

Walks opened the door and cautiously entered, before waving Chione and Ralay through into a little office that was devoid of personnel. There were a couple of desks, each with a smattering of printed readouts on them, a control panel that was a mass of green blinking lights, and a small kitchenette, which housed a sink, a coffee machine, and an icebox. Chione nodded to the icebox. "Told you."

Walks opened it up. "Several pots of Zerren yoghurt, some pretty solid looking milk...." He picked the carton up and gave it a shake. It glooped rather than sloshed. "One can of beer, someone's going to be in trouble for that, half a loaf of long-life bread, and two jars of goodness-knows-what." He showed a jar to the room.

Ralay scrutinised the pot. "From the looks of the writing, I think it's a kind of Liverden curried sandwich spread."

Walks pulled a face, put the jar back in the fridge, and closed the door. "Well, if anyone's down here, they're either getting their food from elsewhere, or prefer to starve to death rather than touch this stuff."

Chione smiled at Walks' words and jumped onto one of

the desks for a better look out of the windows that edged the office, and from his perch, he could see the giant recycling vats. Out in space, water was scarce, and so the liquid waste of several thousand individuals of tens of races got collected and purified. Toxins were removed, bacteria were killed, and the resulting water was ready to pass through people again. Solids weren't wasted either. They were transferred to another tank for a similar treatment, and the resulting, slightly less appetising fluid, was fed through the piping up to the arboretum to fertilise the plants. Biomedical waste too had its own processing facility, where viruses, used equipment, and chemicals, were neutralised, before being jettisoned from the station at such an angle, that when the waste pod hit Zerra's atmosphere, it was vaporised. Occasionally, his sharp eyes caught a small light, weaving its way between the vats. Those lights he knew belonged to the cleaner bots that kept the place spotless. Although the office in which they stood was brightly lit, the main area beyond its walls was dim; a means to prevent unwanted bacteria from gaining a foothold. As a further precautionary measure, the air was kept chilled, despite all the working machinery in the place. For Chione, it wasn't an issue, as he had the eyes and thick coat of a cat, but he figured it was going to come as an unpleasant shock to the two Humans in their thin clothes.

Walks opened the door to the processing plant and shivered noticeably as a blast of frigid air hit him. "Jeez, the air here's colder than my last date," he muttered, zipping up his jacket, and stepping out into the gloom.

"A damn sight less toxic though," Chione added, as a cleaner bot trundled past his paws.

"Very true," Walks said, with a grin.

Ralay showed no inclination towards humour, so Chione set the pace again, his path skirting the edge of the wall of vats. The area they crossed housed the vats that dealt with biomedical waste, and which were taller than a man, but they were nothing compared to other structures in other areas. The ones that dealt with purifying wastewater were as big as houses, and there were multiples of them to deal with the huge output and need of the station's occupants. Chione didn't particularly like investigating either set-up. The biomedical vats may have been smaller, and more spaced out, but the chemical smell emanating from them was, at times, headache-inducing. The waste vats, though surrounded by a marginally more tolerable biological smell, towered over Chione, and created too many dark and hidden corners. When he'd scouted them in the past, he'd always had to be on his guard. Having Ralay and Walks with him made things a bit more secure, but their senses weren't as acute as his, so were at a disadvantage if trouble headed their way.

"Is it true there are big cats down here?" Walks whispered, only to have his voice inadvertently amplified by the acoustics of the place.

"Biggish cats," Chione confirmed. "They're Zerren cats, and they're a bit bigger than me. Mean tempered bastards they are too. They were deployed to keep any rodent population down amongst the food stores in the wheel hubs, only new pests came, old ones expanded their ranges, and so the cats did like-wise."

"Wouldn't the low-grav in the hubs cause them problems?" Ralay asked.

"Surprisingly, no. The Zerren cats are originally from for-ested mountains and have big powerful muscles and sharp grappling claws. They could easily stalk across the mesh floors, and people were surprised by how quickly they acclimatised to the low-grav environment. As for the prey, I think in the hubs the original prey was Zerren rodents, which are descendants of tree climbers with prehensile tails, which meant they coped too. The thing is, these cats are adaptable and smart, and they soon figured out how to get out of the food storage areas, and into other regions of the station that were more amenable to them. But the areas they moved into had their own share of pests, like Ciberian weevils, Toch roaches, and Human rats, brought on accidentally with various supplies, so they were left to their own devices."

They headed to the spot that gave Chione the creeps. It was nothing more than a bend in the wall that led down a narrow passageway roofed with pipes. What they carried, Chione had no idea, maybe chemical waste, maybe fresh water. The area had been meticulously cleaned by the bots, who had, unwittingly, also cleaned up the remains of the dissolved Carl Matthews, after he'd met his untimely fate. Their thoroughness meant no trace of him, or the scorpiad, could be smelt by Chione. "Ensign Matthews was killed here," he announced.

"I guess we push on and see what we find," Walks answered.

They continued forward, and Chione put all his senses on high alert. As they headed away from the vats, the chemical odour that had plagued his senses dissipated, to be replaced by the musty smells of things long kept in the dark. It was a general, permeating odour, which even the cleaner bots couldn't remove. There were other smells too: machine oil, grease, ozone, even a tang of Zerren cat. Sounds of electrical components reached Chione's ears: the tiniest spark, the whir of a motor, the click of a switch. Soon, the smells and sounds became the norm from which Chione looked for deviations. They were walking down the passage he was sure the scorpiad had prowled in its pursuit of its victim; an engineer who'd simply been trying to get the truth to those back home. The ensign had been sending out messages to family and friends, telling them what was really happening on the station, the humanity of those involved, and the questionable nature of the Alliance; corrupting truths the Alliance simply couldn't let circulate. And so, they had used the monster to silence Ensign Matthews.

But where had it come from? Chione wondered. The pipes were angling down, heading into the main structure of the station, and the walls closed in around them, narrowing the passageway in the process. They were heading for a dead end, and soon the route became too narrow for even Walks or Ralay to comfortably follow. *Could I be wrong, and it came from some-*

where else and waited here? Chione considered.

Walks seemed to be thinking the same thing. "There's no way it came from behind that wall. Those pipes wouldn't provide any wriggle room for a giant creature to get around."

I must be missing something, Chione thought. As a precaution, he headed further forward, until the pipes became too low even for him, put his nose to the ground, and began smelling every square centimetre of the floor. Every few seconds he would stop, and pull the scents over his Jacobson's organ, in a bid to extract every bit of information from his surroundings. The smells of machines were still there, along with traces of dust and spores the cleaners couldn't reach. Then, amongst the cacophony of aromas, something registered. He let his mind drag out the information. It wasn't chemical, it was pheromonal. *Toch sweat? Down here?* He turned around to where he'd picked up the scent, and tasted the air again, trying to home in on the source. Ralay and Walks watched, bemusement etched on their faces, as he turned in small circles, stopping every few steps to grimace. Eventually, there was no doubt. He looked to the others. "A Toch has touched the adjoining area of these two floor sections," he stated, pointing with his paw to where two large metal plates edged each other.

Walks got on his hands and knees and shone his torch directly where Chione had pointed. "Looks pretty solid to me." He stuck a fingernail into the minute gap, but nothing moved.

"What about a crowbar?" Ralay asked, looking back in the direction of the office.

"Should be a tool bag somewhere in there," Chione said.

Ralay disappeared and returned wielding what was indeed a crowbar. Chione stood back as she hooked its flattened section in the gap between the plates, and then she and Walks put their backs into it. Chione had the distinct impression that because of Walks' shoulder, Ralay was doing most of the levering. If she was, then the excursion wasn't even causing her to break a sweat, unlike Walks, who, despite the gloom, had gone a noticeable shade of purple. After a few choice swear words from Walks, there was a crunching, ripping sound, and the panel gave way, flipping dangerously over in the air, and landing with a loud clang at their feet.

Chione saw instantly what had caused them the problem. "There's a couple of bolts fixed to its underside,"

"Looks like someone was using it as a trap door," Walks said, between pronounced breaths. "No wonder we never found it."

The three peered over the lip of the hole, and Ralay and Walks pointed their torches down into the darkness below them. No sound reached Chione's ears, but the smell of Toch had gone up a notch. "He was definitely down here," he told the others.

"So down we go," Ralay said.

Walks did not look happy at that statement, and Chione could understand why. Agility was not his defining feature, thanks to advancing age and a knackered shoulder. Plus, though the man was not overweight, he wasn't exactly thin, and there wasn't a lot of breathing space heading down, as wires, pipes, and metal trussing made for cramped going.

If the scorpiad was using this route, it must have been while it was still small, Chione figured, having been privy to Tia's reading of its memory before she had killed it. Despite his initial belief that the creature had somehow been smuggled on board while in its scorpiad form, it had started off as a Human, with the seeds of the scorpiad genome sown within it. It had walked the corridors of the Scientia scouting its victims, before holing up and transforming into a scorpiad; growing larger as it awaited Tia's inevitable return to the station. He gave a shiver, knowing the pit he was staring into had been its home, up until the point it had outgrown it. And it had had company. Mister Ward, a grinning, egotistical telepath, and a thorn in Tia's side, had been its handler. How the man had ended up on the station was anyone's guess, but his body was the only thing remaining from Tia's fight with the Scorpiad. Subsequently, it had been frozen and stored. The knowledge that he was a clone, and an exceptionally well-made one at that, had led to his retention, as Tia still had questions over just who was making telepath clones.

Ralay too had seemed to have gotten wind of Walks' disinclination to go potholing. "You should stand guard up here while we head down," she said, giving no tonal indication as to whether she was taking pity on the man or not.

"Good idea," Walks answered, not bothering to hide the relief in his voice.

Ralay shone her torch down again, giving Chione an idea of his decent. His route mapped, he lightly dropped down, pouncing from pipe to beam and back again. Behind him, he could barely hear Ralay as she followed suit; ninja-like. They landed on the floor, side by side, as softly as each other. The torch beam highlighted a narrow crawl space, so that was where they headed. As they walked, the smell of Toch increased, as did other, less palatable odours: soured food, Human sweat... and excrement.

Even Ralay had noticed the smells. "I believe we have found their hideout," she announced.

Chione tested the air again, trying to delineate between the smells. "It's a bit of a muddle, but all I can sense is Human and Toch, so I guess that narrows things down."

They pressed forward, and eventually the blackness became less constrictive, and Chione used the torch's light to investigate his surroundings. The tunnel had opened into a marginally larger space, walled on three sides by piping. Ralay tried to stand, but the roof was formed from a huge duct, and was too low for her to get fully upright, meaning she had to stoop. After a couple of seconds, she gave up, and took a knee as she investigated the place. There were three strips of foam that Chione took for beds, and the floor was littered with an assortment of food wrappers and tins. He took a closer look. Most of the rubbish was from freeze-dried ship rations, used by those on long haul flights, but amongst the silver foil packages were more familiar products. Chione recognised the smell of a brand of tinned meat eaten by the Tochs, emanating from a discarded can, and several wrappers came from a Zerren candy that was liked by many of the Humans aboard. There were also some take-out tins that smelt spicy, and made Chione think of Liverden curry, and some paper bags that may, by evidence of crumbs, have held sandwiches. Close to one wall were several bottles of liquid, which Chione's nose told him not to go near. *Guess there's not much in the way of lavatorial facilities down here,* he thought, with a grimace, and he warned Ralay not to open the bottles.

"Where do you think they are?" Ralay muttered in the gloom.

Chione did his best to shrug. "I don't know, but if they had left the way we had come, you wouldn't have had that problem with the floor panel." He headed to the furthest corner of the room and found a small crawl space under one of the pipes, which lead in the opposite direction, and that was barely big enough for a Human to crawl through. "Whoever they are, they're not big, that's for sure," he told Ralay. "They also don't seem to be too bothered with being seen. A lot of this food stuff has been bought on the thoroughfare."

"So, we're looking for wiry and nondescript," Ralay reasoned.

"Well, a Toch wouldn't draw any glances because they're Toch, and should be on our side. As for any Human, either they're waiting it out elsewhere or, if they're out and about with a Toch, they won't get questioned because people will presume them to be an ally."

"There should be three assassins on board. Can you tell me what ratio we're dealing with?" Ralay asked.

Chione went back to the makeshift mattresses and sniffed each one in turn. One had the odour of a Toch, one had the odour of a Toch and a Human, and the third had the odour of two Humans. However, the degradation of the scents allowed him to surmise the occupants, both past and present. "There are two Tochs and one Human, all male," he told Ralay. "Further, the bed that now belongs to the Human was once the bed of a smug telepath by the name of Mister Ward." In the dim light, a normal Human wouldn't have noticed anything, but Chione's sensitive cat eyes picked up on Ralay's barely perceptible wince at the mention of the man's name. "The bed that is being used by the second Toch I can only assume was the bed of the man that became the scorpiad," Chione finished, keeping the fact that he'd seen Ralay flinch to himself. "What do we do now?" he asked her.

"Now we wait," she hissed.

****

Chione had no idea how long they'd been waiting; him curled up into a ball, tucked out of sight, and Ralay using the gloom to mask her crouched form. He had only briefly returned to the hatchway, to inform Walks of Ralay's plan to wait the assassins out. The security chief had, unsurprisingly, not been happy about that. He had wanted him, or his men, to take them down, but Chione knew the cramped nature of the place would put pay to that. Walks couldn't get down the tunnel, and any extra bodies that could, would quickly fill up the room, alerting their foe to their presence. Instead, they had to put their faith in Ralay's ability, not only as a fighter, but also to not kill them all.

So, Walks had replaced the flooring panel, effectively entombing them with the soon to arrive enemy, before heading to a quiet spot to radio for eyes on the ground to find two Tochs and a Human. Chione could have left, he knew he should have left, but he felt obliged to watch Ralay's back, and to be a witness to the outcome. He had only whispered one further thing to Walks, as the man had dragged the sheet of metal back over the hole. "Ralay knows Mister Ward." Walks had given a dark look and a slight nod, then the world had gone black.

The minutes ticked by. Chione began wondering what on earth he hoped to achieve by being a part of the waiting party. There were times when he forgot he was a cat, and that below the white fur was a fragile body, easily broken. He had claws, but they were ineffectual against a plasma blast, or a well-timed boot to the face. He hunkered down further in his chosen corner, his eyes barely peaking over his flank, and watched Ralay, while wondering what her deal was. The woman had been squatting for what seemed like hours yet showed no fatigue. She was just as alert, and ready to pounce, as when she'd first taken her spot. Chione figured a normal person's legs would have lost all feeling, but then he didn't think Ralay was a normal person, and not least because she was an Alliance-trained assassin. *Why would someone like her know Mister Ward?* There was only one answer to that question, and Chione figured that Walks had thought the same. *She's a telepath.* Ralay had said she would know the enemy when she saw them. Chione had assumed the reason to that was that their targets would move a certain way, much like Ralay. If they were mercenaries, they would be big and bulky, like Kan, and carry themselves with assuredness. If they were covert, close-combat assassins, they would be lither, and move with graceful ease, in much the same way as Ralay did. However, the more obvious reason now figured out was that as a telepath Ralay would be able to read their minds, at least when it came to any Humans.

Ralay may not have known why her parents were killed, but Chione had a good idea. *Her parents were killed because of her. I'd wager they'd known the truth of her and had tried to protect her from the very people who had taken her, namely the Alliance. What better person to add to their ranks than a telepathic assassin with nothing to lose?*

A noise interrupted his thoughts. It had been real, as Ralay's head had imperceptibly moved in its direction. Chione closed his eyes, not because he didn't want to see what was coming, but because he didn't want his reflective pupils giving him away.

The noise came again, this time accompanied by the low mutterings of echoey voices from beyond the pipes.

"I'll be glad when this is all done. I hate living like a rat." The voice was low, and Human.

"A few more days. We have their routines. Now we have to decide when to strike." The voice was slightly higher pitch, and with a Toch accent.

"Attack sooner. I see many more security when we head back. I think they know something." That speaker had an even thicker Toch accent, and a poorer grasp of the Human language.

"Who'd know?" asked the Human. "These damn rebels have no spies and no intel. They're blind."

Despite his eyes being shut, Chione could tell there'd been an increase in light level. One of them had a torch, and its beam was illuminating the narrow gap under the pipes.

"They have telepath woman creature," said the second Toch.

"Yes, but she is not on the station, and has been gone for some time," said the first Toch. "But you are correct, we should carry out our mission soon. Security has probably been alerted to something else, but their presence will cause us problems."

"Fine," grumbled the Human, his voice now barely feet away. "They have a big meeting in a couple of days, so we strike before then. It'll still be within our window"

"Agreed," said the Tochs, in unison.

There was a scrabbling sound, and Chione's world was flooded with torch light, and despite being in a well-hidden corner, he felt exposed by the sudden brightness. There was a grunt, as the closer individual, the Human, going by the loudness of his voice, wriggled through and up. Chione counted the seconds. He barely got to two when there was a muffled, slightly strangled noise, and a scuffing of shoes on the ground. *One down.* He dared a peek, opening one eye just a crack, and saw Ralay laying down the unconscious Human. His torch deftly caught in her hand. At first, Chione thought she might have broken the man's neck, such was the way his head lolled as she dropped him, but the subtle movement in his chest said otherwise. *Someone knows their pressure points.*

"I will be glad to sit down and have my meal," the first Toch was muttering, his voice getting louder; oblivious to what had just happened, "I haven't had hot food in days. We should have bought more than one canister of gas."

Chione shut his eyes again, just as more slithering noise reached his ears, signalling the alien was making his way into their hidey-hole. But something had gone wrong, he had either caught a glimpse of Ralay, or his fallen comrade's body, and the result was a yell of warning to his friend in the tunnel. Chione was wide-eyed now, watching as Ralay pounced, full force against the man. She knocked him to the far wall, dropping the first guy's torch in the process. The ground hit the torch's off button, and its beam went out. They continued their tussle in the dark, with the Toch as well-matched as Ralay in fighting ability. Blow was met by block, grip was met by twist, and foot was met by counterbalance. Whatever telepathic ability Ralay had, it seemed ineffectual against the rapid parries and deflections of the Toch, as his wiry, tribally tattooed arms mirrored her every move. Ralay had caught the Human by surprise, and had dealt with him quickly, but the Toch was not going quietly. Further, both parties were at an equal disadvantage thanks to the lowness of the ceiling, and occasionally a skull would clang as it hit the intrusive duct.

Movement caught Chione's eye, and he turned to see that the second Toch was making his way into the fray, and thanks to his friend's warning, he was armed with a long thin knife. Chione realised that despite her skill, Ralay was outnumbered, and the cramped, blacked-out nature of the arena was making it hard for her to get the upper hand, especially as she was now having to protect her back. All it would take was a well-timed shove from the fighting Toch to impale Ralay on the second fighter's thin blade. Chione knew he had to even the playing field, and quickly. The armed Toch made to slash at Ralay's side, but despite not having eyes in the back of her head, she somehow sensed the oncoming attack, and arched her back in time. *Definitely a telepath! Chione surmised. I guess his murderous intent was strong enough that she managed to pick up on it, even though she's not a Toch telepath.*

The blade cut through air, the Toch went marginally off balance, and that was when Chione struck. Like a cat out of hell, he launched himself across the room, and as he rushed past the Toch, he unleashed a paw full of his own little blades against the back of the assassin's exposed leg. As the unsuspecting alien unleashed a roar of surprise and pain, Chione darted back under the safety of the pipes. The creature's bare hoofed legs may have been covered in long fur, but that hair had failed to protect him from Chione's claws.

Chione watched as the Toch spun round, casting his blade wildly about at midriff level, instead of pointing it floorward, as he tried to pin down his second assailant. *He doesn't know what's hit him. He can't get a fix in the dark.* Chione took a chance, and attacked again, scooting between the Toch and the fighting duo. Again, his claws sliced into the back of the alien's calf, and the smell of fresh blood reached his nose as he slid to safety. He turned to inspect his damage, and noticed his target was favouring his undamaged leg. He grinned.

There was a thump, and Chione turned to see the other Toch hit the ground, blood spurting from his flat nose. Ralay had finally got her shot in and had floored her opponent. She turned to face her new attacker, while reaching for her own weapon with her now free hands. The Toch picked up on her movement and threw his knife. Ralay gave a stifled yelp as it sunk into her arm. At the same time, the Toch made to launch at her, intending to use her moment of distraction from the pain to his advantage. Chione read the scene as quickly and ran. But this time he didn't go for the ankle, there was too much movement, and he was in danger of being kicked, or missing his mark, instead, he headed for the torch. With a flick of his paw, he turned it round, aimed it at the Toch's face, and hit the switch. The light blinded Ralay's attacker, his purple eyes just as sensitive to sudden brightness as a Human's. He instinctively flinched and stepped back quickly to extricate himself from the beam, while forgetting the damage to his leg. He unbalanced. Ralay, pulling the knife out of her arm, sprung. There was a wet noise as the two hit the deck. For a second, neither moved, and Chione waited, his heart hammering in his chest. Then Ralay rolled off the man, and lay on the floor, breathing heavily, while holding her damaged arm.

Chione carefully padded over to her, taking notice of the knife that was now protruding from the Toch's stomach.

"You okay?" he asked Ralay.

"I've dealt with worse," she muttered, staring at the ceiling.

Chapter 26 - Walks

"Give me one good reason why I shouldn't ship you back off to Alliance space directly?" Walks spat at Ralay. It had been a couple of hours since they'd pulled the assassins out of their hidey-hole, one in a body-bag, and he was still mad as hell. It didn't help his mood that it was late, way past when he would've liked to have been asleep, and he was suffering the head-banging effects of only having had one coffee the entire stress-filled day.

Ralay had been patched up, and she was sat before him in one of the offices used for interviewing criminals, with her arm in a sling. Chione had sequestered himself on a spare chair and was occupied with grooming the grime off himself. *How the hell does his Human side deal with having to do something like that?* Walks shook his head, trying to ignore the distraction, and got back to his fury at hand. "Why the hell didn't you tell me you were a telepath?" *Should've listened to my gut. Should always listen to my gut.* "Have you been happily rummaging through my mind all this time? Who the hell do you think you are?" he demanded.

Ralay looked at him with her cold eyes. "Are you just going to keep throwing questions at me, or are you actually going to let me answer them and defend myself?"

Walks ground his teeth. "Then answer."

"Those weren't the only assassins, there's still another on his or her way, and several more planet side. I am your best shot at finding them, and you know it, so cutting me loose is the last thing you want to do. Secondly, I didn't tell you I was a telepath for just this reason; you freaking out and threatening to throw me off the station. Your own paranoia would've trumped reason and would've led to the deaths of several people on this station. And as for me reading your mind, you have nothing to fear there. I'm not that strong a telepath. I can only pick up on surface thoughts and emotions. Right now, I can tell you're as pissed as hell, but I have no idea what you had for breakfast, not unless you start thinking about it."

"Reconstituted scrambled eggs on toast and coffee," Chione piped up.

Walks shot him a warning look. He was furious, and he desperately wanted to throw Ralay off the station, but she was right about them needing her to find the other Alliance killers. However, he wasn't about to trust her claims about her lack of telepathic skill. "And where does Mister Ward fit into your life?" he shot at her. He had met the grinning telepath only once, when he'd been thoroughly questioned by him as a precursor to Zerra's invasion, to make sure he wouldn't be a problem when the time came to subjugate the race. Luckily for Walks, his interrogation by the telepaths had been before the rebels had taken up arms, and Shar had given him the chance to gain a spine and stay and fight. Otherwise, if there had been a hint of wavering, he'd have been packed up, sent back to Alliance space, and 're-educated' over what it meant to be an Alliance man. That is if they were feeling particularly kind. Considering his previous insurrection, he would have probably ended up sucking vacuum. As it was, there was also a frozen popsicle version of Mister Ward in the Medicentre's morgue, so Walks knew it hadn't been the definitive version of the telepath that he'd met. Especially as Tia had turned his first encountered Mister Ward's brain to mush.

Walks still remembered the skin-crawling sensation he'd felt as the telepath's mute partner, Mister Knight, had surreptitiously waded through his brain, as Mister Ward himself had thrown random questions at him to unfetter his mind. Whether the sensation had been a real feeling, or purely psychosomatic, Walks had no clue. Only another telepath would register a mental incursion, and Walks was pretty sure he wasn't a telepath. Still, he had to wonder if there was a sixth sense thing going on, and he wondered if the lack of sensation meant Ralay had avoided his mind. However, he wasn't about to give her the benefit of the doubt just yet.

Ralay was less than forthcoming to his question. "What makes you think I know a Mister Ward?" she said, coming the innocent.

"Well, first off you're a telepath," Walks reminded her.

"And secondly, I saw you react to his name when I mentioned it in the tunnel," Chione added.

Ralay threw a rare glare Chione's way, but the feline ignored it, and went back to grooming.

"Fine," she relented. "Yes, I know him because I'm a telepath. Every telepath knows him. He indoctrinates us, keeps an eye on our training, and admonishes us if we're not up to par." The word 'admonishes' hung in the air. "And he takes special interest in those who are assigned to specialised areas...like assassination. I got to see a lot of him. A little too much of him...."

Ralay's last sentence made Walks feel unnecessarily uncomfortable. He didn't like the connotation behind the words, and it backed up the nasty feeling he'd got from the man. He chose not to press Ralay any further on the matter, but even though her words had taken the wind out of his anger's sails, he still couldn't bring himself to trust her. "And I'm supposed to just believe you when you say you can't read my thoughts? How do I know you're not lying about that?"

"I would have thought I'd have been able to buy your trust by helping you capture those assassins, but if proof is what you need, ask that barman. You seem to trust him more than me."

Walks exchanged a look with Chione. "Talon? Why him?" he asked.

"Because he's a telepath too."

257

****

Despite the late hour, Walks had decided to answer the call of his body and was downing some much-needed caffeine. "You honestly didn't know Talon was a telepath," Walks asked Chione, between gulps of scorching liquid, as they waited for the man himself to arrive in the office after his shift.

Chione shook his head vigorously. "I'm as surprised as you. All these years...I never knew. I don't think anybody does. I mean, there's never been a whiff of gossip on Tartarus, or this station."

"Tia would've known. Wouldn't she?"

"Definitely," Chione confirmed, "but she kept this information very close to her chest."

Walks saw Talon enter the central office, caught his eye, and beckoned to him.

"So how are you going to deal with this?" Chione asked.

"As he's a telepath, I guess the only way is to get to the point, 'cause he's probably gonna see my question coming a mile off."

Talon entered the office, caught a glimpse of Chione, and looked at Walks. "This looks serious," he said, with his usual hint of sarcastic amusement.

Walks closed the office door behind Talon before speaking. "So, are you a telepath or not?"

Talon's reaction was not what he'd envisioned. He'd expected either outright denial, or an angry rant. Instead, Talon simply closed his eyes and smiled. "I guess Ralay dobbed me in," he said, in a voice of someone who'd just been asked the time, rather than being asked if they were a dangerous aberration.

"And considering that silent stand-off you had with her in your bar, I'm more than inclined to believe her."

Talon nodded his head in understanding. "She was trying to get a fix on my thoughts. I blocked her and pushed back; harder. She didn't like that."

"She claims she's not a strong telepath, and that you can vouch for that."

Talon gave a shrug. "I guess you could say she's about one or two steps above an empath. She can read emotions and surface thoughts, but that's about it. She certainly couldn't block a stronger telepath."

"And what about you?" Walks asked, feeling decidedly uncomfortable at the idea of secret telepaths running about unchecked on the station.

"To be honest, I'm probably not that much stronger than Ralay. Again, surface thoughts only. It's just that thanks to Tia's manipulation, I can block and redirect telepathic intrusion, much like everyone else who works for her." He gave a sideways look at Chione.

"And nobody else on Tartarus knew you were a telepath?" Chione asked.

Talon didn't bat an eyelid at being addressed by a talking cat. "Tia left it up to me whether I'd tell people. In the end, we agreed that keeping it secret would be beneficial, same as with your little secret. The less who knew, the less who would find out. For all I know, there could be other telepaths aboard Tartarus who've decided the same thing."

"How you've always managed to stay one step ahead of people is becoming clearer," Walks grumbled.

Talon smiled amiably. "It certainly helps to know that someone's coming for you before they appear in front of you. It may not be much of a heads-up, but every second helps. But how did you figure out she was a telepath."

"I didn't," Walks admitted, "he did," he said, nodding at Chione.

Talon gave the cat a questioning look.

"I mentioned Mister Ward, and she looked like she'd suddenly developed a bad taste in her mouth," he explained. "It was brief, but noticeable. That and she managed to dodge a blade coming at her from behind, in the dark, while she was fighting another assailant. And for how long have you known I could speak?"

"I overheard you talking to Aben shortly before we shipped off for the dead world."

"Dammit, I thought I'd smelt you, but when I headed round the corner there was no-one in the corridor."

"You're not the only one who knows the Scientia inside and out," Talon smirked.

"Trust a smuggler to know all the hidey-holes," Chione countered.

"Okay, we're getting off topic here," Walks interjected. "Ralay, can we trust her?"

Talon cocked his head. "She's tricky to get a reading on. She's cold, calculating, and extremely guarded, but overall, I got no hint of deceit. Despite everything, I believe she's on the up and up."

"Great, that means she can sit in on the interview with the Human, and hopefully we'll get some usable information out of him."

****

The Human assassin sat hunched in his seat, purple bruising blossoming around his neck and throat where Ralay had worked her magic to bring him to his knees. He was securely handcuffed to the floor by way of his wrists and ankles, and he glared at Walks and Ralay; him leaning against the wall, her sitting upright and prim in a chair to Walks' right. Despite Ralay's svelte size, the man was thinner than her, and was compact and wiry. Ralay believed his trade lay in stealth, and that he was a hunter, not a direct fighter; silently stalking his prey before ambushing them. His more combatant-able friend had been dumped in solitary confinement, after having his nose patched up, but with Toch telepaths not being a thing, he got to wait for Tia's not-so-gentle touch. However, Walks was hoping that he'd glean all he needed from the Human opposite him before Tia showed her face again.

Ralay had confirmed she'd never met the man before, and Walks was sure he'd never seen him around the station, *but then I'd never seen Javin until I'd met him.* He had dirty black hair, deep brown eyes, and an awful lot of stubble. He was also ripe, which made Walks wonder how he expected to creep up on someone. *He'd need one hell of a head wind.* Subsequently, the atmosphere in the interview room had turned rather fusty.

"So, let's begin," Walks announced. "Name?"

"Fuck you traitor,"

"Kim Salcedo," Ralay translated, her eyes never wavering from him.

Kim Salcedo's angry face rounded on her. "A fucking telepath? Are you serious? That's against the law!"

"Whose law?" Walks asked, benignly.

"The Orion Alliance."

"Well, I've got news for you. First, this is Zerren space, and the powers that be are more than happy to have a telepath attend an interview when it regards a matter of national security. Second, the Alliance have never been one for rules, so telepaths in interviews are fair game. And third, just count yourself lucky that ain't Tia sat over there, because you'd already be a mindless corpse if she was." Kim spat on the floor at the mention of Tia's name. "Don't do that," Walks said, casually.

"You're all a bunch of treasonous arseholes who'll burn in hell for turning against the Alliance," Kim ranted.

Walks waved his hand in answer. "Yeah, yeah, we get that a lot. Believe me, I went through hell enough when I was with the Alliance. I consider anything else a vacation." Kim looked like he'd just caught a whiff of himself. "So, tell me, what was the plan?"

"Why don't you ask her?"

"Because I'm trying to give you a chance to co-operate you idiot. Command is all for flushing your worthless arse into space, and I'm more than happy to be the one who presses the door release. A little co-operation, and you could end up happily ever after in a mining penal colony. Who knows, you could even get the chance to escape and live a full and sadistic life somewhere far away from here." That was only part of the reason for Walks chatting to the man. The other part was that Ralay needed Walks to ask the questions to get the answers at the forefront of Kim's mind, otherwise she couldn't read them. However, he wasn't about to let Kim know just how weak a telepath she was, otherwise he'd laugh in their faces and never open up.

"Fuck you." Kim said, trying to cross his arms in finality, and failing miserably when the chains wouldn't let him.

"Seems to be the phrase of the day," Walks said, rolling his eyes in exasperation. "Would you do me the honours?" he asked Ralay.

"They were sent here to take out Ken'va, Captain Sin'ma, and Lieutenant Leo Jackson in a coordinated strike. Though as Lieutenant Jackson is off station, they'd shifted their focus to Commander Veth Herrin."

Walks had a strong urge to punch the man in the face but tried to keep his air of cool and calm professionalism. "What about those on the surface? Who are their targets?"

Kim refused to give him eye contact.

"He doesn't know. Their missions were kept secret from each other."

Dammit. "And what of the fourth man coming to this station? What's his mission?"

Kim gave a nasty grin.

Walks turned to Ralay, who was showing some rare emotion, and wasn't looking happy. "He's coming to blow us all to hell."

Chapter 27 - Sin'ma

"There is a suicide bomber coming?" Despite the late hour, Sin'ma had convened an urgent meeting, and was sat in his office surrounded by Lieutenant Walker, Ken'va, Commander Herrin, and the questionable woman his security chief had introduced as Ralay. "Do we know what species?"

"Yes, and the prisoner didn't know," Walks told him, regret and exhaustion etched on his face. "All Ralay could drag out of him was that his mission was separate to the assassins. They were supposed to take care of you three, bail, and in the resulting panic, in comes the bomber as a final F-U to the rebels."

"That information, combined with what I already knew about another assassin being in transit, means you only have a couple of days before he hits," Ralay added.

Sin'ma sat back and groaned. "It could be anyone, any face, and we would not know until it was too late."

"All my men are on high alert, and all newcomers and papers are being thoroughly scrutinised," Walks assured him. "Could we get more security personnel up from Zerra to help us increase our coverage?"

"If we fail to identify this man or woman, then even more people will die," Sin'ma countered. "So far, we have had one cloned telepath, one mass-murdering scorpiad, and three assassins come aboard, all unchallenged. The only person to send any kind of alarm up is this woman," he gestured at Ralay, "and she walked unhindered into your department."

Walks gave him a look of daggers. "Are you saying my men

are incompetent?" he growled.

Sin'ma winced. "No. I am saying it does not matter how many checks we do, we are operating blind, and a determined individual will find their way onto this vessel. Forged papers, altered faces, back doors we do not even know about. Not to mention the fact the Alliance is employing combatants from among our own allied races."

"What news of the Tochs?" Asked Ken'va, trying to wrestle Walks' glare from Sin'ma.

"I sent their mugshots and DNA to their version of central intelligence. Both were known to them but had dropped off the grid. The man Ralay skewered was a known hitman, who evaded capture a few years back. The guy sulking in solitary was known only through his DNA and is linked to several on- and off-world murders. They want him shipped back to their world to face charges."

"That will not be happening," Sin'ma stated. Everyone nodded in agreement. They all knew his fate.

"So how are we going to deal with this bomber?" Commander Herrin asked, his orange eyes searching the room's occupants for an answer. "We could start evacuating the station, but that would take days, and probably lead to widespread panic. And if we go into lockdown again, the same could be true."

"Dammed if we do, dammed of we don't," Walks muttered. Sin'ma agreed.

"I think we can assume," Ken'va put in, "the bomber is not going to helpfully step aboard already wearing his vest. Therefore, either this bomb is already aboard hidden somewhere, or he will need to make his own."

"I'll get the science geeks to go explosive hunting with their scanners when this is done," Walks said. "And I'll make sure Munitions, Engineering, and Tech Ops tighten security around their equipment. It might not stop the guy, but it might slow him down if he ends up having to resort to stripping the station for parts."

Sin'ma nodded. "Good thinking," he said, trying to undo the damage caused by his inadvertent insult. He didn't think for one minute Walks' security team were useless, far from it, it was that Sin'ma knew all too well how devious the Alliance was. His thoughts went to something Bell'ka had once said. *They are slimy enough to make it through the smallest of holes.* As far as he was concerned, she wasn't far wrong.

The newcomer to their meeting, Ralay, who had been sat back, looking lost in thought, suddenly spoke. "How about an amnesty?"

"To whom?" Sin'ma asked, intrigued. He still wasn't one-hundred percent sure about the woman, despite Walks' support of her trustworthiness. Her presence unsettled him, not least because she was a telepathic killer sat just metres from him. There was a detached coldness about her. She barely showed emotions, or adjusted her vocalisations accordingly, and it put Sin'ma on edge. He had no attraction to the Human species, mainly because he found their hairless skin off-putting; yet it was that same lack of hair that he appreciated when dealing with the species, because it meant their facial cues were easier to read. Humans had a lot of facial expressions, quite often multiples for the same emotion, yet much of the time, Ralay appeared to display just one expression. He believed it was what the Humans referred to as 'poker-face', and her dark eyes and red mouth were inscrutable. Getting a fix on Ralay was like trying to read between the lines on a blank piece of paper. Even Walks seemed to stare a little too hard at her, as if he too were hunting for the briefest flicker to add context to her words.

Ralay had found and neutralised three men who were intent on murdering three key members of Command, which pointed to her being somewhat on their side. However, that didn't mean she couldn't or wouldn't suddenly do a one-eighty and stab them all in the back. She had come aboard because she had been sent; sent to kill. Oddly, Walks hadn't been forthcoming over whom her target was to have been. *Does Walks know, and has chosen not to say? And if not tell us her target, then why tell us we were the others'?* Walks' remarks of an independent corroborator to her trustworthiness hadn't lessened Sin'ma's worry any. In fact, it irked him. He was left not knowing who the corroborator was, and what threat they might mean to the station. *There are too many secrets and lies going on. I am the captain, I am in change of this station, and as such, I should know everything there is to know.* He wondered if it had something to do with Tia. *She is getting worse with her covert behaviour, to the point of becoming like the Karee. Am I to sit quietly by as she and her men work in the shadows, and if not, how do I broach the subject with her?*

"To any underground empaths and telepaths." Ralay stated, as an answer to his question. "Although many races aren't so militantly controlling over their telepaths as the Alliance are, they may still feel the need to hide their abilities for fear of being labelled as freaks or being accused of reading people's minds. There are several species aboard who would fit the criteria and would help reduce our odds if allowed to join security on patrol. They may be able to pick up on who the bomber is if he's of the same species."

"Who would that give us?" Sin'ma asked Ken'va, having no clue which races could be hiding such a thing.

The old priest took a few minutes to think. "Other than Humans, the Panns and Liverdens exhibit telepathy to varying degrees. The Qlaths and Yandakes have something similar, but I believe those individuals get no stronger than a weak empath."

Commander Herrin pulled a face "That's not much help," the Ciberian said. "The Panns are a peaceful people and aren't exactly going to blow us up. And the Qlaths and Yandakes barely ever set foot on this station. If one of them suddenly turned up, everyone would know about it."

"Not sure I agree with you about the Panns being peaceful," Walks chimed in. "I know several are serving on other species' battleships, choosing to go against their own society to fight in this war, but the rest I reckon is true."

Damn, Sin'ma thought.

There was silence as everyone mulled this information over. It became apparent that no-one had anything more helpful to add. "It would not hurt I suppose," Sin'ma said. "Like Ralay says, they may not be able to read the minds of an alien species, but that is not to say they might not pick up on something."

"It's a valid possibility," Ralay stated. "I may not be able to read foreign minds, but I can sometimes pick up on things if the owner's intentions and emotions are strong enough. The desire to slaughter hundreds of people may be enough to sense."

The others silently nodded in agreement.

"We have little to go on, so every extra body helping is one extra tiny chance to avert disaster," Sin'ma added.

"I have a contact with eyes everywhere," Walks added. "He'll get them watching for any questionable goings-on. Chances are, if this guy or gal needs explosives, he'll try to buy some, and we'll get lucky."

"Perhaps there lies the answer," Ken'va mulled out loud, suddenly sitting upright, his eyes shining as an idea coalesced in his mind. "As Walks said, we can make the bomber's task as awkward as possible, so why not turn that to a greater advantage to us? We can block his every route towards equipment and explosives. We secure our tech, remove ingredients like fertiliser off the station, and guide him down one road, a road that leads to our own chosen seller of explosives. Then, when he makes the buy, we will have him."

"And I know just the man you want," Walks grinned.

Chapter 28 - Walks

"**C**an't do it."

Walks looked gob-smacked at Talon. "What do you mean you can't do it? I promised Sin'ma you were the man for the job, the man to help save this station, and you're saying no? What the Hell?"

Talon raised a placating hand. "It's not that I won't help you, it's that I genuinely can't. By now, the Alliance knows who Tia's closest allies are, and there's no doubt I'll be on that list. Hell, my handsome mug's on any number of wanted posters thanks to my multiple indiscretions from way back. The dude gets one look at me, or hears one mention of my name, and he'll bolt."

"Ugh, you're right," Walks said, taking a seat on a stool at the bar, and putting his head in his hands.

"That doesn't mean there aren't other options open to us," Talon said, in an upbeat tone. Walks raised his head and looked questioningly at him. "We just need to find a suitable, nondescript face to play a suitable, nondescript arms dealer."

"A Human wouldn't do it," Walks said, thinking aloud. "Guaranteed the Humans that've come over to our side will be known, or at least won't be trusted."

"Agreed. So, we need an alien, someone good under pressure, and who preferably knows their stuff." Talon suddenly gave a smile.

"Who?" Walks asked, reading it.

"A guy who works weapons on Tartarus. Goes by the name of Azan. He's a Beeden, so from a species that technically has no beef with the Alliance. Plus, Beedens are hard to tell apart, so there's little chance the bomber will know he's talking to one of Tia's men. And as he works weapons, when it comes to knowing the subject, he's well versed. As for staying calm under pressure, there'll be no problem with that. Guy's got a better poker-face than a slab of marble."

"And he'll help?"

"Damn right he'll help. An order from Shar could have the guy mopping the outside of the station with no suit on."

"Let's hope there's no need for that," Walks said, drily. "Don't suppose Shar can come back too? I know he's on watch on your ship but having him skulking around the munitions bay will probably go some way to stopping the guy from raiding our weapons supply."

"What, you think I'm not scary enough?" Talon asked, with mock hurt.

Walks really wanted to say yes to that. Truth told; he did find Talon scary. Not in a brutish way, more in a quiet, never know when he'll flip out and burn everything to the ground, kind of way. It didn't help that he knew the man was a telepath, albeit one who couldn't read his deepest thoughts. Instead, he answered, "grow a second pair of arms and a few kilos extra muscle, then we'll talk scary."

Talon smirked, picked up a pad from behind the bar, and began tapping away. "There," he said, finishing up. "Just sent a message for Shar to give Azan a quick briefing, and for them to head over. I reckon they'll be here within the next twenty-four hours, although I expect they'll take separate ships. They're clued-up on how to behave during covert missions, and we've got a couple of long-distance craft on board, so Azan can use one of them to evade suspicion. Meantime, I'll drop a few subtle hints that there may be an arms dealer of questionable loyalty heading through, that way, when the bomber arrives and begins asking questions, he'll get pointed in the right direction."

Walks nodded in understanding. "Great, now I just have to

make sure every possible explosive chemical remains out of reach."

"How's that going?"

"There are an awful lot of alien races with sweet teeth who are not going to be happy. Add on to that all the random chemicals in the labs, chemicals the scientists have no problems using daily, but can be lethal in the wrong hands, and we've got one hell of a clear-out on our hands. A lot of people are going to start getting real grumpy real soon. Plus, the plants in the arboretum are in for a few rough days with no nutrients."

"Greater good and all that," Talon said, giving Walks a wink.

"It's all right for you, you're not the one who's going to be getting it in the neck when a scientist can't run an experiment, or some Toch has to go without dessert."

"You'll survive."

Walks gave him his best aggravated expression, slid off his stool, and stomped out of the Bar. *Yeah, I'll survive, but with how many health problems?* He felt himself roll his shoulder and caught it mid-movement. *Dammit, that's getting to be a habit.* He knew the discomfort he was feeling was psychosomatic, and that it didn't actually hurt more when he was stressed, but that knowledge didn't stop the pain from feeling any less real.

He headed back to his quarters and stopped mid stride as he rounded the final bend. There, curled up outside his door, was a large white cat. "Chione?" he said, as he approached. Chione, being in a public area, didn't answer. He stood, gave a back-arching stretch, and sat back down before Walks, staring up at him with his luminous green eyes.

Walks opened his door, and the feline followed him in. Once in his sanctum, he addressed Chione again. "Is something up?"

"No. Just thought I'd come by and see if there's any news."

Chione was noticeably giving Walks' quarters the once over. It made Walks feel self-conscious over the piles of clothing on the floor, and the undertone of mustiness he'd got used to over the years, but that was probably all too fresh to Chione's delicate nose. "No news," he said. "Well, other than the fact there's going to be a mad bomber loose on the station any day now, and our fate is in the hands of some guy of Tia's called Azan." As he spoke, he quickly picked some clothes off the floor, and threw them in the general direction of the laundry hamper in his bedroom. Most of the stuff didn't even make it half the distance. Walks swore and began cleaning up the trail. Meantime, Chione had hopped onto his coffee table, and seemed to be watching him with mild amusement. *If I'm like this with a cat, gods help me if I ever manage to persuade a woman to set foot in here.*

Chione finally broke the silence. "Azan? He works weapons on Tartarus. What's his hand in this?"

Walks returned from his bedroom, gave his hands a rinse, and turned on his coffee machine. "We're setting up an old-fashioned sting," he explained, as he waited for his coffee to brew. "We're making it so his only choice is to buy explosives from a dealer, and that dealer will be Azan. He's an unknown face who, according to Talon, knows his stuff."

"He certainly does," Chione confirmed. "He used to be a weapons dealer himself."

"Talon failed to mention that fact," Walks grumbled, pouring himself a cup of caffeine-infused sludge. He caught Chione licking his lips, and without thinking, grabbed a bowl, filled it with water, and deposited it in front of Chione.

The cat took a few laps before speaking. "Chances are, Talon didn't think it was relevant. Azan knows his stuff, and that was the important thing. His past is unimportant. Same for all of us. What we do now is what matters."

Walks knew Chione's present life was in reparation for his past deeds. He may have played his part in the creation of the scorpiad soldiers, but even before he'd met Tia, he'd been trying to make amends. To Walks, his sentence seemed overly inflated, especially as he'd helped create Tia, who was now a champion for the rebels. He figured without her a lot more blood would have been spilt over the years. *But then, Chione seems to be on a longer leash than most of the people who work for her. Is that his perk for having already turned to good?* "How long do you think you have left of your sentence?" he asked, without thinking.

Chione seemed to get downcast at the question. "Who knows. The thing is, before, it never really bothered me. Ten years, a hundred years, it didn't matter. I'd already served so much time, and was used to a prolonged existence, but that was because then, I had my friends to keep me going. I had Tia's companionship, and then I had Aben's too. Now they're both gone. Aben because some arsehole murdered him, and Tia because she and her world are changing fast. I'm kind of left wondering where I'm supposed to fit in to all of this, and whether I'm still needed."

Having evidently touched a fresh wound, Walks felt guilty for asking his question. "As far as I'm concerned, you're still needed." he said, truthfully, trying to raise Chione's spirits. "Without you, we would probably have never known about the scorpiad until it was too late. Without you, chances are we wouldn't have found the assassins nest until it was too late." Walks knew that even with Ralay's help, he wouldn't have found where the assassins had been hiding. Instead, they would have been wandering the miles of corridors, putting their hopes on randomly crossing the murderers' paths. Had it not been for Chione's past recollection, and sense of smell, the trio of killers would have slipped quietly past them, to assassinate two top men in Command, and another from the GR. "Frankly, if anybody should be sitting behind the Chief of Security's desk, it's you," he added.

Chione managed to give a little crooked smile. "I doubt that."

"I'm serious. Hell, if a glorified cat in the form of a Ciberian can be in command of this station, a real cat can be in Security. Let's be honest, the only real difference between you and Herrin is height." Walks was feeling a great amount of pity for Chione, and it struck him that he was seeing much of himself in the feline. They were both very much alone; Walks, because his job took up his waking hours, and Chione, because he was a talking cat who had lost his two closest friends. *At least at the end of the day I get to come home to my quarters, but what about Chione? He either wanders about the thoroughfare on the lookout for scraps, grabs a filthy rat from down below, or he relies on Leo to drop something off for him. Or at least he did until Leo buggered off. He needs a proper home, somewhere he can feel secure again. It could help him regain a sense of purpose.* He thought about having a word with Leo and Pra'cha, but dismissed that idea quickly, realising they had each other to attend to. *They don't need a five-hundred-year-old man-cat prowling around their quarters while they're being intimate.*

Chione was quietly lapping at his bowl of water again. His hunched body making him appear even more dejected. Walks decided to proffer the hand of friendship. "I was about to eat. You want anything? I've got some stuff that's vaguely meat-like in the freezer, and if we're lucky, it might be edible."

Chione perked up a little at his offer. "I wouldn't mind, if that's no trouble."

"No trouble at all," Walks said, returning to his kitchen. "Pra'cha been keeping you fed?"

"A bit, but she just dumps the food and runs. Too busy and too clueless, although that second one isn't her fault."

"She's never spoken to you then?"

Chione shook his head. "It doesn't appear Zerrens have the same desire to talk to animals that most Humans do. I guess they have more literal minds, and don't see the point if we can't answer them back. I doubt it would matter if I was a real cat. As long as they're fed and watered, have a roof over their heads, and a warm blanket to sleep on, they're okay to be left a while. When you're a sentient person who needs verbal interactions to stay sane, then it's pretty frustrating."

Walks gave a sympathetic nod as he fished out a ready meal that contained the Zerren equivalent of poultry. He put it to cooking, grabbed a packet of dried tuber mash, and threw the powdered contents into a bowl filled with water. In a bid to make it taste half decent, he tipped a load of dried Liverden spices into the mix. When everything was ready, he divided the poultry between two plates, then filled his up with the mash, and the smattering of veg that came with the ready meal. He popped the meat-only plate in front of Chione and took his own seat. "Sorry, it's not exactly haute cuisine."

"It smells way more edible than the food Pra'cha has been feeding me, and I'll wager it'll taste heavenly in comparison. Those cans of gourmet pet food she bought for me; dear gods the stuff tastes vile!"

Walks laughed. "What's in it?"

"I have no idea, she always takes the empty tin away, and the full ones are tucked in a cupboard that only height and opposable thumbs can reach. It tastes like I image a combination of Rolst pickled Mowda-fish, raw eggs, lemons, and depression tastes like." Walks inadvertently choked on his food. "The rate things are going, I'm going to end up losing condition rather than gaining any. I'm getting this close to breaking my vow of silence with her." He lifted his paw and curved his dew and digit claws towards each other to highlight his point. Walks chuckled at the imitated Human gesture.

The two men chatted of inconsequential things as they finished up their meals. Walks of his discovery of the Diner and Javin. Chione of the dangers of Zerren cats. Walks of getting his hands on a packet of gourmet Pann 'coffee'. Chione of missing coffee, and what it would do to him if he drank it while in his cat form. The conversation continued randomly as Walks cleared away their dishes and poured himself another coffee. A glance at the clock on his wall told him it was time for him to consider going to bed. Chione picked up on his gesture, and looked at the time too, but Walks decided to make the offer before Chione could say anything.

"Look, you're more than welcome to stay here for tonight. And in all honesty, I don't mind if you want to use my quarters for a base of operations, at least until you decide on a direction. I'll just tell Pra'cha you turned up on my doorstep and seem disinclined to leave."

"I don't want to intrude," Chione said. He was doing his best to be polite and easy-going, but Walks picked up on the tinge of hope and relief in his voice.

"Nonsense, it was nice to have someone to chat to. It took my mind off all the doom and gloom. Besides, now if you find out something important, I won't have to hear it second hand."

"So now you want me to become your spy?" Chione asked, with a hint of mock hurt.

"Which would you rather be, a spy who gets to feed on poultry and steak, or a non-spy who gets to eat a can of sadness every day?"

"When you put it like that...."

"So, it's settled. You can stay here for the time being and pay your way by keeping your ears close to the ground." The arrangement made; Walks put a folded blanket on his chair for Chione to curl up on and went to bed a lot happier than he'd done so in a long time. Even stumbling across Javin hadn't put him in such a good mood. As he lay in bed, drifting off, he began to fathom why. He had gained an important friend. Sure, he had a friend in Shar, but the two men were very different personality-wise, and as Shar was an alien, they had little in common. Their social life revolved around sharing a drink and gossiping about the war. Javin had proven to be a handy friend too. They had similar interests, enjoyed unhealthy food, and could gossip about Human things, but when it came to the intricacies of the war, Walks had to remain mute for fear of secrets being spread. With Chione, he had both. Thanks to his past, Chione could talk of Human things, but was also a part of the inner circle of those who were facing the war, so Walks had someone he could also confide in. True, before Chione there had been Talon, but as the man was a way-past borderline criminal, Walks didn't think it was a clever idea to get too chummy with him, for his sake as well as Talon's. For Walks, things were looking up again. *Which means a shit storm is probably heading rapidly my way!*

****

The next morning, Walks was back to his humdrum and angina-inducing life as Chief of Security, though in better spirits than he had been of late. He was reading a report confirming the emergency removal of four tonnes of fertiliser from the arboretum, plus a host of other chemicals from the labs, when the warning alarm on his computer went off. Crap!

Val'ka's head popped around the open door to his office a moment later, his eyes notably wider than usual. "A suspected Beeden arms dealer has just stepped on board. What do we do?"

All security personnel knew there was a possible suicide bomber on the way, and their patrols and checks had been cranked up in response. However, Walks hadn't told his subordinates about the sting. As far as he was concerned, the fewer people who knew the better. Still, it didn't make him feel any more comfortable about being less than truthful with the young Zerren. "Did the sensors pick anything up from him?" he asked, casually.

Val'ka shook his head. "No. He reads clean. Very clean. If he has been anywhere near explosives, it has not been recently."

"So, what makes us think he's a suspected arms dealer?"

"Word of mouth," his lieutenant answered, truthfully. "There's been gossip on the station that such an individual was heading our way, and there was some mention of identifying clothing. And now this Beeden matching the descriptions has turned up."

"Well, we can't arrest a man based on a suspected past based on clothing alone." Walks stated. "There's no written proof on file that he's an arms dealer, nor is there any chemical proof that he's an arms dealer. Right now, all we can do is keep an eye on him."

Val'ka gave Walks a look loaded with suspicion, but he didn't argue. Instead, he asked, "Should I put a call out for others to monitor his movements?"

"That would be an excellent idea. Send out a verbal warning to our people's communicators."

"That is very public. People could overhear."

"Is it? I suppose they could. Still, can't be helped."

Val'ka stared hard at Walks out of the corner of his yellow eyes. Walks said nothing. *Come on lad, I know you're not stupid.*

His lieutenant reached an internal conclusion, though his look of intense suspicion didn't let up. "I will make the call."

Walks nodded, satisfied. A couple of minutes later, his own communicator went off, and a text message from Talon flashed up, confirming what he already knew; the dealer had arrived.

Walks sent back a quick acknowledgement but made no further input. He put his trust in Talon to continue dropping minor hints to his more talkative contacts, and that, combined with any eavesdroppers to the security message, was all they had to get the information circulating organically. Then it was a matter of waiting. In the meantime, the general populous was receiving official messages. One mentioned a metal frag-ment contaminant in the sugar supply, hence its removal, and another was regards to the fertiliser, and the possibility of it having a plant-rotting fungus. They were unassuming titbits of news that when seeded, would frustrate the bomber, and send him one way.

Nor did Walks think Munitions would get raided for its stock of weapons. Everyone knew who reigned down there, and he was already back on his throne. *Only a desperate idiot would take on a four-armed homicidal lizard for the sake of a haul of explosives.* Engineering was a bit more problematic. Kan was no longer aboard the station, so his reputation couldn't be used to protect the department. Instead, plain-clothed armed security personnel had been quietly added to the roster to keep an eye on things. In reality, Engineering and Tech Ops had no explosive materials, just wires, tools, and other electronic equipment that could easily be found around the station, but which were useless without an explosive component. But as Walks had said, they wanted to give the bomber as awkward a time as possible when it came to making the weapon, thereby pushing them towards someone who could provide them with the whole thing.

Walks' ultimate trust lay in an alien he had never spoken to or seen. Both Talon and Chione had assured him he was up to the job, but their words didn't loosen the knot of worry in his stomach. Without him thinking, his hand went to a draw in his desk, the one usually home to a bottle of inappropriately strong alcohol. The bottle was long gone, and Walks snatched his hand away before it touched the handle. *No! I need to keep a clear head.* But the problem was, he was once again faced with waiting; waiting until things played out in a way that was beyond his control. He hated the not knowing, and the impotence he felt over the situation. *At least during an old-fashioned stake-out I could be watching suspects, taking notes, or snapping photos. All I can do with this is sit and pray it works.* The sense of suspense was already making his skin itch, and the message from Talon had barely arrived five minutes ago. *I wish I at least had eyes on him, then I could know if he talks to anyone.* However, Walks knew that was the last thing he should do, as loitering in proximity to Azan could spook the bomber. Then it hit him. *Chione!*

He grabbed his jacket and weapon and strolled out of his office. "Going to clear my head and grab some lunch from the thoroughfare. You wanting?" he asked Val'ka, by way of an excuse.

Val'ka's look of suspicion had dialled down a notch, but his lack of complete trust was still clear in his tone. "I would not mind a bunch of alkah fruit," he said, before adding, "you can get them from any Zerren store. They are big and purple and come in bunches of six."

"I'll keep a look out," Walks answered, as he made his escape from his second's judgemental stare.

As he traversed the lifts and shuttle, towards his destination, it crossed his mind that he had no idea if the thorough-fare was where Chione would be. The feline had a timetable all his own, and Walks had no idea what he spent half his time doing. *Does he need to sleep as much as a normal cat?* If that was the case, then for all Walks knew, Chione could be hunkered down in a duct somewhere, fast asleep.

He made his way into the main part of the street. *If I were a cat, where would I curl up?* He passed by a movie theatre, making a mental note to try there on the way back if his mission was unsuccessful. *Would be a bit of a perk to be a cat and be able to take in any film for free. That is if you're a fan of Zerren cinema.* He did a one-eighty and went to check the listings. Indeed, the time slots were filled up with a lot of Zerren films. Other race's films were listed under the auspicious title of 'Foreign Films' and filled the less popular times of early morning and late night. Walks recognised a single Human movie title in the mix, but as it wasn't showing until gone ten that evening, he figured Chione was probably not in the building. *He doesn't strike me as someone who's into Zerren romance. I wonder if he even speaks the language.* That was something that had never occurred to him; *just how many languages can he speak? Chione's a spy, and I assume he's good at it, so it stands to reason he should be able to understand a few dialects. Given that he's over five hundred years old, he's certainly had plenty of time to learn.* Walks realised how little he knew about the entity he'd just let take up residence in his quarters. *Hope that doesn't come to bite me on the arse later.*

He wandered down the street, taking his time to check the seats placed outside the various eateries. His search only faltered when he came to a Zerren grocers, but one bunch of arguably expensive alkah fruit later, plus a few tins of what he hoped wasn't Pra'cha's dreaded gourmet pet food, and he was back on patrol, absent-mindedly swinging the paper bag containing his purchases as he went. People of all races wandered by him: Ciberians, Zerrens, Seldens, Panns. A pair of Tings bartered their wares from a makeshift store, a Liverden tried to entice passers-by into his restaurant from its threshold, and a small group of May!en youths, seated outside a café, chatted amiably and animatedly to one another.

Walks watched them with a sombre air. They were oblivious to the danger that had been curtailed, or the danger that was still to come. The arrest of the assassins hadn't been made public for the same reason that nothing had been said about the bomber. Panic would only make the situation worse. If the bomber arrived to mass hysteria, he might rush to make his device, thereby reducing the time they had to capture him. *Better to make him think he can take his time and allow him to take a leisurely stroll to Azan.*

Walks wondered where the Beeden was. He'd stepped aboard the station that Walks knew, but no further news had been forthcoming. He was one of Tia's men, and as such, Walks figured he was more than capable of making himself scarce, despite all of Security's eyes being set towards him. *He's probably already holed up in a dark corner somewhere, waiting. If that's the case, there'll be no point in sending Chione to find him, as he'll probably strike out.* After a few more minutes of aimless walking, Walks was about to turn around and head back to the office, when something caught his eye, and he stopped in his tracks. Through the window of a Pann restaurant, he caught a glimpse of something white on a seat near the back of the room. However, his view was partially obstructed, and he couldn't tell if what he was looking at was in fact a cat, or simply someone's forgotten furry white handbag. He entered, giving the Pann behind the till a nod, and went over to the unidentified blob. It was indeed Chione.

Taking the seat beside the cat, Walks quickly fended off the approaching Pann waiter by asking for juice and the chef's salad. It was the only thing he knew he could get away with asking for without having to spend ten minutes trying to wade through an unintelligible menu. He didn't particularly want salad, he was a carbs and grease man, but as the Panns were either vegan or vegetarian by nature, the likes of steak or fried chicken were not going to be on offer.

Once the waiter had left, Walks angled himself out of eye line of the Pann guarding the till and lent into Chione. "Been looking for you," he whispered.

"Been napping," came a muffled voice from a head that was curled up into its chest.

"Why here?" For the same reason Walks didn't come to the place, it seemed a weird choice for the feline. *It isn't as if he's going to be eating vegetable scraps.*

"Less likely to get kicked out."

"Ah, got yeh." That made sense to Walks. Overall, the Panns were pacifists, and they certainly drew the line at harming animals. Chione had evidently used that to his advantage to get a comfortable and quiet place to crash.

The waiter returned with Walks' meal, before heading once more into the back. The juice he or she had brought him was an alarming shade of brownish yellow, and Walks took a cautious sip, but was relieved to find it was sweet and fruity. The salad was a mass of green and blue leaves, with some unidentifiable pulses mixed in with it. Walks looked at it and found himself desperately wanting there to be something fried on the side, and he regretted not taking a moment to at least look at the menu. He took a mouthful. It was tasty but lacked. He was eating what was ostensibly a giant side order. *I wonder if Jarvin's place does take-out.* His stomach gurgled at the prospect of a greasy evening meal. Between mouthfuls, he quietly muttered to Chione. "Don't suppose you've seen Azan?"

"No. Did have a wander earlier, but no luck." That was something at least. Chione appeared to be on Walks' wavelength when it came to wanting to know what was going on.

"Any ideas where he may be?"

"A few, so not out of ideas yet. Just came here for a bit of shut-eye."

Walks asked one of the questions that had been bugging him. "Do you need to sleep as much as a cat?"

"Not entirely. The cat's instinct to sleep in long stretches has been overridden, instead I tend to power nap, so I can keep going through the day and night. That, and a sleeping cat doesn't draw much suspicion from gossiping conspirators."

"Well, if you manage to find Azan, keep an eye on him from a safe distance for me. I hate not knowing what's going on," Walks confided.

"I don't doubt it," Chione answered, uncurling, and giving a long stretch. He raised his head over the top of the table, stared at Walks' salad, and gave him a questioning look.

"You want some?" Walks joked, pushing a fork laden with leaves in Chione's direction. The feline pulled away, while giving a look of utter disgust, which made Walks laugh. "I'll take that as a no. Don't worry, I've hopefully got you something good for dinner later." He patted the paper bag he'd put on the table.

"Glad to hear it," Chione responded, dropping down from his seat. "Going for a stroll; see you later."

Walks watched as Chione's tail disappeared around the door, then forced the last of the salad down, after which he washed his mouth out thoroughly with what was left of the sweet juice. He made his usual gesture of making to pay, which as usual, was waived away by the individual in charge of the till. *If I was a lesser man, I'd play this, so I'd never have to pay for food again.* Not everyone was so accommodating, like the Zerren grocer who stocked the expensive fruit, but enough proprietors considered Walks' job important enough for him to not be charged for food and drink. He figured he could live a comfortable life, if not for the stress his position caused him.

He took to the street again, and began retracing his steps back to the office, passing his eyes over everyone in a bid to see if they were in the least bit suspicious. Unfortunately, the look of guilt was not universal. Humans he could read, aliens, unless he knew the species well, he could not. To him, everyone was looking as innocent as babes in arms.

He felt a presence close to his arm and turned to find Ralay had fallen in stride with him. She was dressed differently again, this time in a security uniform that had been lent to her, so she could go on patrol to try to sniff out the bomber. Even in a uniform that didn't quite fit her, she had a commanding appearance. Walks felt like a scruff and a fraud in her presence. "Any joy?" he asked, trying not to let his sense of inadequacy overwhelm him.

Ralay shook her head. "I think I've passed my mind over every questionable Human on this station and have come up blank. Sure, there are several individuals radiating guilt over things that aren't at the forefront of their mind, and who your men should have a 'casual' talk with, but none are out to bomb us into oblivion. If they were, that thought would be as clear as day. If the guy's already on board, he's not Human."

"Damn." Walks had been afraid of that. Humans drew attention. Allied aliens did not. There'd been no alert on any new Qlaths and Yandakes boarding the station, so even if they'd managed to drum up empaths from those races, their presence would have been redundant. As it was, their call for help had gone unanswered from what few other individuals of those species there were on board. As for the Panns and Liverdens, only one Pann had volunteered its services. This did not surprise Walks. Telepaths were a rarity as it was, so the odds of finding one wasn't in their favour from the start, and that, compounded by the fact that telepaths weren't eager to be known, made for little help. He figured the Pann had only shown up because its nature to be helpful had overridden its desire to hide. "And no alien's given you cause to question their presence?"

"None that I've crossed paths with. Same for the Zerren I've been on patrol with."

Walks released an exasperated sigh. "It was worth a shot. Now it's up to Azan."

"Yes, I heard the message when we were patrolling the other end of the street. Nice touch, making it audible."

"Thanks. Occasionally I know what I'm doing"

The corner of Ralay's mouth gave a faint twitch, and she gave him a sideways look that wasn't as icy as normal. "I'd better get back to my handler," she half joked. As it was, the Zerren she was on patrol with was as much keeping an eye on her as she was on potential suspects. One wrong move and Walks would see to it that she ended up back in his interrogation room, preferably sedated. He watched as she strode off in her too elegant a fashion and tried to ignore the notion that was encroaching into his mind that he should consider working out. *That woman's so far out of my league she may as well exist in another universe,* he thought, glumly, as he trudged back to Security.

****

The next few days dragged on for Walks. Every morning began with a knot in his gut, as he wondered if that day would be the day. He would have his breakfast, have a passing conversation with Chione, then head off to his office. The day would end with him no more the wiser. There was one upside to all this, the station was still intact, and all concerned felt that the time when they should all be dead had passed. There were two reasons for this being bandied about. Either the bomber had never come aboard, or Walks' plan of making the guy's life awkward was working.

There was good reason to suspect the bomber had never made it to the station, not because he'd had second thoughts, although this too was a possibility, but because the galaxy was a vast and dangerous place. People traversed the depths of space in tiny tin cans that were only as reliable as their parts. Ships could explode, or simply cease to function; jumpgates could fail; or navigation could go cock-eyed, allowing the vast emptiness of hyperspace to suck a person off course. There were thousands of ways a person could get swallowed up by the nothingness, never to be seen again. In fact, it was a miracle that people ever ended up where they hoped to be. Walks spent the quiet times wondering if this was the case, that the universe had delivered, and that the man's lifeless body was slowly mummifying in a ship that was wandering space, forever spurred on by its last burst of momentum. He took a great deal of satisfaction from that thought. However, despite the possibility of a no-show, no one was letting their guard down.

Chione was doing his bit too. A couple of times he'd managed to triangulate on Azan, but both times it had been in public, and he'd never seen the alien talking to anyone else. It seemed the man was as capable as Talon when it came to evading questioning eyes, if not more so. He was a ghost during waking hours, and it had taken quite a bit of cross-referencing, and some on the down-low questionable hacking, courtesy of Pra'cha, to find where he was sleeping. As it was, he had taken up residence in a small hotel room in a cheap establishment run by a pair of Zerrens, who either didn't seem to question his presence or had no intention of questioning it. Subsequently, they hadn't raised an alert to Azan's presence, meaning Security hadn't had cause to go and question him, thereby blowing his cover.

Nevertheless, the desire to talk to Azan burnt bright in Walks, but every day, somehow, he'd resisted the urge to knock on his door and question him. Yet something niggled in Walks' mind, and went back to the fact that, if the bomber had a bomb, they'd already be dead. Just as he had never contacted Azan, Azan had never contacted him, either personally, or by proxy via Talon or Shar. *Surely,* Walks had pondered, *just as I've noted how long it's been, Azan should have done likewise. Why has he not made contact to question the time elapsed, and if his services are still needed?* The only thing Walks could think of was that Azan had been in contact with the bomber, or had heard word about him, and was making sure the lead was solid.

That thought made his stomach tighten, and his heart race faster. Knowing the man, or woman, was likely aboard, and building something that could take out, if not the entire station, at least hundreds of lives, and make the place inoperable for years to come, was an ever-present burden. Walks wanted to hack into the intercom system, and tell everyone to run for their lives, but the station couldn't cope with a mass exodus of that level. He knew the panic and chaos caused would do more damage to people and psyches than a successful suicide bomber ever could. All told, it made him want to pull his hair out.

The fact that he could unburden his stress on Chione made his days a little easier, but not by much. They talked strategies, and drills, and what the hell they'd do if the shit hit the fan, and they had to try to survive as the station crumbled around them. The stark truth was, most of the escape pods were in the bottom wheel, far from the most occupied areas. They were there should something happen in Munitions, and the staff had to make a run for it. As the Alliance had once run the station for Alliance races, the notion that a mad bomber would cause havoc in other areas had barely been considered. And if such a thing were to occur, the few escape pods dotted around the other wheels would have been for senior staff only. In the minds of hose in the upper echelons of the Alliance, underlings were expendable.

It seemed reasonable to Walks and Chione that should the bomber attack, his target would be the thoroughfare. A myriad of races spent their time there, and so a myriad of planets would feel the pain of losing representatives of their species to a senseless attack; perhaps withdrawing their support for the GR as a result. Not to mention the overall resulting loss of life that would be caused if the attack occurred at a peak time. To kill members of command would make them martyrs to the cause, to kill innocents would bring people to their knees. As a result, Walks had double up patrol in key areas with plainclothes officers but had stopped short of carrying out stop and searches, for fear of alerting the suspect.

Time ticked by, with every second teetering between nothing changed, and the entire world going to hell. Powerlessness, frustration, and paranoia entwined themselves in Walks' mind. His hands itched, desperate to have a bottle clenched within them. He could almost taste the brash liquid and feel the burning sensation as it travelled down his throat, to expand in warmth in his gut. His whole body was restless, and a quick drink was a sure-fire way to sooth it. He entertained the idea. *One drink.* Just one drink to calm his frazzled nerves. He would reach for his jacket, and make to get up, before dragging himself back to his seat. When he had learnt of the scorpiad aboard the station, it had been so easy to relapse, in fact, he had welcomed it. Alcohol had blessedly numbed away the knowledge there was a murderous creature on board. But a part of Walks rebelled, and refused to let this time be the same, and he found himself torn daily between the desire to drink himself into oblivion or remaining painfully sober. Walks began to wonder if it were he that was the bomb. Certainly, it felt like he was on the verge of exploding.

When it felt like his heart and mind were about to give out entirely, a single word message from Talon came through on his communicator: Contact.

Walks yelled a ragged cheer, drawing a startled backwards glance from Val'ka. All dark thoughts of alcohol evaporated faster than the substance itself. He shot back a message and waited; his heart so far up his throat it felt like it had his tonsils in a choke hold. Would the bomber be ready to make a deal directly? Would there be more days of planning? His hands shook. His communicator buzzed again and the words, tonight 23:00 water recyc back entrance C, flashed on its screen. Walks had no idea where that was, but that didn't stop him pumping his fist in the air. He brought up a schematic of the water recycling area and located the corridor. It was a secluded area in the lowest ring of the station, reached by winding narrow passageways that passed through nowhere. It was the perfect place to make a deal far from prying eyes…and to tie up loose ends after. *Has Azan entertained the thought he might be killed after this deal?* Walks was thinking it, and he knew they had to nail the guy swiftly, and without trouble. *Time to bring in Ralay.*

****

287

Walks couldn't stop fidgeting, despite the cold glares getting thrown his way by Ralay. He had never worn a protective vest, and he was becoming aware of just how uncomfortable the thing was, especially around his shoulder. It also didn't help that he was ensconced in a tight spot with a woman who irked him because she was a telepathic Alliance-reared assassin, and definitely didn't irk him because she was a woman who smelt of warmth.

The reason for the cosiness was that the two of them were waiting in position behind panelling that fronted a maintenance space that served as access to wiring leading into the recycling area. A few hundred metres down from where they were sardined, Azan was waiting. The idea being to box the bomber in. Both Walks and Ralay were armed. Ralay's wounded arm was well on the road to recovery, and she could hold a weapon steadier than Walks could on his best sober day. There was no knowing if Azan was armed, though Walks figured, considering who and what he was, he was probably packing all manner of weapons.

The minutes dragged on, and Walks spent them with his eye glued to a small hole that had been specifically removed of its screw for the sole purpose of spying. Questions crossed his mind. *What if this isn't the right guy? What if this is the right guy, and he's a telepath, or has some heightened sense, and he picks up on us and scarpers?* Chances where, only the bomber would want to buy explosives from some dodgy guy lurking in a dark corridor. Nevertheless, that wouldn't stop an individual with strong senses triangulating on him and Ralay, especially considering how hot and sweaty he was getting. Rolsts could see infrared heat signatures; Beedens, like Azan, had a heightened olfactory ability, and could detect pheromones; and although Shar wasn't a suspect, the lizard had the sense of smell of a blood hound, and could hear a pin drop from the other side of the station. And they were just the evolutionary abilities Walks knew of. There was no knowing what other races could sniff, see, hear, or taste them out long before they passed in front of Walks' peephole? The odds were not in their favour, making Walks wish dearly that the suspect was a Human they'd somehow let slip through the net.

His view of the corridor was briefly obscured. Someone had walked past his lookout, but so close as to be indistinguishable, and all Walks saw was some dark brown fabric eclipsing his hole. *Well, I can cross off Beedens, Rolsts, and Shar from my list of suspects, though that was my entire list.* He gave a tiny head-jerk to Ralay, and she nodded in comprehension. However, they didn't spring into action directly. They needed to wait until the bomber was occupied, so they could sneak up on him. A few minutes more, and muffled voices could be heard, the sound of their suspect haggling with Azan.

Cautiously, Walks unhooked the panel, and placed it carefully against the outer wall, trying to minimise any metal-on-metal sounds. Then, with weapons in hand, he and Ralay quietly made their way down the corridor; the sounds of talking getting louder as they went. Walks failed to make out the accent. It was thick, that was for sure. The words, though sounding Human to Walks' untrained ear, were faltering and unintelligible. He wondered how Azan was managing to broker a deal with someone so incomprehensible. *Maybe he's another telepath,* Walks hypothesised. *Considering the revelations of late, I wouldn't put it past him.*

At the final bend of the corridor, Walks gave a nod to Ralay, which she returned; a signal to get ready. She mouthed, "not Human," at him, though considering the incomprehensible words that were reaching his ears, he could have figured that out for himself. In silence, he held up his hand, four fingers raised, and counted down. 4...3...2...1!

They burst around the corner, Walks yelling, "Freeze," as they did so. Azan continued to play his part, and instantly raised his hands in surrender. The bomber, race now clear, turned at the word, and made to draw a weapon, but did not consider that Azan was not on his side. With the alien's back

turned towards him for a split-second, Azan took the opportunity, and gave the bomber a solid right hook to the back of
his head, flooring him in one hit.

Walks walked over to the prone form. "Thanks," he said to
Azan, who merely gave a shrug in response. He rolled the man
over with his foot. "Zorstanian?"

"Aldarean Zorstanian," Azan said, breaking his silence.

"That make a difference?" Ralay asked.

"It might," Walks answered. "There are two Zorstanian
tribes. They were at war with each other for over a century
until we brokered a treaty between them. They helped in the
battle for Ciberia after that."

"Not all happy with treaty," Azan remarked, poking the man
hard with his boot.

Walks gave a nod of understanding.

****

Walks watched the Zorstanian sulking in his seat via a live
feed in the small adjoining room. Flanking him, and with their
eyes also on the screen, were Ralay and Azan. Walks found
it a little ironic that both the perpetrator and their saviour
had yellow skin, but that's as far as similarities went, because
though the Zorstanian was staying stubbornly quiet, Azan was
more than happy to supply information. Talon had been right
about him; he had done his job, and he had been exemplary in
executing it. Not only luring the man to his capture, but also
taking time to gain his trust, and learn much about the whys of
his murderous plan.

"Many of his tribe believe treaty robbed them of their right,"
Azan was telling them.

Walks already knew a bit about their history thanks to the
talks that had been chaired by Ken'va and Sin'ma. There were
two tribes existing on their second home planet of Zorstan II:
the Aldareans and the Barothees. In fact, the separation between them had happened so long ago, the tribes could be

considered sub-species, despite their similar appearance. They both had the same, white-dappled yellow skin, blue eyes, and reptilian genetic makeup that gave them a slightly cold-looking countenance, at least to a Human like Walks. The only way to tell them apart, other than to run a DNA test, was that the Barothees wore turbans, while the Aldareans kept their bald heads bare. For Walks' sting, it was fortuitous the bomber was Aldarean, as Azan's chop to the back of his skull may not have been as effective when faced with a thick turban. The two tribes had been at each other's throats for nearly a century over moon mineral rights, each side believing it had a god-given right to mine the riches that lay below their dusty surfaces. Ken'va and Sin'ma had helped resolve the dispute, allowing the races to function as effective allies, yet, as Azan had said, it seemed not all were happy with the arrangement.

"He come here to destroy station as political statement, to tell us to mind our business," Azan explained.

"So, what does the Alliance have to do with his presence?" Ralay asked. "They knew he was coming, so they must have had a hand in this."

Azan nodded, making the tufts of yellow scaly hairs atop his head bob up and down. "He no say directly, but I hear. How you say? Between lines?"

"You read between the lines?" Walks said, trying to clarify.

"Yes. The Alliance helped. Pushed I think better phrase. Word here. Ideology there."

"They groomed him," Ralay suddenly growled, "just like they did me."

The two males looked at her, and Walks saw a thunderous cloud had descended across her face, and for a moment, she looked scary mad. Then, just as quickly, she regained her stoic composure, and the cloud evaporated. Even so, the sight had been enough to make Walks shiver inwardly.

"He say, he do this for his people. More a case, Alliance tell him he do this for his people," Azan continued.

"Do you know how he even got tangled up with the Alliance?" Walks asked.

"His family miners. Lose business because of treaty. Him there," Azan jerked his head at the screen, "look for work elsewhere, but not with rebel races. Get mining job with Nor'kelteens."

"Hence his knowledge of explosives, and his foot in the door with the Alliance." Walks said, the pieces falling into place.

"Yes. Talks good of race. Say how they understand him. Help him. Good friends."

"So, he talks of his distaste for you rebels, and they seed the idea of how blowing you to kingdom come will send a message," Ralay concluded.

"Don't suppose he dropped the words 'virgins' or 'paradise' during his ideological rants?" Walks asked. Ralay and Azan gave him sideways looks. "Play one out of the recruitment handbook. Make it sound like when they die, they'll go to some awesome heaven to party all day and night."

"No. No paradise," Azan responded. "Zorstanians don't believe in afterlife. Wanting praise and accolade during life and after death is something he mentioned."

"They probably promised to build a jewel-encrusted statue in his honour or something," Walks theorised.

"Wouldn't put it past them," Ralay muttered.

"Well, time's pressing. Let's see what else this moron can tell us." Walks said, as he stuck an earpiece in his ear. "If you guys need to chip in..." he tapped the device, then left Azan and Ralay in the little booth, and entered the interrogation room.

The Zorstanian, whose name, according to the papers found on him, was V'zinery, was chained down. However, his mood was much less defiant than the Human they'd had strapped down in the same chair several days earlier. Despite V'zinery's sullen and non-communicative air, Azan had informed them that the man liked to talk, especially about those he considered as having wronged him. Walks just had to manipulate that to his own ends, though he doubted he'd get anything useful out of the alien. He was a pawn, and unlike the hired assassins, Walks was doubtful he was privy to anything beyond the lies the Alliance had fed him to get him to become a suicide bomber.

"So? What did the Nor'kelteens promise you?" Walks asked, straight off the bat. "Eternal notoriety, a bejewelled statue in the centre of their main city, a televised series dramatising your heroics?" Not a peep. If that's what he'd been promised, he was keeping mum. "Money to your family?" The corner of V'zinery's eye twitched. *Bingo!* "You do know that all Alliance assets within Zorstanian control were frozen when Zorstan II aligned itself to the GR, and that no money from any Alliance race can make it into any Zorstanian account? And did you know, anyone found receiving a questionable sum of money, which is later traced back through shell accounts to the Alliance, gets arrested for treason?" V'zinery's eye twitched again, and Walks decided more grim elaboration was in order. "From what I hear, the Zorstanian penal system isn't exactly pleasant. Overcrowding, limited resources, hunger's commonplace, so are rampant diseases. Violence and death are all around, and it can take years before a trial date is even set. One has to wonder, on knowing that, how your family members would fare behind bars while they awaited processing, and ultimately extradition to a penal mining colony. And don't even get me started on the conditions in those, though I have heard the word cannibalism crop up from time to time." V'zinery was wearing a strange expression on his face. Walks wondered if it was his version of crying. "Don't suppose the Nor'kelteens mentioned any of that while they went about grooming you into a bomber?"

V'zinery finally spoke. "Zey would av go monay to familay," he said. His accent was as thick as Walks recalled, but to his ears, V'zinery's words lacked conviction.

"No, they would not have got money to your family," he countered. "Your race's penal system may be an abomination, but their technical ability, not to mention their rampant penny-pinching bureaucracy, is top-notch. As soon as any large amount of money turned up in your family's account, it would have been traced. That is, of course, if the Nor'kelteens had any plans to actually pay out. Part of me says no. They're a bunch of lying Alliance scum who just wanted to see you blow yourself up, while sending hundreds, if not thousands of innocent people to their version of hell. But another part of me thinks they would have kept up their side of the bargain, in full knowledge that it would bring suffering and death to your family. People, who I figure, are just as innocent in all this as the people you were trying to murder and have no idea what you've been planning."

"Zey zay..."

"They say a lot of things," Walks cut in. "Doesn't mean any of it is true. I should know, I was an Alliance man."

This seemed to trigger something in V'zinery, and he raised his head to look at Walks. "Oo waz Allianss?" he asked, seemingly surprised.

"Oh yes. And you can believe me when I say they're full of shit. They tell you slaughtering hundreds of thousands of people is for the greater good; that it will make the Alliance nation better and stronger. All it really does is leave millions of corpses and makes those at the top crueller and more blood thirsty. To be honest, I don't think I've seen the Alliance advance as a race in any way since being in their ranks. Any new tech or science goes into making planet-grabs easier. The resulting wealth gets funnelled to those up high, and those below barely see a whiff of a more evolved future, just as it's always been done. For most of us, our state of living is hardly any better than it was a couple of centuries ago. It's just for some, their crappy state of living ends up being on alien world promised as a new and exciting opportunity, when really it's nothing more than an inhospitable wasteland, populated by dead bodies and resentful survivors."

"I not know," V'zinery responded, hanging his head again.

"How can you not know?" Walks asked, dumbfounded. "This is the one thing everyone knows about the Alliance. At least those who exist outside their brainwashing rhetoric." A warning bell sounded in his head "How old are you?" he asked, "I mean, how many years have you been alive?" he added, for clarification.

"Ahteen years."

Ahteen? Ahteen? Eighteen? "Eighteen years?" he asked, unsure.

"Yas, Ahteen."

Azan's voice sounded in his head through his earpiece. "Zorstanians count from one, have no zero age."

That makes him seventeen. Oh, for crying out loud, this guys just a kid. Walks fumed and turned his furious gaze to the ceiling. *No wonder he doesn't know half this shit. He probably left home while barely a teenager and stayed ignorant to all of it. Fuck the Alliance!* "Did they promise your family anything more than money?" he prodded, looking back down.

V'zinery mumbled into his chest. "Zey Zay all to know my nahm. Familay would ramember me."

"Oh, I can guarantee that would have been true. If you had succeeded, your name would have been remembered as belonging to a kid who massacred thousands of people. And your family sure would have remembered you, as they rotted away in prison, having been framed as traitors."

V'zinery slumped down in his seat. The realisation of what was reality was slowly sinking in. The weird expression returned, so Walks left him to his misery, and went back to the viewing room.

"He's just a child," Ralay said, as he entered, echoing his earlier thought.

"Yep. They took a kid, warped his mind, and sent him off to commit genocide."

"Fucking Alliance," Azan muttered.

"No arguments from me there. Did you not pick up on his age?" Walks asked Azan.

Azan gave a shrug. "I don't know difference between young and mature Zorstanian," he explained. "He come asking for bomb equipment. He knew what he want. He sound confident. I never think he was young."

"In his defence," Ralay added, "I think we all thought he was an adult until you asked."

Walks knew she was right. If V'zinery hadn't shown his complete ignorance about the Alliance, Walks was under no doubt he would have processed him as an adult until his age had eventually been revealed. The small amount of information he'd gleaned led him to believe V'zinery had never had a formal education. He had likely grown up in a mining family, without much connection to the outside galaxy, and his lessons would've revolved around his immediate world, namely mining. He would have been schooled in explosives, not in the fact that there was a mad bunch of races trying to conquer the galaxy by any means necessary. Walks sighed.

"So, what happen to him now?" Azan asked.

"I'll turn him over to the Zerren authorities," Walks responded. "How they deal with him will be up to them. On one hand, he came here to blow us up. On the other, he's just a brainwashed kid. I'll be sure to make that part abundantly clear in my report, and hopefully they'll show him some lenience. Last thing he needs is to end up in a Zerren prison. Okay, their penal system is a lot better than the Zorstanian's, but I doubt he'll be welcomed by the other inmates once word of his conviction makes the rounds."

"He wouldn't last the night," Ralay said, matter-of-factly. Walks nodded. "So, where does that leave us with the assassins planet-side?"

"No bloody clearer as to who and where they are," Walks said, frustrated. "Unless something happens in our favour, we're gonna have to head to the surface and hunt for four needles in a haystack of several billion."

"Why you?" Azan asked.

"Simple maths," Walks answered. "The fewer people that know about what's going on, the less chance there is someone'll say something to tip the assassins off, so the more time we'll have to figure things out."

Azan nodded in understanding. "You could head down with V'zinery," he said.

"As suggestions go, that's not a bad idea." Ralay said. "It would at least give us a cover story for why we're on the surface. Then we could hunt under the radar."

"So, you're still in this with us?" Walks asked, slightly surprised. Ralay nodded and gave a rare small smile. "Fair enough. I'll get us some travel passes sorted."

Azan took in each of them in turn. "And how you gonna find assassins?"

"We'll just do what seems to have worked for us so far. We'll make it up as we go along." Walks said, trying to sound a lot more confident than he was.

Chapter 29 - Tia

R essen hadn't been wrong about the cramped nature of Tia's quarters. Her room aboard the brother's vessel was just as snug as the command room. Unlike the command room, where she was aware of her surroundings, the fixtures of her room were less safe, as when her mind wandered, she was apt to forget what she was. Subsequently, the furniture was getting tested. She'd already managed to dent the metal leg of the table several times with her tail, and having straightened it each time by hand, it was looking exceedingly mangled, and was on the verge of breaking. "Hope the wall brackets are up to muster," she muttered to herself, as she tried to get comfortable on a decidedly uncomfortable bunk.

Beyond the bed and table there was a small locker for clothes, toiletries, and the like. As a Karee, Tia had little need for clothes, as she could change the form of her skin to make herself decent. Nor did she require much in the way of toiletries, as although she didn't sweat, day-to-day grime still collected on her skin, but all she needed to deal with that was a bottle of her favourite vanilla-scented shower-come-hair wash. Rather, her locker was filled with tea, coffee, chocolate, and any other snacks she could think to bring, along with a data pad loaded with books, and some of her favourite old-Earth films. Her mission was important, but that didn't mean she couldn't enjoy the quiet times. *That is if I can get comfortable on this interminable bed,* she grumbled, as she fidgeted in annoyance.

The bed's base was a metal frame, on which sat a relatively soft, single mattress, topped with another carry-on of hers: decent quality sheets. But comfort wasn't the problem, it was the bed's dimensions that were the issue. Thanks to the brother's species' height, it was almost long enough to accommodate her lanky form, though it did come up a bit short, thanks to her crown of horns, so she had to sleep on it upside-down, so her horns were over the foot end, as opposed to sticking into the wall. However, it was the width that was the biggest problem. Her wings were expansive, and if she lay down on the bed, one would get crushed up against the wall, and the other would flop over the edge onto the floor. She'd got into the habit of wrapping them around her like a giant bat in hibernation, which wasn't the most practical position to be in, especially if she wanted to hold her pad to read. Most nights culminated in her being swaddled up like a giant burrito, with her data pad jammed into the three claws of her tail, so she could hold it above her face. She was coming to the point where the idea of altering her form was looking like a sensible plan, and only her stubborn nature was holding her back.

The claustrophobic confines of the room weren't helping either. She didn't begrudge Ressen and Grelt's hospitality, but she dearly wished she had room to, literally, spread her wings. "I need a cup of tea," she decided. A cup of tea meant using the ship's kitchen, which had a bit more space going for it. She got up from the annoying bed and rooted around in the locker until she found a box of teabags. Slamming the door with a little more force than she should have, thanks to her irritability, she caused the datapad that was perched atop it to unbalance and go crashing to the floor. "Crap!"

Unthinking, she quickly bent down to retrieve it, and her action was accompanied by a metallic ripping sound from behind her, followed by a crash. She stayed bent over and unleashed a string of expletives that would have made even the most robust pirate blush. Standing up carefully, she looked over her shoulder to survey the carnage. Involuntarily, she had counter-weighted her bending over by raising and straightening her tail, and it had hooked itself under the little metal table in the process, ripping it from its brackets and floor mounting, and depositing it, and its contents of dinner plate and coffee mug, on the floor.

Tia looked to the heavens in frustration. "That does it!" she exclaimed to the universe. She turned her mind inwards on to herself, becoming acutely aware of her body's structure as she did so, and as she focused, she became conscious of the individual components that made up her form, from the individual cells that formed her skin, to the sensory receptors that criss-crossed underneath it, to the alien substance making up her virtually impenetrable mesoskeleton. If she went further, she could home in on the atoms that made up her being, but that was not what she was after. Instead, she sent a message to the cells in her body that made up her tail and wings, and they obeyed her command. Starting from their tips, her cumbersome limbs began dismantling themselves, returning their energy to her core, and in a little under ten minutes, Tia was stood in her room, wingless and tailless.

It was an odd sensation. She had worn her tail and wings for years. Even on the station, shortly before the battle for its control, when she had seemed perfectly Human to those who'd cast their eyes on her, she'd had them. Then they had been invisible because she had telepathically masked them, now they were physically gone, and it had been some time since she'd been without their weight. But more than feeling lighter, she felt strangely naked and vulnerable, and she gave a little shiver.

She bent over to pick her mug and plate up from the floor, which luckily for them were also made of metal and had survived their unplanned trip to the ground. However, Tia still had to be careful when retrieving them as she was now a tad top-heavy, having retained her horns, and she had to concentrate on the position of her new body, relative to the gravity generated by the ship, so as not to topple over. Then, with dish, mug, and teabag in hand, she left the confines of her cabin, and headed for the kitchen; adjusting her stride and sway to compensate for the absence of her limbs. Her lightened and altered load made walking feel odd for a time, but on arriving at the kitchen, it was as if she'd been devoid of wings and a giant tail her whole life.

The kitchen on the ship wasn't much bigger than the kitchenette in her Scientia quarters. There were cupboards that held dried and canned food, plus crockery and cutlery, and there was a small cooler for the fresh foods that inevitable got eaten within the first week of a journey. Beyond that, there was a sink for washing up, which supplied marginally drinkable cold recycled water, and a boiler for hot water. Tia gave her battered mug a rinse with some water from the boiler, ignoring the more stubborn coffee stains, deposited the teabag in it, and filled it back up with more hot water. As the bag steeped, filling the room with a mouth-watering smell of fruit and herbs, she gave her plate a cursory scrub.

She felt Ressen's presence before he entered the room and steeled herself for the inevitable mental jolt he'd send towards her. She wasn't disappointed, as on seeing her minus wings and tail, a tidal wave of confused thoughts headed her way. Tia turned to see Ressen stood motionless in the door. She went to speak first, feeling the need to reassure him, but he managed to beat her to it.

"Do you ever stay longer than a few days in one shape?" he joked.

Tia felt a little wrong-footed by Ressen's ability to easily accept her abilities. Not since the likes of Shar had anyone been able to deal with her changing form, or her. She smiled in response. "I got fed up with getting numb limbs while squashed up on that bed. That and I accidentally demolished the table. Sorry."

Ressen gave a dismissive wave of his hand. "That's fine. Those tables are flimsy things. This craft was designed for cargo transport, not luxury."

"I never asked; does this ship have a name?"

Ressen looked perplexed. "Its serial number is two-hundred-six-five-nine. Why?"

"I was wondering if it had a more familiar name, like the Scientia, or the Victory."

"No, just its number. Why would you give it a name? It's just a vehicle."

His response made Tia stop and think. "I guess I never thought about the why. It's just something a lot of races seem to do. Humans pretty much anthropomorphise everything. Plus, a name is easier to refer to than a string of numbers."

"I suppose, though I wouldn't know what to name it."

"In the old days of Earth, ships were given female names."

"How about the Tia?"

Tia rolled her eyes extensively and hoped Ressen understood her gesture of mock exasperation. He seemed to and grinned widely back at her. "No," she answered, firmly.

"Your loss. Our mother's name was Eerell, so we could call it that."

"Sounds good to me."

Their small talk had reached its natural conclusion, and they remained awhile in awkward silence; Tia sipping her Tea, Ressen pottering around the kitchen to make himself some food. Tia knew she was under no obligation to stay but couldn't bring herself to go back to her quarters. Instead, she surreptitiously watched Ressen over the rim of her cup, as he poured hot water into a bag of dehydrated who-knew-what.

She couldn't shake the feelings she had in his presence. He was a handsome alien, strong and confident, not to mention resilient, but Tia had, unofficially, sworn off relationships on becoming Karee. She had become an ethereal and powerful being, who was part of a symbiotic relationship with an even older, more ethereal and powerful being. Such a situation was hard enough to explain, let alone conduct a successful relationship around, and things would only be complicated. *To put it mildly,* she thought, bitterly.

Unfortunately, her change had done little to quash Shar's desire for her, and the lizard who caused her so much frustration, ire, and mixed feelings, still saw her as the ultimate prize, and she had no doubt, should she say the word, he would jump into her bed without a second thought. Ressen was a different story. Tia had read enough of his body language over the weeks to know he both feared her and was attracted to her, like many others were, but above it all, and despite all he'd witnessed, he somehow managed to see and treat her as just a normal entity. He didn't cower from her, he didn't kowtow to her, nor did he chase her. There was a kind of benignity about the way he perceived her, as if the way she was, was the most natural thing to him. It was a, "Yes, yes, I know you can destroy the world purely with the power of your mind, here, have a slice of cake," type of situation, and Tia simply didn't know how to deal with his nonchalant attitude towards her, at least beyond feeling slightly funny whenever she was in his presence.

Ressen had finished preparing his meal and took a moment to let it cool. "Grelt says we've made good progress through hyperspace, so we'll be out in four days as scheduled," he announced, "but it will take several more days to backtrack through normal space to catch up with the planet."

"And all systems are still working well?"

"No problems so far."

Tia was pleased to hear that. It was the ship's inaugural flight since getting patched up after its explosions, and as such, the repairs hadn't been properly tested. They'd been flying on a wing and a prayer, but they'd made it across the Zerren system without issue, and the same was looking true of their trip through hyperspace. It was clear the brothers were good engineers.

Ressen began eating his food, but despite there being a small table to sit at, he remained stood up, facing her. There was a teenage awkwardness about the moment, and Tia couldn't quite bring herself to make eye-contact with Ressen, even though she could sense him occasionally looking up from his bowl of food to study her from across the room. Instead, she chose to scrutinise the bottom of her empty mug, and its myriad of brown tidal rings. *What the hell is wrong with me? I can rip stars apart and destroy mighty enemies with no more than a thought, but gods forbid I should look a male in the eyes.*

She dragged her gaze up, to see Ressen looking at her. He gave her an innocent smile, and her stomach felt as if it had dropped ten floors. *Oh for goodness' sake,* she reprimanded herself. She wanted to look deeper into his mind to see what thoughts were massing behind the grin but held back. Translating words for ease of communication was one thing, rummaging through the depths of private thoughts and emotions was another. On one hand, he would never sense her presence, and she would know precisely what he was thinking. On the other, she had trespassed deeply into his mind too much already, and even though it had saved her life, she still felt guilty about it. It was that guilt that held her back.

Instead, she turned her mind to the future, and what awaited them as their mission unfolded. *If things go pear-shaped, I may have to transgress again, for both our sakes.* She debated whether she should tell him. Her men aboard Tartarus had no issue with her being in their heads as it came with the territory; that of being incarcerated under her. Ressen was different, just as Aben had been, and she at least owed him an explanation, and a semblance of choice. Semblance because, if the worst happened, she would override his choice if she saw fit.

Tia took a minute to think about how she would broach the subject, then announced, "I have no idea what, if anything, we will be up against when we finally land on that planet," she said. "And there may come a time when I need to protect you more...intrusively."

"Meaning?"

"We could find ourselves up against telepaths, and depending on how capable they are, I will have to protect you, which would mean me being inside your mind, even to a point of having to manipulate your thoughts and memories."

Ressen considered her words. "I think it would be idiotic of me to not ask you to do everything in your power to protect me, but I also understand the caution you have over messing with my mind. Our minds are our private places, and as such, shouldn't be encroached on without permission." He gave Tia a look that, had she not known better, would have made her wonder if he'd been listening in on her earlier mental to-ing and fro-ing about reading his thoughts. "But let's be honest, you've already been rummaging around in my head."

Ressen's last words made her guilt resurfaced, and she made to protest. Her subconscious, in the form of Emma, had intruded into Ressen's mind without her full knowledge, and her conscious mind had been too wrapped up in primal instinct and insurmountable misery to even register what Emma had been up to. Tia may have often run a cursory glance over peoples' minds, so she could see their forefront thoughts and keep ahead of the game, but Emma had gone layers deeper, even so far as to reanimate a dying man.

But Ressen waved Tia silent before she could say anything and continued. "Believe me, I know what you did was the last, desperate cry of someone in need of saving, and I do not begrudge you being in my head one bit. If the need arises, please, be my guest, and do whatever you need to do.... I will not reject you." That last sentence came with an intense look from Ressen, and it made Tia's insides involuntarily jolt. There was another connotation behind those words, and Tia didn't need to be a telepath to understand it.

Chapter 30 - Leo

So far, Leo's mission had been uneventful. Once clear of the mother ship, Kan had set their scouter to autopilot, and it had headed off towards the jumpgate that would link up to the one near the Endier system. During the short trip, Kan and Leo had been left to their own devices. Leo had read, watched movies on his datapad, reluctantly used the gym equipment to make sure his muscles didn't atrophy in zero-g, and snoozed whenever the desire took him.

Kan had religiously kept up a day night cycle and had advised Leo against his devil-may-care routine. "When we board the Qosec Three you'll regret it," he'd warned. "Chances are, their cycle will be a little different to ours, but it'll still be enough of a shock to your system. Last thing you need is jet lag."

When they had arrived at the jumpgate, it was activated, and waiting for them. The massive, multi-ringed structure had loomed over their tiny craft. Its whole was eleven giant rings, heading off into the inky distance, its centre, an undulating mass of energy, ripping a hole through the fabric of space, into the bizarre grey-blue nether-realm of hyperspace. They had entered at full speed; thereby preventing loss of time through braking, waiting, and picking up velocity again.

Then there had followed the eerie trip through the blue-lit nothingness, carried along by the current of the wormhole created by the jumpgate, their little vessel at the mercy of its pull. Like all ship travellers, Leo and Kan could only hope that this wasn't one of those rare times that the extraordinarily complicated calculations involved in getting them to the exit gate had been cocked-up or corrupted; otherwise, the unseen eddy would eventually weaken, as it's distance from the entrance gate increased, and they would be set adrift, with no means of escape.

Though Kan had deactivated the cockpit's visual overlay, Leo could still look out through the two tiny portholes that were situated beside the two pilot seats. At times, he had sat there, staring out, almost transfixed by the void, straining his eyes looking for the near impossible: another ship. Ships could meet within the void, but to do so they had to have the correct entry co-ordinates, as well as travel speeds, directions, and a host of other rational and irrational numbers to plug into a mind-bending formula. Without this data, the chances of two vessels crossing paths within such an infinite and warped realm was infinitesimal; yet, despite knowing all this, Leo had kept up his vigil.

"I hope you're not going space crazy," Kan had said one day, giving him a questioning look.

"Just keeping an eye out for other vessels," Leo had responded, although after he'd said it, he wondered if his words had been as reassuring and less insane as he hoped.

Somehow, they survived the journey in the small vessel, and in each other's company, and came out as planned near the Endier system. As they made their approach towards their rendezvous point, Kan occupied himself with slowing their speed to a more manageable level, so they could dock with the Qosec Three without punching a hole through it, and Leo made himself useful by checking their food supplies. They had stocked a safe amount for one adult man and one walking mountain, to minimise their payload, and give them a little boost to their travel time. Leo's calculations told him it was a good thing they were meeting up with another vessel, as without it, their food situation would be a little sparse on arriving at Demeter Nine. But once on the Qosec Three, they would restock, and more so. If all went to plan, there would be five extra bodies aboard the scouter on their return leg, and any arguments against excess weight was invalid. Leo hoped the Rotaizians had some interesting foodstuffs, as he was starting to get sick of reconstituted dried pasta meals, jerky meats, and fruit-paste. The fresh stuff Pra'cha had packed for him hadn't lasted long, especially as he'd felt obliged to share his rations with Kan, who hadn't been so blessed.

After a short while, Kan made the announcement, "The Qosec Three has come within scanner range," drawing Leo back to his cockpit seat.

They were still some ways out from the Rotaizian's solar system, where the species' home planet, Lesk, remained unmolested by the Alliance. The jumpgate they had exited was situated close to the system's outer most asteroid belt and was used to provide access to the variously owned mining bases dotted about the region; an operation the Rotaizians made a tidy profit from through mining rights sales.

Kan brought up the live feed and used the scouter's scanners to home in on their intended target. An image of a boxy-looking craft greeted them. The main bulk of it was like a giant steel container, from which sprung the four jump engines that were going to help Leo and Kan make it quickly through the next portion of hyperspace. From the front of the container, jutted a short neck, headed by a marginally smaller steel container, atop which, like a metallic pointed hat, sat a further, tinier container that sported a large plasma cannon. It was a cubic vision in grey, broken up only by a single row of portholes, which travelled most of the length of each box's flank. It was certainly not as elegant or majestic as some ships Leo had seen in the past.

"I'm guessing the Rotaizians prefer function to design," Leo mused.

"Well, it seems to work for them," Kan reasoned. "This is the third in a fleet of twelve, and the oldest has been in service for nearly fifty years and is still going strong."

"We could've done with them at the Ciberian battle. Wonder why they didn't help."

Kan shrugged. "I guess, like a lot of races, they didn't want to draw attention to themselves, believing it'd keep them safe from the Alliance. Most of the races that helped were the ones that had already been up against the Alliance, and had nothing to lose, or had enough presence on the station, and a smart enough government back home, to grasp what shit was coming their way, no matter how deeply they buried their heads in the sand. These guys may not have been at the Ciberian battle, but I'll wager this move to help us is them beginning to get they need to start making friends…just in case."

Leo nodded. The victory at Ciberia, and the capture of the Alliance battleship, had caused a snowball effect. More races were joining the resistance, which in turn was causing other races to rethink their non-committal stance. Slowly but surely, a wall was forming around the Orion Alliance sector, one built of races, linking arms, and taking a stand. At times, Leo would stop and take a moment to focus on just how humbling it was to be amid such a phenomenon, and he hoped he'd live to see it through to the end. And that the end played out in their favour.

The rest of the intercept course was carried out in moderate silence, with Kan occasionally asking Leo to check a readout, or flick a switch or two. After a few hours flight, the walls of the giant steel container welcomed them in, and Kan landed their small scouter among the Qosec Three's own ranks of fighters, which were only marginally more aerodynamic looking than their mother ship.

"They look like giant baths," Leo quipped, as he and Kan collected their stuff. Kan gave a grunt of mirth. "I wonder if we'll have real baths in our quarters," he added. The scouter had a small washing facility, but as it used recycled water, Leo had never felt entirely clean after using it.

"I doubt it," Kan said. "Personally, I'll be happy if their showers don't time out after two minutes, and the water's more than a degree above freezing."

"Agreed. Never mind a cooked meal, I just want a long hot

shower," Leo said, wistfully. "I would image their water recycling is a bit better than this scouter's."

"I'd wager good money on it," Kan said, heaving his holdall onto his shoulder.

They alighted from their vessel, to find an odd-looking alien waiting for them on the hangar deck. Leo had never seen a Rotaizian before. None had ever set foot on the station, and he had never seen pictures of them, but that had been his fault, as he'd been too preoccupied with making plans to stop and search the station's image files. Because of this, he had to stop himself from looking too surprised by their appearance. Overall, the individual stood before them was typically humanoid. He was bipedal, and had two arms, though his fingers were long and tapered. However, it was his head that was unarguably distinct, and he had what Leo could only describe as a bi-chin. They were two, long and pointed chins, which came down from the bottom of the alien's jaw line, and between which was a thin goatee beard that was the same length as these chins. About half of the aliens milling about the hangar had the same beard, so Leo could only surmise it was a sexual characteristic that distinguished the males from the females.

Both genders also sported large, curved structures on the sides of their faces, which spouted out of a heavy brow ridge, and reconnected where Leo assumed would be a cheek bone. They looked ear-like in shape, being round at the bottom, and highly pointed at the top, but Leo couldn't see any holes that would signify an auditory canal. Thanks to these structures, a small inconspicuous nose, and a lipless mouth, the Rotaizians came across as having large, flat faces.

Strange looks aside, their greeter came across as being amiable, and with the help of a mobile translator, he identified himself as Lorkav, and the second in command of the ship. After which, he directed them to their temporary quarters, with them following; slightly jelly-legged from having been away from artificial gravity for so long.

Leo was slightly miffed to find he and Kan would be bunking together but had the decency to appreciate there were probably few available spaces on the ship, and the room, though small and sparsely furnished, appeared to be one reserved for the higher-ups. The main sleeping area consisted of a bunkbed, two small steel lockers for personal effects, and a little seating area, consisting of a small table and a couple of moderately comfortable chairs. In a small alcove was a kind of kitchen, which housed a cupboard stocked full of more dry rations, a sink for water, and a machine that looked a little like an old-fashioned microwave oven. Their tour guide even did a little demonstration to show them how to use it.

"Fresh food?" Leo queried, hopefully.

Lorkav waved his hands enthusiastically and launched into directions that appeared to be for the ship's mess hall. However, thanks to not having the best translator, coupled with his own language's idiosyncrasies, they were chaotic.

Leo glanced over at Kan, who looked equally baffled. "We'll take a stroll later and find it," Kan whispered, as Lorkav headed off into the other room, gesturing for them to follow.

It turned out that Kan's earlier bet had been on the money. Their quarters had a small bathroom, complete with a latrine, sink, and more importantly, a shower cubicle. Once Lorkav had politely left, Leo was the first to try it out, while Kan stayed in the bedroom to organise his gear in his locker. The shower was powerful, comfortably warm, wasn't on a timer, and didn't leave a funny taste on the back of Leo's tongue when he happened to get an accidental mouthful of liquid.

Leo ended up staying in the spray way too long and was finally ushered out by Kan pounding on the door, yelling, "Bloody hurry up in there, I need a piss!"

Leo wrapped a rough towel around his midriff, and regrettably left the bathroom. Kan nearly clambered over him in his bid to answer his call of nature. Leo then used Kan's absence to quickly towel himself down and get a pair of pants on. As he was putting on a t-shirt, the ship gave a violent shudder, and the general vibration of the vessel seemed to crank up a notch.

"That'll be the jump engines kicking in," Kan said, as he came to grab his towel. "I guess we're about to head into hyperspace."

"Oh good," Leo said, trying to sound upbeat. Truth was, entering hyperspace didn't agree with him. It felt like he was on a violent roller-coaster, and his stomach did its best to rebel every time. It had been the same when he'd travelled on the Scientia to Zerra, and it had been the same entering and exiting the jumpgate to meet the Qosec Three. On the Scientia, he'd had the relief of being able to hide the negative effects in his quarters. Not so on the scouter, and he'd been in the uncomfortable position of having to swallow an awful lot of bile to save face in front of Kan.

"Just don't puke on my gear," Kan said, not buying into Leo's strained smile.

"How do you not get sick?" Leo whined.

Kan gave a shrug. "Self-control," he said, before disappearing back into the bathroom.

That's no help, Leo thought, feeling the ship, and then his stomach, shudder again. He concentrated on putting his clothes away and tried to ignore the increasingly rattling fixtures. Just as he was finishing up, the ship gave an almighty lurch. There was a crash from the bathroom, followed by Kan swearing loudly, and Leo only just made it to the sink in the cove.

Leo was rinsing his mouth out when Kan exited the bathroom, rubbing the back of his head, and looking decidedly peeved. "They could at least warn us with a siren," he growled. "Smacked my bloody head on the shower nozzle." He ran his eye over Leo, who was still bent over the sink. "You miss my stuff?" he asked, casually. Leo spat and nodded. "Good lad."

****

Despite the bumpy start, Leo soon came to enjoy his brief stint aboard the Qosec Three. Despite their weird appearance,

Leo found the Rotaizians to be an affable species, and though there was a bit of a language barrier, they did their best to help him and Kan. Once Leo's stomach had settled after the jump into hyperspace, he and Kan had found the mess hall, thanks to a load of finger pointing from the crew. There they had found a palatable selection of relatively fresh food, and spent every subsequent mealtime there, drawing curious glances from the rest of the alien crew.

The only thing that had Leo feeling deflated was Kan himself. He was a man of frustratingly few words, and those he did use were often accompanied by a gruff tone, as if conversing was a major annoyance. As the only fluent Human speaker around, Leo had hoped conversations would have been more forthcoming, but try as he might, Kan could rarely be engaged. Leo wasn't sure if it was him that was an annoyance, or if that really was Kan's general demeanour. Even when Leo had worked under him as an engineer, the man had never fully engaged with him beyond regularly barked orders, and they had certainly never hung out socially outside of work.

When they were alone in their quarters, Leo was relegated to reading, or movie-watching, while Kan huffed and puffed doing push-ups and crunches to keep himself trim as, unlike on the Scientia, there were no gyms aboard the ship. As far as Leo could tell, the Rotaizians were a naturally slender species, with no need of workout equipment, and he'd yet to clap eyes on an overweight specimen. However, it was this lack of gym facilities which finally brought about a breakthrough for Leo when it came to Kan's lack of engagement.

He had been half watching Kan go through his evening workout routine, and half reading a fantasy novel by some ancient Human writer, and while shifting his eyes between the two, Leo noticed, with some disgust, that his stomach was not as flat when lying down as Kan's was, and the inadequate workouts he'd done in the shuttle hadn't kept it toned. Casting his mind back over the previous years, Leo realised his athletic prowess and diet had been boom and bust. Before being promoted to command, he had been relatively fit. He'd not been an Adonis by any means, but his overall physique had been slim and lightly muscled from carrying around engineering components. Then he'd got promoted and had spent most of his time sitting: sitting on the bridge, sitting in interminable meetings, sitting at home.

His eating habits had also gone on a downward spiral. When Pra'cha had left for the mission that had culminated in the capture of the Victory, and the Ciberian battle, Leo had slipped into a depressed funk, and had filled Pra'cha's void with junk food. Then she had returned, but Tia had gone nuts, and he had ended up watching over her monstrous form. During that time, food had not been plentiful, despite Pra'cha and Chione's best efforts, and the enforced fast had gone some way to helping his waistline. There had then been a brief, but healthier dietary lull during his honeymoon, thanks to Pra'cha making sure his nutritional needs were met, and he had, for a time, embraced a pattern of healthy eating.

Alas, his healthy eating hadn't been a permanent state. The food on the scouter, while limited, had been nutritionally dense, to pack as many calories as possible into as small a portion as practical. Leo had eaten more than he'd needed to, and not being the gym-bunny Kan was, had failed to burn the excess off. Conversely, the food aboard the Qosec Three was plentiful, and this, combined with boredom triggered by Kan's general unresponsiveness, meant Leo had been comfort-eating again. There was no getting away from it, his normally thin frame was starting to show the signs of excessive calorie intake, and he was getting podgy.

Leo watched as Kan finished up his routine, and when the man had disappeared into the bathroom to shower, Leo decided to take his situation into hand. He slipped of his bunk, lay down onto the floor, and began his journey to fit by doing some half-arsed crunches. He grunted and strained, and his stomach muscles bloomed with fire on being used for something other than digestion, and after barely a minute, he was winded. *Think I'm going to have to tackle push-ups tomorrow,* he thought, through clenched teeth.

"What the fuck are you doing?"

Leo'd had his back to the bathroom door, and had been straining so much, his ears hadn't picked up on the fact that the shower wasn't running, or that the door had opened. He opened his eyes, and through the spots that were swimming in his vision, saw Kan staring down at him, one eyebrow arched. "Uh, watching you kinda inspired me to get a bit more fit," he explained, thoroughly abashed.

"Not like that you're not," Kan told him. "You've got a better chance of getting whiplash and a hernia, and the last thing you're gonna want is some untrained alien doctor trying to sew your guts back in."

Leo's insides gave an alarming spasm in response. "I don't see what I'm doing that's so different to you," he said, trying to not sound as out of breath as he was.

"Really?" Before Leo could respond, Kan was on him, re-positioning his legs, and unwrapping his unprotesting hands from around the back of his neck. "Try doing a rep now…and without trying to kiss your ankles," he commanded.

Leo tried to do another set of crunches. Although the damage had already been done by his earlier amateurish attempt, he had to admit, it was marginally easier, though his stomach muscles still felt as though they were on fire.

"Now roll over and show me a push-up."

"Ummm."

"You can actually do a push-up?"

"Technically, yes." Although it had been a long time since he'd had to do any, Leo was pretty sure he could complete at least one.

"How the hell did you make it into the Alliance's ranks?"

"I was an engineer, remember? Soldering stuff and checking readouts didn't require me to have muscles like yours. I mean, I was okay fitness wise, at least enough to pass the tests, but the last few months I've been getting more sedentary, and I haven't been eating well either."

"Yeah, married life'll do that to you."

"Actually, the only time I've eaten right and got any exercise has been when Pra'cha's been around." He caught Kan's expression, and blushed at the thought of what he'd just insinuated.

"So, you want to get fit?"

"Yes." That was something Leo was at least sure of.

"In that case, put yourself in my hands, and by the time we get to Demeter Nine, you'll be able to pick up a plasma rifle without falling over."

Leo wanted to say that he could do that already, as a plasma rifle wasn't that heavy, but he knew Kan was only exaggerating for effect.

More importantly, Leo had found his way in. After that day, Kan at last began talking to him more freely. In all honesty, it was more a case of him once again barking orders at Leo, but Leo was perfectly content with the situation. It was some much-needed Human interaction, and it helped bolster the bond between the two men, something that had been missing, and that Leo knew would be needed once they reached Demeter Nine. As the monotonous days passed, and as they continued their journey through hyperspace, he and Kan got into a daily rhythm of eating, sleeping, and working out. Kan even offered, without prompt, to put Leo through some weapons drills. As it turned out, Leo managed to impress Kan with his accuracy, and got a surge of pride on seeing the look of amazement break across the man's weather-worn face.

"I didn't know you were that good," Kan admitted, with clear reluctance.

Leo tried to downplay his skill. "I spent a lot of time clearing out the vermin from our farm," he explained. "They were small and fast, which made for uncooperative targets."

"I guess if we get into trouble, I'm not going to have to worry too much about you."

"See!" Leo said, exasperated, "That's what I tried to tell Sin'ma and Ken'va, but they still see me as some kid who needs to be babysat. I wouldn't mind so much, but Sin'ma's not that much older than me." As it was, Sin'ma was a mere four years older.

"The more responsibility you have, the quicker you age mentally," Kan said, as an explanation.

Leo wasn't finished though. "Not only that, but I held my own during the battle for the Scientia, and Ken'va witnessed that." He was in full rant mode and was determined to air the grievances that had built up while he'd been trying to secure his mission.

"I get your point," Kan answered, unperturbed by Leo's outbreak, "you're a clever and skilled lad, and despite the grief I give you, I see that." Kan's candour took Leo aback. The man had never shared an ounce of approval towards him, at least not until he'd witnessed Leo blast twenty holes into the centre of a moving target. "The thing is, what abilities you possess will be eclipsed by another consideration."

"What's that?"

"Tia."

Leo groaned. "That woman is getting to be the bane of my life," he muttered.

Kan cracked a smile at that. "Welcome to my world," he said. "But seriously, think about it. It was her decision to make you second in command of the station, despite your overwhelming inexperience. By doing that she singled you out as, for want of a better phrase, a chosen one of hers. Don't forget, the Zerrens have an awkward love-idolise relationship with the Karee, and by default, Tia. The last thing Ken'va and Sin'ma would want is for Tia's chosen one to go wandering off on a dangerous mission and end up dead. In all likelihood, if they had agreed on the offing, they wouldn't have sent just one soldier to watch your back, they'd have organised a whole battalion, which, let's face it, would've thrown a spanner into the idea of a covert mission. Yes, they finally agreed when I came on board, partly because of my skill, and partly, I suspect, because as one of Tia's people, any mishap befalling you would be my fault. Therefore, it would be an internal problem amongst her men, as opposed to theirs."

"So, if I die, the way they see it, you will be the one to get strung up, even though they let me go," Leo echoed.

"Pretty much."

"That's comforting."

Kan gave a shrug. "It's how strategy and internal politics work, and why I choose to be on the front line and have nothing to do with it."

"I don't blame you. There are days I miss the monotony of Engineering."

"Your seat's still there, should you ever decide to get demoted."

The two men headed back up to their quarters to shower before dinner. Leo was quiet in thought. He didn't like the idea of the Zerrens in charge treating him like a fragile precious gem, simply because Tia had shown some favouritism towards him. He wasn't completely oblivious to Tia's way of thinking either. On hectic and bad days, he had often taken solace in the fact that Tia had bumped him up the ranks. Not because he was her pet, but because she genuinely thought he was the man for the job and could handle what came his way. That knowledge gave him the confidence boosts he needed to deal with stubborn freighter captains, or marauding, shape-shifting demigoddesses. He just wished the others had more faith in his ability, and the willingness to let him prove it. *At least Pra'cha has my back,* he reflected. With the escalation of war, came the escalation of having to go out on dangerous missions, a situation she was familiar with having done likewise all too recently, so could not veto his request to go, especially as his mission concerned his family.

As they were walking the last stretch towards their room, Lorkav intercepted them. "We come out tomorrow," his translator said for him.

"Out of hyperspace?" Kan confirmed.

The translator burbled at Lorkav, eliciting a facial expression from the alien that Leo couldn't read. "Yes," Lorkav eventually said.

"That was quick, I was expecting a few more days of travel." Leo said, more to Kan than Lorkav.

Lorkav's face was contorted again, either from concentrating on his translator, or from a sudden bout of indigestion, Leo wasn't sure which. The alien came back with the answer. "Travel faster, arrive quicker."

"Fair enough," Kan replied. "We'll get packing, get a last cooked meal, and turn in early."

Lorkav listened to Kan's answer, gave a head-bob, which Leo hoped meant the alien had comprehended what they'd said, and headed off the way he'd come.

"Wonder what time our exit'll be," Leo wondered.

"Well, whenever it is, considering the jump in, we'll know about it when it happens."

"Ugh. In that case, I think I'll give breakfast a miss." Leo didn't fancy getting up close and personal with the sink again.

"You and me both." Kan said, with a grimace.

****

Leo and Kan were once more on their own. The Qosec Three had exited hyperspace as planned, deposited Leo and Kan out in space in their scouter and had jumped back into hyperspace. After which, it was to re-enter normal space, and find a secure place to hide amongst the asteroids of the Transersalan system of Parania's outer belt, as close as it dared to the Alliance-monitored jumpgate that would be Leo and Kan's exit from Demeter Nine's system. There it was to await their eventual return. At least Leo prayed they would return; not to mention in one piece.

Entering the jumpgate hadn't been an issue. They had sent a signal to get it to power up, knowing it wouldn't trigger an alert as, although it was an Alliance-owned jumpgate, there were no security-checking features in place to prevent unauthorised activation, simply because so many differing races within the Alliance used it. Setting up security checks, and ensuring every individual, from cargo captains and scouter pilots to covert mercenaries and spies, from over a hundred races, got any updated passwords or automatic security clearance, was a huge, logistical nightmare. In general, any monitoring that occurred simply noted whether the ship entering the jumpgate was of a familiar design. If it wasn't, nothing happened on the inbound leg. Instead, any check on who or what the unfamiliar vessel was would come when the vessel officially entered Alliance territory, such as on the outskirts of Demeter Nine's solar system. However, Leo and Kan's vessel was a recognisable Alliance scouter, and Kan was banking on the fact that any information pertaining to it being from the hijacked battleship wouldn't have made it to such a secluded outpost. Long distance messages were sent along gate routes, and they weren't the most reliable relay stations. If a fault occurred at an unmanned jumpgate, it could be months until a fix happened, either via long-distance reprogramming, or manually by a repair crew.

If they were made on entering the solar system, then the first part of the plan was scuppered, and they'd have to hightail it to Leo's homeworld, grab his parents and sister, and have a rethink. This was because the first part of their plan was them hijacking the monitoring station that oversaw the gates that were to be their entrance and exit.

As they traversed hyperspace yet again, Leo and Kan talked at length at what might be waiting for them, and how to work round the issues they might face. Kan made it clear that Leo would likely see action. "These will be men and women who work for the Alliance. Chances are, all will try to repel us initially, no matter how weak a support they have for their sadistic overlords. Eventually, some may lay down their weapons, some may even come over to our side, but a few will try to kill us, no matter what, and it's them we'll have to deal with."

Leo felt a knot form in his gut. He didn't want his two

brothers, who were assigned to the station, to be in the latter group. It was bad enough he was probably going to have to kill people, but the idea that his own kin could be amongst them was a terrible thought. However, there was just no way of knowing how far into their brains the Alliance had buried themselves. "Nathan and Marlan better have the good sense to lay their weapons down when they see me," he said. "If they don't...." He couldn't, didn't want to, finish the sentence. He looked at Kan, who looked sympathetically back.

"I promise you, if the worse happens, I will do my best to spare them," he stated, "but not at the expense of your, or my life. If the Alliance has corrupted them, then chances are they won't think twice about killing you, no matter if you're blood. But if they're anything like you, they'll probably be smart about things."

"I hope you're right." Leo looked out his little window at the eerie light that stretched for infinity around their speck of a vessel. He tried to remember conversations he'd had with his brothers before his defection had made communications impossible. Their chats had been typically male. Glossed over workdays, dissections of the latest sports matches, enthusing over the yearly batch of new films delivered from New Earth, and the occasional gossip about a girl that had caught their eye. There had never been any in-depth discussions regarding feelings towards the Alliance.

To them, much like to Leo, the goings-on of the Alliance had been something in the periphery and had no real impact on them. Their jobs had them working as engineers. They spent their days monitoring the workings of the gate, they were paid electronically, and that was that. They weren't embroiled in conquest, or mass genocide, nor did they hear much about those topics, and so long as they did their jobs, everything was fine. But there was no knowing how deep the insidiousness of the Alliance had woven itself into their minds since Leo had last spoken to them. The Alliance ran the monitoring station, which meant there were higher-ups in charge who had a deeper worship of their overlords, and who saw fit to make sure those below them felt the same way.

Leo's thoughts led him to another worry. Though his brothers had mentioned women on and off, there had never been anything serious going on. Relationships were considered a no-go between close members of staff, especially in small teams such as the one at the station, but the rule did nothing to stop casual hook-ups. Sending program updates to the gate, occasional physical repair jobs, regular station maintenance, and stock-checking, only took up a certain amount of the day, after which, boredom was the tool of the devil. Leo knew, from his brief conversations with his brothers, that everyone had pretty much dallied with everyone else. Conversely, working in space kept them away from their home planet, and fresh faces, so finding a new partner, and holding on to her, was problematic. Yet that didn't mean that in the intervening year and a half they hadn't managed to tie down a long-term partner, or wife. If his brothers had partners, Leo was faced with the possibility that they could end up coming too, or worse, prevent his brothers from leaving. Coming meant a severe strain on their refilled rations, staying meant his brothers remaining in danger, and becoming pawns, especially if Leo managed to rescue everyone else. His sister was less of a worry. She was younger than him, and though planet side, she was still working through her carefree phase, and Leo figured that if she was dating, it was by no means serious. Leo turned from his hyperspace gazing, and mentioned his concern of extra bodies to Kan.

The man simply shrugged. "We'll cross that bridge if and when we come to it," he said.

"How can you be so calm?" Leo asked. They had entered hyperspace barely hours ago, but thanks to a multitude of worries, Leo was having a tough time keeping his food down.

"I've been on more missions, and seen more action, than you will ever know, or do," Kan explained. "All you can do is write the plans down and prepare for every eventuality.

Chances are if you're smart enough, and prepared enough, things will run smoothly and to plan."

"And if not?"

"Then you use your brains."

"How many times have you been in such a position?"

There was a long pause. "I'll be honest, most of my missions involved me going into places and killing people." Kan admitted, much to Leo's dismay. "Saving people, and getting them out alive...well, that's only been a recent thing."

"And...," Leo prompted.

"I've managed to do pretty well so far," was Kan's dry response.

****

They came out through the jumpgate on the outskirts of Leo's home system and weren't greeted by a battalion of Alliance ships. Leo unclenched slightly, but what was coming next prevented complete relaxation, and he waited, on edge, as Kan hailed the monitoring station, which was still some distance away, using the scouters ID.

A voice crackled back, "go ahead." The two words failed to indicate if they'd been made.

"This is system-scouter Ess-Ess-Ex-Nine-Omega-Twelve," Kan responded, "requesting temporary docking at your station. Our water recovery system has died, and we need a couple of replacement parts, ASAP." Kan had come up with the excuse of a broken water system to gain access to the station. It meant their predicament wasn't dangerous to the station, such as a problematic nuclear engine could be, but was simple enough that the station would have compatible replacement parts in stock. Further, a water issue would be important enough to allow them to dock, as without clean water, a scouter's occupants wouldn't survive much further into the system.

They waited anxiously, as their distance meant any response wasn't instantaneous.

"What parts you after?" came the brusque response.

"The microbial sensor blew, which wouldn't have been too big a deal if it hadn't taken the UV steriliser with it. I need replacements for both those, otherwise, I've got nothing but what's left in the tank to drink, what with the emergency override stopping water entering that part of the system, and that's not gonna let me make land-fall."

There was another long silence, and Leo began to sweat, wondering if the person on the other end of the line had figured out who they were, and was calling for reinforcements. Eventually the voice got back to them. "We've got replacements we can give you. Once you get to us, head to the red airlock, and we'll meet you there."

"No problem, and thanks." Kan cut the line.

"So, did he sound nervous or suspicious to you?" Leo asked.

"Nope, and I've got pretty good at picking up any strains in a person's voice. I don't want to jinx it, but I think we may be in the clear."

This was good news, as it meant they had a better chance of taking the station and its crew by surprise, thereby reducing the body-count. Unfortunately, they still had a couple of hours travel to reach the station, and the situation could easily change in the meantime. Complacency wasn't an option.

****

The monitoring station was a small, windowless, ring-shaped vessel just big enough to house monitoring equipment, engineering and repair components, and minimal living quarters, while still being of a decent enough size to be able to spin at a sensible speed to produce artificial gravity. It had taken Leo's legs a little while to readjust to the gravity on the Qosec Three, and he hoped his legs didn't fail him when they stepped aboard the station, after having been in the zero-g of the scouter again.

Kan located the red airlock, which was an unassuming red

ring on the station's side. Gradually, he matched their ship's speed and angle to the station's rotational speed, in a dizzying dance that drew them in closer with each orbit. After a two-hour-long waltz, the vessels connected with barely a clang.

Up next was an awkward moment, which was so for a couple of reasons, but mainly because of physics. On attaching to the ring, the shuttle became subject to the same centripetal forces as the station, and that meant they had gravity, which Leo could feel tugging away at him, but the direction of tug was the inconvenient part. Though the station and scouter were technically joined side-by-side, the location of the floor was very different for each. On the ringed station, the floor was the inside of the rim of the ring, with centripetal forces holding the crew to it like laundry in a spin cycle, and because the scouter's airlock was on its left side, attached to the rotating station's 'floor', the right side of the scouter had become Leo's floor.

He watched as Kan gingerly unbuckled himself from the pilot seat and slumped against the right wall. After a bit of shuffling, he stood up, at right angles to Leo. For Kan, it had been an easy manoeuvre, as he'd been next to the wall that was now the floor. Leo was next to the left wall, which was now the ceiling, and he knew full well that on unbuckling he was going to crash sideways onto the wall-come-floor.

"You need a hand?" Kan asked.

"Umm, how am I supposed to do this?" Leo asked, feeling a little panicked.

"Get your legs round to your side as far as possible, then when you unbuckle and drop, you should land on your feet."

Leo scooted his legs and body as far round to the right as possible while still in his seat, disengaged his belt's latch, and dropped. His legs were almost underneath him, but not enough, and he stumbled forward and head-butted the scouter's roof, which was now the wall. "Son of a...!"

"You okay there?" Kan asked, with nominal concern.

"Yeah, fine," Leo fibbed, rubbing his bruised head, and

blinking back tears. He grabbed a jacket that had been pur-
posely lifted from the Victory, with the idea that its Alliance
tailoring and insignia might give him a moment of disguise
against questioning eyes.

"Good…shove this in a back holster," Kan said, as he handed
Leo a small plasma gun.

Leo did what he was told and made sure the weapon was
hidden under his jacket. There was no point jumping out of
the airlock waving weapons, because their current angle made
that impossible. They were going to have to clamber upwards,
out of the scouter, and were going to come out at the feet of the
station's crew. They would be at a complete disadvantage, and
at the mercy of the crew until they were eye-to-eye. That was
when Kan intended to make his move, though he hadn't explained exactly what that move was to Leo.

"You never know, we could be up against a telepath," had
been Kan's overly cautious reasoning.

Kan's own outfit had little in the way of hiding places for
firearms. His black leather vest and pants had several pockets,
but none big enough, or handy enough, to holster his weapons,
and unlike Leo, he had chosen to forgo camouflaging himself
in Alliance garb. Leo wondered if it was because the man was
simply too big for any of the proffered clothes, or whether he
was set against wearing their insignia again, and he watched
as Kan shoved a single large hunting knife in his boot, but his
long, samurai-like swords he left jammed in a corner, along
with his plasma rifles. As far as Leo could tell, it looked like
the man intended to tackle any resistance by hand. Kan stood
up. "You ready kid?" Leo gave a reluctant nod. Kan cycled the
airlock above them, and pushed the door upwards, letting it hit
the floor of the station with a loud clang. Then he removed a
ladder from the wall and hooked it over the rim of the airlock.
"I'm coming up," he shouted, by way of a warning to those
waiting outside, and grabbed the railings. "Follow me straight
up," he told Leo, before climbing upwards.

Once Kan's boots had disappeared, Leo followed suit, and

headed up the ladder. At arriving at the top, he sensed Kan's presence behind him, and turned, to find him and their greeting party, in a stand-off.

Leo watched Kan size up the three men. Two were strangers, the third, with his eyes going wide with surprise, and a bag holding their lied for replacement parts at his feet, was his brother Nathan. All of them had their weapons pointed squarely at Leo and Kan. Leo's stomach sank, and he briefly tasted regret and failure. Then, without warning, his world went black, and he barely had time to register himself pitching forward.

****

"Leo...? Leo...?" The voice was faint, and Leo was having a hard time finding its direction. His world was still dark, and his mind was fuzzy. "Leo!" The voice was clearer, and more urgent now. "Wake up, you dumb kid!" Then a bolt of pain, as his brain registered he'd been slapped across the face, and he came to with a start. He sat upright; befuddled. Kan was squatting over him. "Damn, sorry about that, I thought, what with all her meddling, that Tia had shored your brain up against psychic attack."

"Say what now?" It was then Leo saw the two men and his brother laying prone and hog-tied on the ground. "What the hell happened?" His mouth felt weird, as if his tongue were three sizes too big, and his head hurt, more than it had when he'd smacked it on the scouter.

"It's something I keep handy in case of emergencies," Kan explained quickly. "These studs," he showed Leo the thick black leather cuffs that encircled his wrists, which were dotted with large silver rivets, "are various incendiary devices, and a couple are courtesy of Tia. They effectively short-circuit the brain."

Leo rubbed his aching head. "I told Tia not to meddle in my brain anymore," he told Kan. Kan gave a nod of understanding.

Leo looked over at his brother. "They don't do permanent damage, do they?" he asked, concerned.

"Don't worry, he'll be fine. Though you're both gonna feel like you've got a hangover for a while."

"Wait, can we use those to take out the rest of the crew?" Leo asked, the fog slowly lifting from his mind.

Kan shook his head. "No can do. I only have one left, and their range is pretty weak. They're really an up-close-and-personal-last-resort kinda thing."

"Oh."

"Doesn't matter. We're on their level now, and we have weapons."

"That's a thought," Leo said, looking around quickly, "why haven't the others come for us yet? They probably saw you take us out via the security cameras?"

"I've locked the doors," Kan said, matter-of-factly.

"Okay, so what now?"

"Now we see if we've got an extra pair of hands." Kan walked over to the incapacitated crew men. "This your brother?" he asked, pointing down to the only man of the trio who had dark blond hair.

"Yes. His name's Nathan."

Kan rolled his brother over and tried to try to wake him up by calling his name. When that failed, he employed the same tactic he'd used on Leo, and slapped him. Nathan gave a grunt and opened his eyes. They looked shocked into Kan's face, then went searching for Leo. When their eyes finally locked, Leo gave his brother a weak smile.

"Hey Nath, long time no see?"

His brother gaped at him. "What the hell are you doing here?" he spluttered. "Are you mad? You do realise you've got a price on your head?"

"And do you want to collect it?" Kan asked, in a tone of voice Leo had never heard come out of the man before. It was low, and barely above an animal's growl, and his face had taken on the countenance of a deranged killer.

It had the desired effect. What little colour was left in Nathan Jackson's face drained away, and he shook his head violently. "Oh gods no! He's my brother, I would never hurt him."

Kan remained staring at the lad, purposefully letting the moment drag on. He reached into his boot, and fished out his knife, and Nathan looked like he was about to lose control of his bowels. Then, as if a switch had been clicked, the visage of rage cleared from Kan's face. "Good enough," he said, almost jovially, and he cut Nathan's bonds.

The Jackson brothers exhaled in unison. "Was that completely necessary?" Leo asked, feeling just as unnerved as his brother.

"Yes. I wanted to make sure he wasn't going to stab you in the back," Kan said, somewhat ironically, as he sheathed his knife.

The two brothers got to their feet and came together in a bear hug. "Really, what are you doing here?" Nathan asked, holding Leo at arm's length.

Leo stared into the face of a man he hadn't seen for ages. His brother was slightly taller than him, and his skin was pale, from spending his days away from natural sunlight. Like Leo, he had inherited his mother's unruly hair, but he had his father's green eyes, while Leo had his mother's grey-blue eyes. "I came to rescue you two, mum and dad, and Ellie too."

Nathan shook his head. "You've taken an awful risk. The Alliance knows you're a turncoat, and now there's a good chance they know you're here."

"Did you make the scouter?" Kan asked.

"No," confirmed Nathan. "But there's a chance someone on the crew has recognised Leo from the cameras..." his eyes glanced to where the security camera was now a mangled mess courtesy of Kan, "...and has already sent the message to Demeter."

"In that case, we may be okay," Kan assured them. "I introduced a virus into the station's system after taking out you guys, and with any luck, it'll have blocked communications before they could react and get the word out."

"How long was I down?" Leo asked.

"Long enough." Kan said, smiling. "Like I said, this ain't my first rodeo. And what about these two?" he asked, giving one of the still-unconscious men a prod with his boot.

Nathan grimaced. "I wouldn't trust them. They're directly under Lieutenant Commander Pasqual Zhan, the guy that runs this place, and he's all for the Alliance."

Leo finally bit the bullet "What about Marlan?"

Nathan grinned. "You're our brother, and when it comes to loyalty, you're top of the list."

Leo felt a profound sense of relief wash over him.

"And the rest of the crew?" Kan queried.

Nathan shrugged. "Like I said, Lieutenant Commander Zhan is an issue, as are those directly under him; namely these two, who are out of a crew of five security personnel, and the two department heads. The rest of the crew?" He gave a shrug. "Well, to be honest we don't talk much about the Alliance, so it's hard to say."

A loud bang from the other side of one of the locked bulkhead doors got everyone's attention. *Looks like they're trying to break in.*

"I guess we should make a move and subdue the locals," Kan said, as he dropped back down into the scouter.

"Can we trust that guy?" Nathan whispered to Leo, keeping a close eye on the hatch Kan had disappeared through, while handing Leo a spare rifle, and clutching his own regained gun to his chest.

"Despite outward appearances, yes, completely," Leo whispered back, as Kan re-emerged carrying his swords and rifle. "Man, there's so much I have to tell you."

"I don't doubt it," Nathan replied, inspecting Leo as he did so. "You look like you've gained twenty years in just over five." He looked back to the door, which was reverberating to another ominous bang. "Do you think Marlan is in trouble?"

"I would imagine so," Leo said. "Chances are, they'll use him to capture me."

Nathan grimaced in response.

In the meantime, Kan had strapped his swords to his back, and was fiddling with his cuff. "You may want to back off a bit," he told the brothers. Leo and Nathan did as they were told and pressed themselves against the far door. Whereas Kan headed to the door from which the explosions were coming from. He removed the front of its control panel and fiddled with the wiring. Then, in a deft move, he cycled the door barely a centimetre ajar, and flicked one of his silver studs through the gap, just as a reciprocating shot of plasma whipped past his ear in the opposite direction and scorched the wall close to Leo's head. Kan flattened himself against the wall as a loud bang, and a flash of blinding light, came through the gap.

Kan cycled the door fully open, to reveal the final three security men, their uniforms giving them away, suffering the disorientating effects of the flash-bang grenade. Kan easily ducked and weaved past their flailing arms and guns and took each of the staggering men out with a swift blow to the head from the butt of his rifle.

"Grab a body," he barked, and the three men each dragged a stunned counterpart, to lay next to their prone colleagues. Kan cycled the door closed, and locked it, then disappeared back into the scouter. He re-emerged, carrying a little box. "Can't have these guys coming up behind us," he said, and proceeded to extract a small revolver syringe from the box.

"What's that?" Nathan asked, looking worried.

"Just something that'll keep them quiet," Kan assured him, before injecting the five prone men. Done, he pocketed the capped syringe in his free boot. "Right, no more mucking about. We need to secure this station before someone manages to purge my virus and alert the authorities. Just an FYI, does your brother look like you two?"

"He's taller, blonder, and has more freckles," Nathan explained. Leo nodded the affirmative.

"I'll try not to hit him then," Kan said. "In the meantime;

Leo, you know the score...shoot first, questions later, that's how you survive. Same goes for you Nathan." He headed back to the door.

Leo and Nathan exchanged looks. "You kill many people when you took the station?" Nathan asked Leo.

"More than I would have liked, but as Kan said, it was them or me."

His brother gave a sage nod. "Was it easy?"

Leo could see the fear encroaching in on him. He may have been his older brother, a man who had ten years on him, but as an engineer, in the backwoods of space, he'd never seen action. "To be honest, the adrenalin was pumping, and I was trying to stay alive," Leo replied. "I guess the magnitude of what I'd done didn't sink in until everything had calmed down. I'll admit, despite it all, I regretted taking lives, but I knew there'd been no other choice. In the end, I survived, and so did a lot of other decent people."

Nathan didn't look any less scared, but he hoisted his rifle up with an air of determination. "You got any bars on that space station of yours? Because I'm probably going to need a stiff drink when all this is said and done."

Leo smiled. "Oh, I know the perfect place for that."

"Ready?" Kan interrupted.

"Yes," the brothers said in unison.

Kan once again cycled the door open a crack and took stock of the situation. Satisfied, he opened it enough for a person to get through, and took point, beckoning Leo and Nathan to follow him through. Once in the open of the corridor, they slowly inched their way forward, weapons at the ready. They met a couple more security cameras en route, which Kan simply ripped off the wall. At the end of a short walk, they were faced with another door, this time, as indicated by Kan's annoyed expression, locked from the other side.

"What's beyond?" Kan asked Nathan.

"It's a small engineering workshop, then another bulkhead door, then the control centre. After which it goes mess area, living area-come-Medibay, escape pod and docked station-to-gate vessel, water and refuse recycling, storage, and back round to the docking station. All of which are sectioned off."

Kan nodded. "Then we don't have far to go to get control of this place, and if we keep pushing forward, they're just gonna end up with their backs against the locked door between storage and our scouter." He seemed pleased by that.

"True, but they're not going to relinquish the control area without a fight," Nathan pointed out, "which means they're probably waiting the other side of this door."

"And with Marlan held at gunpoint no doubt" Leo put in.

Kan seemed to be re-evaluating his position. "So, if they're using him, they could either have him up front as a shield, meaning I could accidentally hit him trying to take out any combatants behind him. Or, he's being held at the back, to retaliate for any initial kills." Kan's words made Leo seriously question Marlan's odds. "Well, there's only one way to find out…. You got any tools on you?" he aimed at Nathan. Nathan fished out a multi tool from the tool belt he was wearing and handed it to Kan. Kan used it to remove the panel from below the door's locking mechanism.

"You know what you're doing?" asked a worried Nathan.

"No offence Nath, but he's the best engineer I know," Leo said.

Kan gave a wide grin, as he once again manipulated the wires that snaked into the mechanism. A few moments later, and the door's interface beeped, and the light that had been blinking red, turned to green. "Nathan, I want you watching our backs, okay? Leo, here with me."

Leo did as he was told and joined Kan's side; waiting as the man inched the door open. No weapon's volley came at them. In fact, it was eerily quiet. They peeked through the gap, and Leo's stomach fell. In the middle of the room stood two armed men, whom Leo took for the department heads. One wore the orange uniform of engineer, the other, command white, and both had high-level insignia on their collars. A short way behind them was another armed man in white, his pips show-ing he was Lieutenant Commander Pasqual Zhan. Off to his sides, looking apprehensive, were several other crew members, all with weapons, but all looking like they'd drop them at the first loud sound. But it was who was ahead of them all that made Leo's stomach twitch, because held in the grip of the one dressed in white, with a gun visibly dug into his ribs, was Marlan.

Before the Lieutenant Commander could get his threats out, Kan took charge of the conversation. "So how are we going to play this?" he called out.

"Simple. You hand over the traitor Leo Jackson, and we'll release his brother Marlan, and show leniency towards his brother Nathan, who has clearly been corrupted into acting against us," Zhan answered.

"And me?"

"I think we both know you're dead either way. You are a rebel mercenary, and execution is your only end. But at least if you surrender, Leo's brothers will be spared."

Kan's eyes darted over to Leo, who felt himself grip his gun tightly in response. "I didn't think leniency was in the Orion Alliance's vocabulary." Kan shot back. "I've certainly never seen a shred of it. Let's be honest, they'll be executed along with me to set an example."

"Leo," Marlan suddenly shouted. "If you've got any sense, you'll take Nathan and leave now. Don't waste your life trying to save me."

The head of engineering silenced Marlan with a smack to the back of his head with the handle of his gun. Leo winced as the crunch reached his ears.

"See," Kan said, his voice and face turning dark again, "the problem is, we're not retreating types, and I'm willing to bet you really need Leo alive, so your superiors can torture in-formation out of him regarding certain individuals. Which means his death in crossfire is not what you want, because if he dies, it'll be you suffering the wrath of the Alliance, not us." Despite Kan's almost blasé words about his life, Leo was satisfied to see a moment of doubt flicker across Zhan's face. "I would also like it to be known that if it looks like Leo is about to end up in enemy hands, I am more than capable of killing him myself."

Leo's eyes bugged. "What?" he mouthed at Kan, but the man's war mask prevented Leo from telling if he was being serious or not.

"So how about we finish this conversation face to face," Kan called out to Zhan.

Zhan seemed to have lost his desire to converse, and his jaw was locked in an angry sneer.

"Are you sure about this?" Leo asked Kan. He had accepted his brothers would be used as bargaining chips, as indeed Marlan was at that moment, but it had never occurred to him that he'd become one too.

Kan gave a brief nod. "Listen," he growled. "We're going to play this like surgeons, using quick precision. I know you have a damn good aim, so when I say the word, you take out the guy on our left."

"And what about the guy holding Marlan?"

"You leave him to me."

Leo could only agree to Kan's orders. "And what's the word?"

"Bread." Leo raised an eyebrow. "You'll know it when it comes."

They shouldered their weapons, and Kan cycled the door open wide enough for him and Leo to stand abreast. The two parties faced off. Leo didn't dare take his eye off orange-shirt; whose weapon was aimed squarely back at him. Notably though, his finger was carefully away from its trigger. Leo could feel his palms sweating, and hoped that whenever Kan's signal was coming, it was soon.

Lieutenant Commander Zhan found the power of speech once more. "You will not leave this place alive."

"It's amazing how many individuals, Human or otherwise, have said that to me over the years, and yet, here I am," Kan threw back.

"I will be the one who changes that," Zhan said, starting to look almost rabid in his confidence. "I will present the Alliance with one of its greatest traitors and get the rewards I so justly deserve."

"Let me guess," Leo interrupted. "You're pissed off with having to oversee a tiny little station in the middle of nowhere, and think you're deserving of a battleship command?"

"Damn right! I've had enough of ordering around a bunch of dumb, backwater hicks." Zhan's comment drew dark glances from the crewmen about him, though in his fervour, he didn't notice.

I think he's just lost his backup, Leo surmised, gleefully.

Kan gave a protracted sigh. "And there's me thinking we could sit down and talk this out, share a drink and, I don't know...break...bread."

Three shots went off almost simultaneously. Leo's caught orange-shirt full in the torso, caving in his chest, and sending him flying in a spray of blood. The other two were Kan's, and Leo watched in horror as both white-shirt and Marlan were sent lurching backwards. Leo was rooted to the spot, and the image of his brother, crashing to the floor, seared itself into his mind. Zhan rose his own weapon, and aimed it at Leo, but Leo's world was lurching, and he couldn't find the wherewithal to react. A blast came from behind; the ball of broiling plasma sailing between Kan and Leo and removing Zhan's head.

Leo's world was still spinning, and he was barely registering anything. "No...no...no...!" He ran over to his fallen brother, to find his freckled face screwed up in pain, and his left hand gripping his right shoulder. "You're alive?!"

"Considering the pain I'm in, I should bloody well hope so!" Marlan answered, from behind clenched teeth.

Leo's head whipped round to Kan. "What the hell?"

"I couldn't get a clear shot, so got him out of the way," Kan explained, without a hint of remorse. He had his weapon aimed at the rest of the crew; however, none of them appeared to have any desire to retaliate. "I knew you wouldn't want to take the shot."

Leo couldn't close his mouth.

Despite what he'd seen, Nathan still had control of his senses. "Get a medikit!" he barked. One of the crewmen gratefully dropped his weapon, grabbed a pack from the wall, and rushed over to Leo's moaning and swearing brother. Nathan joined them and proceeded to deal with his brother's scorched shoulder with a burn kit. "We'll need to get you to the Medibay and patch you up properly." He told his brother.

"Am I going to lose my arm?" Marlan muttered.

"No, but I don't think you're going to be throwing any pitches for a while," Nathan joked, giving his brother's healthy shoulder a supportive pat.

Leo could see too, that his wound, though painful, was expertly done, and not life-threatening. Kan had caught him enough to spin him out of the grip of White Shirt, while allowing him to get a clear shot at the man himself. This was confirmed by the fact that his head was several feet away from the rest of him, having been severed by a calculated blast to the neck. However, this did little to quell Leo's anger, and he rounded on Kan. "You could have warned me. I mean hell…you could have killed him."

"Firstly," Kan said, in a level voice, "I didn't tell you because you would've tried to stop me. Secondly, you may be a good shot, but I'm better, and I knew he would be relatively fine."

"Relatively fine?" Leo parroted, his cheeks flushing. "He could have still been shot."

"Yes, but his spin was enough that even if that bastard had got a shot off, it would have glanced his side, as opposed to turning his internal organs to mush."

Leo stood, aghast. He was under no illusions to what Kan was, namely a soldier and killer, but he still couldn't grasp the fact that the man could easily shoot a non-combatant, even if it were to save his life. "Just promise me," he snarled, "you won't pull a stunt like that with my elderly parents." Kan didn't answer straight away. "Promise me!"

Kan seemed to relent, though his face showed he wasn't happy to do so. "Fine. I promise."

Nathan came over to them, having overseen his brother's trip to the infirmary. "So, what now?" he asked, trying to break the tension.

"Did they manage to get a message out on our arrival?" Kan asked.

"No," Nathan confirmed, "the system's still gummed up with your virus, so no alert's been sent to Demeter, or the monitoring station covering the gates on the Alliance-side of the system. However, according to one of the guys who works command, a ship identifying itself as a government agency vessel entered the system about a week ago and hasn't been registered as having left."

"Which agency?" Leo knew 'agency' could mean anything from mundane animal and crop inspectors to problematic intelligence gatherers, the latter being the ones gunning for him and his family.

"Apparently, they weren't overly forthcoming with that information."

"Which means we can assume they were covert individuals as opposed to busy-body bureaucrats," Kan surmised.

"That's my thinking," said Nathan.

"In that case, we'll go on and assume your family is being watched, if not already being guarded over. Nathan, do you think you'll have any problem holding this station until we get back?"

Leo's brother shook his head. "As long as we can confine everyone to the living area, me and Marlan should be fine guarding this place. It hardly needs a full team to keep it ticking over."

"And what if a battleship or something comes in?" asked Leo, still seething.

"We're not exactly anybody's first port of call," Nathan said, in a conciliatory tone. "Chances are, anything like that will head straight to Demeter, just like the 'inspectors' did."

"In that case, we'll grab you on the return trip," Kan said. "We'll be escaping through the exit jumpgate at this end, so we'll swing by for you."

Leo had another thought. "Where's Ellie? Is she at our parents, or still in the town?"

Demeter Nine had no real cities to speak of, not throughout its entire land mass. It had been colonised for only a couple of hundred years, and despite what its external defence structure would have people believe, most of its one giant southern continent was either untamed wilderness, or farmsteads. Occasional hubs of commerce had formed, where food stuffs arrived, locals gathered, and necessities were bought, but they were nowhere near being bustling metropolitan capitals. A few entrepreneurs had set up cloth-making factories, making direct use of the cotton and hemp that was farmed, but they tended to be no bigger than large sheds. The other businesses tended to be small and locally owned; potters, vintners, cosmetic-makers, and the like. There were only three big complexes on the planet that Leo could think of. The first was the main space port. It was situated at the point that had been first landing and was the main destination for freight on and off the planet. The second was a TV studio, which covered the entire population, and beamed out weather and farming reports, low-quality independently made dramas, and the occasional movie blockbuster. The other....

"In our last conversation, she told me she'd moved permanently to the Comma Facility." Nathan said.

"What the hell's that?" Kan asked.

Leo explained, "It's the site that monitors the defence satellites around Demeter Nine, and keeps in contact with the off-world bases. It's basically a self-contained facility, stationed around a giant radio telescope, way out in the sticks." He turned to his brother. "I guess she got fed up with commuting."

"Basically," Nathan replied.

"I take it it's a military base then," Kan said.

"Oh yes. Soldiers and guns kinda place." Nathan elaborated. "Not many, but enough to cause you problems."

"Right. Which means the last thing we want to do is rescue her from there," said Leo.

"What about if I disable the virus? Could you get a message to her to get her to your parents?" Kan asked.

"Sure. It won't be suspect either. Me and Marlan often get her to send stuff to us, usually new casual clothes we've ordered. Because of her connections, she can get them on the faster resupply pods, instead of us relying on mum and dad to send them by inter-planetary freight, which can take bloody months to arrive."

"Good, we'll do that then. Even if they're all under guard, at least they'll be so together, and we'll have a better chance of grabbing them all."

So, with the help of burnt and pissed-off Marlan, Leo and Kan rounded up the crew and locked them securely in the living quarters. Leo was relieved to find none wanted to protest or put up a fight. He hoped that, when he and his family had left, the Alliance wouldn't treat the survivors too harshly. They had willingly let Leo slip through their fingers, but as Kan pointed out to them, "You'll have plenty of time to come up with a believable story." Leo doubted any story would bare the scrutiny of a telepath, and he felt a pang of guilt over what would be their fate. "Just as a side note," Kan added, as if he'd read Leo's thoughts. "If the worst comes, the Transersalans over in the Paranian system, would probably take you in...if you can get your hands on a suitable escape vessel...just saying."

Meanwhile, Nathan sent a message to their sister, telling her he had a parcel of new clothes and work boots heading to their parents that he needed sending on to him ASAP. To cover his lie, he placed the order too, making sure the delivery time coincided with Kan and Leo's planet-fall. That done, Kan reactivated the virus, just in case, and the group said their goodbyes.

"No hard feelings over the arm?" Kan asked Marlan.

Despite the earlier disgruntled looks he'd shot Kan's way, Marlan shook his head. "Nah, though it still hurts like a bitch."

"Mind your language," said an aggrieved Nathan.

"Hey, you weren't the one who got shot in the bloody arm, remember?" countered Marlan.

Leo couldn't help but smile. Listening to the banter of his bullish mid-brother, and his more uptight older brother, made him realise just how much he'd missed them. The feeling of family unity buoyed him, and he was sad to leave it after such a brief time. But he was only halfway through his mission, and the lives of his parents and sister were still in the balance. Hands were shaken, and brotherly bear-hugs were given, before Leo sadly trudged after Kan back to their little scouter.

After some mutter-infused clambering, Leo managed to get himself back into his seat, and after a brief pre-launch check, they were off. Before them stretched another two days of uncertainty, as they headed into the heart of the system to what Leo hoped wouldn't be his final showdown.

Yet Leo's nervous excitement at being back in his old home solar system was mollified by its interminable void. A road trip home, cross-country, would bring with it familiar sights. There would be known towns, random landmarks, and recognisable scenic vistas that would inflame the butterflies of anticipation with every encounter. A trip home via space was a different, almost soporific journey. To Leo, it was no better than the journey through hyperspace, but instead of the weird blue light, Leo was faced with hours of unending blackness, speckled with distant constellations that never changed.

This was because the system that held Demeter Nine was small on planets, but big on diameter. At its heart, beat a young A0V white star; twice the size of Zerra's little yellow sun, and considerably hotter. As a result, the system had expanded out further than those that had more 'normal' suns, and as they sped through the system, Leo didn't glimpse a planet or an asteroid; the spacing between bodies meaning nearly all but their destination would remain hidden from direct view.

The system itself consisted of a measly four planets. At the outer reaches of the solar system was a ball of rock and ice, and any mineral wealth it held was hidden deep below a layer of frozen water, and little had been done to crack its shell. As such, it was an unguarded world, and Kan had no issue with flying close to it. Though close was a relative term, and Leo would have been hard-pressed to pick the dirty snowball out from the black void.

Next in was a belt of asteroids, but with several thousands of kilometres between each hunk of rock, Kan easily plotted a safe course through it. Once through, they crossed the orbital path of another small rocky planet. This one was devoid of ice, and a small mining outpost had been set up on it, shortly after the colonisation of Demeter Nine had allowed it to be regularly supplied. However, as its orbit had it on the opposite side of the sun to them, there was no chance of one of its satellites picking them up.

Then came another asteroid belt, followed by the behemoth of the system. It was the only other planet Leo could make out, though even then it was indistinguishable from the other stars in the void and was just another pinprick of light to him. It was a huge orange gas giant, plagued by violent storms, and encircled by eleven moons. It reigned over the system, and swept it clean of rogue comets, and in so doing, it had kept the last planet of the system safe, so much so that primitive life had managed to get a foothold. That planet was Demeter Nine; its inflated number a result of being the ninth planet colonised by the interplanetary company Demeter Corp., which specialised in mixed farming-based colonisation.

Kan pulled the scouter to a stop in the shadow of the dark side of Demeter Nine's only moon. Unlike the more established colonies within the Orion Alliance, Demeter Nine's system had little in the way of off-world infrastructure. Along with the mining base on the rocky world, and a few machine-run bases on a few of the Jovian moons, Demeter Nine's moon had its own small base for mining. However, it consisted of barely a handful of structures, all on the opposite side to where Kan had parked, and most were underground.

Kan scooted their vessel as far round as he could, to get a peek at Leo's home world, and cut as much power as possible, to make it harder for an unforeseen satellite to spot them. The temperature in the scouter plummeted, and Leo got goose bumps, despite having put a jacket on in preparation. Most of the power that was left, Kan used for the scanners, and he started up the algorithm.

"How's it looking?" Leo asked. He knew what Kan was doing. His program was surreptitiously listening in on the satellite's communications, looking for a pattern, a gap, or a blind spot that would allow them to land undetected.

"There's a viable option by the coast in quadrant seven."

Leo checked his map. "That's about a hundred kilometres out from the farm. If we land there, we'll need to find transport, and I don't fancy our chances heading back over such a distance once we've played our hand."

"Fair point," Kan muttered. He carried on looking, as all the while, the atmosphere in the cockpit got colder and tenser. After an hour, he exclaimed, "Got it!"

"What?" Leo started, realising he'd dozed off.

"We come into orbit above this ground-monitoring satellite," he pointed to a tiny dot, blinking merrily away on the screen that was displaying a mock-up of the planet below, along with its satellite entourage. "Then, at this longitude, we drop in a little way behind it, and follow a diagonal trajectory down. That way, we stay just out of its sensor range, while keeping ahead of the satellite following on behind it. We'll land here. It's about six kilometres from your farm, but it's on the edge of this forested gully, and hopefully the branches and crags will hide the scouter from view."

"I know that place," Leo confirmed. "It may be only six kilometres in a straight line, but the sides of that mountain are pretty steep. It'll be hard going."

"Nevertheless, I think that's our best option. Any closer to your farm, and we may get picked up by geosynchronous satellites, or by ground radar."

"Well, I just hope mum and dad have kept fit while I've been away."

"They're farmers, I'm sure they'll do fine. Besides, they'll probably have transport to take us most of the way back."

"That's true. Dad has a four-by-four. If it's still running, it should do the job, though not quickly." Leo remembered the vehicle well. He, his dad, and his brothers, had spent many a night tinkering a way on it. Its speed never seemed to improve, nor did its rust-to-metal ratio, but it stayed running, had a healthy purr, and could tolerate some serious off-road use.

"We'll find out soon enough; our window arrives in 30 minutes."

****

Kan's plotted course kept them true, and after a nail-biting hour, their scouter came to rest on a small plateau. Then they sat and waited, scanning the area for any incoming vehicles that could spell trouble, but nothing appeared. From his window, Leo could see the trunks of the large trees that covered the mountainous region, their huge branches causing the scouter's interior to be bathed in a green-tinged light. Eventually, Kan gave the all-clear.

Leo gratefully, and shakily, got up and made it to the airlock. He opened it and was greeted by blessed fresh air. It was biting cold, like the hangar in the Qosec Three had been, but this air was filled with clean, earthy and pine aromas that didn't catch in the back of the throat. Leo took deep lungfuls of it until his chest hurt from its chilliness, then gingerly stepped out onto the plateau; his feet touching home soil for the first time in nearly ten years. About him, the trees sighed gently, as the wind moved their boughs, and the planet's version of birds twittered unseen amongst the branches. It was an eerily peaceful moment that lasted mere seconds.

"Those are some big-arse trees," Kan uttered, as he stepped out of the scouter.

Leo gazed up too. The trees reached two hundred meters in height, and the girth of their trunks were close to thirty metres. "They reckon these trees are several thousand years old," he said, remembering his botany lessons. "Early settlers even carved their homes into them because they were much more resilient to the weather than their pop-up habitats."

Kan gave an impressed low whistle in response. "Kind of reminds me of a race I once met…. Don't suppose they'd mind if I water them?"

Leo gave him a sideways glance. "Wanting to mark your territory already?"

"Something like that," Kan replied, before disappearing rapidly behind a trunk.

Leo stood for a moment more, taking in the tranquillity. Then, *to hell with it,* and he too went and found a willing trunk.

The two men regrouped at the scouter, as the shadows slowly crept across the ground. "We'll head off at dusk," Kan said. "By my reckoning, we'll reach your farm well after dark."

"Don't suppose you've got a more in-depth plan?" Leo asked.

"'Fraid not. We'll have to play it by ear."

As the sun set behind the forest, Leo and Kan gathered their gear, and holstered their weapons. As the sun's rays weakened, the air became as cold as their scouter's cockpit had, as they'd waited behind the moon, and Leo instinctively grabbed a jacket, although not the one emblazoned with Alliance insignia. Kan, who hadn't given warm clothing a second glance the first time around, shrugged his own jacket on too, but made sure he still had access to his weaponry by putting it on under his vest and cuffs. This fashion choice, while practical, made him look like he was wearing a life vest.

Leo looked to the horizon, where the sky was taking on a yellow hue. "Looks like the sun's on its last leg. Guess it's time to make a move."

Kan checked his swords were secure on his back, slung his

plasma rifles over his shoulder, and pulled the scouter's door shut, making sure to lock it. Then, with Leo in the lead, as he knew the area better, they skirted the edge of the forest until they could find a clear way down. Leo soon found the route he was looking for. It was an unstable region of mountain marked by old rock falls; the giant boulders and loose gravel having prevented any trees from gaining a foot hold. Scree covered the ground, making the going slippery, and he and Kan had to resort to taking a zigzagging approach to their descent. Occasionally, their boots would cause a mini rockslide, and little pebbles would stream off before them, but despite the instability of the ground, Leo wasn't too worried about a big fall. The huge boulders that peppered the way were covered in thick blankets of lichen and moss, indicating that they hadn't moved for centuries, and although the place appeared barren, there were plenty of animals, large and small, that called the mountain home, yet they had done nothing to perturb the rocks. It was going to take more than two tiny Humans to cause the mountain to come crashing down.

By the time they reached the bottom, dusk was on its last gasp, as was Leo, whose legs were on fire from the awkward descent. He leant against a rock and took a well-earned drink.

Kan consulted a map on his pad. "It looks like cutting across the fields diagonally is our best bet," he said.

Leo recalled his farming days and did some crop rotation maths. "If my memory serves me correct, we'll be heading across wheat fields for most of the way. Thankfully, it's still early in the season, so it won't be too scratchy."

After a short jog across open pasture, they hopped the fence that bordered Leo's parents' land. Kan stopped a moment to look through his night-vision binoculars. "I see some sheds off in the distance," he stated.

"That'll be the hay barns and machine storage," Leo answered. "Tractors, combines and the like."

Kan nodded. "I think it's best if we skirt the edge here, and curve in behind them."

The weather was with them, and the overcast sky meant their journey through the fields was done under the cover of darkness. Soon, that darkness took shape, and the great steel barns loomed up ahead of them. They carefully made their way to the edge of one, and glanced around and there, just within view, Leo could see the lights shining through the windows of his parents' homestead. He felt a great swell of homesickness at the sight of the warm, beckoning light. It reminded him of long-forgotten evenings curled up with a novel on his datapad, as his brothers and sister playfully squabbled, and the smell of stew and dumplings filled the air. But that light had taken on an edge. Once it had been a beacon of homeliness and security, lighting the way of a mad dash from barn to dinner. Now it held unseen dangers.

"I can't see any movement inside," Kan was saying, his binoculars glued to his eyes.

Leo grabbed his own binoculars and had a look. The lights shone brightly through the windows, but even after adjusting the focus, he couldn't see anything that would tell him if his family were inside. "They could be having a late dinner," Leo theorised. He moved his vision beyond the house and caught sight of something that instantly worried him. "The hen coop is still open!" he hissed.

"What?" grunted Kan.

"The hen coop is still open. At this time of night, the hens should be roosting in the coop with the door shut, to keep them out of reach of predators," he explained. "Dad turned off the door timer when stragglers kept getting left out, so it has to be shut manually once they're all in." His parent's hens weren't Old Earth hens, they were some hen-like species his mum had picked up in the market years ago. They were dim, had no sense of urgency, and were apt to wander the length and breadth of the farm, which meant they often failed to make it safely back before dusk. Still, Leo knew even the slowpokes should have returned hours ago. "There's no way mum or dad would have left it open unless...."

"Unless someone's preventing them from doing so," Kan finished. "Looks like we're not gonna be doing this the easy way."

Leo's stomach sank. The one thing he was hoping against, namely a shootout, was looking more likely. "Please tell me you have some way of dealing with this situation," he asked Kan.

Kan seemed to mull over his options. "I still have one close-range psychic grenade, several flash-bangs, and some higher-end explosives. Trouble is, all these things are designed for missions involving breaking into places…or escaping. They're designed for carnage, not precision extraction."

Leo didn't like the idea of using concussive devices or explosives anywhere near his parents. "What about if we cut the power to the farm? If we cut the lights, we can attack in the dark using night-vision."

"It's a valid plan, but I don't like that fact that I don't know who we're up against. If it's a couple of suits, fair enough. If it's soldiers, I'm worried any crossfire will endanger your parents. And don't get me started on if there's a telepath in there."

Leo sat on his haunches, stumped for any ideas. Then, a thought came to him. "What if we could have a quick peek inside remotely?" Kan gave him a questioning look. "When I was living here, we had a set of drones that we used to check on the crops in the further fields; saved us having to travel all the way over there. They should be in one of these sheds if my memory serves. They weren't too noisy, at least not enough to be heard through metre-wide stone walls and double glazing. We could use them to check on what's what." Kan gave an expansive grin.

Cautiously, they edged round the side of the barn, and darted across to a second, smaller shed. There, they found a regular, Human-sized door, protected by a security keypad. Without thinking, Leo entered Marlan's birthday. The door gave a quiet beep, and noiselessly opened, allowing him and Kan to quickly enter, and shut the door securely behind them.

"All the sheds and barns have our birthdays as the security

codes," Leo whispered, as he fumbled his way around a moth-balled robotic berry-picker, so he could reach a bench in the far corner. "Thank the gods my parents are not ones for changing tradition."

They were in his father's electronics shed, where he stored and fixed all the small and medium-sized electronic tech. As Leo's eyes grew accustomed to the gloom in the building, he started to make out the shape of equipment. There were racks on the walls holding soldering irons, screwdrivers, and volt meters, and the benches were littered with circuit boards, chargers, and boxes of archaic transistors and screws. *Organised chaos as always dad,* he thought, seeing much of himself in his father's mess. He made out a laptop missing its screen, and what appeared to be the remnants of an automatic sprinkler system from one of their small greenhouses.

Going along the row of tables, Leo soon found what he was looking for. On a large metal bench were clustered four small quadcopters, each barely bigger than his hand, and he was relieved to find they were all in one piece, and with their controllers lying next to them. He picked up the closest one and gave its power button a flick. A little green light came on, meaning it was good to go. Leo turned off the device, and he and Kan retraced their steps, leaving the shed for the shadow of the main barn. Once there, Leo took a moment to smear dirt over the tiny, yet conspicuous, LED.

"You know how to fly this thing?" Kan asked, as he watched Leo switch the drone back on.

"This isn't my first rodeo," Leo answered, with a knowing wink, and he powered up the machine. Its four blades rotated with barely a hum, and with a couple more button presses he brought up the drone's camera feed on a little screen in the centre of the controller. Satisfied, Leo launched the drone, and guided it towards his old house.

It was a simple, two-storey building, built from the grey rock that littered the area. Though Leo hadn't been around when his parents had taken over the land, they'd told him much about their early days, when they'd lived, with their own parents, in an inflatable habitat provided by the Alliance. Even though the planet had been occupied for two centuries, the land was sparsely populated, and his parents and grandparents had been akin to pioneers. The womenfolk had tended over the farmland, with the help of autonomous machinery, and as his father had matured, he'd divided his time between the Space Corps, and helping his grandfather build their home from the rubble the ploughs had removed from the fields. It had taken years to build, but it stood strong against the elements; a legacy from Leo's long-departed grandparents.

Despite having travelled the galaxy, and the wonders he'd seen, Leo had often had moments when he'd reminisced fondly over his childhood home. It had been solid, welcoming, and cosy. Leo guessed his parents hadn't planned on having so many children though, as the place only had three bedrooms. Leo and his two brothers sharing one, his only sister getting the third to herself. When his grandparents had been alive, he and his siblings had needed to share one between them. All of which had meant a lot of suspiciously long showers as they'd got older. The bedrooms and bathroom were naturally upstairs, while the ground floor consisted of an open-planned kitchen, dining room, and lounge. Although it was built primarily out of rock, the open-plan nature meant the bottom half of the house was always toasty, thanks to its two fireplaces, and the huge old-fashioned stove Leo's mother had used for cooking their equally huge family meals.

Leo carefully guided the drone around to a small window that sat at the kitchen end of the house, and that allowed him to see the length of the building. Immediately, he saw his parents, looking a lot greyer than when he'd left, and his sister, sat on a sofa in the lounge at the far end. Standing guard over them were three men in suits. However, they looked distinctly un-bureaucrat-like, and were too well-built and suspiciously tanned to be office workers, plus each sported a lot of stubble. *Dammit, how did they know to be here now?* he wondered. Despite his and Kan's covert behaviour, the Alliance had somehow beaten them in the race to his family.

Leo's family all had their backs to him, so he had no idea if they were cuffed. "I count three questionably buff government agents," he relayed to Kan, before guiding the drone to the upper floor. He checked each room in turn and found no more strangers.

"Are they armed?" Kan asked.

"I couldn't see any rifles lying around." Leo brought the drone back to the kitchen window. "Their jackets, apart from looking ill-fitting, look a little on the bulging side, so I'm guessing concealed arms." He piloted the drone out of line of sight.

Kan nodded. "They'll have played the parts of suits to gain entry. Turning up on your parent's doorstep with huge rifles wouldn't have helped them get over the threshold. That's something at least. With any luck, we'll have more firepower."

"Yes, but they're standing right over my family. They don't need big guns to cause problems."

"Which means we need to take out three men before they can react."

"Well, you showed with Marlan that you can shoot two men in quick succession."

"Yes, but that was at close quarters, not through a window at dispersed targets. Plus, I shot your brother first, and I can't do that with your parents. Things are a little trickier here, especially if the guys watching them are skilled soldiers. What's the layout?"

"The end the drone's at is the kitchen, which kinda merges into the dining room, which is basically just a big table and chairs, after which is the lounge."

"Points of entry?"

"Kitchen door this end. The front door is round the other side, in a little porch that is about where the dining room becomes the lounge."

"Are the fires lit?"

Leo launched the drone to have a peek. "The one in the

lounge is, the dining room not."

Kan gave a sigh. "Damn, could've used the one in the lounge. Anything else?"

Leo thought hard. "Wait...." A memory came to him. "Just before I left, dad had started working on a cold storage cellar under the house. It was going to be a big basement for storing meat and preserves over the winter, so they could be a little more self-sufficient. The thing was, though he planned to have the main hatch in the kitchen floor, he was going to make another entrance that came out in the milk shed over there." He pointed to a barely discernible dark mass in the distance that had, when he left, housed three creatures called ilt, which produced milk. "That way, he could make the cheese and butter in there, and roll the full barrels down the slope into the basement." Leo manoeuvred the drone back to the window for a quick look. "Yeah, I can see the outline of the trap door in the kitchen floor. I mean, it's pretty well camouflaged by the way the wooden slats lie, but I can tell it's there. And it's hidden from their view by the kitchen counters."

"Looks like we have our way in," Kan said, with a hint of relief.

Leo landed the quadcopter below the window, and left it on standby, so they could use it again to check on the situation once under the trapdoor. Then he led Kan to the milking shed, and they entered via the back door, his mother's birth date giving them access. The smell was the first thing that hit him. It was a heady mix of hay, hay-based dung, and musky animal scent, as the original inhabitants of the shed were still alive, albeit rather grey around their muzzles. The mini herd was off to the side, secured in a roomy pen strewn with straw. They padded to the gate to see who the interlopers were; their four, clawed paws, making barely a sound as they jostled for prime viewing position. The animals stood taller than Leo, and were covered with short, coarse brown fur. They regarded him with small placid eyes, as he gave the pointed snout of the closest one a little scratch as he passed. It flicked its large, curved ears in contentment. Leo had no idea about their planet of origin, yet despite being non-native, they did well on Demeter Nine. They were hardy creatures, and survived well on the short, nutrient-poor grass that thrived in the colder regions. In return, they had provided Leo's family with nutrient-rich milk for many years.

Leo lined himself up with where he believed the kitchen's trapdoor was and began searching the floor on his hands and knees, praying that what he was running his hands through was just straw. A couple of minutes of side-to-side sweeping, and he found the ring to pull up the access hatch, which opened to reveal the gently sloping dirt floor of a tunnel barely bigger than a barrel when laid on its side. "I guess dad had no intentions of entering the cellar this way," Leo said, ruefully. "I think it's going to be a bit of a squeeze, especially for you."

Kan gave a shrug. "If the worse comes to the worse, I'll use your dad's butter to grease me up."

Leo grimaced. "Well, you'll get no help from me if you do." He got on his belly and wiggled into the tunnel. The cold stone walls encased him, and the strong farmyard pong gave way to the fresh aromatic aroma of earth and damp rock. Despite his eyes having adjusted to the moonless night, Leo couldn't see even a millimetre in front of him. "This kind of reminds me of when I was making my way to the arboretum when we were under siege," he whispered. "Fun times," he added, sarcastically. Behind him he could hear Kan huffing and puffing away, his muscular girth making his going harder.

After five minutes of claustrophobic shuffling, Leo was suddenly aware that the subconscious feeling he'd had of the ceiling had lessened, and he cautiously got to his feet. The roof of the cellar brushed the top of his head. "I'm in," he said, in a hushed voice to Kan, "but be careful when you get here, the ceiling is really low."

A moment later, he could about make out Kan's form as he squeezed himself out of the tunnel. "Now I know what it's like to be born," Kan murmured, as he got himself to a stooping upright.

Leo felt around on the ceiling until he found the wooden frame of the kitchen trapdoor. "What now?" he asked Kan.

There was a strange rustling coming from Kan, which Leo couldn't figure out. "Now, I'll open this door a crack, and you reconnect with the drone," Kan said. "If the men are still in their original positions, I'll enter, use the kitchen counters as cover, and do my best."

Leo cringed inwardly but didn't say anything. He pulled the drone's controller out of his coat pocket. "Ready."

Kan gently eased the trapdoor upwards, and a small shaft of light illuminated him. Leo saw what the rustling had been about; Kan had removed his bulky coat...from under his vest. *I though that's something only women could do.* Leo regained his train of thought and proceeded to do a weird little dance around Kan, as he desperately tried to get the wireless signal of the controller to connect with the drone, the machine having become disconnected thanks to several feet of soil and rock suddenly appearing between them and it. A tiny bar of signal eventually appeared on the screen, but it was enough, and the drone took flight. "Everyone as is," he mumbled, under his breath.

At the same time, Kan briefly regarded the controller's screen, and as the word 'is' left Leo's mouth, Kan pushed silently upwards and out, not bothering to use the ladder in front of him. Despite his great bulk, he pulled himself effortlessly and silently through the hatch, having ensured the door hadn't made a noise as he'd laid it on the ground. Leo could hear everything but Kan: the house creaking as it settled, his father giving a suppressed cough, a barely audible whimper. *Mum?* His vision returned to the controller screen. There he could see Kan hunkered down behind the counter, readying his rifle. He could only imagine that at his glance, Kan had mapped out the field of battle before him and was calculating his shots. Leo held his breath; afraid the soldiers would hear it. His hands were shaking as his vision bored into the screen.

Then, in a fluid movement, Kan stood up, aimed his gun, and fired three quick shots in sweeping succession. Only the third man managed to make a move for his concealed weapon, but his hand never got closer than the fabric of his ill-fitting suit. In a heartbeat, all the men were heading towards the floor, dead.

Leo bolted up the creaking ladder, up towards his family that were now getting to their feet and turning around in shock to see who had killed their captors. Cuffs were round their wrists, but Leo barely noticed them as he charged the length of the house, flung his arms around his astonished mother's shoulders, and buried his head in her neck.

****

Once Leo's parents had run through the emotional gamut of horror, confusion, and delight at seeing his return, and once Kan had removed their cuffs and secured the premises, conversation quickly turned to the hows and whys.

For his part, Leo explained his reasons for coming. His fears proven true by the presence of the three mercenaries that Kan was presently piling up behind a barn. The look of relief on his family's faces, when he told them of his brothers' safety, was palpable.

"You took a great risk coming here son," his father told him. Despite his advancing years, his face was still young, with only his greying dark blond hair giving away his age. His green eyes were full of concern as he looked at his youngest child.

"I know," Leo confessed, "but I've had a great partner watching my front." He nodded to Kan, who had re-entered the farmhouse, and was wiping blood off his hands with a shred of cloth torn from the suit of one of the men. Leo saw his mother wince at the sight, and he took her hand and gave it a squeeze. "So how did the men get in?"

"They arrived the day after Ellie," his mother explained, her eyes still bloodshot from crying. "They said they were here to get an estimate of this year's crop yield, so Amos let them in."

The look of regret on his father's face was instant. "It wasn't your fault dad," Leo quickly assured him. "They would have gotten in any way they could."

"I should've tried to fight them," Amos responded, ruefully, "but I'm not as fit as I used to be, and I'm dammed if I can remember my combat training."

"Dad, if you had fought them you would've died," Ellie reminded him.

"Anyway," his mother continued, "they've been here for two days, watching over us. The only time we could leave the room was to go to the bathroom, and even then, we had an escort."

"I wonder what forced their hand?" Kan said.

"They said something about a lack of communication from the monitoring station," Ellie answered, "which is odd, because I got a message from Nathan a couple of days ago saying he needed some clothes picking up."

"That was down to us," Leo explained. "We needed to get you here for when we came to rescue you, so Nath sent you the message. But once it was sent, communications were shut down."

"They also mentioned something about a telepath," Leo's mother piped up.

"What?" said Leo and Kan in unison.

"It was while I was in the bathroom. I heard two of them talking, saying something about waiting on a telepath who was coming across from the main space port." She checked the clock over the mantle. "I think that means he should be getting here today."

"Oh gods, they're coming to interrogate you." Leo said, feeling himself blanch.

"In which case, we need to leave. Now!" said Kan.

Panic gripped his parents, and Leo could see them looking this way and that, figuring out what they could take. Kan stepped in. "No! Leave everything. Just grab a coat and get moving. We don't have time to pack stuff. We need to get to our ship before they even make it to the house."

His mother looked torn at having to leave her world behind, but Leo's father had grasped the enormity of the situation and put his hand on her shoulder. "We have our lives and those of our children," he told her, "We don't need anything else." She nodded, but Leo could see her eyes were welling up again.

"Do you still have the off-roader," Leo asked his father. The man nodded. "Good, we'll need that."

"I'll go get it started. Ellie, I'll need you on the doors." Ellie nodded, grabbed her jacket, and followed their father outside.

"Can I make one call?" his mother asked, meekly.

"What?" Kan asked, suspiciously.

"We can't leave the animals unattended. They'll die. I'll leave a message with Bryan and Kale from down the valley to come and get them. I promise I won't say why. I'll make something up about us heading into the city for a few days and that they need to be put out to graze." Kan, seemingly happy with her request, allowed her to leave.

Leo looked around the lounge as he waited. It hadn't changed one bit since he'd left. There was the same tatty mauve three-piece suite, the same worn brown rug, and the same mismatched wooden side tables. The fireplace mantle was still full of photos of his family, and he went in for a closer inspection, remembering the moments when they'd been taken. *There's a hell of a lot of innocence in those eyes,* he thought, catching sight of a pre-pubescent Leo in his old school uniform.

"Take one," came Kan's gruff voice from behind him. Leo turned to look at him. "It's not like it's gonna make much difference to our energy consumption."

Leo picked up a family portrait. It was the last one taken of them all together before Nathan had headed off-world. His parents were young-looking, and grey-hair-free, and the family stood together, with their varying shades of blonde hair, all except Ellie, who sported light ginger hair. Behind them, strong and unyielding, was the farmhouse, framed by a cloud-free sky. The scene was a moment of domestic happiness, and a time Leo dearly wanted to return to. "When this is all done," he said, more to the house than Kan, "I'll bring this photo back."

"We all will," chimed in his mother, having returned from her call. "This house has stood against blizzards and hurricanes…it's not going anywhere."

"We're good to go," came Leo's father's voice from the porch.

His mother picked up her coat, and gave a last lingering look round her home. "I'm going to miss this place," she said, her voice cracking.

"Now you know how I've been feeling for the last ten years," Leo said, giving a sad smile. His mother gave him a hug.

They left the house, making sure to lock it up as they did so, and in depressed silence, they made their run for it.

****

The return leg of their journey had involved less planning of counter moves so had been relatively quicker than their route onto Demeter Nine. They had driven full pelt back to the mountains and had managed to gain some distance up it thanks to the off-roader, which had allowed them to put all their physical energy into the dash up the scree-covered path towards their hidden vessel. Kan had scouted ahead, to make sure their vessel was still undiscovered, and it mercifully was, so Kan, Leo, and his family, had crowded in for the long journey back to the monitoring station.

Talk during their journey had revolved around catching up. Leo told his family stories of his part in the liberation of the Scientia, the fleeing of the Alliance fleet before the Karee, his promotion, and of course, Pra'cha and Tia. His father and mother had looked at him with immense pride as he had told them he was second in command of a space station, and eyebrows had been raised at his announcement that he was married to an alien. His family's stories had been less impressive. Talks of farming and neighbourhood gossip seemed to pale in comparison to what Leo had done, but he hadn't minded, he was just happy to have his family around him, and to talk of menial things.

They had then re-docked at the monitoring station to collect Marlan and Nathan; the two brothers just as delighted to see their family again as they were to see them. Only after their arrival at the station did Leo get a sense of the danger following them.

"We've been monitoring communications," Nathan had told them, gravely. "You've got two military vessels on your tail, but as they're not designed for long-range missions, they've had to refuel a couple of times. I reckon they're about a day behind, and if they're to make it to the jumpgate, they'll need to refuel here too, which considering the mess we've left, will slow them down even further."

As it was, the enemy never made it within scanner range of their scouter, and they'd headed to the exit jumpgate that connected with the gate in the Paranian system, and which Kan had ensured was turned on well in advance of their arrival, so they never had to slow their speed. He had also made sure it became deactivated as soon as it was safe to do so as a final act to delay their chasing foe.

As they passed through the exit jumpgate, new stories were exchanged: of Leo and Kan's rescue of their parents, and of their rescue of the brothers. Then there had been the more awkward conversation of what Leo's family had been told about him and his defection away from the Alliance. It turned out his parents had been supplied nominal information. They had simply been told that Leo had committed treason against the Alliance, was a wanted man, and that should he get in contact with them, they were to immediately alert the authorities. To prevent themselves from having to do that, his parents had made the unenviable choice not to contact him; a case of hear no evil, no having to reluctantly report alleged evil. A situation that Leo grudgingly appreciated. Leo's siblings had been another matter. They were amongst other Alliance personnel, and had been privy to the details, and their colleagues' opinions, not to mention the exaggerated half-truths and fabricated lies. The way they'd heard things, anybody would have thought Leo had taken out a planet full of Alliance soldiers single-handedly, while laughing manically like a deranged supervillain.

But as Ellie had pointed out, "we all know you, and none of us believed a word, at least not the worse stuff."

As it was, they too had kept the gruesome details and lies from their parents, not wanting to make them any more worried, or involved, than they already were. However, Leo had felt terrible about having to admit that he'd taken his fair share of life in the battle for the station. He didn't want to have to confirm what the Alliance had been saying about him, if only a little.

Marlan had put his arm around his young brother. "Let's all be honest right now. If any of us had been in your position, we'd have done the same thing."

A chorus of nodded heads had come from the rest of the family.

"Agreed," Nathan had added. "None of us have any real love for the Alliance, and if we'd been given the chance to fight for freedom, we'd've taken up arms too."

Again, the head bobs confirmed all of Leo's family members were on the same page, and it made him feel indescribably glad to finally have the support and presence of his close-knit family around him.

After the return journey through hyperspace, during which time the air in the scouter had become exceedingly ripe thanks to the extra bodies, and the food and entertainment options had become decidedly monotonous, they had exited the jumpgate, and after an encrypted hail, had rendezvoused with the Qosec Three close to their original drop-off point, behind an irregular shaped meteor that was large enough to be called a dwarf planet.

On docking, Leo quickly got up from his seat, and opened

the hatch. The air of the hangar was as cold and metallic as he remembered, but it was a blessed relief from the pungent aroma of seven barely washed bodies, and all the unfortunate extra smells that came with them. He stepped out of the craft, to see Lorkav waiting to greet them once again.

Leo's mother was next to step out the shuttle, and he heard her catch her breath as she looked around the hangar. "I have never seen so many ships," she uttered. Then she caught sight of Lorkav, and her eyes bulged. Leo had to remind himself that, despite being a colony within the Alliance, which encompassed many alien races, Demeter Nine was isolated, and rarely visited by non-Human species. Those that did come, came to visit elected officials, not farmers, and though his siblings and father had seen aliens because of their time spent in service to the Alliance, his mother never had. The alien bovine-like ilts under her care seemingly hadn't prepared her for face-to-face first contact.

I guess because they weren't uniform-wearing sentient bipedals. Leo opined, with some mirth. He figured he should do introductions. "Mum, dad, this is Lorkav, second in command of this ship, and a Rotaizian." His mother remained glued to the spot, her brain failing her; however, his father gingerly stepped forward, and held out his hand. "Thank you for giving us sanctuary aboard this vessel," he said, calmly.

The alien regarded his gesture with clear confusion. "It's a human greeting," Leo quickly explained to the alien, hoping his translator was fast enough to convey it wasn't a threat. "You take the offered hand, and shake it with your own, as a sign of friendship."

Amos remained poised, with hand outstretched, while Lorkav's translator garbled. At the last guttural sound, Lorkav grabbed Amos' hand, and pumped it so vigorously that both parties' fingers practically became a blur. Leo winced. "Sorry dad," he said, as his father regained his arm with a pained expression. "Quite a bit of what we say gets lost in translation with these guys. I guess I should have said 'gently shake'"

Leo's siblings, who had been watching this exchange from the safety of the scouter's hatch, laughed.

Lorkav took in the crowd of people. "Your mission success," he stated.

"Thankfully, yes," Leo answered. "Do you have rooms for them?"

"Yes," Lorkav responded.

Leo turned back to his family. "Who wants a hot shower?"

Five hands raised, accompanied by a muffled and gruff, "Hell yeah!" from inside the scouter.

****

Within a few hours, seven freshly washed bodies converged around a table in the mess hall of the Qosec Three and began shovelling fresh food into their mouths.

"I don't know what I'm eating, and frankly I don't care so longs as it doesn't taste of grit," Marlan announced, between mouthfuls.

Murmurs of agreement followed. Though they hadn't starved during their flight back to the Qosec Three, the enjoyment of having a daily intake of freeze-dried food had worn a bit thin. Leo'd had double what his family had had to put up with, thanks to doing a round trip, so was especially glad of real sustenance. The water in his mug tasted a damn sight less suspect too.

"So, are we having to enjoy this while we can, or are we heading all the way to your station on this ship?" Leo's father asked.

"From what Lorkav was saying before he left," Kan said, "I think we're doing the full journey back via ship."

"Yeah, I think that's what he meant," Leo added. "Though it's a bit hard to tell with his translator. From what it sounded like, they've had word from their government to go to the station and request membership to the GR."

"The GR being?" Nathan asked.

"The Galactic Revolutionists," Leo explained, cringing slightly at the phrase. "It's kinda what we call ourselves."

"It's an overly dramatic name for a disorganised bunch of rebels," Kan put in, with a slight sneer.

"That's as maybe," Leo interjected, "but people are willing to rally around it, and so long as worlds are joining the cause, I'm happy to refer to us as the GR."

"And what about you?" Ellie asked, directing her question to Kan. "How did you come to be a part of this galactic revolution?"

Leo, to his credit, hadn't failed to notice the doe eyes his young sister had been making in Kan's direction, and the days trapped in a confined space with him hadn't seemed to diminish her interest. Conversely, Kan hadn't noticed, or wasn't biting. Leo found it hard to imagine the former was true. *Considering his vast history with the ladies on the station, he probably knows every alien come-on imaginable.* Kan's conquest throughput did seem to have stagnated in recent months, and Leo hadn't got wind of much gossip in that area. *Perhaps it's because he was AWOL for nearly 6 months, then had to deal with the whole Shar mess, so hasn't had time for hanky-panky.* But even once back on the station, and once everything had returned to relative normal, it seemed that Kan had become a bit more monkish in his lifestyle. *Could it be he's ready to settle down and is looking for The One?*

Ellie was certainly no ugly duckling. Her light ginger hair was shaped into a practical bob, her pale skin was heavily freckled, and her eyes were a similar green to Kan's. She had put on a little weight since Leo had last clapped eyes on her, due to her spending her days sat at a control terminal, instead of running about the farm, but what weight she was carrying gave her a curvy, womanly shape, as opposed to making her look unhealthy. Although Leo didn't like the idea of Kan and his little sister getting intimate, he found the notion of Kan having no interest in her irksome. *Seriously, he could do a hell of a lot worse!* he fumed, before getting creeped out by his line of thinking.

The only other thing Leo could think of was that Kan was being conscientious. Reciprocating Ellie's flirtatious advances, while in the close confines of the scouter, surrounded by her entire family, would have been inappropriate by any decent man's standards. On the Qosec Three they had more room to spread their wings, but as they were the only Humans aboard, they would undoubtedly converge together to eat and socialise. Leo guessed that Kan didn't want to disturb the family dynamic. *If they did get together, and things suddenly went south between them, then it could put a strain on the group, and knowing my luck, I'd get it in the neck for bringing him. Despite the fact he saved their butts.* He tried not to give a noticeable eye-roll.

Kan gave a shrug in response to Ellie's question. "Proximity to an unstoppable natural force," was his cryptic response.

Ellie glanced at Leo. "Tia," he clarified for her.

"The demi-goddess person," his mum said, remembering their conversations in the scouter.

"That's the one," Leo confirmed. "Though she's not actually a demi-goddess, that's just how some Zerrens think of her because she was a servant of an ancient race who they saw as kinda like gods. Though I guess as she's now evolved into one of them, they see her as more a full-blown goddess. It's all very convoluted. At the end of the day, she's just an alien, but with some powerful abilities, which means you don't want to piss her off."

"Will we meet her?" Amos asked, with a hint of concern to his voice.

"I expect so, as long as she hasn't gone and got herself lost again," Kan said, a little exasperated.

"Sounds like she's a bit uh…wayward," Ellie said. Leo figured she may have wanted to use the word 'unreliable'.

Kan seemed to pick up on it too, and he shot Ellie a look that made her shrink a little. "Tia's done more for the likes of me than you can ever imagine. I owe her my life. And despite everything, I know she has my back, along with that of every free race. Yes, she's had her own crosses to bear of late, but each time she's come back stronger."

Just as the last words came out of his mouth, Kan's eyes seemed to glaze over, and he sat with his cup halfway to his mouth. Leo exchanged worried looks with his family, who had all noticed the same thing. It was an unnerving spectacle. Kan's eyes flickered, and the corner of his mouth twitched, and Leo was at the point of going and finding medical help when Kan uttered loudly, "Bloody woman!"

Chapter 31 - Tia

They had crept within scanner range of the rogue world, and Tia crowded into the small cockpit of the newly named Eerell with Ressen and Grelt; her lack of extremities making things less dangerous. Before them, on the ship's screen, was a fuzzy image of the planet.

"What do you think?" Ressen asked. "There's not much to see."

To Tia, it was as the Zerren scientists had postulated. It was a nondescript, grey, rocky world, out where it shouldn't be. Scans showed it was marginally smaller than Zerra, that it had minimal atmosphere, and crucially, there were no discernible signs of multi-cellular life on the surface. No lights, no concentration of gasses, no thermal signature. "I'm more interested in what I can't see," Tia said. "Its course was tracked back to the red dwarf star system of Dece Twelve. As far as we can tell, nothing untoward has happened near that system, no supernovas, nor an interaction with another star or giant planet. If Dece Twelve is indeed where this world came from, the only other way it could have been flung out is a collision. In which case, I'd expect to see a bloody huge hole in it from where it was knocked out of orbit, but apart from the occasional meteor dent it's spherical."

"It could have come from beyond that solar system," Grelt postulated.

This was a fair assumption on Grelt's part. The system of Dece Twelve was uncharted, at least by any race in an information-sharing mood. The Zerrens only knew of it through their own early exoplanet hunting days, with Dece being the telescope that had found the star dimming in time to a circling planet. Twelve indicated it had been the twelfth planetary system discovered by Dece. The Zerren's early observations had only discovered the gas giant, anything smaller, if indeed there had been anything smaller, had failed to be discernible. Tia's innate knowledge was more complete than the Zerrens, and she knew that the system of Dece Twelve had a rocky planet; however, there was presently no way of knowing if what they were looking at was one and the same.

"True," she said to Grelt, "but if this world had passed close to the system, one would've expected it to have got pulled into it. There's a gas giant circling the star, and with all that gravitational attraction going on, by rights, this planet should have become its new moon, rather than passing right on through. Then again, Dece Twelve had a rocky planet, and there's always the chance that some interaction with its gas giant could've kicked it out, but no further observations have suggested there's been an upheaval in the solar system. For now, I have no reason to assume that I'm looking at a different body. One that is travelling a rather suspicious path."

"So, we're back to it having had a helping hand," sighed Ressen.

"Afraid so," Tia said.

"So, here's a question," said Grelt. "If what we think is true, that it had help with escaping its orbit, and those orchestrators are on it, probably underground as we can't find any surface trace of them, how do we find them? I mean, I could land anywhere flat, but there's no guarantee that's where they are, and I'm pretty sure you don't want to have to wander the surface trying to find them. That could take years."

"I have no doubt they sent this as a message to me, and there's no point in sending a message if I can't read it. There must be a way." Tia sensed Ressen and Grelt exchanging glances. Then the idea hit her. "Pull back out of scanner range but keep following in its wake."

"What are you going to do?" Ressen asked, as she made to leave.

"I'm going to take a closer look...I hope." She left before Ressen could get out the barrage of questions that were forming in his mind and headed to the storage bay; a place that was much less cramped than her quarters. Once there, she locked the door to ensure privacy. It was dark and cold in the bay, and she left it that way, choosing not to turn on the lights, or environmental controls. Instead, she sat cross-legged on the floor, closed her eyes, and let her mind drift. She was about to attempt something she'd never tried before, at least not outside the confines of Morrígan; she was going to try to remotely view the planet.... All of it.

As an A'daree, she'd been able to psychically view ahead of her, altering her perception to look through walls to see the enemy, but the distance she could see had been short; meters as opposed to kilometres. As a Karee, and with the help of Morrígan, she had been able to expand this ability exponentially, and she could see and do much more. She could traverse the galaxy, wander through the beating hearts of planets like they were nothing more than fog, and connect with people's minds as if they were stood next to her. However, all that she had done whilst joined with Morrígan, and she was still unsure how much influence her vessel's presence had on her ability to do things. Her plan was to observe the planet ahead them, just like an orbiting, multi-sensory satellite, but whether she could, was waiting to be seen.

Tia expanded the touch of her mind and let her consciousness envelope the ship. Within it, she could sense Ressen and Grelt, and she could feel their heightened alertness as they watched the sensors in case an attack came from the planet. There were other sparkles of life within the ship too: insects, bacteria, a small rodent stowaway hidden away amongst the piping. Then Tia pushed her mind beyond her vicinity. Because of her orders to Grelt, she knew where she was in relation to the planet, and in theory, it was just a case of moving her mind forward; however, between her and the planet were several thousand kilometres of emptiness. She concentrated on the thought of the planet, and let her mind break free of her body.

No matter how many times she did it, the initial feeling was always unsettling. It was like dangling from a cliff with one hand, in the middle of a moonless night, over an unknown void, and overriding the body's base desire to hold on for dear life, choosing instead to drop. As she homed in on the planet, the galaxy whooshed past her, the stars leaving streaks in the void. Yet, in barely two heartbeats, she had arrived at her destination, and was floating, disembodied, a few hundred meters above its surface.

The planet was no more interesting close too. Its pock-marked surface was still grey, though of more noticeable differing shades, and in some sheltered craters, ice crystals twinkled. Tia let her mind pass over the surface, looking for anything that would mark out something as being abnormal.

Tia altered her vision, looking at the infrared, the ultra-violet, and the patterns of deposits on the ground. Craters merged with craters, in some places the ground was hard, in others, powdery, but frustratingly, just as it had with the sensors, nothing stood out. *There must be something, or am I just completely wrong about this world? Is Grelt right, and it's just a wandering planet that happened to pass close to Dece Twelve? Or is it the planet from Dece, and its companion planet just decided to send it on its merry way?* She focused her mind and brought herself in closer to get a more detailed look at the ground below her. As she 'walked' the surface, she could see individual pebbles, no bigger than her thumb, but nary a track or trace of anything untoward.

As the world rotated below her, an ancient rift valley came into view. It was a giant deep wound in the planet's surface, and she paused a moment on its edge to look down into its gaping maw, where millennia-old, solidified magma coated its sides, making the depths appear even blacker. She was debating on whether to head into the dark unknown when something flitted in the periphery of her mind. It was similar to what she'd felt when the presence of the scorpiad had intruded into her mind during her remote viewing of the Scientia, many moons ago. Forgetting for a moment that she was an incorporeal entity, she looked around and saw nothing. The twinge happened again, but instead of subsiding, it remained, and it pulsed steadily in her head, as if blood were rushing in her ears. *Okay, that's not normal!* There was an unsettling connotation to the feeling, and a familiarity, but unlike with her first mental discovery of the scorpiad, she didn't shy away from the sensation.

Tia 'stepped' off the edge of the rift valley and floated over its cavernous depths. She allowed the intrusion to remain in her head, and used it to triangulate, and for its part, whatever, or whoever was causing her mental disturbance didn't retreat. It was the beacon she needed, and she passed her gaze over the walls of the valley, allowing instinct to guide her. Her eyes fell on an area just below the lip of the cliff, and she pushed her mind towards it. At first glance, it was just the same as every other square meter of wall, and its surface was a swathe of obsidian; all shiny and black. She looked deeper at its structure, homing in on the molecules, then the atoms, and found what she'd been searching for.

Even the most advanced sensor would have struggled to find the way in, as barely an atom's width separated the edges of the entrance from the rest of the cliff wall. However, once Tia had found it, she could make out the square of the hatch. *That's some seriously advanced engineering,* she thought. What's more, whatever was sending the mental signal was secreted behind it. *Target acquired.*

She quickly shut her mind off to the signal and pulled herself back into her body. When she opened her eyes to the gloom of the storage bay, she half expected to feel Morrígan's body a hair's breadth from the end of her nose. Instead, the distant looming shapes of storage boxes greeted her, and she briefly let herself have a swell of pride at knowing she could project herself without the assistance of her vessel. She got to her feet, and returned to the control room, to find Grelt and Ressen still in their seats.

"That was quick," Ressen said.

"Really? How long was I gone?" Tia had no concept of time when in her out-of-body state.

"About twenty minutes," Grelt answered, checking his controls.

"It felt longer." To Tia, it had felt as if she'd spent an hour or more scouring the planet before she'd stopped by the rift. What had then happened once she'd been alerted had felt like minutes. *I always figured viewing time was close to real time, but I guess I was wrong, and there's a good deal of randomness to it instead. Perhaps it speeds up or slows down depending on how focused I am on the moment. Interesting.* "I found where we need to go," she added. "There's a rift valley that cuts deep into the surface, and whoever sent this planet is hunkered down in its side."

Grelt checked the scans of the planet, and Tia pointed out where the entrance was situated. "There's a flat area just here," Grelt stated, pointing to a shallow basin close by. "I can land there, and it will be about an hour on foot to where you want to go."

"I don't suppose you have any climbing gear?" Tia asked the brothers. They both shook their heads. "Claws it is. Ressen, check your space-suit, you're going to need it down there."

"What about you?" Ressen asked.

"It'll take more than a lack of oxygen and frigid temperatures to slow me down," Tia answered, grinning.

****

Tia watched as Grelt lifted off, to follow the planet at a safe distance, after having left her and Ressen on its surface. What little atmosphere the planet retained barely raised the surface temperature above a few degrees, and though Tia had no need for external protection, as the freezing effects of space had no real impact on her, she could feel the air's cold bite. Likewise, the lack of oxygen wasn't an issue for her, and she simply held her breath, and recirculated the air within her. Conversely, Ressen was decked out in a cumbersome space suit, because without it, it was toss up of whether he'd freeze or suffocate first. Tia looked at him. "Ready?" His helmet nodded.

They made their way up the gently sloping wall of the basin, Ressen in an oddly bouncing gallop because of the reduced gravity, Tia in her ever-purposeful, lack-of-gravity-defying stride, their steps leaving deep footprints in the silt. On reaching the rim, Tia could hear Ressen breathing heavily, and she took a moment to wait for him, using the break to survey the grey world. For what was a reasonable sized planet, its landscape was more moon-like. There was no hint of plant life, or complex animal life, just the occasional energy spark from some hardy bacteria that been too small for the sensors to pick up and were determinedly defying the odds. Tia had noted gullies in the sides of the more mountainous areas, but without a spectral analysis, there was no knowing if ancient rivers had caused them, or by something disturbing the planet's thin surface layers. From what she could tell, it was a world that had never become.

Beyond Ressen's laboured breathing, the place was deathly quiet. Its ground was covered with a thin covering of dust, which would rise with each foot fall, sometimes hanging for a second, bound by electrostatic charge, before slowly drifting down again. However, the eerie silence held within it secrets of a more violent past, and Tia could feel the effects, even as she stood still. The dust in the air, tiny particles barely visible to the naked eye, patted against her, and she could feel the little motes trying to cut at her, like minuscule daggers. The planet, though at rest, bore on its surface the scars of meteor strikes, and the dust told the same tale. Micrometeorite impacts had formed the grey silt; reducing the planet's rocks to dust and vaporising the ground so that each cooling mote was covered with a tiny layer of glass. Tia's skin could regenerate itself in time to the bombardment, and her hardened carapace was impenetrable to the tiny attackers, but Ressen's space suit could not, and the longer he stayed outside, the less protection it would afford him, as the dust slowly wore away at its layers.

"Tired already?" she asked, a little cheekily, as he drew level with her.

Ressen took in a couple of deep breaths. "It's not so much the distance and terrain...as this awkward gait," he panted "I know the gravity isn't that much below normal, but it's enough to throw out your stride. If I'm not careful...I'm going to fall over. I'm having a full body workout right now."

"Just try to let the bounce do the work for you,"

Ressen gave her a look of indignation. "That's easy for someone who isn't affected by the laws of physics to say."

"They affect me, I just choose to ignore them." Tia said, glibly, before starting off again.

As they carried on the journey, Tia could hear Ressen muttering away, and occasionally releasing expletives when he stumbled over a rock, or over-bounced. Admittedly, she felt sorry for him, but there was little she could do other than give him a piggyback ride, and she knew he would find that demeaning, though it was going to have to happen anyway once they made it to the rift.

As they drew nearer the target, the ground became fissured, making the going hard for them both, and even Tia ended up having to leap from one piece of ground to the next. Finally, after an exhausting game of hopscotch, they came to the edge of the crevasse.

Ressen leaned carefully forward to peek, and Tia made sure she was in grabbing distance of him in case he overbalanced. "That is one deep crack," he murmured. "Where's the entrance?"

"Just below us," Tia informed him. What she didn't tell him about was the nagging feeling, which had returned, and was once again trying to enter her mind. Whoever was waiting for them was still broadcasting to her, and it desperately wanted to be allowed in, but she was having none of it.

"And just how do we get down there?"

"With these," Tia answered, showing him her hands. Ressen looked at her, confused. Then his eyes went round as Tia flexed the muscles in her fingers to extend her claws. What had been black polished nails, manicured into points, had extended a few centimetres out from her fingertips, revealing themselves to be thick black talons. What's more, they were an extension of her hardened mesoskeleton, were razor-sharp, and could gouge lumps out of the hardest of rocks. They weren't the only tools in Tia's crampon arsenal though, as before they'd made planet-fall, she had regrown her armament of wings and tail. Her bat-like wings were tipped with their own grappling claws, just as equally sharp and strong, and although her tail's middle claw was used as a poison-injecting weapon, when combined with the pincers either side of it, it was just as capable of grasping hold of objects as any hand.

Ressen took it all in. "And me?" he queried.

"It's piggyback time."

"It's what time?"

"You climb onto my back, hold on around my neck, and grip on with your thighs." Ressen looked dubious. Tia wasn't sure what had him the most worried; being dangled over an abyss on her back, while she clambered down a shear face, or the over-familiarisation of having to cling on to her body. "You'll be fine," she added.

"Oh, I trust you not to drop me. It's just that my nerves are doing their best to override that trust."

"Well, the more you dwell on things, the worse it'll become, so let's make a move before you run, screaming for the hills." Tia curved her wings around the front of her body, and leant forward slightly, and with some difficulty, Ressen jumped onto her back, and caught her neck in a vice-like grip with his arms. But his spacesuit caused him problems. The fabric was slippery, and it prevented him from getting a good grip with his legs, so Tia resorted to wrapping her wings round her back, and him, to hold him tightly in place. She could only imagine how they appeared. *Like a bipedal dragon carrying a giant glass-headed baby in a papoose, no doubt.*

With Ressen secured, she eased herself over the rim of the cliff, and using her talons and tail, slowly made her way down to where she knew the entrance to be. The obsidian and rock were no match for her augmented claws, and they dug into the wall of the chasm as if it were no harder than sandstone, and her nails, steel. Her feet she used to brace herself as she went down, the rubber soles on her boots providing much-needed traction.

As she came within about a meter of the secreted hatch, her acute hearing picked up a click that came from inside the wall of the cliff. A moment later, a vibration travelled through her hands. Then, with and exhaling hiss below her, the hatchway opened downwards, providing her with a landing platform on which to jump.

"Guess they know we're here," came Ressen's muffled voice in her ear.

"It would seem so." Tia didn't like the idea that her nemesis had the upper hand. *Do me a favour, from now on, if you need to say something to me, do so through thought alone,* she projected to Ressen. She felt him mentally agree. Then she weaved her way into his mind, barricading it the best she could from unwanted telepathic intrusion. However, she had to wonder if it would be enough against whoever she found inside the inviting lair. *If they can block and alter my perception, chances are, they're doing likewise with him. I may as well be trying to stop a forest fire with glass of water.* Having done what she could, she dropped, landing with unnerving silence on the platform, and faced the dark, cave-like entrance into the planet, letting Ressen dismount from her back as she straightened up. A slight hum met her ears, and her senses told her the atmosphere was richer inside, and the gravity, a tad stronger, indicating that something, somewhere, was generating breathable air and artificial gravity.

"What do you see?" Ressen asked.

There was no lighting, or rather, none was switched on, but her eyes didn't need bright neon light to see, and the stars gave enough illumination for her pupils to pick out shapes in the gloom. *"I see a couple of small, unmarked craft docked in front of us,"* she told him, looking around. *"They're similar in design to Voleth fighters. Voleths are an Alliance race,"* she clarified. *"Beyond them is a rock wall with a door in it. I'm guessing that's our route in. The atmosphere inside is breathable but keep your gear on just in case someone decides to make it otherwise."*

Once again, she held back from telling Ressen the whole truth, because despite pushing her mind forward, she couldn't sense anyone in their vicinity, and yet someone was still merrily hammering away at her mind, trying to gain access. She led the way into the cave, hearing Ressen draw his weapon as they threaded their way between the Voleth fighters, which towered over them like metallic vultures, and where, size-wise, blatantly overcompensating for the small stature of the ugly aliens that used them.

They got to the door, and Tia placed her hand on the archaic handle, pausing a moment to see, one last time, if she could get a read on the situation. She pushed her mind beyond the rock wall, and it yielded, fading into nothingness as it did so, and she found herself looking into a deserted lit room full of consoles. And yet, something was amiss; something she couldn't put her finger on. To her, it was as if there was a heat haze in the periphery of her vision, distorting, ever so slightly, what she was seeing.

Tia focused hard, trying something she'd never done before, but had been thinking about since her remote viewing of the world. She'd always had the notion that the passage of time seemed to contract when she looked beyond the now. As an A'daree, she had been able to glean moments of detail within the space of a heartbeat, reading a room out of sight in barely a second. Her out-of-body foray to the planet had confirmed this too, and what had seemed like hours of work had, according to Grelt, taken mere minutes.

Time was not fixed, she knew that. It was a construct, created by sentient creatures to mark the passage of their existence that was mere seconds in the grand scale of cosmological ordered chaos. Tia was not so constrained. Time truly was relative to her, and she could see before her in rapid time, or interact with it in normal time. The thing was, her disregard of the passage of time had never been a conscious act, it was just what happened when she decided to scope out a room or watch the comings and goings of a far-off place. She seemed to unconsciously dictate when time needed to pass quickly, or normally, like a person submerged underwater instinctively knows not to breath.

Standing, with her hand on the door handle, while needing to know what she was blind to, was different, and a casual glance was not going to cut it. It needed to be a conscious effort, with her overriding her innate handling of time. She needed to breath underwater. So, in the same way she homed in on the atoms that made up her surroundings, she homed in on time itself. As she did so, her immediate environment seemed to distort, and expand outwards, as if everything were trying to speed away from her. Ressen appeared at once close beside her, and at the same time, hundreds of metres away. It was a nauseating sensation. Time convulsed. Time slowed. Time stopped. And there it was, a moment of time, infinitesimally small, frozen in place for her to see. And within it, finally exposed, were her adversaries.

Tia had to admit that whoever, or whatever, was concealing her opponents was unnervingly good. The mental camouflaging of them was fast enough to outwit an ordinary eye, and even to Tia, the haze had been barely discernible. But the obscurer couldn't compensate quick enough against her near freezing of time, and three individuals now stood revealed before her. One was a nondescript Human female, who was tall, slender, and had thin, long brown hair. However, despite being

Human, she was decked out in the lieutenant garb worn by the race of the second individual. It was a turquoise-skinned creature, with four black, soulless eyes, and no nose or lips. It was a Bardak, and its mouth-breathing gross countenance was instantly identifiable.

The third person was another odd-looking alien, one of a race Tia had seldom encountered, and whom she recognised as Juvan. It was clothed in what could only be described as a leotard, and its yellow-skinned feet, legs, and arms were bare, although it was wearing black gloves over its three-fingered hands. The alien's skin-tight apparel was interwoven with tubes, which fed through to what looked like a small pointy hat attached to the back of the creature's hairless, elongated head. However, Tia knew the hat thing was what was keeping the Juvan alive, and that it was in fact a respirator, which toned down the nitrogen-rich atmosphere the other two individuals were adapted to cope with. Confusingly, although the Juvan breathed out of the back of its head, it had nostrils on its face, but these were for olfactory use only. Its unusual appearance was finished off with a pair of huge black rectangular eyes, which sat either side of its head, and a tiny little mouth, which sat below its non-breathing nose.

The problem for Tia was that none of the three looked to be of the kind that could cause her so much trouble. Neither the Bardak nor the Juvan had telepaths. Conversely, the Human female, if she were a telepath, would have been proudly sporting the X-pin of her ilk, and even if, for some reason, she was going incognito, and was a high-level telepath, she'd be nowhere near strong enough to cause Tia any bother. The trio were not the ones physically and mentally cloaking themselves from her gaze, and they were not the ones capable of knocking continuously on her mental door. Whoever that was, was still capable of hiding themselves from her, and she couldn't get a fix on them. *Hell, they could be the other side of the planet for all I know.*

All three were facing the door, yet none had their weapons

drawn. There was no doubt they were waiting for her, but not to kill her, at least not for the moment. However, even though Tia was sure she could push through the mental barricade given time, as reality was frozen, so too were their thoughts, meaning they would be unreadable. It was time for Tia to face her foe. She brought herself back up through time and looked at Ressen. *"There are three unarmed assailants behind this door,"* she told him, *"but be aware, there could be others I don't see."* He gave her a nod of understanding and gripped his gun tightly in his hand.

Tia pushed on the door handle and opened the metal door to the once again empty-looking room. Without thinking, she positioned herself in front of Ressen, in case any of her unseen assailants decided to take a shot at them. She could take a bullet or a blast, he could not. As she stepped into the room she announced, "I know you're standing in front of me. Kindly have the decency to deal with me face to face." The haze on her periphery shuddered, and in the blink of an eye, the three people were revealed. Behind her, Ressen drew in his breath, telling her he too was seeing what was real.

The Human female stepped forward. "I am lieutenant Toray Caloo of the Bardak Space Legion. We've been expecting you."

No shit! Tia thought, with utmost sarcasm. She didn't respond to Toray's obvious declaration, as she had just noticed the infernal hammering in her skull had stopped. Instead, she cast her mind as far and wide as she could, searching for a possible familiar presence. Again, she came up empty.

"Well?" Toray asked her, sounding a little put out by Tia's underwhelming response.

"Sorry, I was looking for a new old friend."

"There will be no Mister Ward this time," a deep, rasping voice said, as a new face entered the room. Although Tia had no idea of the owner's race, she instinctively saw him as the bigger threat, and angled herself between him and Ressen. Whoever he was, he was as tall as she was, and his limbs were long and muscular, and his fingers elongated and bony. He wore brown slacks, and a thread-bare, white V-necked vest, which exposed his barrel-like torso and pallid skin. His face was hard and angular, with small sunken eyes, a flat nose and chin, and a barely lipped mouth. Sparse, wispy hair covered his head, which bulged outwards at the back over a large brain case.

The creature's mind was slightly open to her, and as she cautiously swept her psyche across his, she felt as though she was looking in a mirror, albeit a distorted one. The creature radiated an energy and presence she had felt before, specifically during the battle for Ciberia. It tasted of the black alien crafts she had fought, and she had no doubt that the creature was like her, a symbiont of one of the unknown vessels. It gave a vicious smile, sensing her realisation. "You guess correct," it stated, "and this time, as I have the upper hand, things are going to play out very differently to our last confrontation." It was then Tia recognised who he was. He was the symbiont of the ship she had wounded and released.

"So, the goddess of war and death is amongst us finally." Tia felt an involuntary chill go through her. She had been prepared for the worst, but coming up against an old nemesis, with more knowledge of her than she would have liked, left her with a feeling of dread. Tia kept a close eye on him as he strode towards his compatriots. "Politeness dictates I should make introductions," he added. "You have already met Lieutenant Caloo, so let me introduce her commanding officer Commander Zho Wanuuk, also of the Bardak Space Legion, specifically their land infantry division. And this is Admiral Ujiri," he gestured to the Juvan, "a member of the Alliance High Command." The admiral was the only one to give Tia an involuntary head-bob of greeting.

"And you?" prompted Tia.

The alien gave a sneer. "I am Werldon, and you know my race." For the briefest millisecond, Tia lost her poker face, but it was long enough for Werldon to pick up on, and the look of glee on his face was unmissable. "You mean to tell me you don't know my species? Ah the Karee and their guilty little secrets, as always unwilling to deal with their past."

"If you know me as well as I think you do, then you'll know that I'm not one for vague talk and long speeches. Kindly get to the point."

Werldon bowed sardonically. "Duly noted." He then raised his arms wide. "I am Karee."

Tia's mind went into shock. "How can that be?" she asked. "I felt your presence at the Ciberian battle. Your energy is different to the Karee...."

"And yet, so alike," Werldon finished. And to prove his point, his dark, deep set eyes, transformed into shining green stars, flecked with red, which had the effect of making the pallid skin on his face look even more sickly. The overall effect was that it made him look like a lanky demon, a stark contrast to when Tia's eyes glowed blue.

Tia couldn't fault his statement, or his display. There was a sense of familiarity about him, one that spoke of Karee, and his words seemed annoyingly truthful. Yet the differences were too big to ignore. Her mind rebelled at the idea of him being Karee. Their ships were different, their behaviour was different, their presence was different. A notion popped up in her head, hearkening back to her botanist days aboard the Scientia. Among the various plants she had studied, several had off-shoot populations that could exist in different biomes to the main species. Their outward appearances were similar, but over the centuries, their genetics had changed just enough to allow them to survive differing environmental conditions. "You're a different ecotype," she said.

Werldon considered her labelling of him. "Ecotype, subspecies, either is an accurate description," he answered. "My brothers and sisters and I are Karee, but we dispensed with that name many millennia ago. Now we have no true name, just those that are given to us by other races. Personally, I like the one bestowed upon us by the Voleths: Zah'r'raith. It translates loosely to 'hand that guides', or the grammaticality better 'guiding hand'. So, we are Zahraith, and so, I feel, are you."

What? "What?"

Again, Werldon smiled at her confusion; an act that was starting to annoy the hell out of her. He turned to the trio, who left without a word. It was clear he had sent them a telepathic command, but Tia had been unable to intercept it as their minds were blocked from her. What she did notice was Admiral Ujiri did not seem to share in the pompous determination of the other two. They strode off with purpose, he slunk along after them.

"I think it's time you learnt the past of the Karee, a lesson you are sorely in need of, and when you have heard it, I doubt you will be so inclined to follow in their wake."

I'm hardly following in their wake, Tia thought, recalling all the times she'd disobeyed them, and the fact they weren't speaking to her anymore, but she held her tongue. She was eager to hear what Werldon had to say for himself, and about the past of her once leash-holders.

"I don't entirely know what you've been told so, for completion's sake, I shall go back to the beginning...to the birth of the Karee...." And so Werldon said his piece. It made Tia's mind spin. It made Ressen's head fill with a multitude of questions. But most importantly, as far as Tia was concerned, it was the truth.

****

The race of the Karee was old, that Tia knew, but how old was only just being revealed to her. They had been at the birth of the universe, they had seen the creation of time, and all because they had witnessed the death of their old universe. They had been the oldest race within that universe too. They had been the first race to crawl out of the primordial goo, to think, to debate the stars, and to touch other worlds. Their intelligence had become renowned. They mastered time and space, and to those species below them, what they did had seemed like magic; god-like. Yet the Karee were dissatisfied. They sought to master more, and more importantly, they sought to master themselves.

Travelling across the expanses of space in metal ships was one thing, to do it unfettered and free was another, and so they poured their knowledge, and themselves, into becoming something better. They became the engineers of their own evolution, and became the ageless, organic ship-like creatures of Jarell and Morrígan. Unconstrained by the fragility and limitations of a humanoid form, they could explore the cosmos anew, and gaze upon it through different eyes, and when their universe began drawing its last breaths, instead of going quietly into the night, they pushed forward, and crossed the boundary between multiverses. Yet the new realm they found themselves in was not Tia's. That was still a universe away.

They explored every inch of their new universe, and they watched as suns, planets, and life formed, but something was amiss. As ship-bound aliens, they could interact with other races. They could teach and learn, and their lives had been filled with fascinating encounters with other lifeforms, but as space-faring ships, that ability had been lost. Therefore, the Karee sought to change themselves once more; welcoming into their bodies a symbiont; an alien they could interact with and use to interact with others; a landing craft, an away mission, and an emissary all rolled into one. That achieved, the Karee were renewed, and their involvement with other races began again.

However, a rift was forming. While all within the Karee ranks saw aiding the advancement of a lesser race as an important obligation, the line of where to begin and where to stop was being hotly debated. Was it wrong to seed life onto a barren world that couldn't seem to get bacteria right? Was it right to help a race vanquish the competition so it could become the dominant species a little sooner? When did aiding become interfering? When did natural succession become genocide? Some wanted only to nudge a species in the right direction. Others wanted to shove.

When the time came to move on again, the divide had grown, and as the Karee entered Tia's little corner of the multiverse, the split finally happened. The Karee that were 'Karee', for a time, chose to aid the lesser races, just as they'd done before. But the Zerrens were their swansong, culminating in a fought and won battle over the protection of Zerra from the Zahraith's questionable interference. And so, the damage was done, and the fuzzy line between hands-on and hands-off became too contentious, so the Karee took the easy way out, and stopped involving themselves altogether. That was until the Zahraith once more crossed their path.

While the Karee had lamented over the ethics of their involvement, the Zahraith had held no similar compunctions, and had pushed, cajoled, and controlled, wherever they could. From that meddling, the Orion Alliance had grown, creating a select group of races that saw themselves as superior successors to the galaxy, and ultimately, the universe.

Tia understood why the Karee had pulled themselves out of hiding to protect Zerra, when they had sworn to interfere no longer. It may have been the Alliance knocking on Zerra's door, but it was because their own kind were pulling the strings, threatening Zerra's existence once again. Old wounds had become exposed, forcing the Karee's hand into taking a hazy moral high ground to protect Zerra. A situation that included destroying, in spectacular fashion, Alliance battleships.

Slowly, other parts of the puzzle began fitting themselves together in Tia's mind. She knew the rule that stipulated no Karee should kill one of its own kind, and finally, some of their earlier behaviour made sense. The Karee had refused to go after the orb because they had known one of the Zahraith ships would be there and hadn't wanted to end up in a battle with their brethren. Instead, they had made the questionable choice of allowing one of their own, rare new-borns to fall into enemy hands, to be used as a powerful weapon of war. Luckily for Morrigan, the situation had been turned on its head thanks to Tia's waywardness. Similarly, Jarell had refused to fight the ships at Ciberia, because he was part of the old guard, and couldn't bring himself to fight his kin.

It also made Tia wonder something else. "Are the Karee afraid of you?" she asked, when finally able to get a word in edgewise.

"Yes," Werldon stated, without hesitation. "The Karee follow the old law, one of those rules being that one Karee should never attack another. That rule was written down when we still walked on two legs. But over time we Zahraith developed a different view. We see ourselves as successors, as an evolutionary advancement, and as such, we have no problems with superseding the lesser form."

"An evolutionary advancement?" Tia queried, trying to keep her eyebrows level.

"The Karee sequestered themselves away in isolation over a thousand years ago, and as a species, they have stagnated. The Zahraith have continued advancing forward, gaining knowledge, and developing new skills and technology. What is that if not evolving?"

I'm sure my biology textbooks would have something to say about that, Tia thought. True, the Karee and Zahraith could be classed as separate species, but that doesn't mean one is more evolved than the other. They are both spacefaring, highly intelligent, organic creatures, and are pretty level pegging when it comes to advancement. So, one has a greater compunction to kill, and can turn that aggression on a similar species, that's hardly a basis for labelling one as more advanced than the other. However, as Werldon was a font of knowledge, she didn't want an argument over morals and evolution to cut him off, so she kept quiet. Instead, she asked, "So, are you intending to kill me too?"

"Straight to the point as always." Werldon teased. "Oh, there are many who would dearly love to see your rotting corpse, so they could spit on it, including those three cretins in the other room."

"Charming!"

"But you and I can see the bigger picture. Your death would

solve a lot of problems, there's no doubt about that, but in life, you could do far more for the Zahraith than you realise."

"Care to elaborate…?"

"For so long, the Karee have shunned us, trying to pretend we're a problem that doesn't exist, but no more. Our choice in ideologies may have separated us, with our interactions with Zerra forcing them into acknowledging our existence once again, but there's more to it than that. An inescapable bond has been created between our two species, and in that, the Karee have no one to blame but themselves." He looked pointedly at Tia. "You see, your existence is as a direct result of the Zahraith, after which, the Karee begrudgingly welcomed you into their fold for their own ends."

Tia had a good idea what he was insinuating, and she didn't like it one bit. "You created the scorpiads."

Werldon gave a huge smile. "Guilty!" he said, with some relish. "We gave the irksome Humans a method of creating an unstoppable army to sort out their rebellion problems, though they never knew it was us that had provided them with the know-how. The information found its way to them by way of the Pyr'mu, likewise the Alliance's new engine shielding."

Tia knew of the Pyr'mu race. They were old and aggressive warmongers with an eye always towards the next effective method of wiping out a race. Little wonder the Alliance hadn't questioned where the information had come from; the scorpiads had all the hallmarks of a Pyr'mu weapon of mass destruction. And Werldon's statement over developing the new Alliance battleship shielding explained something else. *No wonder Jarell never picked up on it. It wasn't just because it wasn't turned on, these bastards managed to cloak the components just enough so neither he, nor I, realised they were there unless we went looking for them. Just like the entrance to this place.* There was no doubt in Tia's mind that the Zahraith were a dangerous foe within the Alliance's mix.

"Of course, some Karee would say the blame lies with the Humans for not listening to us, by trying to create female-based scorpiads," Werldon was surmising. "Had they not messed around; you wouldn't have been created."

Tia's thoughts momentarily turned to Chione, and the hand his previous incarnation had played in her existence. Despite him having made the call to use Emma's body, she couldn't find the level of hatred for him as she had for Werldon.

"But after you ran amok, it was the Karee who saved you," Werldon continued. "What they should have done was eradicate you on the spot, no offence, but instead they decided to again take the questionable moral high ground. Perhaps they felt sorry for you, recognising our handy work. Or perhaps on recognising our handy-work they decided to prepare themselves to combat us in the future by fortifying you." Werldon waved his hand dismissively. "Whatever the reason, they took you in, and now the fates have made you a Zahraith construct in a Karee vessel. A half-breed of both worlds, and an inhabitant of neither, but so much more like us than the Karee would want or tolerate." He gave Tia a knowing wink.

Tia's heart sank. She knew her past had been less than rosy. Before the Karee had caught up with her, she had near wiped out a ship full of scientists. Further, her deployment by the Karee implied she had destroyed countless other lives while under the effects of the Scorpiad's mind, even if she couldn't remember the particulars. Yet knowing her brutal actions had been as a direct result of an alien race who were pushing others to wipe out countless species for the sake of evolutionary domination was hard to stomach. But Werldon had made a mistake, despite her past, she was not Zahraith. At least that was the idea she clung to. The Zahraith were who she was fighting against, not who she'd joined forces with. "I am not like you." She told him, trying to sound like she meant it.

"Oh, but you are. You proved that after your birth from fire, and again at the battle of Ciberia. You killed several of my brothers. In particularly spectacular fashion I might add. A Karee would not have done that, a Karee would have run and hidden, or would have refused to fight us." Tia knew Jarell was being hinted at. "The truth of who you are is even carved in stone...."

Tia's stomach clenched. A giant effigy of her likeness hewn from the inside of a mountain flooded her vision. Her men had labelled it the hall of gods. It had been a huge cavern on the Ethtas' old and barren home world, filled with statues of aliens, proclaiming them gods and goddesses: of healing, of justice, of helplessness. And at the end of the rows, there had been her likeness, and the proclamation that she was the goddess of war and a harbinger of death. Just as Werldon had greeted her. "How do you know about that?" she asked, feeling a little weak. "And what do you know about it?" As far as she knew, the Zahraith had never set foot on the planet. If they had, they'd have taken the Karee egg long before she'd managed to get hold of it.

"We hear things," was Werldon's vague response. "As for what, well that all made sense when the truth of the orb was finally revealed in all its world-shattering glory. I'll be honest, we hadn't realised it was a Karee egg. We assumed it was some highly advanced power source, and we came to the planet to take it, and reverse engineer it for our own ends. The truth regarding its initial discovery had long been lost, and even the stories regarding your statue were a little hazy, though I don't think there is any question to their validity anymore." He gave Tia what she could only describe as a 'once over' and a cheeky wink.

What the hell kind of creature are you? She had her suspicions, the way he talked so easily, his hand and facial gestures, his nauseating wink. Somewhere, under the messed-up form she was seeing, was a Human.

"The orb," Werldon continued, "contained the energy and essence of a Karee, and though not properly formed, it could still interact with the universe. There are intriguing, albeit muddied fables of the engineers of the generator becoming worshipped and revered. A religion sprang up around them, with individuals being indoctrinated into their now-closed ranks. Some, including modern Ethtas, put it down to the fact that they had managed to save the Ethtas civilisation through the 'creation' of this infinite energy source. But it has since become clear this is not the full story. One narrative that keeps cropping up within these fables is these 'holy men' had visions. Of course, stories get more outlandish with each telling, but the cavern of statues insinuates there is some validity to this. The truth as I know it is, these men were reacting to the orb's presence. Being in proximity to it for days on end affected them, and its innate knowledge, its ability to read the cosmos, and its potential energy, leached into their minds, allowing them to see echoes of the galaxy past and present. It led them to create the statues. It led them to seeing you."

Tia took in everything Werldon had to say. It was a lot of information, and it raised more questions in her mind, but more than that, in the thirty minutes or so she had been talked at, she had learnt more about herself, and about the Karee, than she had during the last five hundred years in their service. Not even Morrígan had been forthcoming about Karee history, and although it may have been nothing more than an egg for a good part of it, it still knew considerably more than Tia ever had. To say she was irked by the whole situation would have been an understatement. "And do you believe the statue's proclamation of me?" she asked.

"I have no reason to doubt it," Werldon replied. "I believe many more bodies will be piled up at your feet before this is all over."

Tia felt Ressen wince behind her. The forgotten eavesdropper in their toing and froing. She couldn't bring herself to focus on his emotions, as she didn't want to know what he was starting to think of her. Here she was, being outed as a mass murderer, with an active career still ahead of her, but there was one important thing the statue didn't state, nor did Werldon know, and that was just whose bodies would end up at her feet, if indeed the prophesying of her was true. Werldon's words hinted that he believed they would be his enemy's, lead into battle by her, but they could just as easily be his own compatriots, bested by her and the other members of the GR. "The trouble with relying on these kinds of prophesies," Tia stated, "is they tend to be vague and open to interpretation. There's no guarantee that the bodies will fall in your favour."

"They will if you are one of us," Werldon said, with a sickening smile.

Tia knew he was waiting for her inevitable question. The cue he was desperately after to put her whole reason of being there into action. The air around her felt oppressive, as if it knew what was coming. She did all she could to prepare. She held firm onto Ressen's mind and steeled herself. "And why would I join you?" she finally asked.

"Because you will have no other choice," Werldon replied.

Hell swarmed her. Fire and ice burned into the cells of her body in an agonising crescendo. Being separate from Morrígan meant she was short a formidable shield against one of her own kind, and the rage she'd weaponised to best Werldon's brothers first time around was lacking. Werldon's mind hammered at hers, and she desperately tried to hold her ground against the onslaught. Teeth clenched against the pain, she unleashed what she had in response. She sensed Ressen turn tail and run but had no time to call after him. She felt the air crackle around her in response to her summoning of her energy within. She released it at Werldon in a bid to rip him from the universe. The room illuminated in blue brightness, and there were explosions as some of the surrounding machinery shorted out, but through it all a voice, Werldon's voice, said in a triumphant tone, "not this time."

It was as if the whole universe just froze. Space, time, feeling, sights, sounds, all ceased to be. Blackness rushed up to greet her, but before consciousness left her, there was the briefest of moments when the darkness in her mind shone with thousands of suns. Green suns, flecked with red. To Tia's horror, Werldon was not alone in his fight against her. The cavalry was with him. Whether hidden from view in the skies above the nomadic planet, or thousands of light years away, it didn't matter. They had her. She heard Ressen yell out her name in panic, but there was nothing she could do. She crashed to the ground, out cold.

****

"Tia?" A voice, barely discernible, croaking.

I know this moment. I've done it before. I'm in the arboretum.

"Tia?" The voice again; at once both rasping and gentle.

But last time I was with Aben. There was a dream. What happened to the dream?

"Tia!" This time it was urgent and demanding.

Tia came to with a start. She felt light-headed. She felt... light-bodied. She rolled onto her back with a groan.

"For the love of gods Tia, get up!"

This time she recognised the voice and bolted upright in blind confusion. "Ressen?" The memory of pain came flooding back to her, its residual presence making her woozy, and with it came the reminder that she'd been defeated by Werldon and a fleet of Zahraith.

She looked around her, and found she was on the cold, concreted floor of a cell. Its walls were bars, and through them, she could see Ressen in the next cell, and as she focused on him, her heart fell. He was chained up to the wall, and had been worked over, either by Werldon, or one or more of his cronies. Bruises and cuts covered the alien's naked torso, and one of his eyes was swollen shut. Tia could smell the pungent odours of the incarcerated, coupled with the metallic tang of blood; Ressen's blood.

She scrambled to her feet, with a mind to bring the cell walls down, and make Werldon pay for everything he'd done, and nearly fell flat on her face, her centre of gravity well away from its norm. It was then she realised why she felt so light and out of place. Everything was missing: her horns, her wings, her tail, even her height. She looked down at her arms, to see pale skin devoid of silver lines.

"Werldon said he's regressed you," Ressen said, in a cracking voice in dire need of water.

Tia didn't know what to say. She just stared down at herself, her small, fragile, Human self, clothed in a hessian shift and nothing more. Her legs buckled, and her backside hit the concrete floor with a thud. She looked up at Ressen, completely devoid of words.

"Hey Emma, nice to meet you in the flesh," Ressen said, trying to lighten the mood, and failing miserably.

How? Tia couldn't feel herself, not the way she used to. Her ability to focus in on her cells and change her form was gone. Her mind was incarcerated in her skull. "How long have I been out?" Her circadian rhythm normally would've been able to tell her the time, but whatever had happened to her had kicked it out of kilter. In her befuddled state, she couldn't figure out how long she'd been unconscious, though, judging by Ressen's wounds, it had been some time.

"I'd say about twelve hours," he croaked, confirming her suspicions, "but that's just going off how hungry I am."

"Did he say how he regressed me?" she asked, barely able to raise her voice above a couple of decibels. She tried to think. She doubted they had made her truly Human. That would have required some major genetic manipulation, and would have taken ages to achieve, and that was speaking from experience. The Karee had not changed her from scorpiad to A'daree overnight, nor had she gone from A'daree to Karee overnight. What was more likely was the Zahraith had done much like she had done back on Ressen's ship, and had forced her body to change its shape, stripping her of her adornments, including that which resembled clothing. Then they had walled up her mind, to make her a prisoner in her own body.

"No," Ressen said, answering her question. "All he said was, if you wanted to be Karee again, then you'd have to join his side. That, and if you wanted me to live."

Tia jerked her head up to look at Ressen. "What did they

do to you?" she asked, looking again at his damaged body. She couldn't discern much about his injuries, but a particularly nasty bruise encircled his left side, likely marking the presence of a broken rib or two. Beyond that, it looked like they had taken whip, hammer, and fist to him, and his blue and white striped body was a mass of red welts and large purple bruises. But amongst the carnage something shone. Tia's pendant was still around his neck, and resting safely on his chest, moved only by his laboured breathing.

"No more than I've endured in the past," he answered, with more than a little bravado.

Something occurred to Tia. She stood up, went over to the bars that separated them, and whispered, "How come I can still understand you?"

Ressen looked a little taken aback. "As far as I'm aware," he said, under his breath, "I'm talking my own language."

"We speak of this no more." Tia answered, hurriedly. Ressen gave a slight nod of understanding. *A crack, a crack in the wall.* Somehow, despite everything, a part of Tia's mind had stayed connected to Ressen's. But was in by accident or design?

Tia felt the cold, smooth steel bars in her hand, her fingers unable to detect any imperfections. Less than a day ago, she would have felt every microscopic fissure and bump, and would have been able to melt them and the bars into nothingness. Now, they were an unyielding barrier. She wanted more than anything to take the coolness of the metal into her hands, reach out, and numb the pain that would be pulsating through Ressen's body, but he was well out of arm's length. "I'm sorry," Tia sighed, resting her head against the bars.

"You said we could be walking into a trap, and I chose to follow you. You have nothing to apologise for."

"But they're using you to blackmail me into joining their side."

"Well, that would only really work if you had strong feelings for me," Ressen answered, in a tone that made Tia's stomach squirm. "But even if you do, my life is insignificant in the

393

grand scheme of things. I understand that. You can't join the bad guys just to save me."

"How do you do what you do?" Tia said, with frustration. "How can you continue to be so blithe and calm in the face of all you've seen and experienced."

Ressen smiled, which made his cracked lips begin to bleed. Tia almost felt like crying at the sight. "I guess it's just my nature," he said.

"I wish it was in mine," Tia answered. "I seem to spend my days teetering on the brink of rage and madness."

"Is that such a terrible thing?" Tia gave Ressen a questioning look. "Considering what I've heard of your successes, rage and madness seems to work for you."

Tia took a moment to think about what Ressen had said. It was a plausible notion. Going back over the last couple of years' events, her victories did seem to have been spurred on by her unhinged emotions. Leaping after the orb, after Aben had thrown it down a near bottomless pit, could only be described as pure madness, and the destruction of the Zahraith ship, and then its brothers at Ciberia, were as a direct result of her rage. Inner peace certainly didn't seem to do her any favours, at least not in a confrontation, as proven by the fact that Werldon had bested her, albeit with help. Knowing that made Tia feel even more guilty. She had been calm, even curious, while in Werldon's presence. For years she had yearned for the knowledge he had shared willingly with her; his giving it to her on a silver platter causing her to drop her guard. If she hadn't been so relaxed, she may have at least been able to do more to protect Ressen.

But, yet again, she had failed to protect a close ally and friend, and the result of her failure had been callously strung up for her to see, as a visage meant to break her spirit. What was coming next for Ressen, Tia barely dared think about. She felt her heart pound in her chest, and desperately wanted to wail for all to hear, just as she had with Aben's passing, but something inside her held her voice back. Ressen was still alive, and she still had the tiniest of chances to save his life.

A noise made her look towards the main door of the cell block, and the entity Werldon had named as Admiral Ujiri entered, carrying a tray of what Tia hoped was food. The creature kept his head cowed, unable to bring himself to look either Tia or Ressen in the eye. He came close to Tia's cage, and she moved to intercept him. A savoury smell hit her nose, telling her the tray's contents was indeed food, and not implements to use on Ressen. Ujiri bent over, and made to push the tray under Tia's door, but she stopped it with her foot.

"No!" Alarmed, Ujiri jerked his head up to face her. "You give that food to him," she said, gesturing in Ressen's direction.

Ujiri vocalised a string of clicks in response. A moment later, his translator took up the batten. "Food is for you. Alien gets none until you give in to our demands."

"Your demands won't even be on the table unless he gets food and water," Tia responded, angrily. Ujiri looked torn. His head flickered in Ressen's direction, and he hunched a little more. *There's regret and guilt there. Despite his position, he doesn't want to be a part of this, and a plan is only as strong as its weakest link, and for Werldon, it's this creature.* Tia reigned in some of her wrath. "At least give him some water, otherwise he'll be dead before a deal can be made," she pleaded, as sweetly as possible.

The desire to keep their bargaining chip alive seemed to do the trick. Ujiri took the container of water off Tia's tray, and opened up Ressen's cell. Tia paralleled him and watched as Ujiri gently poured the water into Ressen's mouth. "What's the plan? To torture him until I give in?" Again, Ujiri winced at the reality he was being made to face. "You know, for someone in the upper echelons of the Orion Alliance, you don't seem to have much of a stomach for this," Tia said, conversationally. "Let me guess, you gave the orders, but never had to get your hands dirty...until now. What? The results aren't as palatable as you'd imagined?"

Ujiri approached her side of Ressen's cell. "I have killed

people," his translator announced. "I have been in the heart of battle and cut down charging foe."

"Charging foe is one thing, it's another to beat a restrained man to a pulp. He's not even your enemy. He comes from a world far beyond the border of the Alliance."

"All those beyond our border are considered enemies until we decide otherwise."

"Where's that from; page one of the Orion Alliance hand-book?" Tia asked, mockingly. "Enemies are those who would attack you, not those who are simply minding their own busi-ness, trying to live their lives in peace. Hell, the Alliance has been eradicating races who don't even know they exist...like the Filteth. Tell me, how were a bunch of farmers, on the other side of the galaxy, the enemy?"

Ujiri had no response for her. He slammed Ressen's cage door shut and left the cell block as swiftly as possible.

"He didn't like that," Ressen said, with a nasty wheeze.

"I just hope it was enough," Tia answered, trying not to grimace at Ressen's voice. "I don't think Ujiri wants to be here. He was probably sent as an observer to oversee Werldon's plan."

"He certainly didn't want to be a part of my torture," Ressen confirmed. "He hid in the shadows and winced every time they hit me."

"And just who were 'they'?"

"That big ugly creature punched me with metal things on his hands, the woman whipped me, and Werldon...."

"Werldon what?"

Ressen pulled a face. "He got inside me...made every nerve in my body scream." Tia wanted desperately to reach out and give him comfort. "But joke was on him. Been there, done that...and survived," he gave Tia a half-hearted grin.

"Stop trying to be a damn hero," Tia said, tersely, and she went to check the food Ujiri had proffered her. It didn't look appetising. There were puddles of brown gruel, a desiccated potato-looking thing, and a lump of orange jelly that smelt slightly of petrol. Tia's stomach both turned in revulsion and gurgled in desire. She put the lid back on the tray. "So not hungry for that," she half lied. In truth, had Ressen not been there, she would have inhaled it, jelly and all, but she didn't want to consume it in front of him and make him feel worse.

"You can eat it, I won't mind," Ressen said, seemingly reading her mind.

"Nah, I'm good," she told him, pulling a face. "You may not mind seeing it go down but coming back up is another matter."

They heard the door to the cell block open again, and Tia turned, half expecting to see Ujiri looking for another lecture, but it was Werldon. He strode over to their cells, giving off an air of self-importance. Beyond him, through the crack in the cell door, Tia could see a table covered with the implements they had used on Ressen. Blood was on them. Tia wondered if Werldon had specifically left the door ajar for her to see them. Tia's own blood boiled. Werldon ran his eye over his handiwork on Ressen and gave a sneer. Then he focused on Tia. "Well?"

"I'm not going to join you."

Ressen released a soul-wrenching scream, his body straining and contorting as Werldon did his thing. Tia's heart felt like it was going to shatter at the sound. Her body convulsed, as though she was sharing in his pain.

"Enough," she yelled over the sound. Werldon let go of Ressen's body, and the alien sagged from his shackles, barely conscious. Her own body unclenched in time to his. *Did I really feel his pain, or was that just sympathetic? There's some connection still at work between us, that's for sure, but is it enough to do that?*

"Shall we try this again?" Werldon asked, smugly. "Will you join us?"

Tia fumed, and her building rage flush her cheeks. "If you want me to join you, what's the point of torturing him? Just threaten to leave me in this state, that would be enough."

"Ujiri said something along those lines. Said we should use this creature as insurance against you rescinding on any loyalty you promise us."

"Ujiri sounds like he has brains," Ressen mumbled, his head still sunk into his chest.

"Ujiri is a weak-minded coward," Werldon spat. "He may have gained his seat within the Alliance's high command through victories in his youth, but he's grown soft with age. He has more conscience than is seemly, and his questioning of Alliance actions is going to see his position terminated, sooner than expected."

"And where better to have his career terminated than on a rogue planet in the middle of nowhere?" Tia gave Werldon a questioning look.

He feigned innocence with a shrug. "Space is a dangerous place, especially on a planet with a wayward Karee."

Yeah, I bet that'll be it. Either I change allegiance and you have me kill him as a sign of good faith. Or I don't, and you kill him anyway and blame me, having already killed me, Tia mused.

"Here's the thing," Werldon said, "I think you care more for him than you do for your own predicament. Your soft spot for worthless cases is well-known, so me threatening to leave you incarcerated in your own body may hold some fear for you, but not enough. No, the imminent death of this creature, I think, will be enough to sway your mind. As for keeping you under control, I think we've proven we can do that."

Ressen gave another blood-curdling scream, as pain rocked and twisted his body. Tia's insides burned as her anger raged. "No!" she screamed above Ressen's cry. Ressen silenced, and his head lolled in unconsciousness. Tia held back her own sobs and looked pleadingly at Werldon. The stress she was feeling was giving her something akin to heart burn, and her chest spasmed in pain.

"Last chance," Werldon said, with a vicious grin, and his eyes began to take on an ominous a green glow.

Tia felt consumed by fury and helplessness. Ressen had said his life was worthless compared to the cause, but his life was not worthless to her. But if she denied Werldon's offer, he would be dead, and she was under no illusions she would be likewise. Werldon may have been threatening to leave her as 'Human', but there was no way he'd risk her vessel finding her and undoing his handiwork. The only choice Tia had, was to accept his offer, and hope that she could find a way to escape the Zahraith once she'd been returned to her Karee form. The thought of that sent the fiery spasms in her chest down into her stomach, so much so, she had to hold onto the bars to prevent herself from doubling over as pain rocked her abdomen.

Her fingers picked up the minutest tremble travelling through the metal bars, but she put it down to her own hands shaking through a combination of grief at Ressen's treatment, and pure ire at her own. She tried to bide some time to collect her thoughts. "If I come, Ressen comes too," she growled, through clenched teeth. Her insides were throbbing, and white spots swam in front of her eyes. *What is wrong with me?* She felt as though she was in the grips of a fever. *Have they made me so Human that my appendix can rupture, or is it some residual illness that once ravaged my Human body re-establishing itself?* It certainly felt like her appendix was on its way out. Pain and heat radiated out from her core, and she was sure she was visibly sweating, though if she was, Werldon was paying no attention to it.

"Of course," he said, benignly answering her request.

But Tia could see the lie etched in his eyes. The moment she was under the Zahraith's thumb, Ressen would be dead. She could not trust the man, she could not trust the Zahraith, and she could not allow herself to become a willing and destructive pawn of the Alliance. She considered her final choice. *Shar and Kan have become as near as dammit to good men under my watch and can lead without me. And the likes of Sin'ma and Leo have been set on the right path. They have the GR, and themselves, and they can continue to strive forward. Morrígan will watch over them, and I'm sure Jarell will do likewise. May Ressen's death be swift and may Grelt forgive me in time.*

With the last of her strength, she drew up her height, and

bolstered her resolve. "No," she said, with terrible finality.

Werldon almost did a surprised double take. "No?"

"No. I will not be your plaything or your tool. You will not have me. You will not have control over me."

"You can't say no, it's your destiny. The truth was taken from the universe and carved in rock."

"Prophecies are just fragments and glimpses glued together into some bastardised whole," she snarled. "They are not truths, just maybes. I am not destined to become a destroyer for you. I am Karee, and not now, nor will I ever be, Zahraith."

"You are not Karee," Werldon sneered, all pretence at pleasantries finally gone. "You are just some screwed-up mongrel symbiont, shunned by the very creatures who helped make you what you are. And don't think for a minute they didn't know what they were creating, they knew all too well. That glorified statue of you appeared long before the Karee collared you. They knew who you were, what you were, and what you would become, and they lied and manipulated you to become the very same. They could have destroyed you, but instead they chose to bolster the prophecy. They made you the bastardised whole, set you loose on the galaxy, and hid behind their wall of self-imposed righteousness." His face contorted in disgusted, making his features appear even more angular and repugnant. "But right now, you are just a half-breed wastrel creature with no strength or abilities. You are what you should have always been. You. Are. Nothing."

Tia's skin felt unbearably clammy, as the fever, triggered by whatever organ stood on the brink of failing, took hold, but it was a mere backdrop to her madness. More than anything, Tia wanted to be free. Free of the pain, free of the blackmail, free of the cell.

Flight.

In a few seconds, she knew she would have that freedom, but at a price. In the face of death, her brain and mouth ran away from her. "You are wrong." She yelled, banging the bars of her cell, making Werldon step back, at last a look of concern materialising on his face. To be nothing, meant to be some insignificant speck, all alone in the darkness. It was a ridiculous fallacy to insinuate that she was nothing. She had helped free Zerra, she had found the orb, she had defended Ciberia, and she had achieved all that because she had friends who trusted her, colleagues who worked with her, and lovers who would do anything for her. She was worshipped, respected, cherished, and followed. She was something to an awful lot of people; some she knew, thousands she never would.

A voice floated into her head, the tone belonging to Ressen, *"You are Tia, and you are Karee."*

She had no idea if it was truly his thought finding its way in somehow, or just her own, desperate subconscious taking on the countenance of someone she cared deeply about in a bid to bolster her strength. Whatever its source, it gave her failing mind and body one last boost. "I am not **nothing**." she hissed, through clenched teeth. "I was born of Karee, I led as Karee, and I will die as Karee. I am Karee! I am everything. I am…."

Tia barely had time to witness the look of shock on Werldon's face as the bright spots in her vision consumed her sight. The fire and pain that had been building inside of her finally consumed her, rushing out through her body like a tide. *This is it. This is how it ends.* She accepted her fate. A sense of calm washed over her. She would not fight the end, because the end would bring freedom.

Flight.

She would except her next chapter, just like she always did, whether that chapter was an unknown afterlife, or infinite nothingness.

Existence seemed to stop. The last moment she'd seen before her eyes had died placed itself before her, frozen. Werldon, Ressen, even the walls of the cell, seemed to stretch out; at once beside her, and at the same time, far away, much like the world had been when Tia had stopped time to spy on her foe. *So, this is what death is like,* she mused. She wasn't sure what she'd expected. People talked about life flashing before their eyes, bright lights, or the voices of long dead relatives beckoning. Technically, Tia had died once before, when she had joined with the orb to become Karee, but that had been less tunnel of light, more burning and exploding inferno, and neither that time, nor this, was matching up to what others had claimed to have seen whilst on the brink.

Is this it? Is this the moment I'm destined to see for all eternity? she wondered, casting a ghostly eye about her. Everything seemed so clear, to a point where it was almost surreal in its intricacy and clarity. Colours shone crisp and bright, and Tia was sure within them, if she tried hard enough, she could see the individual cells and atoms making up the scene, like tiny pixels in a photo. Smells that had been hidden from her came into sharp focus, and beyond the smells of blood and waste she could pick up on the subtleties of the planet's dust speckling the floor, and the off-key scent of petrichor as Ressen's sweat mingled with it. Then there was the sharp tang of steel from the cell bars, the familiar smell of machine oil, the garlicky undertones of the remnants of Ujiri's sweat, and the chemical aromas of ozone and plastic, and these and many more odours accosted her senses. Details within the tableau seemed to step out one by one to show themselves to her, like performers in a show taking their final bow. There was the look of horror on Werldon's face at Tia's end. *No doubt pissed that I'm not dying by his hands.* There was the handsomeness of Ressen, heightened by his slowly healing scars; a sight that made her soul ache. There was the bent bar of her cell where she'd hit it in frustration....

Wait...that's not right.

Time imploded back in on her.

Death ran from her.

The fire that had burnt inside her still radiated through her, but there was no more pain, just a strangely comforting hotness.

She could see. She could see **everything** again. The walls the Zahraith had built had been broken, *I'm Karee again.* Yet the look of shock on Werldon's face was still present, and the heat she felt spoke of something else. Tia was struggling to make sense of things. She could see, but all she could feel was an omnipresent warmth. She felt disjointed, from herself, and her surroundings. Her eye briefly caught Werldon's. Time jarred to a stop again; a phenomenon that now seemed to be driven by her whim, rather than the application of concentration. She concentrated on Werldon's eye. There was a reflection, a reflection of light. She focused in on it, just as a photographer zooms in on spot in the distance, but for Tia, the image lost none of its detail as it expanded.

Is that...me?

Her mind spun.

What she saw was unlike anything she'd seen before, though a distant, instinctual memory thought it was all completely normal. Captured in Werldon's eyes was a creature of white light and raw energy, floating a foot off the ground. Its body was sinewy and snake-like, with no arms or legs, but it had wings; wings that came out from rudimentary shoulders, and curved downwards towards its, for want of a better word, waist. Their edges undulated, as if moved by unseen currents, as did the tip of the being's tail. It had a neck, atop which was an oval head, and above a barely visible nose and mouth sat two huge blue eyes that radiated with their own light. The head was crowned with a bony, horn-like structure, which began where its ears should have been, and curved round the back of the head.

Tia blinked.

Time reasserted itself.

The reflected creature's eyes dimmed briefly in time to her blink.

Two familiar voices wafted into her mind, vocalising unspoken thoughts.

"*Tia?*" Ressen's, whose one word conveyed the exasperated tone of, 'Oh gods what's happening now?'

"*How is this possible?*" Werldon's, whose face and thought

were of someone who was completely off-guard, and who had no idea what was going on.

Tia, realising she had the upper hand once more, decided to make it count, as the last thing she wanted was for Werldon and the Zahraith to take her down and devolve her again, that is, if they still could. Acting, rather than thinking, had always worked for her in the past, and her attack on Werldon was born from just that.

When she had been A'daree, and enemies had shot their energy weapons at her, she had instinctively taken and turned that energy against them. The same was true when she'd taken on the Zahraith at Ciberia and had used their own weapons' power against them in a panicked bid to save her own life. Werldon hadn't used a weapon on her, but she didn't need his input, she had her own reserves.

She looked within, found the energy she knew was swirling around inside of her, and without much thought, shot it out at Werldon. The bars before her vanished in a shower of molten white droplets, and the creature that was Werldon vaporised without a scream. A good chunk of the wall behind him was also turned into a molten mess, and it emitted loud pops and hisses as the frigid cell air rapidly cooled it. Tia looked at the devastation in stunned silence. She had carried out a level of attack that, up until that point, would have required Morrígan's help.

She turned her attention to Ressen. He had fully regained consciousness, and was looking at her in astonishment, and her ethereal form reflected at her from his dark blue eyes. Tia wanted to release him from his shackles but didn't dare try in case she inadvertently vaporised him too. *I need to change back, but how?* Nothing had prepared her for what was happening. Morrígan hadn't hinted at such an ability, and the vessel's innate knowledge, though often portioned out to Tia on a need-to-know basis, had never hinted at anything like what she was experiencing. Yet there was the small, nagging feeling that her current predicament was a perfectly acceptable occurrence in the grand scheme of things. Tia didn't believe for one moment that Morrígan had failed to tell her or had intentionally withheld the information from her. It seemed too big a deal for it to have slipped its mind, or be a case of, "she'll figure it out when/if it happens." The look on Werldon's face, and his thoughts, certainly seemed to imply that whatever had just happened to her, shouldn't have.

Tia concentrated on herself, swapping between reasoning and instinct as her guide. When she'd wanted to change her form as an A'daree or Karee, she would simply focus on the body part she wanted changing, and command the cells to do what was needed, such as grow, or disassemble. In her present, frankly unnerving form, she wasn't even sure she had cells anymore, yet she was somehow still a thinking creature, fully aware of its thoughts and emotions. She looked once more within her, and found the mass of potential energy, but not much else. Knowledge told her it had the ability to become more, and that the surrounding atoms could be drawn together to form elements, chemicals, and ultimately cells, but that was a huge building project, and she was at a loss as how to begin. She was an architect in desperate need of a blueprint.

A glint caught her eye. It was the light shining off the pendant around Ressen's neck. When Tia had given it to him, it had been insurance against her mind rebelling against her, and as she contemplated its usefulness to her present predicament, she appreciated it had indeed fulfilled its purpose. The little crack in the door that had kept her mind connected to Ressen's, allowing them to speak freely, had been because of the pendant's influence, as it held within it her psyche, or at least a very good approximation.

The first time she'd created such a device, she'd been nothing more than an A'daree, so the necklace Ressen had brought to her, to cure her of her madness, had been nothing more than a crude reboot disc. But she had created Ressen's pendant while as a Karee. As a Karee, her mind was so much more, and Tia had known it would need so much more to be revived, and so she had poured so much more into the crystal. The result was that it was near as dammit to being aware. Not as self-aware as Tia and Ressen were, rather, it was more instinctual awareness. It was a programmed facsimile, just like a higher life-form. It had its rules, and it followed them, and if it ran into problems in following those rules, it could problem solve.

And that's what it had done. As her mind had been walled up by the Zahraith, it had reached out without asking, and had held on to her, just enough so it could worm its way into her mind if needed. That was the crack. That was what had allowed her to talk to Ressen unhindered. It had become an extension of her 'self', acting as a translator, and funnelling their words through it so they could communicate.

Tia wondered how much of her current predicament was down to her mind within the pendant. *Did it start breaking down the walls, allowing me to become this? Or did I achieve this on my own?* For it to do the former, would mean Tia knowing she could become what she'd become, and programming it into the crystal. That was not the case, but that didn't mean it hadn't played some sort of part in her transformation. Keeping the door open to the Karee part of her, even just a fraction, may have tipped the balance as Werldon had fuelled her fire with his abuse of Ressen.

Although Tia knew the pendant could reboot her mind, in terms of her body she dismissed it as useless, as it didn't have the necessary information; however, seeing it had triggered another realisation. *Ressen has my blood.* The blood she had shared with Ressen to heal his wounded body, and to help his future healing, still pumped through his veins. He held within him Karee cells, her Karee cells. Like nanobots, they were robust, self-replicating, and more importantly, something akin to stem cells that held her template. They could be triggered, by her will or by necessity, to create any tissue or organ. From skin cells to brain cells, they could do it all, all they had to do was read the lay of the land and decide what needed repairing and how. Within Ressen, they could heal him based on his genetic code, as opposed to hers. All Tia could do was hope they could read and respond to her energy signature in the same way and recreate her once more. If not, the galaxy was going to have to brace itself for another Ressen.

She moved in Ressen's direction; his expression turning to a mixture of shock and horror as she passed through the bars that separated their cells. She wanted to reach out for him but had no hands. *Only one thing for it.* She had no idea if what she was about to do would hurt Ressen, in fact, there was a distinct possibility that she was about to turn him into highly energised gas. *"There's something I need to do,"* she told him, with no clue whether she could still communicate with him.

"You do what you have to," was his answer.

It took her a couple of minutes to better connect her mind with her movements, and she kept checking her reflection in Ressen's eyes to see what thought moved what part. As far as she could tell, physical and ethereal movements were the same, and her desire to move her old wings moved her new wings, and her desire to move her now-gone corporeal tail moved her ethereal one. Eventually, with caution, she carefully brushed her snake-like tail across the surface of Ressen's bruised and battered left leg, with the idea being if she did cause him harm, it would be moderate, and hopefully fixable.

Ressen winced and shivered, but miraculously, nothing untoward happened to his leg; however, the effect of the act on Tia was instant and tangible, and she at once felt heavier, as the cells she'd skimmed from Ressen's wounds quickly began multiplying. She could even sense them growing within her, and rapidly, a tingling, almost itchy like sensation replaced the weightiness. Much like the heat, it started at her core, and rushed outwards, like a thousand tiny fire ants surging out from their hill to wage war. Limbs returned. Her feet found the ground; her hands, Ressen's torso, as she tried to prevent herself from falling over again as her body tried desperately to narrow in on its rapidly changing centre of gravity.

In what seemed like barely a minute, Tia was solid again,

feet planted firmly, and her recognisable human face reflected once more in Ressen's eyes, crowned by her black horns. Her skin was covered with its own garb, replacing the hessian shift that had been incinerated by her change, and as she flexed her muscles, her tail and wings answered in response. Tia couldn't help but give a wide and victorious grin.

"That was impressive." Ressen stated, nonchalantly.

Tia was overwhelmed with relief, and for a moment she forgot herself, and pressed a heavy kiss on Ressen's chapped lips, holding his face in her hands as she did so. Ressen, for his part, didn't pull away. Instead, Tia broke the moment, feeling unnecessarily flustered.

"You'll forgive me if I don't hug you back," he said, breaking the awkwardness between them by rattling his cuffs.

"Yes...right," Tia muttered, taking his steel cuffs in her hands, and pulling them apart easily, as if they were made from fresh dough.

Ressen stumbled on to his feet, and Tia held him while he regained his bearings, his legs shaking from too long spent dangling. "So, what in the universe was that?" he asked, while carefully bobbing from one foot to the other.

"Your guess is as good as mine. I have no idea what that was, how I did it, and whether I'll ever be able to do it again."

"Werldon seemed as surprised as me."

Tia remembered the intonation behind the words that had floated into her mind after her transformation. "To be honest, I think he was even more surprised than you. From what I could tell, what I just did wasn't supposed to be a viable option."

"Lucky for us," Ressen said, finally supporting his weight with a grimace.

"Well, as enlightening and fun as this has been, I think it's time we get going. We'll get back to the ship, and I'll contact Morrígan to come and incinerate this place."

"Not that I'm not eager to get back to my brother, but there has to be more to this place than a welcoming bunker and torture cell."

Tia considered his statement. The room they had first entered had been filled with control panels, and they had to have been controlling something. "Point well made. Let's do this quickly before Werldon's back-up comes."

"Do you think they'll come?"

The last thing they'll have seen, if they were monitoring Werldon's thoughts, is whatever the hell I was, vaporising him. They may not want to mess with that. "Let's err on the side of caution." A noise caught Tia's ears, and she stopped to listen.

"What is it?" Ressen asked, looking worried; his hearing not as sensitive as hers.

Tia placed the sound. "Sounds like a vessel powering up. I guess Werldon's entourage aren't in the mood for a fight."

They headed out of the cell block, and into the room that held Ressen's instruments of abuse. There were a pair of bulky knuckle dusters augmented with blunt spikes, and something akin to a cat-o-nine-tails, complete with metal tips. Ressen looked at them with revulsion. Tia's opinion of them wasn't much better. She studied their structure, noting for a moment the congealed blood splatter on them. Then, under her watchful eye, they disintegrated, as she pulled their atoms apart.

"Good riddance," Ressen muttered, as their matter merged with the universe.

They exited out of the room and found themselves once more in the room of control panels. They were also greeted by the sight of Ujiri's body lying sprawled out on the floor, the signature burn-mark of a plasma weapon hit emblazoned across his chest. "Looks like they at least accomplished that part of their mission," Tia stated, and she stepped over to him to check for signs of life. A barely perceptible wheezing sound came from the creature's gas mask.

"Is he alive?" Ressen asked, taking a moment to sit on a bench, his body still weak from his ordeal.

"Barely," Tia told him. *"Admiral Ujiri,"* she projected into him, *"why did Werldon send this planet?"*

Ujiri couldn't answer, his mind was too much a muddle of thoughts and pain, and the image of Toray firing an energy weapon at him replayed itself in a loop in the background. Regret weighed heavily on him. Regret over the things he'd done, and the things he should have done. But Tia's question had brought thoughts to the surface: his quiet questioning of the direction the Alliance, his disdain over the presence of the Zahraith, a thought that he should join the resistance. Tia rooted around, and eventually managed to piece together the smallest of answers. There had been sudden orders to oversee the coercion of Tia, but even then, Ujiri had been oblivious until the last. As to why they had manipulated the planet's trajectory, the answer Werldon had given Ujiri had been a shoulder-shrugging response of, "Why not, it'll get her attention."

"They really didn't trust you, did they?" she whispered, frustrated. Ujiri moved one of his hands glacially slow towards her. For a moment, Tia was unsure of his intention, but then she picked up on a fragment of thought and moved her own hand to intercept. She felt the data crystal drop into her hand, just as Ujiri's breather silenced.

Ressen came to her side "Anything?"

"He was kept in the dark as much as we were, and it wouldn't surprise me if his fellow high-ups sent him to die here. There was one interesting titbit though, apparently a resistance is starting within the Alliance."

"That's good."

"Yes, if it can gather momentum, but not if the Alliance manages to snuff it out. He also gave me this," she showed Ressen the crystal.

"What's on it?"

Tia let the object roll around in her hand, watching as the light reflected in it, then she grasped it tightly, and let her energy connect with that held within the crystal's facets. The data it held, drifted into her mind. "It's a decryption algorithm," she announced, loosening her grip on the crystal, and handing it to Ressen for safekeeping. "It may be the key to decrypting the Alliance's secret communications." Tia knew, if she were right, it would be a breakthrough for the GR. As such, their recent actions had been because of other races calling in unusual Alliance activity, which meant they'd been running to keep up. With the crystal, the GR would know what the Alliance knew, almost as soon as the Alliance knew it. *Another chink in their armour,* Tia mused.

"And are we any clearer on knowing why this planet is hurtling through space?"

"Nope. Werldon told Ujiri it was a case of, 'why not?' Considering what he was like, that doesn't surprise me. But like you said, what's the point of all these controls?" She looked around at all the electronics. "Those other two may have been able to tell me more, but they've scarpered." Tia had to admit, it was suspect. Even if she had been persuaded to join the Alliance, the likes of Jarell, or even a well-organised vanguard of the more powerful GR ships, would have been able to turn the planet into ineffectual asteroids before it caused Zerra any problems. She turned her attention fully to the technology.

Several control terminals near the exit sat dead, victims of her first, failed attack on Werldon. There were also several large towers that looked like servers, and their faces displayed row upon row of memory drives and motherboards. Some had LEDs blinking merrily away, others looked to have been shorted, and they emitted a noticeable smell of burnt plastic and electronics that she could catch a whiff of even at a distance. A further, unmarked tower hid its true purpose, and was nothing more than a sleek black box emitting a low frequency hum. Off to the side was a large barrel-shaped structure that Tia could instinctively tell was a power cell, thanks to her senses picking up on the energy radiating out of it. There was also an uncomfortable energy that permeated the room, which made her skin tingle.

A large assortment of wires snaked along the wall, joining the computer servers to a single terminal in the far corner that appeared to be inactive, as opposed to being another victim of her attack. She looked at the rear of the server towers, and saw more wires disappearing into the stone walls of the room. "I think this is a monitoring station of sorts," she decided, out loud. Ressen joined her, to see what she was looking at. "See these wires? They go through the rock. I guess to transceivers hidden on the surface."

"Why didn't you pick up on them when you investigated the surface?"

Tia went over to the surviving control panel and flicked a switch. Its screen lit up, and Tia picked up on a simultaneous change in energy flow around her. "Because they weren't turned on," she told him. "I guess once they detected our vessel coming into range, they deactivated them." The text on the control panel was Human, and she quickly began manoeuvring around the information held within the computer. There were files and files of communications linked to the rebel races. "They've been spying on us," she said, as she trawled through them. "There's stuff here about ship movements, what races have joined, and even mundane things like personal communiques sent ship to shore. There's even stuff from Zerra and the station." She calculated the significance of the find. "This is dangerous stuff in the Alliance's hands. They can link fighters to family members, and decide who are strategic targets, and who can be blackmailed with whom."

"Those must be some pretty powerful receivers up there," Ressen said, jerking his head towards the surface.

"Indeed. This is data from all over the place, and a lot of it is from races that aren't even in this planet's eye-line. I think this is a main hub of collection, with some data coming here from other monitoring stations, and other stuff being directly picked up by the receivers. It looks like they're sending the data to here for collation."

"So why send the planet to Zerra if it's going to get destroyed."

"First, I would assume this data is getting relayed out, so it's no big deal if it gets destroyed. Second, I reckon it was a two-birds-one-stone kinda deal. They send the planet here to get my attention, and do a show of strength towards Zerra and the GR. While they're about it, they try to get nice and close to Zerra and the Scientia to pick up suitable intel. With the Karee and the other races patrolling the region, setting up monitoring stations anywhere nearby would be close to impossible, so this is their go at listening in on us." Not that Tia now had any confidence in the Karee to take out the planet if it officially crossed into Zerren space. Their cowardice at facing up to the Zahraith had become clear. "Dotting the relay stations around its surface would help boost the signal, which is why they've gathered so much data at such a distance."

"So, this whole planet could be one huge listening device?"

Tia nodded in confirmation as she turned her attention to the unmarked tower. It was taller than her two-metre-and-a-bit frame, and twice as wide. Its coating seemed to be one of darkest black plastic, with no visible seams, and it backed directly onto the wall of the room. Tia noticed a single wire snaking from it to the other server towers, but not the control panel. As she approached it, the uneasiness she had felt increased, and images fluttered in the periphery of her mind; shadows that she knew would take form, if only she could focus on them, but every time she tried, they dissolved into nothingness.

She must have pulled a strange face, because Ressen asked, "Are you all right?"

Unanswered questions niggled at Tia. *The kind of receivers needed to pick up on distant signals are no small things. If there are relays or receivers on this planet, how come I didn't notice them? Are they under the surface? In which case, they would need to be incredibly sensitive to pick up the signals through rock. Or are they as well camouflaged as this place was? Even if they were turned off, there should have been some residual energy I could've picked up on. But then I didn't pick up on this place until Werldon hammered on my mind.* She cocked her head to one side. The black material of the tower took on a barely perceptible redness. She reached out a hand to touch its surface, and at once her skin began to itch violently, and a sense that she shouldn't touch it leapt unbidden into her mind. She withdrew her hand quickly, and at that moment, she knew what she was facing. The giant case wasn't housing a computer, it was housing a brain, one like the brain that controlled Tartarus, though more remedial. The itching sensation she was feeling was its defence mechanism, and the images she was seeing were rudimentary thoughts leaching into her mind. Tartarus had them too, though as its brain was more advanced, so too were the images, as those who trespassed into his its vicinity knew only too well.

Ressen had been right to claim the planet was a huge listening device, but it was so in a completely different way to what he, and she, had envisioned. Tia walked over to the wall near to the brain, placed her hand on it, and concentrated. It was faint, but it was there. *Life.* It was scarcely above the signal given off by microbes, but it was there nonetheless, and it permeated the rock. Frustratingly, Tia had noticed it, but without the realisation she'd just had she had simply passed it off as nothing more than a hardy bacterium colonising the planet. What they were in wasn't just a ball of rock, it had been converted into a living planet. Zahraith cells were spread out amongst the tiny cracks and fissures and were hiding amongst the dust up on the surface, allowing communications to flow through the planet. They had turned it into a huge sensory organ that could home in on the faint radio signals that pervaded space. Afterwards, Tia figured it transferred what it had heard to the giant data banks, either for future transmission to the enemy back out through the rock, or to be downloaded by Werldon and his cohorts shortly before the planet got obliterated. The contained brain controlled it all, and just like the Zahraith, it could camouflage itself and any of its parts from Tia. It hadn't just been Werldon disguising the location of the cave from her, it had been the planet too.

Tia took a step back, grabbed hold of a set of wires that

snaked out from the back one of the normal computer towers, and yanked them down, ripping them out of the stone wall as she did so. The entire planet shivered in protest.

"What the gods?!" yelped Ressen.

"This place is alive," Tia explained quickly. "It's not some random world thrown out of orbit, it's a Zahraith construct. In a way, it's like my old vessel Tartarus, but on a grander, and yet more simplistic scale. It's like a giant cell, designed to detect and respond to a stimulus, in this case, radio waves. Once its picks up on one, its cells relay it down to the servers for cataloguing." She studied the wires she'd pulled out of the wall and found them to be a mix of biological and steel components, complete with a dash of Zahraith cells.

"I'm surprised those two didn't set this place to blow when they ran, to prevent us from figuring this out, and to take us out in the process."

Tia headed back over to the control panel, but despite her rummaging through files and drop-down menus, she failed to find a programme for a self-destruct command. She did, however, find a voice interface programme and booted it up. The word 'ready' blinked onto the screen. "How do I activate the self-destruct command," Tia asked the computer.

"Self-destruct can only be initiated by Elder of the Zahraith Werldon," it recited.

"How is the self-destruct initiated?"

"Self-destruct is initiated through a direct mental command to the mainframe's brain by Elder of the Zahraith Werldon."

Tia gave a humourless grin. "Zahraith ego strikes again." *I guess he didn't trust the others not to inadvertently destroy this place. It's a good job I killed him when I did.* She glanced back over the files on the control panel. "There's no knowing right now how much of this data is in Alliance hands. But as they'll no doubt use it to attack us, we'll use it to shield us."

"You're suggesting we take all these memory cores with us?" Ressen asked, looking at the ranks of hard drives. "That's not going to be easy." He stuck his head out the door, to investigate the hangar. "There are no ships left out there, and our ship is too big to land on the platform."

Ressen was right. Even if one Voleth vessel had remained, Tia knew it would have had barely enough room for a spare packed lunch, let alone several hundred bulky hard disks. They were designed for combat, not caravanning goods and people, and were all engine and weapons, with toileting and nutrition coming to the Voleths via their spacesuits. Chances were, if Ujiri, the Bardak, and the Human female had arrived on the planet in just two ships, the Bardak and woman had paired up. It would have been a snug journey for the two of them, especially as the Voleth were about half their size, but with Ujiri dead, they could take a ship each. It would have still been a tight squeeze, but certainly preferable to facing whatever the hell had happened to Werldon.

Tia contemplated her options as she ripped the remaining wires from the backs of the server towers, and from the towers to the Zahraith brain. *No point in giving it more time to relay data than necessary.* Her actions elicited more planetary shivers as she did so, and Ressen flinched as stone and masonry rained down from the ceiling. That done, she approached the brain itself, and her skin began to itch again as it tried to fend her off with its limited awareness. However, Tia had been through enough that day to be able to ignore the sensation, and its desperate attempts to sway her mind away from it failed. She unsheathed her nails, and with a swipe, sent a chunk of the plastic-like casing flying across the room, revealing its insides.

Inside it looked like a mass of wires, but Tia could tell they were fully biological components, and the electronic impulses of cells sparked before her eyes as they travelled up and down the living wires. *Brain don't fail me now.* She got up close to the box, but it was not going to let her get at the information within without a fight. Its defensive imagery accelerated into a maddening cacophony, designed to disorientate and distract her, thus prevent her from getting a read on the stored data.

It was not like reading the mind of a mentally defenceless Human, this was Zahraith technology, designed to be near impenetrable, and it was not making things easy for her. But Tia was no one-trick pony. She plunged her hand into the organism, commanded her own cells to entwine with the living wires of the computer, and allowed the sparks of its life to directly mingle with hers. She had physically jacked herself into the brain, and all she had to do was let the information flow.

She had experienced a download before, when she had stepped aboard Tartarus after her prolonged absence, but the data the brain stored was so much more. It was akin to melding with Morrígan for the first time again, and the digitised content of conversations, documents, plans of attack, home plans, meetings, and personal calls, surged into her mind. Tia did her best to let the digitised words and voices wash over her, choosing not to focus on the individual information, but rather to just let it become a part of her already extensive knowledge. Once back with Morrígan or Tartarus, she could easily transfer the information to them, allowing it to become converted back into computer-based knowledge for easy sharing with rebel mainframes across the galaxy.

As the last byte became fixed within her own neurons, she yanked her arm back, thrusting forward a mental attack as she did so. There was no two-ways about it, Tia's powers were getting stronger, and despite its earlier uncomfortable attempts at dissuasion, the brain had nothing that could defend itself from her attack. Its neural network collapsed in on itself, and life stopped pulsing through it. Tia let the dust settle in her mind and looked at Ressen.

"How are you feeling?" he asked.

"Like my head is full of wool," she replied. She was having a little trouble focusing on him. "I suggest we contact your brother, then head back up to the surface to get picked up."

"Finally!" Ressen exclaimed. He practically skipped over to the corner where his spacesuit had been unceremoniously dumped, picked up the helmet, and put it on. Tia could hear his muffled voice as he contacted Grelt, and she sensed his change in demeanour as hearing his brother's voice elicited immense relief. Then she felt him clench again. He took off his helmet and looked at Tia, worried. "Good news, bad news time," he said.

"Go on, good news first."

"Good news.... Grelt destroyed the two vessels after they escaped the surface and headed straight for him. I guess they weren't expecting him to be the marksman pilot he is. They barely had time to register what was going on."

"Bad news?"

"Unfortunately, one of them registered it just enough to get in a lucky shot. The ship's engines are damaged again, and now he can't land. We're stranded!"

Tia rolled her eyes. "Bloody marvellous!"

****

In truth, Ressen was stranded. Given a long enough run up to accumulate an adequate amount of kinetic energy, a few beats of her powerful wings, and a quick disagreement with the laws of gravity, Tia could break free of the planet's weak pull and leave its surface. She could even achieve the same with a piggybacking Ressen. Then it would simply be a case of drifting towards the Eerell to be scooped up by Grelt. However, while the airless, frigid brutality of space would have no effect on her, Ressen's space suit wasn't designed for such extreme exposure. It was designed for terrestrial planets with a suitable environment, but questionable air, and even then, it was barely suitable for the rogue planet due to its thermal layering not being thick enough. If Tia took Ressen into space, his components would freeze, then he would freeze, and if his components froze, he would suffocate as well. The suit he required to survive in space was tucked safely in its alcove aboard the ship, where it was integrated with a large cumbersome jetpack for when minor external repairs were needed.

There was only one option, and as Tia explained her plan to Ressen, he didn't look impressed. "So, you're going to leave me here, while you launch yourself into space, and fly to Grelt." Tia nodded. "And what if you overshoot?"

"This will not be my first time flying through space unprotected," she assured him. "I will make my target." This was true. On defeating the Scorpiad aboard the Scientia, Aben's simultaneous death had caused her to break out of the side of the wheel she'd been in, head several miles up, and then enter through the side of another wheel. Her actions then were still a blur, but she remembered the exhilarating feeling of whooshing through chilly space, and controlling her direction seemed to have been a non-issue. Therefore, Tia had no reason to believe she couldn't make it to Grelt's ship, and once there, she would grab the spare suit, and bring it down to Ressen.

"Won't re-entry cause you to burn?"

Tia shrugged. "The atmosphere is thin, so any heating will be nominal. Besides, my mesoskeleton can handle a hell of a lot of heat." As it was, all her organs would be protected within the confines of her mesoskeleton, and a lack of oxygen wasn't an issue. It was her skin that was going to endure the worst of it. In space it would freeze and coming in it would burn. Tia knew she was going to have to forgo looking marginally normal for a while, and she just hoped that Grelt was as blasé about her changing form as Ressen.

She made to head out the door, to make her way back to the surface.

"What should I do while you're gone?" For the first time, Ressen looked unsure of himself. Despite his heroic front, the day had frazzled his nerves, and he had the air of someone who desperately didn't want to be left alone.

Tia went over to him, and breaking with protocol, lightly kissed his cheek. "Keep the door shut, and I'll be as quick as inhumanly possible." Ressen gave a little smile at her joke.

She headed through the hangar, now devoid of vessels, and as she made her way towards the platform, she commanded her body to absorb her skin cells to reveal her self-grown black armour. Once on the platform, she flexed her talons, and with the help of her tail and wings, she traversed swiftly up the cliff face. With her feet back on silty ground, she looked up to the heavens, and with no lights, and barely any atmosphere around, the sky was crisp and clear, and billions of stars dazzled. More importantly, one of the shiny dots was a space craft, and she adjusted her vision across the spectrum of light to find the odd dot out. Grelt's ship was still there, several hundred kilometres out, trailing along in the wake of the rogue planet through a combination of thrusters and gravitational tug.

Tia tested the planet's pull on her by bouncing up and down; letting her body re-acclimatise to the low gravity that had been missing from inside the Alliance base. The sensation was almost as weird as having a Zahraith brain info-dump, and on one landing, her feet nearly went out from under her. A flail of wings, and a thrusting of her tail into the surface saved her from landing on her backside in the dust. There were no two ways about it, what she was about to do was going to be tricky and inelegant.

And so, like some spiky, gangly, black bird of prey, she half ran, half bounced across the surface of the planet, beating her wings in huge arcs as she went. She placed all her energy and strength into her jumps, and each bounce got higher and faster, as the energy of the previous bounce was channelled into it. With each up, the curvature of the planet at the peak of her bounce increased, and she could feel the chill of space reach her a little more each time. It was exhausting work, even for her, and she was glad she wasn't having to do it with Ressen clinging to her neck.

Then, when she felt her speed and trajectory was right, she shifted her centre of gravity, beat her wings, and broke free of the planet's grip. She was flying, and it was as exhilarating as she remembered, and the hows of it came back to her as easily as if she were riding a bike after a short break. She did a barrel roll, just for the hell of it, then struck out in the direction of the vessel. As she travelled, she beat her wings, and her body responded as if she were a bird on the wind. However, a bird in space would have gone nowhere fast, its wings ineffectual in the vacuum of space, yet Tia moved through the void with ease. Space was a vacuum, but it was an imperfect one. Neutrinos and atoms of hydrogen peppered it, dark energy wove itself through it, and gamma and cosmic rays sped across it. Their barely perceptible presence was enough for Tia to push against, allowing her to propel herself through space, and each thrust of her wings gave her more momentum, and in no time at all, the ship was easily discernible.

She pinpointed the airlock that would allow her entry, but misjudged her speed, and collided with the hatch with force, and even though sound couldn't permeate space, she felt the ship vibrate in response to her broadside, and she was sure a loud clang would have resonated through the ship in response. *No time to worry about that now*, she thought, as she ignored the dent she'd caused, and keyed in the unlock code. The door opened, and Tia swung herself in. She closed the door behind her and waited as the pressure inside the small room equalised.

The light finally gave her the all clear, and she quickly cycled the inner hatchway that would give her access to the ship. As she did so, she felt a presence just outside it, and gave a little smile to herself. She opened the door cautiously and was met by Grelt aiming his weapon at her. His eyes went planet-sized as he gazed upon Tia's shiny black, insect-like form.

"Put the weapon down, it's me," she said.

Grelt still looked alarmed, but he holstered his pistol. "I thought one of the pilots of the ships I'd destroyed managed to escape and had broken in," he explained. "What happened to you?" he added, giving her an extensive once-over.

"I had to dispense with skin to get up here. I came for the space suit and jet-pack so Ressen can get back."

"Oh.... And Ressen is all right? You two have been gone ages, and he sounded strained over the radio."

Tia didn't want to go through the whole story, she had a rescue mission to fulfil. "He's had a rough day, but he's been through worse," was all she was willing to say.

Grelt still looked worried, but let Tia pass, so she could gather up the bulky spacesuit and jetpack.

"And you're going to take that back down to him?" Grelt asked, looking sceptical.

"Yep. I'll wrap my wings and tail round it, and with my back to the planet, head in like a lander. There's enough juice in the jet-pack for Ressen to reach escape velocity, and I've already achieved the same under my own steam."

Grelt gave her a questioning look. "That's fine, but what then? I don't have the equipment needed to fix the engines."

Tia mulled over whether to contact Morrígan or Jarell to give them a tow, but as far as she could tell, they were still scouring the galaxy for crystals, and she didn't want to call them away. What the two Karee vessels were doing was vital to the success of the GR's new ships, and although their little ship was damaged, it was in no danger, and neither were they. They had enough food and energy reserves to keep them alive for months, and they even had a backup location, in the form of the planet, should an important system suddenly fail. There were always the Zahraith; however, Tia had the distinct impression that she would feel their presence even more acutely after what had happened to her, but as it was, they hadn't retaliated, which was something they should've done, on the spot, and with lethal precision. She couldn't sense a thing, and as far as she was concerned, they were going to remain a no-show. She sighed. "I guess the only thing to do is send a signal in the direction of any neighbouring neutral or rebel planets and ask for help."

"That could take months!" Grelt exclaimed. "And that's if they pick our signal up. Our broadcast range isn't that good, and I know the jumpgates aren't reliable."

"Well, on the plus side, we're being pulled along by the planet, so we'll eventually come in range of someone," Tia halfheartedly joked. Then realisation hit her. She gave a big grin, which, given Grelt's reaction, must have been terrifying thanks to her lack of Human features. "Sorry," she said, quickly. "As it happens, fate is even more on our side." *What better way to make a long-distance call, than with the help of a planet-sized communicator?*

****

"Explain that to me again?" Ressen said, as he jumped and shimmied into his bulky spacesuit.

"I'm going to see what's out there, and if anybody can help," she said, jerking her head in a random direction to indicate the galaxy. Pieces of experience had fallen into place for her. She could remotely view places, even without the presence of Morrigan, and she could interact with people when doing the same, which she'd found out by accident during an earlier foray. She wasn't sure if she could project herself over vast distances without her vessel, but then that was where the planet came in. Having fried its neurons, it was equivalent to a brain-dead Zahraith vessel, so she would be its new brain. She would tap into the living cells that still permeated the planet, listen to the signals criss-crossing space, and then make direct contact with a likely ship.

Tia placed her hands against the cool rock of the planet and reached out to the bacterium that trailed out towards the surface. In her mind, she could see the pattern of them as they interlaced the planet, like a giant, three-dimensional spider web, warped so the room in which she stood was the centre. The electrical impulses from the cells came thick and fast, each microscopic flash a tiny bit of binary data, transferred cell by cell, axon to dendrite, down the line for translation by the now-dead brain.

She closed her eyes, and let the signals hitting the planet find their way to her. Many she could ignore. Some were weak, and were either from too far away, or were too old to be considered. Many others were Alliance messages; either call signs transmitted from the ships of its member races, or encoded signals that would take too long to crack without the help of Ujiri's dying gift. However, there were still plenty more to be considered. Soon, Tia began wondering if she even knew what she was doing, and it became clear to her that the brain and computers had undoubtedly erased a lot of data they had received automatically because it had been useless. *They probably used keywords, or specific signal frequencies so they didn't end up saving a whole load of crap.* She started to regret her premature destruction of the brain, as she could have used it as a filter, yet she persevered. She picked up television and radio shows, a random signal that she could only assume was a pulsar, and a wealth of personal communications that had no bearing on their current predicament. It was maddening. A thousand voices chatted aimlessly in her head, and billions of words flittered past her closed eyes, in an unending stream of information that Tia began to believe would take decades to wade through.

Worse, she could feel Ressen's presence in the corner of her mind getting gradually more impatient. *This may have been a mistake.* She was getting worried that she wasn't going to achieve anything other than delay their rescue. Their SOS would have been weak, and the jumpgates hit-and-miss at relaying it, but it would have eventually hit its mark, leading to an eventual rescue by either a friendly race, or by Jarell or Morrígan when they had finally finished their task.

Tia was close to admitting defeat when something occurred to her, *I've been a telepath for centuries, I know how to do this. The trick is not to analyse every message, but rather to turn my analytical mind off to the noise, and let instinct pick up on the important cues.* She relaxed a little more, and instead of focusing on every word, she allowed the signals to wash over her, letting them be no more than white noise in her mind. The result was an indecipherable mess; a babble of scripture in hundreds of runes, overlapping with words said in a hundred different tongues, with Tia as one person, stood in a giant auditorium, stuffed to bursting point with people and paper trying to get their point across all at once. *There!* It had been no more than a phrase in a sea of billions, but it triggered something, like a person hearing their name being said amongst a thousand others. *Where do I know Qosec Three from?* She searched her memory and found the information amongst the data she had absorbed from the brain. It was a short, simple message, confirming the rendezvous of the Qosec Three with an Alliance scouter, and the welcoming aboard of two GR representatives; one Lieutenant Leo Jackson, and his companion Kan. Tia couldn't believe it. *What in gods' name have those two been up to?* But answers could wait, she had her filter, and the rest of the incoming information became nothing more than a minor distraction.

She shifted her consciousness, and stepped outside of the flow of data, so she could evaluate what she'd found. The message that had caused her recollection was a brief communique stating the vessel should head to the Scientia as an envoy. This provided her with little other information, other than the fact the ship was heading where she and the brothers needed to go, that is if they had received the message. But the information she dug up on the Qosec Three from her memory came with a wealth of other tagged-on information, namely a rough positioning co-ordinate, and some energy signatures from the region where the message had originated. The energy signatures gave her one big ship of an unknown species, with jump engines, and a weak signature that had some resonance of an Alliance craft. *The Alliance Scouter,* Tia reasoned. Tia reached out to the flow of data again, expanding her filter to include the energy signatures. However, whoever was captaining the Qosec Three had made sure to send no more messages or trigger any more monitoring posts. At least not any that had been able to transfer the data back to her in time. The scouter was a different story. It had triggered another monitoring post within a decent broadcast range, twice. Tia scoured for, and found, the co-ordinates, but they told her nothing. She needed a map but didn't dare detach herself from the stream of information in case she missed something. *This would be so much easier with Morrigan in the driver's seat,* she ruefully thought.

Portioning off a part of her consciousness, so she could talk to Ressen, she reeled of the co-ordinates to him. "Find out where that is," she barked. A moment later, she heard a muffled conversation, as Ressen relayed the information to Grelt through his helmet.

"It's between a pair of jumpgates located just outside of the Alliance border." That didn't help her much, and she let Ressen know. There was more muffled conversing, and she heard Ressen tersely say, "but where does it go?" She waited for what felt like an eternity. "Grelt says, from the information that was uploaded to our system, the gates lead in and out of a system on the edge of Alliance space. There's not much to it, just a mining outpost, and a small farming colony on a planet called Demeter Nine."

Demeter Nine? The light bulb went off. "Leo went to rescue his family," she said, incredulous. "And if the jumpgate picked up their signal twice, that means they got in and out, and with Leo's family with any luck." It also meant, that if the Qosec Three was Leo and Kan's main mode of transport, it was probably already on its way home to the station, and would be heading their way, albeit through hyperspace.

Tia broke free of the planet and saw Ressen's expectant expression. "We have a vessel," she told him. He smiled in relief.

"When will it get here?" he eagerly asked.

Tia gave a grimace. "That's still an unknown. Given what I know, it's somewhere in hyperspace, and I still have to contact it, but I don't want to use this planet in case someone picks up the signal." *Not that I'm paranoid, and don't trust the Zahraith not to take a retaliatory shot at people I care about.* "I'll make direct mental contact with someone I know is on board."

"And you can do that?"

"Yes." For once, Tia was unwavering in the certainty she had in her abilities. Until the trip with Ressen and Grelt, she would have baulked at the idea, believing she needed Morrígan to augment her strength, and to guide her silently through the process. However, her pushing of her abilities and finding them eager to obey her command had her questioning her need of her vessel. She had mentally circumnavigated a planet, stopped time, and had substantially altered herself twice, all under her own power. She didn't even feel the need to sit in a darkened room to aid in concentration, she simply closed her eyes, calmed her mind, and focused on the man she was looking for...Kan.

She fixated on the man's energy, his personality and presence, and stepped her mind forward. The rocks of the planet blurred past her, as she reached out to the galaxy, and were replaced by darkness and stars. As she concentrated, and tried to pinpoint his position, the dots of light began to circle around her. She knew he was probably in hyperspace, and at that thought, the stars began expanding outwards, rapidly spinning around and around, more and more, until their individual streaks of light became indistinguishable, until Tia was faced with a glowing universe, as if she was stood in the centre of a bubble of pure light. Gradually, from the centre of the spinning orb of brightness, the colour of the light shifted, from the beige of a billion stars and galaxies smeared into one, to the blue of hyperspace. Its change expanded outwards, just like the stars had done, until Tia was bathed in a blue glow.

Yet she didn't break concentration, and she held within her the feeling of Kan, and used it to pull her towards him, and though the blue light lacked any detail to make the movement visually perceptible, she could sense lateral movement. Then, within a realm devoid of landmarks, she saw dot. It was barely a speck on her vision, but she knew instinctively what it was. *The Qosec Three*. The dot came racing towards her, taking shape as it did so. It was a large, boxy craft, and its jump engines sent ripples through hyperspace as it warped time and place around it. But its break-neck, head on collision path towards Tia didn't stop, and for a heart-stopping minute, its huge metal flank came careening down on her. She instinctively flinched, but the steel wall simply passed through her cerebral presence, swiftly followed by several more bulkheads as Tia triangulated on her target.

The motion stopped, and there he was before her, sat at a table with Leo, and surrounded by several other Humans who, by way of appearance, could only be Leo's family. Kan looked to be having a terse exchanged with a red-headed girl, and for a fraction of a second, Tia felt a twinge of jealousy at seeing a man she cared deeply about being in the line of sight of such an attractive young woman. Then she remembered Ressen, and regretfully let go of the feelings she had for Kan. He had a right to his desires, and she knew she had no say in them, and had not done so for longer than she cared to admit. Instead, she focused on the mission.

Now for the ultimate test, she thought, hoping she hadn't come all the way for nothing. *"Kan?"* she spoke into his head.

Kan stopped what he was going, and Tia felt the jump of surprise in his stomach. *"Tia?"* he answered, in complete bewilderment.

Relief. *"Yes, it's me. I see you and Leo have been busy."*

"You're here?" Tia could see his eyes dart subconsciously in a bid to find her.

"Yes and no. Long story short, I'm on the rogue world, but the vessel that bought me and the Yaldren brothers..., Ressen and Grelt..., is damaged, and we need a lift."

"Let me get this straight.... I'm finally on my way home after a hell of a journey, and you need me to turn this damn ship around and come rescue you?" His friendly mocking of her was unmistakable, and extremely missed.

"Yes."

"Bloody woman!"

~ ~ ~ ~

Chapter 32 - Kan

K an was fully aware that his breath on the back of the head of the Rotaizian manning the tug's grappling hook was making the alien nervous. Good, he thought, it'll make sure he treats it and its cargo carefully. The individual in question, name and rank incomprehensible without a translator, was undertaking the final procedure to lock on to Tia's small, crippled ship.

Kan watched the feed being sent from the end of the grapple as it slowly reached out toward the vessel. With a pace that was almost slow motion, the six-pronged grabber encircled itself around the side of an engine, the tips of the claws barely contacting its outer casing. Then, in the blink of an eye, it sucked itself on, triggered by the activation of an electromagnet in its centre, and the claws came together, locking into place around the engine.

Kan, satisfied, sent his thoughts towards the vessel. *"We've got you. There's no escape now,"* he joked.

Tia's voice came back to him as clearly as if she were stood beside him. *"I kind of figured. No problems I take it."*

"None. The guy on fishing duty was quaking in his seat, but he did his job."

"Were you keeping an overly close eye on him?"

"Of course." Even Tia's exasperated mental sigh was audible to him. *"It'll take the tug a little while to manoeuvre you safely to the docking bay's entrance. Once there, you'll be able to bring yourself in with your thrusters."*

"I take it there's room."

"Oh yes. They're having to move some furniture around, and it'll be a bit tight, but we'll get you in. It'll be safer than lashing you to the roof." He heard her laugh. *"Anything you need to tell me in the interim?"*

There was a longer than normal pause before Tia answered. *"Tell, yes, but not quite yet."*

"Why? What's happened now?" It was Kan's turn to be exasperated.

"I'm not sure."

"That doesn't sound good."

"Then again, it's not bad...I think."

Kan rolled his eyes at the obscurity of it all and headed off the bridge.

Back down in the mess hall, a group of eager faces met him. Leo was first to speak. "So? Everything okay?"

"Seems it. Her ship has been wrangled, so she should be on board in a few hours."

"You don't look convinced by everything?" Leo's father said, catching Kan's frown.

"Something's happened to Tia, again."

"Any idea what?" Leo asked, worried.

"The way things are, I'll just be happy if she hasn't grown a second head." Kan said.

****

The Eerell looked like a huge gravid queen surrounded by her tiny offspring. It sat snug in the hangar of the Qosec Three, surrounded by the smaller craft that had once been spread out neatly, but which were now relegated to getting cosy with the walls. If the smaller vessels needed to head out for some reason, it was going to be in single file.

Kan had overseen the Eerell's docking. Decked out in a space suit and hanging over the railing on the upper floor of the hangar, he had watched as the small tug had helped her line up with the entrance. Then her pilot, with remarkable skill, had used her thrusters to gently manoeuvre her bulk into place; Grelt's command of his vessel impressing Kan. As the hangar's door finally clanged shut, and oxygen was pumped back into the bay, Kan loosened his helmet, and shed his bulky suit, leaving them in an untidy heap on the gantry. He bounded down the stairs, making good headway, and arrived several heart beats ahead of the rest of the welcoming party.

Lorkav was once again present, representing the Rotaizians, and Kan was a little miffed that the captain was a no show. He considered Tia to be deserving of a welcome by the man himself, but it seemed that his presence was a permanent fixture on the bridge. Beside him came Leo, minus his family, as although they were eager to meet Tia, this first greeting was a time for formality and business-like discussions. As such, familial introductions could wait, and so Leo had left his relatives safely in the mess hall.

Kan gave a head-bob of greeting to the others, Leo followed suit, as did Lorkav, who did it in such a way that it was obvious he was copying their behaviour, whilst not entirely sure of its meaning. Kan looked to Leo. "So, what do we reckon? Two heads? Four arms? Changed into a Qlath?"

Leo laughed. "I'm not sure I want to put money on any of those. I may win, but I wouldn't be happy about it."

Kan answered with a grunt. He just had his fingers crossed that whatever stepped out of the craft was more than just vaguely Tia-shaped.

A clang from the Eerell told them someone was cycling the outer airlock, and the three men stepped back a safe distance just as the hatch swung open at head height, and a large familiar form dropped down onto the floor of the bay. As it righted itself, Kan was faced with the remarkably unchanged vista of Tia. He beamed at her, and she responded in kind. Two more bodies dropped down behind her, albeit a little less elegantly

"Should've told us you needed a ladder," Kan said, as Grelt and Ressen picked themselves up off the floor after the long drop.

"I would've thought it was implied," Tia answered, huffily, but with a smile in the crook of her mouth. "Hello Leo, how are you and your family?"

"All in one piece, thanks to Kan and the Rotaizians," the lad said, not asking how she knew.

Tia turned her attention to Lorkav. "And you are second in command of this ship," she stated. Lorkav didn't wait for his translator to finish and answered in his own tongue. To his indecipherable burbling, Tia nodded, before adding. "Give my warmest greeting to your captain, and my extreme thanks for coming and rescuing us."

Lorkav seemed happy and understanding of her response and headed off without another word uttered.

Kan raised an eyebrow at Tia. "The hell did you just do?"

"Any message given to a Rotaizian captain must be delivered immediately, and in person, by the courier." she explained.

"I'm rather surprised he didn't come here to greet you himself, especially considering your reputation," Leo said, uttering Kan's earlier thoughts. "I've been starting to wonder if he actually exists. We've never clapped eyes on him, and all our dealings have been with Lorkav."

"That's down to Rotaizian space-faring superstition backing onto a maritime superstition." Tia explained. "It's considered unlucky for the captain to leave the sanctuary of the bridge, and that a grievous occurrence will happen if they do. At sea, a ship will sink. In space, it'll explode, or get lost in hyperspace. That's why they have their quarters and office directly attached to the bridge. Technically, a captain's bedroom and bathroom are considered part of the bridge, though I doubt any member of staff would take it upon himself to just wander in there uninvited." Leo's expression took on an air of bemused understanding.

"Good to see you're still the font of all random knowledge," Kan ribbed. "I guess it's not your brain that's changed."

Tia took a second before answering. "Well, no...and then

again, yes."

"I'm guessing there's a hell of a story behind those words," Kan said. "So, how many lives lost, and solar bodies destroyed?"

"Am I getting that predictable?" Tia asked, amused.

"Shit woman, you were causing havoc long before you became Karee, and that's just the stuff I know about. I'm sure if Shar was here, he'd back me up. He knows more of your past than anyone." Tia gave what Kan felt was only half a conceding nod. "With you, chaos and death are business as usual."

"Four lives lost, only one down to me this time, and no obliterated worlds, although that'll change once I get back inside Morrígan."

"And those two behaved themselves?" Kan asked, casting an eye over the brothers.

Tia turned back to where the two brothers were loitering. "They went above and beyond," she said, her voice softening as she regarded them. It was then Kan noticed the cuts and bruises on the closest brother, the one he recognised as Ressen. He also recognised the look in his eyes, one that was missing from his brother's. Whatever had happened on the planet had left its mark, physically and mentally. He gave a questioning look to Tia, who answered it with a non-verbal raise of her eyebrows, and her mouth pulled tight. Her face relaxed. "I think a snack and a meeting, then a proper meal. We've been too long without fresh food, and I know this vessel has hydroponics. I think a nice salad would do wonders for the soul."

Kan stared at her, stumped. True, they'd eaten fresh vegetables occasionally alongside their reconstituted or canned foods, but he'd surmised they'd been frozen in some industrial freezer, not that there were hydroponics going on, and he'd figured the reason the servings of them had been so small was down to simple rationing, not because the stuff needed to grow. "How?" he asked.

"I can smell the dirt," Tia said.

"Your senses have been ratcheted up a notch."

"I guess they have," Tia answered, sounding more than a little surprised herself.

****

After some discussion, they ended up having their meeting in Kan and Leo's quarters, which meant it was a cosy affair. Leo and Grelt sat on the top bunk, hunched over, Ressen, the bottom, with the alien brothers leaning at an angle to slot in their extra height. Kan leant casually against the door frame that led into the bathroom, his arms and legs crossed as he listened. Tia stood, her wings and tail wrapped carefully around her, her horns nearly scraping the ceiling. "This is…snug," she murmured, as she nibbled at a green fruit Lorkav had procured for her from the hydroponics bay. The brother's each had one too, though theirs were now nothing more than sticky cores.

"There're other rooms aboard, but I know this one's secure," Kan explained. Although he didn't envision any covert shenanigans from the Rotaizians, old suspicions died hard. He'd investigated the room top to bottom during his and Leo's first night back aboard and had come up empty-handed. No bugs, nor odd holes in the walls, and further checks had been equally fruitless. Tia hadn't mentioned anything on entering, and Kan figured, with her senses, she'd be able to pick up the electronic buzz of even the tiniest of listening devices. As far as he was concerned, the room was clean.

"So?" he prompted. And he stood and listened with the others as Tia went about describing their going to the rogue world, their discovery of it being a huge spying device, created by another ancient and powerful race in league with the Alliance, and her and Ressen's capture by the representative of said race.

Kan contemplated the mechanics of the eavesdropping world. He knew signals took ages to traverse space, even with the help of relay stations, yet here was a device that could readily collect signals from pretty much all over the galaxy. Sure, the closer it was to a target, the easier it was to get a signal, but the delays involved would render most tactical information obsolete before it even got picked up. All of which made Kan wonder just how powerful the planet was, and whether the Zahraith had hidden other, smaller relay stations about the galaxy. He voiced his thoughts to the room.

Tia took a bite of her fruit, which left sugary juice on her lip that she absent-mindedly licked off. A simple action that made Kan's chest ache more than he wanted. "They have the skills, and compared to the Karee, the wherewithal," she explained. "Even I didn't comprehend what the planet was until I'd investigated it in more detail. I wouldn't be surprised if there are other worlds, moons, and asteroids with covert devices on them, listening to our every word. The race has been here long enough, and are capable enough, to do such a thing."

"I wonder if that planet was what tipped the Alliance off to Kan and my trip," Leo said.

"Could be," Kan answered for Tia. He nodded in her direction, "If you picked up on enough intel to find me, chances are that same info could've given them enough of a head's-up." Tia pulled an expression that conveyed that she believed his and Leo's idea weren't an impossibility.

As Tia spoke further about her and Ressen's run in with the Zahraith, Kan watched the expressions behind the words, not just from her, but from Ressen too. It was something he'd become adept at over the years; learning to see when chunks of text went unspoken, especially by an alien who kept things very close to her chest. Tia's talk of discovering who the alien was, and being taken out by the Zahraith, created a wordless void. Kan knew Tia. She was pragmatic and could be blunt way past the point of rudeness. At times, her frankness could put plain-speaking Panns to shame, which is why she was left out of delicate negotiations with obstinate races, so when faced with the Zahraith, she would have talked, he knew that. Her need for answers would have been insatiable, especially when dealing with a dangerous enemy who was collaborating with the Alliance.

Yet, as she stood and talked, little knowledge was forthcoming from her. Ressen's expression was tense, as if he were waiting on words that never came. A frown of confusion here, a cocked head there. He had been with her, he had heard the words that were going unsaid, and it was clear he was quickly learning that he too needed to remain silent. Although, as he still seemed to be struggling with the Human language, Kan figured his input would have been nominal anyway. Whatever secrets Tia was keeping were for another time, and for behind a different closed door. Conceivably somewhere on Tartarus.

Then came the part Kan had been waiting for. Tia's vague comments, hinting at change, bore fruit, and they all listened, Leo with wide eyes, as Tia told them of her transformation into the ethereal being, and the death of Werldon.

"What triggered it?" Kan asked. If there was a trigger, there was the chance of it happening again.

Tia took a moment. "Pure anger," she finally said, her eyes flickering towards Ressen.

She hadn't said it, but the wounds on Ressen indicated torture. Kan was all too familiar with them because he'd left similar marks on other people during darker times. Before Tia had left for the planet, gossip had been circulating, about Tia and Ressen being an item. Kan had heard it mentioned in work, in the gym, and in bars where he'd been trying to have a quiet drink. There was no denying their closeness, after all, Ressen had brought about her reawakening, but Kan questioned how much of an item they truly were. He didn't think, at least not by body language, that any paring had been consummated, though that didn't mean it wouldn't be later. He recognised the look of adulation Ressen cast Tia's way, and he noticed the softening of Tia's expression when she looked at Ressen. It was on the cards, and if Werldon had been abusing Ressen in front of Tia, there was no doubt she would have snapped big time.

"It's not the first time," she suddenly admitted.

"Are you talking about the time with Aben?" Leo asked.

Tia shook her head. "No, that was different. That was losing my mind to darkness. What I'm talking about is something else, something that happened during the battle for Ciberia."

"When you took out the Zahraith ships?" Kan asked, remembering a vague conversation he'd had with a drunk Talon a while back.

Tia nodded. "They made me so angry as they poured scorn on the ones I love." She caught Kan's eye, and his stomach twisted. "They were mocking, and their thoughts too vile to put into words. It enraged me, and somehow it charged me. I'm not even sure what I did, whether it was physical energy I threw at them, or whether it was purely mental, all I know is, it killed them outright. I think what happened with Werldon was similar. Though somehow, with me being away from Morrígan, it manifested itself a different way."

"You think Morrígan was somehow suppressing your ability the first time around?" Kan asked.

"Maybe it was suppression, maybe it was a case of her channelling that potential energy into a more useful counterattack, I simply don't know." The frustration was clear in her voice. "All I know is, this time my physical body evaporated, but I still had control over me, and my mental abilities."

"How the hell did you turn back?" Leo asked, aghast.

"Ressen holds within him my cells from when I healed him. I took some back and regrew my body."

Tia made it sound so simple. First, she was a frightening creature of pure energy, then, with the flick of her mind, she wasn't. But Kan was under no illusions, Tia may have figured some things out for herself, not least how to become corporeal again, but that didn't mean she was a hundred percent in control of who and what she was. Experience told him she spent her life walking a thin line between having it together and outright mayhem. She had been dangerous as an A'daree soldier, she had been more dangerous as a Karee, *and now?* Well, his guess was as good as anybody's. Chances were if something worked her up again, people would need to duck for cover, fast.

Tia was scrutinising him out the top of her eyes. *"You listening in?"* he asked her, unsure if she was scanning his thoughts.

"A little," she responded.

"And?"

"I'm scared."

Kan kept his face a mask, but inside, his heart jolted. Tia rarely admitted fragility. There was no denying she worried about things. Outcomes that relied on the toss of Fate's dice concerned her, and she fretted over the future and safety of those around her, but being scared for herself, if she ever felt that way, was not something she freely confessed to. She was nigh-on indestructible, so being afraid was not something she seemed to consider, as evidenced by all the times she'd run headlong into a melee or jumped into a bottomless shaft. Yet there she was, wrapped up in her wings, as if she were trying to hide under the blankets, a distant look etched on her face. Tia being scared was something Kan had to take note of.

"So, then what happened?" he asked, filling the silence that had been caused by their private exchange.

"The others escaped, and were dealt with by Grelt, but they damaged our ship in return. I used the planet and its stored data to locate a rescuer and came up with you. I reached out to you, and you know the rest."

I'm not sure I do, but okay, Kan thought to himself.

Tia gave the tiniest arched eyebrow, showing she was still listening in.

"What now for the planet? Is it still collecting data?" Leo asked.

"No. I've downloaded what it had, destroyed its brain, and wrecked its computers. It's obsolete. The Zahraith know I know about it now, so it's doubtful they'll come for it. For them, it's nothing more than a lost asset."

"So, can we use this ship to destroy it before we head back into hyperspace?" Grelt asked.

"Yes and no," Tia answered. "The weaponry on this vessel would probably make a significant dent in it, but probably not enough to break it apart. And even if it did succeed in blowing up the planet, instead of one big planet charging through space, we'll end up with multiple large chunks charging through space. If we dodge all that shrapnel, it'll be a miracle. Then there's the fact that many of the chunks will carry on their course towards the Zerren system and put it in danger. Better I and Morrígan vaporise it."

"So, what's the plan?" Kan asked.

"We head back to the station, as you were already doing. Zerra is under no direct threat from this planet, so once my vessel returns, I can come back and deal with it."

"In that case, I can think of no further reason to delay dinner," Kan said. There were vigorous nods from Leo and Grelt. Ressen looked confused, but then hopeful when his brother whispered to him.

"Agreed" Tia said, as she eyed the remains of her morsel. The others extracted themselves from the bunk beds, and she moved out of the way to let them pass. "A moment," she directed at Kan.

Here we go. He gave a nod to the others to carry on without them. Leo looked irked that he was not going to be privy to whatever Tia had to say, but left without protest, and ensured the door closed behind him. Happy they were alone; Kan was the first to talk. "Is this where you fill in the blanks?"

"You know me too well," Tia retorted, with a smile.

"No arguments from me there. You failed to mention who or what the Zahraith are, and you're right, I do know you, and I know you would have found out by any means necessary."

"Lucky for me, Werldon was a chatty bastard-come-emissary full of his own self-importance, and that of his race."

"I take it that means he basically told you their master plan."

Tia gave a heavy sigh, the closeness off the walls and ceiling seemingly causing her discomfort. "He told me enough, for now."

"And?"

"The Zahraith are related by blood to the Karee," she revealed.

"Great, so this is turning into a family dispute with us in the thick of it," Kan grumbled. The news wasn't that much of a revelation to him, as he'd always had a weird feeling about the black vessels. They'd triggered a notion in the back of his head, and Tia's statement confirmed what he'd always, subconsciously, thought.

"I am also Zahraith," she added, with a detached air.

Kan gaped at her for a moment. "The hell you are!" he exclaimed. "Yes, you're a crazy bitch, but you're not a genocidal crazy bitch."

Tia looked at him "Am I not?" she asked, coldly. Kan's heart sank. "I have a dark past, darker than most, which is even now hidden from me. Why else than if I had been a killer? I was bound into servitude to the Karee for centuries, I answered their command for over five hundred years, and I had many more centuries ahead of me. Only Shar has come close to me in terms of that kind of sentencing. His charge was the murder of billions by his order. I was a primal monster once. I gave no orders, I simply acted, but I am under no illusion that there isn't blood ingrained on my hands, just like the Zahraith."

Kan shivered, trying to get his head around her confession. "That may be true, but I can't agree that you are Zahraith."

"I am their creation. The key to the scorpiads came from them. I am a Zahraith construct, in a Karee ship, waging war, just like them. So much so they wanted me to join them."

Kan inhaled deeply and stared at his feet. He knew how to deal with broken electronics, and how to stay alive in the middle of battle; deep soul-searching discussions were not his forte. In his gut, he knew Tia was no Zahraith, but how to explain why was not easy. "If you're right, and you've killed billions, then that is not your fault. You said it yourself, you were an unthinking creature, reacting to primitive urges. Why? Who knows? But the crux of it is, it was because you were a scorpiad, not because you were Zahraith. In my opinion, if that is truly the case, then the Karee had no right to sentence you. What next? Sentence cats because they kill mice, or sentence fish because they consume plankton? Where does that particular thread end?"

He looked up. Tia was staring at the ground, sucking the remnants of juice out of her fruit's core, but she gave a small nod, signalling that she'd heard and understood his point.

"And now? Yes you fight, but you fight for freedom, not to conquer. You love, and you don't throw scorn on those who do likewise. You care, not for yourself and your own glory, but for others, and their right to exist."

Tia glanced his way, and he caught and held her eyes. Her expression was inscrutable, but she was looking deeply into him, he could feel it, and he wondered what thoughts and conflicts were going on in her head as he said his piece.

"Being on Tartarus has taught me that there is no purely black and white, no only good and evil; instead, we all exist in shades of grey," he continued. "Even though your actions may not be those of the Karee, everything I've seen of you, everything I've seen you do, even the darker stuff, points to you being anything but a Zahraith. You are you...." He searched for a suitable title to imbue her with. "You are Karee two-point-oh," he finally announced, albeit a tad lamely. "And it's starting to become clear that both sides are running scared because of it." He looked at Tia, searching for a hint of a response from her.

"But how can you be sure? You saw the statue on the Ethtas' homeworld, and the Zahraith knew about it. That was part of why they came for me," she said, still sounding unconvinced.

"And it's the belief that you are Zahraith that scares you?"

"In part. I am the goddess of war. What is that if not a Zahraith title? It was the very title that Werldon acknowledged me with."

"Wars have two sides, if not more. That statue's proclamation made no indication of which side you were on," Kan reasoned.

"But I'm the one who's guiding the races into battle. What if, by doing so, I fulfil the second part of that title, that of harbinger of death, and lead everyone to wrack and ruin."

"Or you could just as likely lead the Zahraith to wrack and ruin. You've said it before; prophecies are fuzzy at best. You have a scary title, so what? I think it's up to you what that title refers to."

"You are right." Tia pulled herself upright. "I've let the hunters poke the bear for too long. It's time to turn around and strike. Let them know I will no longer be a pawn in their petty ancient squabble."

"You intend to take on the Karee and the Zahraith?" Kan asked, with some shock. He was all for taking the fight to the Alliance, but not taking aim at a couple of races who were near omnipotent. It really would result in Tia being the Harbinger of Death.

But whatever fears he had; Tia seemed to be envisaging a different scenario. "The Orion Alliance was guided into place by interference from the Zahraith, and they were there at Ciberia, yet they didn't attack directly, choosing to watch from the side-lines rather than engage; however, it's only a small step from viewing to participating. There's a good chance that with me in the mix with the rebels, they'll actively join in with future battles, which means we need to take them out of the picture before that happens."

"How in gods' name do you intend to do that?"

"With the Karee." Kan gaped at her. "The Karee are up to their necks in this, no matter how much they claim to have a hands-off approach. I'm proof of that. They threw me into this war to goad the rebels into action under the guise of providing guidance against the Alliance. I see that now. If the rebels win against the Zahraith, all's good; no more Zahraith to worry about. If the rebels loose against the Zahraith, all's good; no races left to complain about being trodden under foot by the Zahraith. And they did this in full knowledge of the prophecy about me, as they were allied with the Ethtas, who created my statue. Now it's time for the Karee to stop hiding, take control of their wayward siblings, and make amends for their own misdeeds of lies, manipulation, and turned blind eyes."

"That's a hell of an order," Kan said.

"I have two vessels on my side. One who is part of the old order. If Jarell can see the bigger picture, chances are, others will too."

"I'm sure I don't need to tell you just how unconvinced I am that this will work."

"I know, but this is what needs to be done. For too long the Alliance has been safely suckling at the Zahraith's teat. Time to rip it away. And the knock-on effect may just turn things in our favour. What bigger show of strength than taking away their strongest ally?"

Kan was lost for words. Convincing the Karee to go into battle against the Zahraith was going to be a tall order. Tia may have been stubborn, but they were immovable. "You know I'll follow you into any battle, no matter the odds, but I'm not sure this is going to see success?"

"Then what do you suggest as an alternative to fighting a greater power than us?" Tia asked. Kan's brain couldn't answer her question. "At the end of the day, this battle is mine. I know you, and Shar, and the others, have no qualms about taking on challenges bigger than most, but when dealing with the Karee, your words and actions will be ignored. As you say, I'm Karee two-point-oh, and they can't ignore me any longer, so it's up to me to make this play. I just need to know you have my back and will follow my command."

"Always."

"Then when, if, a time comes, help keep the rebels safe, help keep them together, and help keep them fighting."

Kan felt a weight fill his soul at Tia's word, but he nodded. "You have my word." Tia gave him a sad little smile, lent forward, and kissed the top of his forehead. Kan felt his neck flush slightly. "I missed you," he said, without thinking.

Tia gave him a sideways look. "I would have thought your

mind too distracted by Leo's flame-haired sister," she said, in what Kan could tell was a probing-for-information tone.

Kan choked. "She just a child."

"She's old enough."

"Compared to me, she's just a child."

"So, you're saving yourself for a what…? A fifty-year-old?"

Kan did some quick mental arithmetic. Though his outward age was thirty-five, he had been with Tia for close to sixteen years, which meant her guess was, unfortunately, spot on. Although fifty was technically middle age for a Human, for many it was still considered old, and Kan preferred to date those closer to his outward age. Then again, for some alien species, fifty was still young, but those aliens tended to live in a slower state of existence. He wasn't going to let Tia have him beat. "Depends on how good they look for their age. I mean, I know a five hundred plus year old who barely looks a day over thirty." He gave Tia a cheeky wink.

This time, her smile was a little brighter. "You do know that boat has sailed?"

"Oh yes. Apparently, she's got her hands full with some big blue alien dude."

"That obvious?"

"You turned into a rock-melting energy demon because of him. It's **that** obvious."

"So then, you're free to date whom you so desire, young or old." She said, in a way that made her sound like she was affirming her decision to herself rather than him.

"If only it was as easy as that."

"How so?" Tia looked confused.

Kan turned his mind back to a conversation he'd had with Shar shortly after the battle for Ciberia, and about how Tia's hold on them was even stronger after copulation. *Does she really not know.* Kan suddenly felt embarrassed about having to say the words, but there were no airs and graces when faced with Tia, at least not for the likes of him, so he decided to be himself. He took a deep breath. "After we have sex with you,

you have us in a choke hold. I know I'm not alone in this as Shar confessed the same, albeit reluctantly. You may walk away from us, but you leave us mired. Nobody comes close to you, our brain idolises you, and your face fills our vision. Shar copes by drowning himself in females. I cope by existing in a world of what-ifs. If you've let us go, then you need to let us go."

Tia stood motionless and silent for so long, Kan thought he'd somehow broken her. "I had no idea," she eventually said, quietly. "I thought your and Shar's behaviour was led by alpha male tendencies and too much testosterone. It never occurred to me it was something deeper."

"It's not something you're doing on purpose then?" Tia shook her head. In a way, her admission relieved Kan. Whatever it was, Tia wasn't doing it out of spite, or desire for further control. "So? Can you unhook us?" he asked, tentatively.

"I hope so, for everyone's sake, but it's something I'll need time to investigate. The answer isn't close to mind, which means it's either something I don't know, or something I do know that's being blocked. Personally, I'd put my money on the latter."

"So scorpiad related?"

"Possibly, but that's something we'll deal with later. For now, all that needs to be said has been, and I believe it's time for me to be introduced to the people you recklessly went to save."

Kan led the way.

~~~~

Chapter 33 - Tia

Tia half lay, half curled on her bunk. Her eyes were closed, but she wasn't sleeping, not strictly speaking. She was resting her mind. Her thoughts were clear. No images, no words, nothing intruded. Her body was still, and her heart barely beat. Without Morrígan to enshroud her, she had to recharge the only way she knew how, the way she used to as an A'daree, and in her catatonic state, her body and soul recouped from the day's stresses and strains.

Slowly, the bubble lifted. First the words, as people's minds, in a constant hive of activity, wafted their thoughts into hers. Gently, and without thinking, she closed them out, like closing a window onto a noisy street. Then she opened her eyes, and took in her room, letting the details slowly drift into being. Further and further, down and down, detail upon detail, until the hyper-reality of what she saw would have given a normal person a week-long migraine. She blinked, and her surroundings returned to normal. There were no atoms, no bright energy, no strange smells, just a bed, a table, and a chest of drawers. Mundane things made of mundane materials to the passing eye of a mere mortal.

Her room was much the same as Kan and Leo's, but without the problem of a double bunk. It had been a double bunk, but strong hands and a flick of her wrist had seen to that. She checked the time on the digital clock on the wall; it was seventy-two minutes past eighteen. She frowned and checked the pad she had collected off the Ferell, which was tied to Zerren time; it was a few minutes past midnight. Being cooped up on a ship again made her feel restless, and the walls were closing in. It was a strange, contradictory sensation for her. While in Morrígan, the vessel encased her body, with barely a millimetre between it and herself, yet she felt so much freer. Being able to merge her consciousness with Morrígan meant being able to see the universe as Morrígan, and as the vessel, she had billions of kilometres of free space all around her. On the Qosec Three, much like on the Eerell, she was constantly running the risk of causing damage, and she had to be eternally aware, and duck and weave her way along the corridors, and within narrow rooms, lest she cause disaster by inadvertently taking out a control panel with a wing, or an air duct with her horns.

She stretched, turned on her back, rested her feet on the sink at the end of the bed, and stared at the grey ceiling. She let her mind drift, on the off chance that she would pick up on Morrígan, but the airwaves stayed silent. *Where are you?* she wondered. She could probe the galaxy deeper and find her vessel, but she was hesitant, and wasn't sure why. Being part of the vessel still unnerved her, but that feeling had become less as time and experience had forged ahead. There was the question of finding out about what had happened to her when confronted by Werldon, but again, that didn't scare her. It was the not knowing that scared her, and learning the truth, whatever that was, from Morrígan was what she needed, as the knowledge would guide her next move. So, it wasn't that staying her mind.

I wonder what Ressen's doing, if he's not asleep, she suddenly thought. Tia contemplated sending him a message, to see if he wanted a late drink or snack but decided better of it. Their time spent together whilst waiting to be picked up by the Qosec Three had been, for Tia, frustratingly nominal. He had spent most of his time sequestered in his quarters, healing, and Tia suspected to try to make sense of things. He had suffered greatly at the hands of Werldon and the others, and it was not only his body requiring time to mend, so she had chosen not to push him.

But in his absence, their kiss had gone unexplored, and the words behind their glancing looks had gone ignored. Tia knew there was something there, but she also felt Ressen's reticence. She was an immortal creature of energy, he, just an alien, easily bruised and broken. At the same time as he inched closer towards her, she also felt him stepping back, mirroring her own hesitant, almost denying approach to what was going on. At night, alone in her quarters, Tia had often desperately wanted to be close to Ressen, to hold him and comfort him, both mentally and physically. But each time she had held back, just as scared as much for him as for herself.

Over dinner, while Ressen had been quietly eating his meal, she had got to know Leo's family. His quarrelsome brothers seemed at ease on the alien ship, as did Leo's father; their time spent in the Space Corp. having prepared them for the unusual sights and sounds, and they bickered and teased as only male relatives could, unperturbed by the odd looks thrown their way by the Rotaizians. Conversely, Leo's mother was wide-eyed and quiet, absorbing everything, and she'd often bring a smile to Tia when she caught herself ogling one of the aliens. She was a dichotomy of motherly love and quiet fear. At one moment she would be tutting, fussing, and haranguing her family, as if they were the only people around, the next, smiling shyly at Tia, barely able to form a sentence as she regaled the table with home-spun tales.

Then there was Leo's sister. As much as Tia tried to take a pragmatic approach to the woman, it still irked her to see Ellie cast her eyes forlornly at Kan. Kan, despite their earlier conversation, paid the girl scant attention. Tia wasn't sure if it were because Ellie wasn't his type, or whether the issue they'd discussed was so deeply ingrained in him that he really couldn't side-step it the way Shar could, and the unnecessary feeling of relief she felt at his disinterest annoyed her. She began wondering if the same hold she had over Kan and Shar had a reciprocating hold over her. It was something she dearly needed to get to grips with, as much for their sake as her own.

How was she ever to be an honest partner for Ressen if her mind, heart, and urges, kept wandering back to the other two men?

At that thought Tia's mind returned guiltily to Ressen, and her heart yearned to reach out to him. Then it dawned on her what had been niggling at her and preventing her from finding her vessel. It was Ressen. With Morrígan back, she would be back in Morrígan, with little time free to interact with the alien. Their barely spoken of barely-there relationship would stall, maybe even go into free fall, and Tia found herself not celebrating that idea. After their kiss, she had come to realise that was exactly the opposite of what she wanted, despite the exasperation it caused her. The signs were all there and were undeniable. Their shared looks made her stomach leap, and he kept popping up in her thoughts without warning. She had to hold herself back from reading his thoughts when he was around others, especially other females, thereby refusing to answer the call of the green-eyed monster that had taken up home in her brain. It all pointed to a strong romantic obsession with him, something that made her understand a little more what Kan and Shar were going through over her.

It wasn't the first time she had been mired in desire. Shar had been the first, and she had accepted his advances willingly. Kan had come about through a mixture of weakness and curiosity. To her, they were both strong, capable, and handsome males. Yet they had only had her once apiece. After which, as Kan had said, she had walked away from them, knowing further dalliances would complicate things. They had been one-night stands to rid herself of centuries of tension. Ressen was different. Ressen was not someone she wanted to walk away from, and responsibilities, namely Morrígan, would interfere with that.

"But if I don't go back to Morrígan, I can't rope in the Karee and deal with the Zahraith," she told the ceiling, as if it was it preventing her from doing what was right. The ceiling remained silent and grey. "You're no bloody help," she told it.

449

She had to face facts; she needed her vessel. *At least if we rendezvous at the Scientia, I'll still have some time with Ressen,* she considered. A dark, and unwarranted thought slipped into her mind; *I could sleep with him to keep him true to me.* She at once felt wretched for thinking such a thing. "I won't," she reassured the ceiling.

She closed her eyes, focused her mind, and let her unconscious being slip the confines of the ship. She homed her thoughts onto her vessel, sending them forward like a bloodhound in search of its prey, and the blue nothingness of hyperspace gave way to the vast beauty of the galaxy. It began to spin around her, the stars blurring in their chaotic dance, until their light too became merged and as nondescript as that in hyperspace. She called out with her mind *"Morrigan,"* and waited, letting instinct do the rest. The surrounding light became brighter, more determined. Soon, it felt as if she was getting warmer, literally, though she knew it was merely a phantom feeling, or at least that's what she told herself. The maelstrom of starlight eventually eased, first to distinguishable streaks, the path of each star traced in the universe as it spun, then to individual stars slowly spinning around her, their temperatures picked out in hues of reds, yellows, blues, and whites.

Soon, everything came to a standstill, and Tia, despite all her years, found herself catching her metaphysical breath. She had arrived in the centre of the galaxy, and stars filled her vision, gas burned brightly, and dark dust drew strange shapes by blocking out the light of the myriad of burning suns behind it. She had never set foot in the galaxy's heart. Most of the stars were too old, and the planets were either inhospitable, or long departed. There was no life for the Alliance to challenge, so no life for her to protect. But here, amongst stellar birth and death, she knew one species did exist: The Karee. Somewhere, hidden from view, she knew their civilisation was holed-up, and considering her earlier declaration to Kan, the irony of finding herself in this place was not lost on her, but she had not come for them...yet. *"Morrígan?"*

"I am here."

A tingle ran through her at Morrígan's voice, and its eyes opened within her mind to reveal two blue stars, bright against the many old red stars burning around her. They looked like her eyes when she got mad, or wanted to show her power, or randomly turned into some divine energy being.

The Karee of the Inner Sanctum, despite having been her keepers, or based on Werldon's intel, orchestrators, had never lowered themselves to entering her mind. And Tia doubted they ever would, especially after her recent changes. Instead, during the few times she'd needed to hold council with them, rather than go find them, for they would never deign to make themselves locatable either, she'd had to mentally call out to them. Back during the days of her prior form, the Karee would have been monitoring her...their precious tool...and eventually they would appear as giant apparitions before her. Tia figured that the Karee had never stepped into her mind because they'd thought it too primitive and distasteful, despite everything she'd been through as a Human and an A'daree. She wasn't complaining though. She had never particularly wanted the self-righteous buggers transgressing in her thoughts anyway.

The only Karee who had willingly set foot in her tumultuous mind was Jarell, and he too manifested himself with blue eyes, so Tia had always assumed his were the colour of all Karee eyes. But Morrígan's eyes were subtly different to Jarell's. Hers were a touch more turquoise-blue, whilst his were blue tinged with white. *Is it a coincidence that Morrígan's eyes became like mine, or was it meant to be?* Questions always came to Tia when she was faced with her Karee vessel. She knew so much, then again, when it came to herself and what she was becoming, she knew so little. *"How goes the crystal hunt?"* she asked, casually.

"We have had success and have secured enough for ten Zerren battleships."

"That's something at least."

"You are troubled?"

Tia snorted. *"You think? If you're not reading my thoughts right now you should, because as recaps go, that's the best course of action."*

Morrígan didn't say anything, but its eyes dimmed, a sign that it was concentrating on something. A moment later, they returned. *"Interesting."*

"That's all you have to say on the matter?"

"No."

Tia rolled her eyes. Trying to get coherent facts out of a Karee vessel was like trying to get blood out of a burning sun, and despite its manner of birth, Morrígan was no different in that respect. *"Would you care to elaborate?"*

"You are Karee." Morrígan stated.

"Is this in answer to my argument with Kan?"

"No."

"Then what?"

"It is in answer to you."

"Well, that's cleared all that up," Tia responded, in a tone that was two-hundred-percent sarcasm. Morrígan didn't respond. Tia was wondering if it had failed to read her tone. She gave it a nudge *"So, I'm Karee, as opposed to...?"*

"...Being a symbiont."

"Wait, what?" That was not the end of the sentence she was expecting. She had expected to be told she was not a Zahraith, confirming Kan's words, and her hope. What Morrígan was telling her was not making a lot of sense. The Karee were an amalgamation of ship and symbiont, but the ships had come first, and some existed without symbionts. Indeed, Jarell's standing had a big question mark over it. Tia had never interacted with a symbiont from it, or heard it mention one. The ships were Karee first and foremost. For Tia to say she was Karee was a statement of her existence in partnership with a vessel. For a vessel to say she was Karee, and not a symbiont, was something completely different, not to mention odd. *"Are you telling me I'm one of you? A vessel?"* She asked, hearing the

absurdity in her words. She was not a ship, that she was sure of, because that would mean she was a vessel, who existed within a vessel, and that was bordering on Russian nesting doll weirdness.

"Yes and no," Morrígan answered.

"So, I'm Karee, but not a Karee vessel?" Tia echoed, trying to unravel its vagueness.

"Yes."

"Well now that's nailed down, would you mind explaining to me just what you mean by that?"

"You know our history now. The creature Werldon explained it to you,"

Tia replayed Werldon's long speech, trying to pinpoint the answer. *"Before your species became host to others, you were something else. The answer is between when you were mortal humanoids and space-faring creatures, yes?"*

"Yes."

"And that's what I am now?"

"Yes. There was a time in our manufactured evolution when we walked the line between corporeal and energy forms. We were creatures of energy, cloaked within a shroud of skin-like energy. Should we choose, we could break forth from that cocoon, to become the creature you did. We still carry that ability within us even as vessels. It allows us to warp the fabric of the universe and gives us the power to do that which even great battleships cannot...like destroy rogue planets. And, to a lesser extent, the symbionts within us can display such power, should we choose, though not to a point where they can become creatures of pure energy like us. You were given access to such power as an A'daree. It is that which shines from your eyes, allowed you to embrace the energy from plasma weapons in combat, and went some way to protecting you as we merged."

"Yet I couldn't transform like that after we first joined, otherwise, on finding Aben dead, things would've played out differently," Tia pointed out. On tackling the scorpiad, she had become a scorpiad, and on finding Aben's lifeless body, her scorpiad transformation had gone into overdrive.

"Indeed. Your form was still following A'daree instruction then. What happened on the rogue world, for whatever reason, tipped the balance another way. It awoke the Karee within you and re-wrote your being."

Tia knew what Morrígan was alluding to. If she had access to her memories, she had access to her feelings and actions over Ressen. It wasn't just Werldon's dismissal of her that had triggered her transformation, but also his treatment of Ressen. On entering Tia's mind, Morrígan would have become aware that Tia had strong feelings for the alien, though she didn't mention her feelings or Ressen by name. *"Am I in an A'daree-like body, or a Karee-like body now?"* she asked.

"That depends on what you chose to be."

Tia tried to mentally weigh her body back on the Qosec Three. When she'd used her blood from Ressen to solidify, she had concentrated on her A'daree-like form, as that was what she knew, and as far as she could tell, she was as borderline cumbersome as always. She certainly didn't feel like an energy creature teetering on the brink between solid and gaseous, kept in check by some thin covering. *"I'm A'daree,"* she confirmed, more to herself than anyone. Morrígan didn't feel the need to respond. *"So that's why Werldon was surprised. As a symbiont, or as an A'daree, or whatever mix I was supposed to be, I shouldn't have been able to change."*

"It seems our unconventional joining has had implications beyond even what I envisioned," Morrígan stated, with surprising candour.

That was the thing; symbionts were people, aliens, who already existed. They were trained, prepared, and once ready, they joined with a needy host. It hadn't always been like that. Tia knew in the early days, symbionts had just been interesting individuals who had joined willingly with a Karee vessel, but the Karee, being who they were, had wanted more control over their symbionts. They wanted the 'right sort', those who possessed the desired level of predictability, so along came the training and stringent preparations. But through that time, one thing had remained consistent, and that was the symbionts had been fully formed individuals. Sure, there were tweaks here and there to make them more 'reliable', as it wouldn't do to have a symbiont who could easily die, and aliens, no matter their race, tended to be fragile things when compared to the likes of the aeons-lived Karee. The crux of it was symbionts entered their fully formed vessel as solid creatures.

Tia's transformation into a symbiont had been completely different. She had been consumed by the energy of the emerging Morrígan, which had been followed by a heady bath in the centre of a planet. She had been broken down and rebuilt in some phoenix-like happening of epic proportions, which had, apparently, screwed up her DNA something fierce. Human, scorpiad, A'daree, and Karee combined; she genuinely was some mongrel creature, with no idea of what lay round the next corner in her development. *"Do you think I can do that again?"* She already knew Kan was worried about her getting triggered, and she joined him in that fear.

"Yes."

Great. That meant she was going to have to keep herself in check more than usual. *"And do you think I can do that again if I choose?"* That was the big question. If it were encoded within her, could it be repeated, the same as when she chose to become a scorpiad, or dismissed a limb.

"Yes."

That was good news. If she had some degree of control over her transformation, it meant she wasn't going to inadvertently melt people when ticked off. The confrontation with Werldon had even provided her with warning signs. *"I'm guessing they didn't need some lackey around to siphon skin cells off if they wanted to be solid again?"* Although having Ressen around permanently was something she was all in favour of, she didn't think he'd appreciate being something she had to harvest.

"No. They commanded the energy within their bodies to rebuild cells."

Tia had thought as much when she was trying to figure out how to be corporeal, but she had been against the clock, and had gone with what she knew: blood. *"The Karee aren't going to like this,"* She muttered to herself, realising this new occurrence was going to count against her when she went to try to negotiate with the Karee down the road. *"Though truth be told, the Karee can't hate me more than they already do."*

"The Karee don't like anything." Morrígan retorted, with what seemed so much like humour that Tia raised an eyebrow. However, the two glowing orbs remained unchanged, and she was left wondering whether it had been a dry barb, or simply an astute statement of fact.

Tia was mulling over her next question when something twinged in the back of her mind. It took her a moment to twig to what it was, as it was something that had yet to happen. *That's Hanno Delao.* Thanks to everything else that had gone on, she had forgotten his existence. Aben's murderer, turned her spy, had been sent to root around the back doors of the Alliance, unaware a part of his brain was watching and recording everything he did and saw. Now he was phoning home, which meant something important had been unearthed. Tia switched her vision, and a hazy outline of the man appeared, suspended in the galactic void like a free-standing hologram, and with the stars shining through him, it looked like he was wearing a star-covered onesie, complete with face-paint.

"Report," she snapped.

"Four spies have infiltrated Zerra. Their mission is to instigate a nuclear winter through corruption of high-ranking operatives. Two turn-coat rebels are trying to covertly uncover them, and are under close surveillance, with the command to dispatch when appropriate."

Tia's heart started to pound. *"Who are the two rebels?"* she asked. Were they her men, or had two unknown people just opened a can of worms that was about to get them killed?

"Defector telepath Ralay," that name meant nothing to her, *"and ex-battleship commander John Walker."*

Tia's stomach lurched, and she snapped the vision of Hanno away. The Karee would have to wait. Zerra was on the brink of destruction, and with no clue. She just hoped she could arrive in time.

Epilogue

Walks placed the cup of something-with-a-hint-of-spice down on the table before Ralay, then took his own seat opposite her. The café in which they'd chosen to meet was Javin's last haunt, so the Zerren staff regarded the pair with marginally less suspicion than in other places they'd stopped. This meant their conversation was less likely to be snooped on.

Walks talk a sip of his own concoction before speaking. "So, anything?" he asked Ralay.

She half-shook her head. "Chione thinks he has something from his covert listening, but it's hard to follow up on things without garnering suspicion from both allies and enemies alike."

"I hear that," Walks lamented. "We can hardly go up to officials and ask, hey, know of any suspicious arseholes who may want to cause havoc in the name of the Alliance?" He took another sip of his drink. "I managed to speak to one of my kind in what goes for immigration down here today. Asked him causally if any Humans, or at the very least members of known Alliance races, had turned up recently, with the excuse that it was part of future security measures I was working on for the Scientia."

"And...?"

"Nada! So, either we're looking for members of allied or presently neutral races, like we had on the station, or they're Alliance races, and they've taken a back-door in."

"I would imagine any face belonging to an Alliance race

would immediately get flagged, which would make it a lot harder to infiltrate sensitive areas," Ralay theorised.

"Didn't stop a Human from trying to cause havoc on the Scientia," Walks reminded her.

Ralay shrugged. "The Scientia is akin to a frontier town. Down here, there's much tighter security in governmental buildings."

"Thanks," Walks retorted, in a voice that was not the least bit thankful for her slight.

"I tell it like I see it," Ralay responded, nonplussed. "Chione's bit of information may help confirm things though. According to him, two high-ranking Maisak emissaries turned up shortly before we arrived and are guests in the residence of one of the local politicians."

"Which one," Walks asked, his intrigue overriding his being irked.

"Ka'mec, I believe."

Walks racked his brains for what little Zerren political news he'd managed to digest over the last week or so. "I think he's the lead guy of the opposition party here. Been on the news quite a bit recently, ranting against the influx of refugees, and how they're a danger to the planet, and how they're being used to build battleships instead of good honest Zerren labour."

"Oh, that guy," Ralay confirmed, nodding. "Yes, I saw him last night lambasting the current leader for even allowing the ships to be built. Says it's a waste of funds that would be better spent setting up a global defence grid, and refugee colonies on outer moons"

Having a thought, Walks grabbed the café's waiter as he wandered past to clean a newly vacated table. "You speak Human?" Walks inquired. The Zerren nodded. "Can you tell me please, how is Ka'mec doing in popularity?"

The Zerren thought for a moment. "Good, I think. He is very close to leader Hen'cal now."

"You like him?" Ralay asked.

"He talks a lot about things that worry Zerrens at home. He

plays on fears. Stretches truth. I do not like him. I knew Javin. I understand what goes on out there." He waved his hands to the sky. "But other people, lots of people, they do not. They forget. Then they are given new fears."

Walks nodded in understanding as the waiter ambled off. He leant back in his seat. "So, hypothetically, what damage could an anti-refugee, anti-battleship-building individual do if elected to a position of power?"

"A lot," Ralay stated, simply. "More so if he's been brought under the sway of the Alliance. This is the biggest country in Zerra and holds the biggest allocation of power amongst the unified nations, both physically and politically."

"And elections are...?"

"One month away, I believe."

"Great, we're in the shit now."

To be continued....

ABOUT THE AUTHOR

K. Llewellin

I grew up in the 80's to 00's, during the heady days of terrestrial TV sci-fi. Long-running cult series, combined with re-runs of kitsch 70's shows, ensured I spent my evenings permanently glued to the TV. This had a profound effect on my fertile imagination, and it wasn't long before strange, strong-willed characters were evolving in my mind, clamouring to have their stories told. I've finally given in to them. Now I'm simply along for the ride....

Printed in Great Britain
by Amazon